Pemberton LTD.

ANTHONY GLYN

THE DIAL PRESS NEW YORK

Printed in the United States of America

Part One

1

THERE WAS A diffident tap at the door. I swiveled around, sitting on the floor. "Is who?"

"Is me, suh."

"Is what?"

"Is your next pants, suh."

That at least was a rare variation of our routine. "Bring them in," I called.

Jailall came in, my trousers over his arm. I took them, considering whether they should go in my sea luggage which I wouldn't see for at least another month, or my air luggage which I hoped to keep under sixty-six pounds. I put them into the sea luggage.

"Nearly finished," I said. I was hot and tired, and I have always detested packing, even those glorious packs, the end of term packs, the eve of holiday packs. And this was every bit as glorious as those.

"Yes, suh. Shall me finish it, suh?"

"Yes, boy. I'm sick of it. Everything in that heap and on the bed goes into these grips, and the rest in the trunks."

"Yes, suh."

"And you'd better take the grips to the rum-store when you've finished and get them weighed."

"Yes, suh." He began to pack. I stood up, my dressing-gown clinging stickily to my back, and went into the shower. The water was unpleasantly cold. I hated cold showers, even in the tropics; each time I nerved myself to go under it, I felt as if it were costing me a day of my life. Never mind, I told myself, soon, very soon now, you'll be in a place where they have hot water on tap.

Jailall was still packing when I got back, and I stood for a moment watching him. He was a typical Hindu boy, with the round face, the round nose and the straight shiny black hair. His brown hands were folding my clothes quickly and neatly. I was quite proud of him; he had never been a houseboy before he came to me.

He glanced up at me. "When you come back, suh?"

"Oh, I don't know, boy. A year or more."

"All of we hope you come back soon," he said shyly.

I smiled. "Next time it won't be for so long. Only two or three months."

Jailall glanced at the photograph of Diana lying on the bed, ready for packing. "And shall you bring the mistress?"

"Oh yes, Jailall, I hope so."

"Me like to see her. She proper beautiful, boss."

Involuntarily I looked at the photograph too. "Yes, she is." And then I wondered whether she had changed. I had not seen her for eighteen months.

"Shall you bring the pick'nies too, suh?"

"Oh, I shouldn't think so. They're rather young."

"Perhaps you soon have a next pick'nie, suh?"

He grinned at me impishly. I started to snub him and then thought better of it. I shrugged, trying to look noncommittal. Jailall went on:

"Jehorah having a next pick'nie."

"Heavens!" I exclaimed. "Another! You don't know when to stop. That's four, isn't it?"

"Yes, suh."

Four children. And he was only twenty.

"That's too many for a boy your age."

He made a sulky mouth. "What can me do, boss? God send-a them a-we." For the first time since he had come in, his voice had the familiar Indian begging whine.

"Have you a next job?"

"No, suh."

"But I thought you were going to Mr. Reynolds."

"No, suh."

"But why not? He wants a houseboy doesn't he?"

"Me no know, suh." The face was very sulky now.

"Well, for heaven's sake! What went wrong?"

The boy said mulishly, "He no treat-a we like you."

"In what way?"

"He say 'bearer' and he talk-a we in Hindi. Me no understand Hindi."

I couldn't help smiling. Reynolds had recently come to us after years in India and he prided himself on his understanding of East Indians. The overseers, a little weary of his expert knowledge, called him The Sa-heeb behind his back.

"What a chota-peg, suh?"

"I think it means a whisky and soda, boy. And you'd better go and get me one."

"Yes, suh."

He pattered off, and I stood staring out through the mosquito screening. My bungalow had a view up the road which was lined with cabbage palms. I could see nineteen cabbage palms from my window; I knew there were nineteen, I had counted them many times, and I hated every one.

I heard the flip-flap of Jailall's feet; it was the only noise he made as he materialized before me. He poured the soda into the glass and I watched him, wondering. He was not yet twenty-one and he supported a wife and, soon, four children on eighteen dollars a month. And I thought I was hard done by on five hundred pounds a year. Of course coolies in the tropics don't need so much, I told myself. It was one of those comforting thoughts like the lower classes not feeling pain to the same degree. I decided to give him ten dollars conscience money as a parting present.

I took the drink and sipped it. It was cool and invigorating and the ice in it bumped against my lip.

"What are you going to do if you don't go to Mr. Reynolds?" I asked.

"Me want to go to the factory, please, suh."

"The factory, h'm?" That was where they always wanted to go. It was dry in the rainy season. But houseboys were thought to have an even better job.

"Will you like that?"

"Yes, suh."

He might do well, I thought. He was intelligent and neat with his hands.

"You'll have to start right at the bottom, you know." That familiar deadly phrase. "Do you know what they will pay you?"

"Seven cents an hour."

Seven cents an hour! Of course there would be overtime and cost of living bonus. But seven cents an hour!

"And you'll be able to manage on that?"

He grinned cheerfully. "Me go try, suh."

"And how much more pick'nies are you going to have?"

"Me no know, suh. God send-a them."

"Oh, don't be silly!" I suddenly felt very weary. "All right, I'll speak to Mr. Ingram."

"Oh, thank you, boss. God bless you, boss."

"And now you'd better go and let me dress."

He was gone in an instant and I heard his feet flip-flapping across the living-room floor. I dressed slowly, for haste was very heating, and between garments I pottered about the little white wooden room that was so familiar. It was sparsely furnished, everything cheap and makeshift except the magnificent mosquito net which rose like a pillar of cloud over my bed. It was the ordinary overseer's furniture supplied by the company, and I think Walker had expected me to refurnish the bungalow to suit my own tastes. But I had never felt like spending money on that. If Diana had been here, I should have done it, but alone it didn't seem worth it. I had meant to hang some pictures, but somehow I hadn't got around to that either.

It was, I supposed, my last day in the room. Next time I came to Natividad, I should stay at the Directors' House. The whole VIP treatment would be laid on for me, cars and chauffeurs to meet me, bulging brief-cases awaiting my urgent attention, the overseers calling me sir. I tried to whip up some enthusiasm, but it didn't work. I should then be only a carbon copy of Justin, and at no time had that ever seemed to me the pinnacle of human achievement. All you could say was that it would be more comfortable, more titillating to my ego than my immediate monastic incarceration in my little white bare cell.

Not that it was so bare at the moment. Clothes, belongings, trunks lay about in a mess. My old school trunk was there, after all those years in store. On the last day of the half we used to bounce on it to shut it, singing:

> No more Latin, no more French,
> No more sitting on a hard board bench.

The circumstances now were even more favorable, but I couldn't work up the same ebullience.

I put on my dark grey linen suit, and continued prowling. Beyond the trunk was my black tin uniform case, which had once held my Army uniform. More recently it had been protecting, fairly successfully I thought, my dinner jacket and my English clothes against the ravages of silver fish and the green mold which had ruined my brown shoes. Beyond that was the packing case containing my books, and, as I bent over the case, I caught the whiff of mustiness, the smell of books that have been through two rainy seasons. I picked up Dostoevsky's *The Idiot* and flicked through it reminiscently. Further down, buried in the moldy darkness were Proust, Conrad, Flaubert, Hardy, Emily Brontë, Tolstoy. My secret hoard of treasure, or, as I believe it is technically called, my escape mechanism. Not that the escape was complete even here. In my hoard were the books I had acquired locally, Prinsen Geerligs' *Cane Sugar,* Noel Deerr's *Sugar and the Sugar Cane.* I had read them with perhaps less excitement than the others; their pages were stained with damp and tunneled through with bookworm, but they were among the others now, honored and incongruous.

On top was a folder containing my own scribblings of the past eighteen months. I thought for a moment and then transferred it to the suitcase. It was slender enough in all conscience, three literary articles, a couple of short stories, the first chapter of a novel. Possibly not a very impressive output of my spare time activity, but still it was something, the proof that my intellectual ambitions, though sick and frail, were not quite dead. I might as well have it with me.

I put the folder on top of the packed suitcase. Immediately below was the photograph of Diana. I pulled it out and stared at it once again. It had been taken shortly before our wedding; Diana had on her green evening dress that she had later so little opportunity of wearing. The photographer had posed her three-quarter face with a dawn effect behind her and there seemed to be a misty veil between us and her, blurring and softening the hard edges. She looked incredibly lovely. Her eyes were soft and gentle—softer and gentler than they were in real life. Her cheek-bone slanted enticingly upwards in a strange highlight. Her lips, parted serenely, were full and black and shiny. She was as desirable as the night we got engaged.

I felt the hot wave of fury rising in me like the murillo of an enraged bull. I closed my eyes and steadily fought the resentment down till, with tight mouth and clenched fists, I had myself once again under control. There was no point in going over all that again. It was an injustice, a calm deliberate injustice on Justin's part, but I had accepted it when I had accepted his terms. It was sheer waste of adrenalin to let myself indulge in impotent anger now that it was all over. The eighteen months of enforced separation were over. Nothing could give them back to us. Only the future could compensate us and that must not be spoilt with an orgy of regret. The only possible thing to do with a sacrifice was to forget it, your own or anyone else's.

But how the hell were Diana and I ever going to bridge that eighteen month gap?

I walked across to the club by the short cut that led between the Mosque and the soil lab. With the approach of the rains, the wind was in the south-west, instead of the usual trades, and it blew the sickly smell of the sugar-house and the roar of the mill across the compound. Tonight there were plenty of mosquitoes about.

The club was crowded and everyone was duly carrying out his usual role. It was like seeing a play for the five hundredth and forty-fifth time. Not that I ever had seen a play five hundred and forty-five times, but I could imagine the sensation perfectly. Occasionally a character missed his cue and someone else ad-libbed, or an understudy took over for a spell. The play itself never changed in its essentials.

I sometimes wondered if it struck the rest of the staff the same way and if they were content that life should be so monotonous. Did Mrs. Ingram, seeing her own chair once more, feel that first pleasurable astonishment renewed again?

The womenfolk sat by themselves in the corner, gossiping and reading the ancient magazines on the table. Ingram, Harvey, Hughes and Miller played bridge. Campbell and McDonald played a wild local version of snooker. ("Ha! The revenge for the massacre of Glencoe!" was Hughes' line as they began. It never failed to raise a smile.) Williamson fiddled with the gramophone; later he would strum unendurably on the out-of-tune piano, hoping forlornly that people would start singing, to be finally silenced by Ingram who could not concentrate on his bridge. The rest stood in a little cluster at the bar.

They were all in their places tonight. The gramophone was playing "Tiptoe through the Tulips." Later we should get "Give Yourself a Pat on the Back" and "Horsey! Keep Your Tail Up." Justin had recently turned out his record cabinet and sent his discards out to us. I had a fondness for them; they were to my mind infinitely preferable to "The Dream of Olwen" which otherwise tended to be our staple fare.

I smiled vaguely all around and ordered a rum and soda at the bar. I detested rum and soda, but it would have been up-stage to order whisky in the club and Justin had been very emphatic that I was to be one of the boys. I took a quick gulp and greeted Pattison, the head overseer.

"Good evening, Pattison."

"Good evening, er."

No one ever knew what to call me. Justin had laid it down that I was on no account to be called sir or Mr. Pemberton. Equally I was not to be called by my Christian name. I think he felt that this would bring the whole Pemberton family into excessive and rather distasteful familiarity, and provide a chink in his own aloof glassiness. I was, therefore, to be called simply Pemberton like a schoolboy. However nobody seemed to be able to bring themselves to do that, apart from Hughes, the accountant, who called me Pemberton as loudly and frequently as possible. The rest of the staff called their equals by their Christian names and their seniors by their initials. I was not supposed to be anybody's senior, but this might have served for me had anyone been able to get their tongue round my initials —H.W.S.P. In the general hiatus I was usually addressed as er or I say, or even, sickeningly, old boy.

Reynolds, our new Deputy Manager, standing beyond Pattison, said "Evening, er," and nodded. He was a big middle-aged man with a ginger moustache and a little pattern of red arteries on his cheekbones. Apparently I had interrupted his conversation with Pattison.

"Take it from me," he was saying, "the only way to deal with coolies is to think out a fair line and then stick to it through thick and thin. No one wants to do down the poor little beggars, but if you start messing about and changing your mind you're sunk. And I ought to know. I've seen enough of them in twenty-four years in India."

Pattison nodded noncommittally. Words rarely passed his lips.

Deliberately I interrupted Reynolds' lecture. "All my stuff will be out of my bungalow by tomorrow morning, so you can move in when you like."

Reynolds turned an irritated eye upon me. "Oh, thanks. But A.J. told me to hang on for the moment where I am."

"Mr. Walker said that?" I always refused to call him A.J. "When?"

"Just before he left the office this evening."

"Did he give any reason? I thought it was all fixed."

"No. I suppose something new's brewing. I haven't been told yet."

It was a dangerous remark, likely to spark off a train of rumor and speculation. I was not altogether sorry to be interrupted. Swijter, the Dutch chemist, and his wife arrived at the bar.

"Is it true," he asked, "that this is your last night here, that home you go tomorrow?"

It was the first time anyone had mentioned the point this evening. I said yes, it was. Swijter beamed at me and seemed to bulge further through his tight white suit.

"Ah, you must be very seduced."

Swijter's English was still a good deal less polished than his chemistry and he labored under the delusion that "seduce" was a synonym for "please." No one had ever corrected him, out of politeness or ignorance, and it was now too late to do so. I had the suspicion that someone, probably his sensible wife, must have enlightened him by now, and that he had kept it on as a personal eccentricity or as a joke.

"Oh yes, I am, very," I answered, poker-faced.

"And your wife, she will be seduced, too?"

"She will indeed." There was no glimmer of a twinkle in any eye. As a joke it was hardly uproarious.

Swijter raised his rum and soda to me. "Pros't."

I drank back, and moved to make room for Allen, the dark and wiry second engineer and his wife, a blond and fertile woman who should have been into a maternity smock weeks ago.

"All packed up and ready to go?" said Allen. "You lucky man! I wish we could go home every eighteen months."

It was a remark barbed with envy, just the sort of envy Justin had told me to avoid. "Oh well, we all get our lucky breaks," I murmured pacifyingly. "Compensation for being a grass widower."

Allen said: "Huh! I'd willingly leave Laura behind in England if it meant leave in eighteen months."

"You'd do nothing of the sort," said Laura Allen firmly. "I think a wife should be with her husband wherever he goes. It's her duty to make a home for him." She looked me hard in the eye and said, "You don't mind my speaking frankly, do you?"

I disliked Laura Allen enormously. "Yes, I rather do," I said. But she did not hear me. She rarely stopped to listen.

"It's all wrong for husbands to dump their wives and call for them later when they're wanted. It isn't fair on them."

I reflected that if Allen had dumped his wife somewhere, his own chances of promotion would have been much higher. Mrs. Allen's peevish voice went on:

"People say that this isn't a good country for women and children. Nonsense, that's what I call it. Just look at me. I'm the answer to that one."

One of my heavier crosses in my exile was the total inability of anyone, except Walker, to understand why my wife was not with me.

"You mustn't assume it's my fault," I said. "I'd have liked her out here."

Mrs. Allen must have heard that one, for she changed her attack. "Well, you should have made her come then. Tell her from me there's nothing to be afraid of here. It's a good life."

"Oh, she wanted to come badly." I felt I owed it to Diana to defend her from this unjustified attack. "But overseers aren't allowed wives in their first tour."

Allen said: "But you're not an ordinary overseer, old boy. You haven't been near a canefield for a year."

"I know. But Major Pemberton said I was—"

"Christ! He's your cousin, isn't he? Surely you can work it with him?"

It was a widely held belief, among both white and colored employees, that I could twist Justin round my little finger. Blood was thicker than water, I was his heir apparent, I only did an eighteen months' tour of duty. No one would have understood or believed the weakness of my own position or the subtleties of Justin's sadism.

"Beats me why you didn't put your foot down," Laura Allen was saying, "and that goes for you too, Charles Bolton."

Bolton, diffident and short-sighted, started violently.

"Oh, but I—I—I have, Laura," he said. "Audrey's coming out as soon as the flat's rent is up next quarter day. I had a letter from her this evening."

He pulled it out of his pocket, in case we might not believe him. Of course we didn't. Mrs. Bolton was always coming out after next quarter day or after the summer or after Christmas. She only saw her husband every three years.

Mrs. Swijter, kind and perspicacious, changed the conversation. "It must be very exciting for you seeing your children again. How old will they be now?"

"Just two," I said.

"Oh, walking and talking. They must have changed a lot. I wonder if they'll recognize you."

Swijter laughed chestily. "He's a wise man. He will bring them presents. That will seduce them."

"What are you going to bring them?"

"That's what I mean," Mrs. Allen burst in triumphantly. "They have learned to walk and talk since you've been away, and you've missed it all. You've lost it for good. Now I insist on George's sharing every bit of the kids' emotional development so that later he can't say. . . ."

In the middle distance I could hear Reynolds' voice, "I remember in Coimbatore when I was first made head overseer . . ." In the background was Ingram's: "Bad luck, partner. Two short. If you'd only led a round of diamonds and then finessed his queen . . ." On the remote skyline was "The Dream of Olwen."

"Excuse me," I said. "I've got to see Ingram."

"Your deal, J.B.," said Harvey. "It must be, it's the blue cards."

"Tense struggle this, Pemberton," said Hughes to me as I came up. "Close fight. Oh well, say not the struggle naught availeth."

That too we heard every night.

"Darling, your supper's going to be spoilt," said Mrs. Ingram plaintively.

"What about points for unfinished rubber?" suggested Miller. I don't think he really liked bridge.

"No, finish the rubber," said Ingram sharply. "You can do it in one hand if you play properly. Boy, bring me a drink."

Mrs. Ingram smiled seductively at me.

"Bad luck!" I murmured. Sometimes the wives had to wait till ten or eleven o'clock for their supper.

"Oh, it doesn't matter," she cooed. "It's only macaroni cheese and he always hates that."

I waited till Ingram had finished dealing, and then I spoke to him about Jailall. He went on sorting his hand while I spoke.

"Good boy?" he said without looking up. "Not just one of these trouble makers wanting a cushy job?"

"Oh no. I've found him quite a good boy. He's very quick and neat with his hands."

"I don't care a bloody —— what his hands are like."

Hughes murmured archly, "Pardon my French."

"What I want to know is will he turn up every shift, rain, fine or shine?"

"I think so," I answered. "He's never let me down."

Ingram flipped the tip of his finger round the fan of cards. "All right, send him along to me. One heart."

I stepped back and talked to the women. They said all the right things. How excited you must be, you lucky man, never mind next year we go home on leave, and, my dear, next year we shall be able to say next year we go home, well give my regards to the old country, how exciting for you seeing your kids again, my goodness they will have changed you won't know them, don't you frankly think it's rather a pity now you didn't bring your wife out, we were all so looking forward to meeting her, I expect she's very excited too, is it all settled that W.A. is moving into your house, are you dining with A.J. tonight, J.B.'s always a bit intense when he's playing bridge isn't he, for God's sake tell Williamson to turn off that bloody row, I heard the Hudsons haven't been invited to the Trafalgar party, Ramnarine held a meeting on the bridge this afternoon, just where we can't get at him, what did he want, strike first Monday of the new crop unless, partner when I lead a spade I mean that I want you to lead a spade back to me, Jean told me that Peggy is having another baby, boy bring me drink.

I stood and let it all flow round me. A scene from a ballet came into my mind. The man stood in the center of the stage while the other dancers weaved and circled round him. What were they? Tempters? Ghosts of past loves? Symbols of destiny? Images from the mocking world?

"I saw our Laura giving you a spot of the old and bold."

I looked Mrs. Hughes straight in the eye. Mrs. Hughes had once spread a rumor that Allen wasn't the father of his wife's current embryo. She had been made to apologize to Mrs. Allen and had never forgiven her.

"She meant well," I said.

Mrs. Ingram cooed, "My dear, what a damning thing to say."

I finished my drink and said my farewells. Everyone wished me the best of luck. Even Ingram paused to wish me a good trip.

Mrs. Ingram caught my hand and squeezed it. "Have a lovely time, Hugo. Kiss your babies for me."

I gave a sickly leer. I was never certain if Mrs. Ingram was in love with me, or whether she was merely trying to advance her husband's career.

In the doorway I turned, one hand on the knob, like Madame de Tornquist or was it Fräulein von Kulp? I gave a coy little wave.

"Good-bye, all."

They replied in semi-chorus, fugally. "Cheerio! So long! Have a good time! So long! Cheerio!"

I had avoided saying cheerio for five hundred and forty-four days and I wasn't going to start now.

"Good-bye."

"You sound as if you weren't coming back," said Bolton.

"Oh, don't worry, I'll be back."

2

As I walked up the road, a figure slipped out of the shadow of a palm tree.

"Morning, boss."

In Natividad it was, salutationally speaking, morning all day and night. I paused and recognized the chubby-faced, gap-toothed face of Ramnarine, the local rabble-rouser. I nodded curtly and walked on, wanting no truck with him. After a lot of trouble and divided counsels, he had been put off the estate a year before and trespass notices served on him. However, the main road through Malmaison and the bridge were public ground and he used to visit us on his rounds of the colony, playing a sort of Tom Tiddler's ground.

"Boss, boss."

I hesitated and then stopped. "Yes, what do you want?"

He came and stood shiftily before me. "Boss, we hear you go home tomorrow."

"Yes?"

"Boss, we proper sad to see you go. You are our little father. Your brother, Massa Pemberton, he our big father."

"Is that what you were saying at your meeting this afternoon?" I asked. "And he's not my brother."

"Me hold no meeting, boss."

"Nonsense, Ramnarine. Lots of people saw you."

"They lie, boss, they lie, God strike me dead."

The mosquitoes were stinging me and I walked on. He ran beside me like a yapping dog.

"Boss, you tell Massa Pemberton how the Man'ger and Massa Ingram punish-a me. They no let me work. Boss, me got nine pick'nie. Boss, they take away me house, they no let me work."

"Well, whose fault was that?"

"No me, boss, no me," he whined desperately. I reflected that his tone, if not his command of language, was very different when he was haranguing a crowd to strike for their rights. "Boss, you tell your brother to tell the Man'ger to give me job. Boss, me need job." He dropped his voice to a murmur I could barely hear above the croaking of the frogs: "Oh, boss, give me job. Oh boss. Oh boss."

"What, and have you bring all the cane-cutters out on strike again?"

He exclaimed indignantly: "No, boss, me never do that. Me proper good workman. Oh boss, we look to you."

I turned off the road where he could no longer follow without trespassing. I heard his voice droning on as he called to me: "Oh, boss, me look to you. You are our little father."

Walker, being a director as well as General Manager, could, I suppose, have lived in the Directors' House, if he had wanted to. But the Directors' House was only used by Justin on his periodic flying visits and the rest of the time stood empty. Walker lived in his old house next to the factory. This was pleasant enough normally, but now, with the rain wind from the south-west, it was very noisy and smelly.

Walker greeted me at the door, slapping my shoulders with a fly-whisk.

"Come in quickly, Hugo," he said. "And don't bring the mosquitoes in with you."

We went in to the brightly lit gallery.

"I hate this rain wind," said Walker. "It makes the house hardly fit to live in. Still the crop's nearly over now. It'll be better after we've ground off. Sit you down there. Molly will be down in a moment."

He poured out whisky from a full decanter.

"I had a little chat with our friend Ramnarine outside," I said.

"Oh? What did he want?"

"He wanted me to tell Justin what brutes you and Ingram are. He wants his house and his job back."

"Not bloody likely. You know he's trying to bring the whole estate out on strike the first Monday of the new crop?"

"I heard something about it. Striking for what?"

"The usual. Higher wages all round for the field workers and the unskilled factory people. Conditions generally, details unspecified. Every estate worker to own his own plot of land. Ramnarine to be the Workers' Representative on the Joint Committee. That sort of thing."

"And what has our tough energetic union to say to that?"

Walker laughed sardonically. "Damn little—as usual. I saw Maraj

Singh this evening. They're going to urge everyone to work as usual. Not that anyone will pay any attention to them."

"You think we'll have a strike?"

"Oh, I expect so," said Walker casually. "A braying donkey could bring them out on strike at the present time. Well, never mind that tonight. I expect you're feeling pretty good, aren't you?"

"Very happy," I said, trying to convince myself I was.

"Packing go all right? We'll post anything on to you that you can't get in."

Molly Walker came in at that moment and I rose to greet her. She was a dumpy grey little woman and I had always liked her a great deal. Almost alone of the Malmaison wives she wasn't always running someone else down or grinding her husband's axe.

"This must be a great day for you, Hugo," she said shaking hands. "Are you very excited?"

"Just like the end of term," I said. "Almost too excited to eat."

"Steady now!" said Walker. "You've got to keep your strength up for the great reunion. And for all the farewells at this end."

"I've said most of them. I looked in on the club just now to say good-bye."

Walker grabbed the decanter and poured me out another drink. "Quick!" he said. "Emergency treatment. You must need it badly."

"Oh, it wasn't too bad. At least, not worse than I'd expected."

Walker poured himself another drink and set the glass carefully in its condensation saucer. "Was McDonald there?"

"Yes. He always is. He was playing snooker with Campbell."

"Did he say anything?"

I couldn't see what he was driving at. "Not specially. Why?"

"And no one else said anything?"

"Well, they said quite a lot. Nothing about him, though."

Walker shook his head. "Mrs. Hughes must be losing her touch. Never known her so slow on the scent."

I asked, "Why, is something happening to McDonald?"

Molly Walker smiled at her husband. "If you like, I'll tell Mrs. Hughes. If you think she needs starting off."

Walker smiled back at her and then turned to me. "No. McDonald's got a girl in Maidstone into trouble. Portuguese girl. He wants to marry her and asked Justin for special permission. He got the answer this evening."

"Turned down flat, I suppose."

"Oh Lord, yes. With a lot of heavy stuff about concentrating on his job and not messing about with women. He can marry her on his leave or on his next tour of duty. Fat lot of good that'll be. The kid'll be getting on for two by then."

"Supposing he goes ahead and marries her?"

"Contract voided," said Walker grimly. "Home on the next ship and refund a portion of his passage money."

I tried to visualize McDonald arriving at Dunoon or wherever he lived, with a pregnant Portuguese wife, no job and a debt to the firm.

"He's one of the few promising overseers we've got," I said. "I should have thought it would have been worth while stretching a point to keep him."

"M'm, yes. But Justin would never stretch that particular point. At least not stretch it that way. If he'd been going to stretch it for anyone, he'd have done it for you." Walker paused and lit a cigarette. "You know, I wrote to him when you started work in the factory, suggesting that as you were no longer an overseer you ought to be allowed to have your wife and kids out here. After all, it's only overseers who aren't allowed wives in their first tour. I said that as you were now working under Swijter and Ingram, you ought to be treated in the same way."

"But it didn't work."

"No. Justin said he'd made his arrangements with you and it was too late to alter them now. Besides he was most anxious not to show you any undue favoritism."

"What I need is a spot of nepotism," I said bitterly. "I'd like to be smothered in it. It would make me feel more secure, more wanted."

Molly Walker picked up my allusion. "I know, all this stuff about wives getting in the men's way is terribly bad for me too. Not feeling wanted."

"It isn't only us, you know," said Walker. "All the other companies have the same three-year rule for overseers. They have it in British Guiana too. It's the tradition. Saves houses, too," he added drily.

"How did they come to leave out the chemists and engineers?"

"Had to. Just couldn't get the men. By the way, young John Finlay starts his spell next week."

Finlay Brothers were a rival company and John was their heir apparent. I knew him slightly.

"Poor wretch!" I said. "What's he going to do, start at the bottom and sink slowly?"

Walker grinned. "Same as you. You've set the pattern."

"God, how he must loathe the sound of my name."

"Well, at least he isn't married."

Molly Walker rose. "Let's go and eat," she said. "Don't gulp your drinks. Bring them with you."

It was a pleasant meal. Molly Walker clearly didn't want us to talk shop, and it was unthinkable to gossip about other members of the staff. They asked after Diana and the twins; Molly was intrigued by the technical problems of managing them and questioned me closely. Unfortunately in the intervening months I had rather lost touch with these problems, since Diana found them of little interest and did not often write about them. I was, therefore, rather ill-informed on the subject, but I promised I would find out and let her know.

I then asked about her two sons who were both at a public school in England. I interrogated her about the organization of the school, the method of choosing the school eleven, the particular routine followed by the boys each day. Unfortunately they were both poor correspondents and Molly had to confess to considerable gaps in her knowledge. However, she would find out and let me know.

"What about your boy?" said Walker suddenly. He had been taking little part in the conversation, his mind clearly on something else. "Your houseboy, I mean."

"Jailall? He wants to go into the factory. I've told Ingram."

"What's he going to do there?"

"Oh, sweep up bagasse, I suppose."

"H'm, pity. Still we can always get him back when we want him."

"He's only going to get seven cents an hour," I said. "And he's got four children. Or almost got."

"Four?" Walker looked scornful, and glanced up at the boy who was waiting on us. "Moses Khan, how much pick'nie you got?"

The boy grinned. "Fourteen, suh."

"There, you see," said Walker. "Jailall's got some way to go yet."

"Don't worry, he'll get there," I said, "if he doesn't starve first."

"He won't starve, you know," said Walker. "They never do. And at least he isn't trying to send his kids to an English public school, like yours truly."

"Strong words, but true." I persevered. "But, joking apart, don't you think the basic apprentice rate should be raised?" I had that seven cents badly on my conscience.

Walker looked at me calmly. I noticed for the first time that he was tired and possibly ill. "No," he said. "For three reasons." He ticked them off on his fingers. "One. The firm isn't in a position to raise anyone's wages at the moment. Two. If you start tinkering about with one grade, you upset the whole wage structure for the whole industry. Three. The union haven't asked for it. No point in giving it away till then."

"But if it's fair, why not? If they know they're never going to get anything except by asking, they'll be saying give, give, give the whole time."

"Hugo, after eighteen months in the colony, I should have thought you would know the answer to that one. Or has Ramnarine been having an effect on you?" He paused and swallowed some paw-paw. "If you give the laborers something without the union having agitated violently for it—not asking quietly, but agitating—you merely discredit the union. The money has come without their efforts, therefore they're useless. Then you really are piling up trouble. The union are weak enough already without damaging them further."

"But——" I protested.

He smiled and held up his hand. "Look, go and argue it with Justin. He's the person who decides all this. I'm just the good little boy doing what I'm told. You go and bombard London office with a memorandum on factory pay. And put in all those other points you're always thinking up—the loco-line extension and the Barbados seedling and what was it?"

It was a new urinal in the factory, but I didn't like to mention it in front of Molly.

"You put it all up to Justin. It won't do any harm. It won't do any good either," he added.

"Let's go and have our coffee in the gallery," said Molly. "It's cooler there."

We drank our coffee and made conversation on the lines of well-I-expect-you'll-miss-all-this-won't-you. Walker asked after my luggage arrangements; I explained that Stevens, the manager of our office in Port Catalan, was looking after it all for me. Moses Khan brought glasses and the decanter of whisky which had been filled up during dinner. After a while Molly made her excuses and farewells.

"I'll leave you men to have a good chat. But don't be too long, dear."

She gave me a grave smile, looked fondly and, I thought, rather anxiously at her husband, and went upstairs. I heard the mosquito doors bang behind her.

"I've got an early start tomorrow," I said, "so I'll only stay a moment or so."

"Oh tarry a while," said Walker. "Last night. Sit you down again."

Walker pierced and lit a cigar and while he did this, we sat in silence.

"Get a letter from Justin today?" he asked at last.

"No. Why?"

"I had a long one from him."

"About McDonald?"

"Partly."

"About me?"

"Well, no. Practically nothing about you, except confirmation of your traveling arrangements. That was why I wondered if you had heard direct."

I shook my head and drank some whisky. I wondered how Walker managed to find such good whisky in the colony.

"One thing Justin said in his letter was that he didn't think Reynolds should move into your house after all."

"Oh yes. Reynolds said something about that this evening. Why not?"

Walker stared across the room with a puzzled unhappy look. "Justin said he thought it should be kept for your use."

I froze sickeningly, my glass in mid-air. Then I carefully put it back in its saucer.

"But—but I'm not going to be out here again for quite a while and then it'll be——"

"I know. And we're short enough of accommodation as it is, without locking up a house empty."

I sat, not seeing anything. Whenever I am anxious or apprehensive or hearing bad news, I get a tight little ache in my face on either side of my nose. Other people say they get it in the pit of the stomach, but for me it is always in my face, just below my cheek-bones. I had it now.

"I don't think you need worry about it too much," said Walker. "It may not necessarily mean anything. Justin dictates these letters, probably after a good lunch, throwing off odd ideas. I've given up trying to read between the lines long ago."

Yes, maybe it was all right. One shouldn't look for hidden meanings everywhere. Justin could make himself plain enough when it suited him.

Walker said: "You see, this is where we do the work and make the money, but it's the London office where the orders come from. That's where we need the new blood and without being disloyal I think we need it pretty urgently." He paused, not looking at me. "From my point of view the ideal arrangement would be if you took over the production end from Justin. The day-to-day administration, leaving him to cope with policy and co-ord, or whatever he calls it. I could trust you not to bombard me with letters countermanding everything, couldn't I? Or couldn't I?"

I smiled wanly. "I think you could."

"We might be quite a good team." He waited and then asked, "Has it ever been explicitly stated that you were to be made a director on your return?"

"Well, it's been pretty well understood," I said. "Justin practically said as much to me before I came out. And to my mother."

"Ye-es," said Walker slowly. He flicked off his ash. "I'd got that impression too. But is there any specific promise? Anything in writing, for instance?"

I thought for a long moment, rubbing my cheek-bones with my thumb and forefinger. "No," I said at last. "I don't think there is."

"Pity," said Walker.

There were voices on the road outside. Looking through the window I saw the Ingrams, the Hugheses and the Harveys saying good night. The bridge four had at last broken up and were going home to their dinner. It was past eleven o'clock.

"I gather the bank are being a bit tiresome," said Walker.

"Oh Lord!" I exclaimed.

"Well, we're twenty thousand over the overdraft limit, and it's bound to rise further out of crop."

"What happens now?" The ache was there in my cheeks again.

"Oh, nothing special. They're very polite. They want to know when we can bring it down to its limit. And then they want to drop that down fifty thousand."

"And supposing we can't? Is that the end of us?"

"Oh no. They don't want to break us. We're much too good an investment for them. Anyway we might be able to raise some money somewhere else—might," he repeated dubiously. "No, all they want, according to Justin, is reassurance. I'm getting out a lot of figures about the amount of produce on hand and what it should realize. That should keep them quiet for a bit. Apparently they're also a bit anxious about local conditions here, labor, politics and so forth."

"With some reason."

Walker smiled and stubbed out his cigar. The atmosphere, a blend of Hoyo de Monterry and caramel from the factory, was peculiar. I was aware of having drunk a lot of whisky. Walker poured out some more.

"Well, maybe. But they're to be reassured about that too. That's where you come in."

"Me?"

"Yes. Justin is going to produce you like a rabbit out of a hat, his tame expert hot from the colony, brimming over with optimism and reassurance."

"Huh. And how am I to raise that?"

"Easy. Have a strong drink first."

"But supposing I won't play ball for Justin like that?" I wondered if I had at last a weapon against Justin. For a brief illuminating flash I visualized myself playing power politics, a tough adroit bargainer.

"Oh, I would," said Walker. "It's too dangerous to start playing about with the bank. We don't want them to lower the overdraft limit any further."

"No." Reluctantly I let my bargaining counter go.

"We've got to keep their confidence. They're a bit anxious about our board too, I gather."

"Our board of directors?"

"Yes. It looks all right on paper, but in fact Justin and I are the only ones who do anything, and we live four thousand miles apart."

That was true. The other directors were old Mrs. Wright who was almost blind, Sir Arthur Graham, an imposing person who knew nothing of the sugar trade and rarely came south of the border, and Muir, Stevens's predecessor in the Port Catalan office, now retired in a bungalow in Barbados. It was a board nicely calculated to give the minimum of trouble to Justin.

"I can think of someone to strengthen it," I said.

"You. Yes, but the bank apparently want to have their own representative on the board. Justin says they think they can find a suitable man for us."

"Civil of them. I shouldn't think Justin's very pleased by that, is he?"

"Well, he doesn't seem to mind as much as I'd expected. He says the new man will be a help to him in matters of finance."

I could see the set-up. The bank man would be allowed to push figures to and fro between the general and the special reserves, and if he showed any signs of interfering elsewhere Justin would descend on him and overwhelm him with a dazzling oration about first ratoons and second massecuites and percentage invert sugar.

"What I mean," said Walker, "is that if you are meaning to push your way on to the board, this seems a good moment."

"You mean try and get the bank to back me instead of their man?

Or as well as? I don't quite see how to organize that, except by——"

"Oh, for goodness' sake, don't start doing a deal with the bank behind Justin's back or you'll get the sack. No, the idea should strike them independently when you do your stuff with the optimism and the enthusiasm. I'll write to Justin myself, suggesting that you would be a welcome addition to our board. Just in case it's slipped his memory."

"Thank you very much."

"Not a bit. Sometimes I rather enjoy sticking my neck out at Justin."

The decanter was three-quarters empty and I was feeling terrific. Just brimming over with optimism and enthusiasm. I was calm, authoritative and immensely competent, handling my affairs, my destiny, with brilliance, precision and unerring skill. I was like a rider mastering a restless thoroughbred, a yachtsman assessing all the factors, judging superbly the exact moment to go about. My mind was as clear and cool as rainwater. Only my words had an irritating habit of coming out in a rather jumbled form, and this was both tiresome and unfair.

Walker seemed much less tired and ill than he had seemed before dinner. He was smoking a pipe now and reminded me a little of a bad photograph of J. B. Priestley. He was having no difficulty with his words, but a strong Yorkshire accent had appeared like a giant sea-monster breaking surface in familiar seas. I kept expecting him to say Naay laad thee's champion, choose how, or something. He had also taken to emphasizing his points by prodding me with the stem of his pipe.

"You're coming up to the cross-roads, Hugo," he said. "And you've got to know before you get there exactly which way you want to go."

He gave my patella a sharp jab. It hurt rather, but I tried not to show it. I was thankful that my solar plexus was out of his range.

He said, "You've got to look ahead to yourself at sixty-five looking back to yourself now and remembering how you imagined you were going to be at sixty-five."

I couldn't unravel that one, at least not immediately, so I said simply, "Yes."

"The trouble about these cross-roads is that you don't usually realize what they are till you're past them."

"That's very true," I said. I began to corroborate his theory with a parallel experience of my own, a description, fairly detailed I suppose, of the steps by which I became a signals officer in the Army without ever quite meaning to. For a time we both spoke together.

Then my account becoming a little too involved, I lapsed into silence.

"My own cross-roads," Walker was saying, "was when I signed on for a second spell out here. My first spell didn't mean much. I wanted to travel, I wanted adventure, something out of the usual, just for the moment, just for fun. That was all right. But I signed on for my second spell much too easily. I didn't think about it enough. And then after six years out here it was getting a bit late to start on anything else. I was getting dug into the place. I was getting used to hot weather and cheap rum. And some of it was good fun. Besides, I wanted to settle down. Christ!"

I had never heard him talk like this before. "But you don't regret it, do you?" I asked.

"Oh, I've done very well for myself, if you look at it one way. I've started from nothing and I've got to the top—or as near the top as I can get without being in the family. I've got an interesting and responsible job, a bit too responsible at times. I'm making enough to send my boys to a public school. But where does all that get you in the end? If I'd realized that it would mean spending the whole of my life in this hole, I'd never have signed on again. I can see it now, but could I see it at the time? Why is it you only ever know what you wanted, after you've missed it?"

I tried to think of something helpful to say, but I couldn't find anything. I was painfully embarrassed and I stared at the floor, carefully avoiding his face.

"I can see now that I ought to have cut loose. It would have been worth any risk or any hardship to have got clear. But why couldn't I see it in time? That's why I'm not letting Mike and Billy come out here any more. Justin's offered me jobs for them out here when they've done their National Service. But I'm not going to let them come. I don't want them to make the same mistake as me. And that goes for you too, Hugo."

"Me?"

"Yes. There's nothing in the world, nothing, nothing, nothing at all at any time or at any age so bad as getting to my age and waking up one morning and knowing that you've wasted your life. It's your only one and it's gone and you've wasted it. Don't do it, Hugo, don't do it!" He gave a little gasp and broke off. He poured out two more drinks. "I've never said any of this to Molly." He paused and then added, "but I've an idea that she knows."

"Oh, but surely . . ."

"The world was my oyster when I was twenty, and I had to go and bury myself out here." He was becoming maudlin with bitterness and self-pity. He seemed to realize this for he suddenly sat up, prodded me on the knee-cap and said in a brisker tone:

"I'll tell you something else that no one knows. I'm going to retire. Just as soon as Billy's through the Varsity I'm getting out. And right out. I'm not going to stay here and hang around the Country Club like Wyman or Gotch. I'm not retiring to Barbados either, like Muir. I'm going home to England. And I'm not going to hang around all the other retired planters in Tunbridge Wells or Cheltenham or wherever they live. Or Kensington. I'm not going to hang around the West India Club. I want to go my own way. I'd like a little cottage in Yorkshire, somewhere in the Derwent valley, near Malton, that's what I'd really like."

"Why not?" I said. "It sounds delightful. I'm sure you could find one."

"The trouble is I've lost my roots in England. I don't know anyone there except Justin and the boys, and I'm not going to hang around them. Molly may not like it, and I don't know how we'd manage those Yorkshire winters now."

"Oh, they aren't so bad. I'm sure you'll make lots of friends very soon. They're very hoshpi, hopsi, hotsi, you'll be all right."

"Yes," said Walker slowly. "I'll be all right."

There was a long silent pause. There was a singing in my ears, and beyond it I could hear the crash of a bundle of cane falling from the scales into the carrier, and the rumble of the crushers and the hiss of steam from the cane-hoist.

"What do you think of Reynolds?" Walker asked suddenly. "Do you think he'll make the grade?"

It wasn't an easy question to answer on the spur of the moment. I had no great opinion myself of Reynolds, but I didn't want to crab him with Walker.

"The Sa-heeb," I said vaguely. It came out as Sashbeeb.

Walker glanced at me and went on: "I've got to have a good man to take over here when the time comes. Reynolds ought to be all right. Twenty years on a sugar estate in India; he ought to know all about handling coolie labor." He sighed. "If only he'd stop holding forth for a moment and listen. Things are different here, and he won't be any good till he's found that out. Perhaps he's too old to start learning again now. Maybe we ought to have tried one of our own chaps. But who?"

"Pattison?"

"Too weak. Not enough authority. Harvey, too lazy. Miller, too junior. Ingram, I don't think that would really work. His heart isn't really in it any more. No, there isn't anyone, we just had to go outside. But it's a pity, makes bad feeling, people feel an outsider has jumped the queue. Ingram certainly does. Great pity."

Reynolds is a fool, a know-all and a bore, I thought. It was a great mistake ever taking him on. I didn't say it aloud.

"Pity he isn't more tactful," said Walker. "Oh well, there's time yet. Perhaps it'll work out."

He gave a deep sigh, picked up the decanter, looked at it thoughtfully and put it down again. It was empty. There was a long silence.

I don't remember much more about that evening. In particular I don't remember what Walker and I said to each other when I left. I wish I could; I've tried hard many times to bring it back, but it won't come. It's one of those irritating and rather disturbing blanks like a name or a number that's evaporated. There was, I admit, some reason for it on this occasion, but I should like to bring it back. I suppose we said the usual bon-voyage-take-care-of-yourself stuff. But I'd like to know for sure. We might just have said something important, something I would want to remember.

But I do remember some other things. I remember that the road back to my bungalow seemed unexpectedly narrow and twisting and hilly. I remember a large frog sitting under a lamp-post, blocking my path. I wagged an admonitory forefinger at it and said in that special voice: "Good frog, then. Heel! Heel, sir! Good frog. Good boysie-woysie."

I remember finding a pile of letters waiting for me in my living-room. I remember standing there, leafing through them, with the room beginning to spin dizzily. I remember looking up to see if a sudden draught had caught the lampshade.

I don't remember whether I reached the bathroom in time (though I knew later that I must have). My last memory of the night is of standing, breathing heavily, mopping the sweat from my forehead and thinking:

That pile of letters. There wasn't one from Diana. It's over a month since she last wrote. The bitch.

3

I DIDN'T FEEL too bad the next morning, all things considered. I suppose the quality of Walker's whisky had something to do with it. Anyway I didn't need more than one Alka-Seltzer and I made a very creditable effort at the fried egg and bacon that Jailall produced. I was also able to concentrate on my mail.

There were six letters. Two of them were receipts. Two were local, illiterate and anonymous; I had received a good many of these during my time, my various correspondents having a touching faith in my credulity and my disciplinary powers. One of these stated, after an extended preliminary knock-up, that Allen had had a factory hand dismissed because the man had detected Allen in his practice of locking himself into the engineer's office on night shift and going to sleep; and that the head pan-boiler, the foreman and the lab supervisor, who all knew of this practice too, were held to silence by a complicated series of bribes and counter-threats. It was, I supposed, possible, though unlikely. The other letter related, a trifle crudely, the amatory adventures of Williamson with various members of the Estate Weeding Gang (Female) in the fields of high cane. It appeared that he was aided in these exploits by the Gang Driver, an Indian named Harry Persaud, who arranged everything in return for a modest fee. One of the surprisingly large number of women to be so violated had been my correspondent's wife; it was not stated whether or not she had submitted willingly.

I put the letters on one side, staring out of the window and recalling my own days as overseer in charge of the weeding gangs. I had had to plunge into fields of cane grown to a height of eight or nine feet and argue with a crowd of squawking women, most of them pregnant, most of them with halitosis, and all complaining loudly that their particular row contained an exceptional number of weeds and should be paid for at an exceptional rate. No breeze could reach there and I was always soaked through in a matter of minutes; the toothed edges of the cane leaves scratched my bare arms and knees.

There were always mosquitoes; sometimes snakes and rats too. It had never seemed at the time that it was a *convenable milieu* for establishing a love-nest, but perhaps Williamson had greater energy, resource and desire. I wished him every happiness.

I picked up the next letter, saw that it was from the London office, hesitated with the ache back in my cheek-bones, and laid it on one side. It was almost certainly from Justin, and I felt a sudden disinclination to know the answers to the various questions troubling me. They say that it is always preferable to know the worst at once, but I have never seen that. While there is doubt, there is hope, and without hope I am only half myself.

The sixth letter was indisputably and triumphantly from my mother. It was written from South Meon and was, as always, enormously long, written in green ink on what seemed to be pale green tissue paper. She expressed delight at the prospect of my return and certainty of my own excitement at it. She was pleased that I had recovered from an earlier chill and was convinced that I needed a good holiday. She herself was blooming. It was a lovely hot summer and the garden was looking lovely. She related a number of sayings, opinions and experiences of Mason the gardener (she spent a lot of time in his company, seeing in him a typical example and even a symbol of English rural character, and as such of commanding interest). Her begonias were likely to win first prize at the flower show (she did not necessarily mean begonias: despite the hours she spent in Mason's company she never knew one flower from another). Bella (her golden retriever) had been having an affair with the publican's labrador and the worst had happened. They were having to raise two thousand pounds to repair the church roof; there didn't seem anything wrong with it to her. She missed me very much and sent me her love and blessings. It was, in short, the letter she had written to me every week for the last twenty years.

One passage, however, marked it from its predecessors:

You must be longing to see Diana and the twins again and I can imagine how excited they must be. Perhaps you'll bring them all down here for a week or two when you get back. The children would love it here—they could run wild all over the place. They must be terribly cooped up in that London flat, whatever Diana may say. I haven't heard from Diana for some time now, but I'm sure I should have heard if they hadn't been well or anything. I expect she's terribly busy. I heard from someone who'd met her at a cocktail party that she seemed to be dashing about all over the place. I think she's wonderful doing all that sort of thing as well as giving the children the amount of attention they must need.

One of the complications of my life was the mutual antipathy between Diana and my mother. Diana went to South Meon reluctantly and rarely, and my mother retaliated with thinly veiled disapproval. At least "retaliated" is not quite fair to Diana; my mother had started it. I remember the first time they met. I had brought Diana down for a week-end at South Meon just after we got engaged. They were both on their best behavior and I thought all had gone well. But my mother had disclosed her true attitude in one of her "little talks" one night when Diana had gone to bed.

"She's an absolute darling, isn't she. Oh, Hugo, I do think it was clever of you to find her. She's so lovely, and quite terribly in love with you. It's sweet to see you together. I do hope you'll be happy. Of course you know she's pituitary-adrenal?"

Fighting down the panic this sort of remark always gave me, I had asked for clarification.

"Oh, it probably won't matter at all. But I'd always hoped that you'd marry a sensory-thyroid. On the whole I think they make better wives. More domesticated. Pituitary-adrenals tend to be a bit harder, you know, more ambitious, career-girl types. They're more fine-drawn and, of course, their looks don't last quite as well. They get a bit, well, bony later on. But Diana's so beautiful I don't think it'll affect her."

I hadn't enough physiology to know if my mother's glandular information was accurate, but it was a pretty shrewd analysis of Diana. I had wondered, though, at the time, whether my mother would have found something wrong with any daughter-in-law. In any event, one cocktail party, reported at third hand, was hardly evidence of riotous living. Diana was probably extremely busy; twins must make a lot of work. And she had always been a poor letter-writer.

The station-wagon was waiting at the door and Jailall and the driver were loading my luggage. I took ten dollars from my note-case, put it in an envelope and gave it to Jailall. He thanked me with profuse and, I thought, genuine gratitude. I stared for a brief farewell at the factory, its two tall chimneys smoking in the morning sunshine.

"Let's go," I said.

For the first ten miles we lurched along the narrow pot-holed road between canefields, and later, after we passed the Malmaison boundary, through coconut groves interspersed with scrub. There were houses all the way; the Negroes' wooden and often raised off the ground, the Indians' usually made of mud and cane trash. The little red triangular flags, for keeping off evil spirits, fluttered in the light breeze at the top of long bamboo poles. Occasionally there was a gothic horror, with turrets, battlements and stained-glass, the stately home of some Indian big-wig, and I wondered, not for the first time, by what method the owner had amassed so much money.

At Maidstone we turned on to the Parkway, the fine road built by the Americans during the war, which linked their naval base at Chelmsford on the far side of the island with the airport and Port Catalan itself. And as we swooped smoothly along the concrete road, I forced myself—yes, forced myself—to read the letter from London office.

It was, as I expected, from Justin. The official writing-paper of Wright, Pemberton & Co., Ltd., Sugar Merchants and General Agents, was impressive enough with its handsome embossed lettering, its wealth of detail about codes and cable addresses. But Justin's own paper was also embossed in copperplate *From the Chairman's Office*.

My dear Hugo,

I think this will just reach you in time to wish you *bon voyage* and to welcome you home after finishing your apprenticeship. I am sure that you now realize how essential it was for you to spend this time in Natividad and that what you have learned there will make you of far greater value to me. However, you are now entitled to a period of leave, in accordance with our arrangement, and I have no doubt that both you and Diana will be looking forward to this.

As I think I mentioned to you when we last met, it will be necessary for you to spend some of your leave here in the London office so that you may thoroughly master this end of the business too. It is, however, my wish that you should have three weeks complete break first, so you need not report here till Monday, July the 27th.

I hope you have a good journey home. The *Atalanta* is a lush ship. I have traveled on her several times. The purser is a man called Oldfield. He has a lot of very funny stories, so it is worth while buying him a drink one evening and getting him to tell them. Mention my name to him and he will see you are well looked after, especially over getting ashore quickly.

I have asked Burgers to look after you in New York. Their president, R. P. Mills, is rather a bore, but he has a very pretty daughter! I have also left cards for you at the Racquets and Knickerbocker Clubs, so you can use these as much as you like. There are always a lot of amusing chaps in the Racquets Club if you call in there in the evening. The Knickerbocker is a nice place to dine in summer looking out over the Park. They have a Piesporter Goldtropfchen 1949 which may please you.

Yours ever,
Justin P.

Leave, *mon prince?* Leave! you bastard! I was coming home permanently, not on leave. I re-read the letter, hoping that we might be saying the same thing in different words. Value to me. It is my wish. Mention my name. I have left cards for you.

"Oh, for God's sake, stop showing off!"

"Yes, suh?"

"Oh nothing. Not you." I shifted in my seat till the driver could no longer see me in his mirror.

I have always liked Port Catalan. It is noisy, vital and picturesque, unless you happen to find that sort of thing squalid. There are old Spanish villas, modern concrete office blocks, little wooden shops belonging to Indians or Chinese or Portuguese, parks, avenues, cricket grounds, slums, docks. Its narrow hot streets are crowded with gaudy shouting pedestrians, with donkey carts, bicycles and enormous American cars. Everywhere is the smell of petrol, drains, curry and the sea. It is, I often think, the Tower of Babel in reverse. Here are the races of the world—Anglo-Saxon, Latin, African, Oriental—living together in what passes for harmony, all speaking the same language, or what passes for a language.

The offices of Wright, Pemberton were in Main Street, the commercial heart of the town. It was the usual tropical office, with everyone working in one room, the clerks crowded down at one end, Stevens sitting in solitary state at the other, flanked by empty desks kept for Justin and Walker. In the month I had spent learning the work of the office, I had sat down with the juniors. It was hot, smelly, noisy with typewriters and electric fans and in full view of anyone who might stroll in from the street. I had found it very difficult to concentrate.

"Oh hullo, er," said Stevens, rising to greet me. "Had a good ride down?"

Stevens was a lanky efficient man who suffered intolerably from the heat. He had a big jug of iced water on his desk, which he drank continuously. He mopped himself with a towel every few minutes. It was not yet ten o'clock and there were great wet patches in his white suit.

He wrung my hand with a vigor which must have cost him another half-pint of sweat and waved me to a seat.

"I came in the station-wagon," I said. "My heavy luggage is in the back."

"Fine. I'll get Mackenzie to deal with it."

There was a commotion at the far end of the room. A huge Negro in a bright blue shirt had come in and was shouting:

"Yes, you, Mr. Stevens, me want to see you. You got to repent now. All of you got to repent. The Lord go proper punish all of you miserable sinners. He go purge all of you miserable sinners. Yes, miss, you laugh but you is a miserable sinner. You no go laugh when the Lord punish you."

The typists were looking terribly shocked. Mackenzie, the porter, and Gopal Singh, the Chief Clerk, had rushed up to him. Stevens and I looked away and concentrated furiously on each other.

"This is your air ticket to Trinidad, and this your one on to New York. This vast document is your Atlantic steamer-ticket. Your passport is at the American consulate waiting for you to swear not to overthrow the American Constitution. Your dollars are waiting for you to collect at the bank. I don't know if there's anything else you want done?"

"I don't think so, thanks. I've got some shopping to do before I go."

"And when the Lord sits on His big throne, me go say 'Lord, look there Mr. Stevens, he a proper sinner, you go proper purge him with your holy fire, Lord.'"

"I was wondering if you'd like to lunch at the Country Club."

"Very much indeed. Thank you."

Could he afford it? Yes, surely. He was paid far more than I was.

I stood up. Stevens dried his hand and wrung mine again.

"This south-west wind is awful," he said. "I shall almost be glad when it starts to rain."

"Never mind. Perhaps we'll have air-conditioning soon."

He looked skeptical. "I wonder. Even Finlays haven't got it yet."

"Even Finlays? We're meant to be just as go-ahead as they are."

"Yes, I know," he said hastily, suddenly remembering who I was. "I didn't mean that at all."

Of course he did. I said, "See you later," and went out. The black evangelist had been persuaded to leave.

I did my various chores and bought a couple of light-weight toys for the twins. I looked for a present for Diana, but nothing struck my fancy and anyway she would probably rather have something from New York. Then, suddenly remembering my humble duty, I went to sign the book at Government House.

Government House was a large Spanish villa, enlarged and encrusted by a megalomaniac Victorian Governor. Inside I understand that it was of indescribable inconvenience, but outside it was awe-inspiring and I never approached without trepidation. The sentry gazed at me with deep suspicion. Inside the hall was the book, and above it an old yellow notice telling you to ring for the book if it was not there, to write your name in block capitals, to add the letters PPC after your name if you were departing from the colony.

I read it through and meekly did as I was told. The ink blurred and would not take properly on part of the page where there was a still damp sweat stain, made presumably by the hand of my immediate predecessor, a Mr. Montrose Obadiah PPC.

"Rum punch or pink gin?" asked Stevens.

"Oh, pink gin, please." I was beginning to remember my state last night and was glad of some stimulus. There were a fair number of people in the bar of the Country Club; outside was the sound of shouting or splashing from the swimming pool. I could have done with a bathe myself—it was an unexpectedly rare luxury at Malmaison, involving a long drive to Chelmsford or Port Catalan—but my suit was packed away somewhere.

"I see Finlays are here in force," Stevens said.

"Yes. All come to do honor to their new overseer."

They were all there in a group in the corner, McDougall, Butler, O'Hara, Beale, with attendant womenfolk. In the middle, smiling shyly, was John Finlay, their future boss, still wearing a much too hot suit.

"He's getting the full treatment. The inaugural lunch. Do you remember the one you gave for me here?"

Stevens smiled nervously. "Yes, I do."

"It was the first time I had met 94-proof gin in one and a half ounce tots." I caught John Finlay's eye and waved.

"Of course you know him," said Stevens. "I haven't met him."

"Come along then."

John Finlay had been at the same house as me at Eton, but he was three years younger, that almost unbridgeable gulf. He still seemed to be greatly in awe of me. As I came up, he sprang to his feet and stood watching me with attentive deference, as if I were fagging him to the far side of Port Catalan for a pound of sausages.

Indeed, I rather think that was what I said to him the last time we spoke.

"Hullo!"

"Oh, hullo, er." John was the only person on the island, apart from Hughes, who had ever called me Pemberton, and even he seemed to have lost that gift now.

"We meet in passing. You're just starting, I gather."

"Yes. Yes, that's right, I am." He nodded several times.

"What are you going to do exactly?" I asked.

"Oh, exactly the same as you, I think. My father has been having long talks with your cousin."

"Yes, I suppose he would."

"He says your cousin's given a lot of thought to it all."

"He told me that too. Are you here for eighteen months?"

"Yes, oh yes. Yes, of course."

"Why of course?"

John blinked at me very fast. "My father says it's the absolute minimum. He says even you have found that, and I'm not as bright as you. There's so much to learn."

I said, "It's a good tip to ask yourself every night before you go to sleep, What have I learned today that I didn't know yesterday?"

John nodded fast. "Yes. Yes, I see, I'll do that. Fix it in your mind."

"Oh no. Just to see how often the answer is Nothing."

He blinked at me. "You mean, it doesn't take so long?"

"If you put your mind to it, you could do the whole thing in six months, including learning how to play bridge. But the great thing is to take it slowly. Otherwise you'll be bored stiff later on."

"Oh! Oh, I wish you'd say that to my father."

I shook my head. "It wouldn't do any good. If I couldn't get myself out of it, I could do even less for you. Oh, don't worry. Time keeps passing, that's the great thing to remember. You may quite like it."

He was blinking hard. "Oh! My father said I'd like it out here. Won't I? Your cousin said you had."

"Did he? Oh well, it might be worse. Being single, I expect you'll have a wow of a time. The estate wives will be all over you."

Stevens, who had been talking to O'Hara, appeared at my elbow, and I introduced him. I stayed for a moment, and then I moved over to talk to McDougall, Finlays' senior local director and the most distinguished Chinese in the colony. The Natividad Chinese are not such a tightly organized body as the Indians, the blacks, the Portuguese, or, for that matter, the whites. But they play a large part in the commercial and professional life of the colony; they own all the laundries, some of the shops and restaurants; they are doctors and dentists. It is, however, rare to find one in such a high position in a British company and I sometimes wondered how McDougall had done it. Perhaps he had started as a clerk and had worked his way to the top through sheer ability.

"Passing on the torch, I see," he said, nodding at John.

"More or less. I gather he's been told to follow exactly in my footsteps. I feel I can't be his favorite character."

McDougall smiled a quiet crinkly smile. "Surely we are meant to reverence pioneers and explorers, aren't we?"

"I think John's done quite enough reverencing of me for one life," I said. "We were at school together."

"I know. He told me." McDougall stood and looked me up and down for a moment. He was very short, a stocky wizened yellow little man, and I felt he was sizing me up. "Well I expect you'll be glad to be going home," he said, "though I'm sorry we haven't seen more of you. But you'll be coming out again, won't you?"

"Oh yes, certainly. But not for such a long spell again."

"When are you actually off?"

"This afternoon, by the four o'clock plane to Trinidad."

"Oh really?" He looked at me in surprise. "My daughter's going on that plane too."

He nodded at where she was standing, laughing at something Butler was saying. She was a pretty girl, taller than her father, square-shouldered, full-breasted, seeming taller and slimmer than she really was in her long-bodied tussore frock of powder blue and white. She was carefully made up and her black hair was worn in short casual waves, the sort of hair-style which, according to Diana, was too informal to be true. I had met her once or twice before; what on earth was her Christian name?

She laughed again and we went over to her. She looked down affectionately at her father and smiled at me.

"Mr. Pemberton is going on the same plane as you this afternoon," said McDougall.

She seemed delighted. "Oh, how nice! You can hold my hand if I get frightened."

"Only if you get very frightened," I said with mock severity. "I'm on my way to a long-lost wife."

She laughed again. It was a lilting, attractive laugh. I grinned back at her.

Stevens gave me an enormous lunch: grape-fruit, crab-backs, pepper-pot, steaks and paw-paw, and we washed it down with iced lager from Holland. My tentative hang-over vanished and I felt in fine, confident fettle. Stevens seemed to enjoy it too, and he mopped away with his napkin. He couldn't have had a dry stitch left on him.

We talked mainly local politics and he told me a number of things which were new to me. Ramnarine, the agitator, was forming a new trade union for sugar workers to be called the Natividad Labor League and he would be recruiting members, at the expense of the established union, during the out-of-crop break. Dr. Marshall, an elderly black vet, foolish and wrong-headed, who yet managed to have a large popular following, had been persuaded to be President and various left-wing politicians, some of them members of the Legislative Assembly, were to be Vice-Presidents and Treasurers.

"I saw Ramnarine yesterday," I said. "He pleaded with me to give him back his job, as his children were almost starving."

"He's got packets of money," said Stevens. "Enough to run this new racket and an office and a printing press which pushes out those pretty seditious leaflets."

"But where does he get it from?"

"Oh, in the end he'll get it out of the laborers—poor dupes. But in the meantime—" He shrugged. "Your guess is as good as anyone's."

"And you think he'll make trouble?"

"As much as he can. I don't like the sound of it at all."

"Walker thinks they'll come out on strike next crop."

Stevens nodded. "The trouble is that Government are determined to stay on the fence. Oh well, nothing much can happen out of crop, and in two months' time the picture may well have changed. These people always start falling out among themselves, given time. Still, I think you're well out of it."

"I'm not really out of it, you know," I observed.

"No, no, of course you're not," Stevens said hastily. He always seemed to be making little gaffes like that. But he was no fool and I was sorry he took such a gloomy view of the outlook. I wasn't in the mood for being depressed at that moment.

"I expect we'll get by," I said. "We've had labor crises before and we always manage somehow. I expect we shall again."

We went out, and the sun hit us like a blackjack. On the steps of the club I said good-bye to the Finlay crowd; they all hoped I'd be back soon.

"See you at the airport," I said to Fiona McDougall. That was her name, Fiona.

"Ah yes. My escort. Makes me feel very grand."

Stevens insisted on driving me down to the airport, though I begged him not to.

"It'll be cooler than stewing in the office," he said. "I'll catch up with the work later."

"After that lunch, what we both need is a couple of hours blanket-pressing."

"Blankets!" He groaned, took a clean towel out of the dashboard pocket and mopped himself.

"To me," I went on, "one of the saddest things in tropical life is the way people have given up the siesta. You'd never get the Italians or Spaniards doing a thing like that."

"Oh, agreed every time," said Stevens fervently. "I could drown the man who first decided he was too busy to sleep after lunch. And then of course we all have to follow suit."

I murmured drowsily: "I wonder if there's any connection between the too-busy-to-sleep movement and the white-man-go-home movement. Interesting case of cause and effect."

He wrinkled his eyebrows. "They'll probably make a siesta compulsory after we've gone. Oh well, good luck to them. Here we are."

He turned in at the airport gates, yawning hugely as he did so. We hadn't a lot of time; I could see the squat twin-engined Lockheed on the runway and a couple who might have been the McDougalls, kissing each other good-bye.

We got stickily out of the station-wagon.

"Well, good-bye," I said, "and thanks for the lunch and for seeing to everything for me."

"Not at all. I'll get your heavy baggage on to the boat and I'll cable the London office that you've left. Anything else?"

I hesitated. "Would you mind also cabling my wife? I think she'd like to hear direct."

It would wake her up into the realization that she was about to have a husband on her hands again—that is, if she needed any waking up. And the firm would pay for the cable.

"Yes, certainly. We've got the address, haven't we?"

I nodded. He dried his hand and wrung mine with convulsive agony.

"Well, good-bye, er, have a good trip. Have a good time in England."

"Oh yes, you bet I will," I said, without complete conviction.

I didn't hold Fiona McDougall's hand in the plane, not because of any deliberate ungallantry, but because we weren't sitting together. My drowsiness, too, was all-conquering. Once we were up above the Caribbean, with blue, intense endless cobalt blue, above, about and below me, I let myself fall asleep. An hour and a half later, stupid, stretching and with a mouth like the inside of an old boot, I stood on the tarmac of Piarco airport in Trinidad.

"Too bad you weren't next to me," said Fiona McDougall.

I started, then looked at her and smiled. "Much too bad," I agreed. "Did you need me?"

She gave her lilting laugh. "Terribly. I was very frightened when we took off. I always am. And the man next to me never noticed." She looked at me solemnly. "Do you think chivalry is dead?"

"Not that sort of chivalry. Only sleeping."

The sun was low in the sky and it was much cooler. We had two hours to wait before the big four-engined plane came in from South America.

"I suppose we stick around here," I said, "or do you want to dash into Port of Spain?"

"Not worth it. There might be some coffee inside there."

"Or tea."

She shook her head firmly. "The coffee's much better. It's American."

We went into the building and got some coffee, sitting at a little glass-top table. I began to feel much better. Indeed, I remember that moment as having a special pleasure of its own, a sharp tang as distinctive and as exciting as the taste of an oyster. At last the end of term feeling (though now I am a little doubtful if it was that exactly) was beginning to arrive.

I pulled a cigarette halfway out of a packet of Chesterfields and offered it to Fiona.

"I don't smoke, thank you. You must be feeling very excited with life."

"Oh yes. At last the prison gate's opening." I blew a great cloud of smoke at the ceiling.

"Yes, I suppose it must feel like that. Though I think it's a pity that you should think of Natividad as a prison. I think it's rather a nice place, but then, of course, it's my home. I suppose it's inevitable for you."

I thought for a moment. "I look on it as I look on the various army camps I was in. No special hard feelings now it's all over, but I just don't want to see any of them again."

"But you will be coming out here again, won't you?"

"Oh yes. I daresay I shall be as fond of it as you, in the end. But I've had enough of it for now."

She nodded. "I expect John Finlay will feel the same, only of course, he isn't married. I expect you'd have enjoyed it much more if your wife had been out too."

"It would have made all the difference. Well, perhaps not all, but a good deal."

"What a pity she couldn't come! We were all longing to meet her."

I braced myself for it.

Fiona went on, "I suppose you weren't allowed to bring her."

I relaxed and smiled very gratefully. It must have been rather a puzzling smile for Fiona. "Exactly," I said.

"It does seem hard. Had you been married very long?"

"Just under two and a half years. Some people think that a break at that point is quite a good idea." "Some people" meant my mother, but she may have been only trying to reconcile me to the separation. Justin had persuaded her of its necessity much more easily than he persuaded me.

"But for so long," said Fiona. "I don't know how you stood it."

I said nothing. There were too many things I could have said and none of them fit for unburdening to a comparative stranger, even such a sympathetic one.

"It amuses me," she said, "trying to imagine how it would feel to have a husband home again after a long gap. Of course it must often have happened before with sailors and prisoners of war and other people, but I do wonder what it would feel like. Do you think you'll go on where you left off, or will you have to start all over again?"

"Personally I hope we start all over again. I mean," I went on hastily, "I enjoyed getting married. It would be great fun to do it all over again, sort of make up for everything."

"I don't know what it feels like the first time," said Fiona, a little sadly.

It was dark now and we went and stretched our legs outside. There were the peculiar airport lights like diseased lightning, and at intervals we were drowned in the roar of an aircraft taking off. I found an official, reassured myself that our plane was not amongst them, and reported back to Fiona.

"How far are you going?" I asked. "New York?"

"Well, for a couple of days. I'm going on across on the *Atalanta.*"

"Me too."

She laughed again and this time I thought I detected in it a note of irony, concealing possibly something else as yet unidentified. "Of course. I wondered if you might be. Now you can look after me all the way."

"Charmed, I'm sure." It was rather a pleasant prospect.

"But it's all right, I'm not a bit frightened on ships. Not even sea-sick. Still we shall be able to play decktennis together."

"That I do find frightening," I said. "What takes you home?"

Home? Was that the right word to use to her?

"Oh leave. We're due for it this year, but Daddy's been postponed at the last minute. Some crisis or other. He's coming on later. I didn't want to go without him, but he insisted."

I nodded. Walker too was always having his leave postponed or curtailed by some crisis. It was one of the penalties, an unnecessary one I thought, of high office.

Fiona was saying: "In a way I'd rather go to America for my leaves. I mean, I was educated there and know far more people. But Daddy says we're British and to Britain we must go. Anyway he always has to have long confabs in London office."

"If you're at a loose end," I said, "you must come round and have a meal with us. See how we're getting on with our second honey-moon."

"I'd like to very much. But it's all right, I shan't be lonely. The Finlays will look after me, and I hope to go abroad. And of course I must go to Scotland."

"Must?"

"Oh yes. You see, I'm Scots."

I looked at her out of the corners of my eyes. In the half-darkness I could see she was grinning broadly.

"Yes, of course you are."

"I know all about clans and the Bruce and tartans and reels and highland games—though it's a bit early in the year for those."

"Have you got a kilt?" I asked.

"No, no," she said with surprising scorn. "It's men who wear kilts. Women wear tartan skirts—though I'm not sure if I've quite the nerve to wear mine," she added with sudden diffidence.

"Certainly you must. I'm sure you've much more reason to than many people who do."

I wondered again how she had come by her surname. Had some progenitor of hers simply assumed it because he liked it, or had there in fact been some Scottish planter who had been bewitched by the almond eyes of a Miss Pong Chow?

"Have you ever been to—" I was going to say "China" but some strange feeling of delicacy made me alter it to "the East."

"China?" Fiona had no inhibitions. "Heavens, no. I've never been farther east than London. Well, I suppose Davos—I went there once for winter sports. And, going the other way round the world, Chicago. That's the best I can do, I'm afraid."

I mumbled something incomprehensible.

"It's funny," she went on, "everyone seems to imagine—everyone at home that is, I mean in England and sometimes America too—that just because I'm Chinese, I must have been brought up in Pekin and be an expert on T'ang pottery or Chiang Kai-Shek or Confucius."

"And you're not?"

"No more than you. Why should I know about Confucius? We're Church of Scotland. No one's ever taught me anything about China, either at home or at school. Why should they?" There was a touch of defiance in her tone. "But I could tell you an awful lot about John Knox and Mary Queen of Scots. Daddy did that. Not that he's at all a Scots nationalist," she added. "He's very keen on the Act of Union."

"Oh good," I said, uncertain whether I was meant to laugh.

"People think it's something in one's heredity and bloodstream," she said reflectively. "I suppose there's something in it. I daresay I could pick up Chinese culture or philosophy more easily than you, for instance—that is, if I wanted to, which I don't. But it's a bit like assuming that you must automatically be an expert on Early Britons just because you're British by descent. You aren't, are you?"

"Not a bit. Not my period. I've got some Scottish blood too, but I'm not a bit good on John Knox."

"Well, there you are. And I know nothing about the oriental mind except for sundry Natividadians, and I'm never a bit sure how oriental they still are. Should we go in again?"

I took the wee Highland lassie's elbow and piloted her inside. I was intensely aware of the feel of her arm, warm and surprisingly dry. She smiled at me, her slanting eyes narrowing. Very pretty. And not only pretty, terrific sex-appeal. Sensory-thyroid, I thought suddenly.

4

New York the next morning came as a jolt. I think any large city would have done it to me at that time. A Natividadian had once said to me, "You can't think how odd it feels never to have seen any city larger than Port Catalan." It was eighteen months since I had been in a big vital noisy city, and New York is bigger, noisier and more vital than most.

It gave me a liberated holiday feeling; partly because it was so different from Natividad—at last I was getting somewhere; and partly because it struck a nostalgic chord. But it was staggeringly hot, hotter than Port Catalan before the rains, and this posed a sartorial problem. I had only one dark tropical suit with me. How would it look by the following evening? My hotel room, however, was air-conditioned and cool. When I opened the window I was blasted by a wave of heat and noise. I peered cautiously down at Madison Avenue twenty stories below me and then retreated into cool silence. I poured out a glass of iced water from the tap marked Iced Water, reflected how Stevens would have appreciated this luxury, added some ice cubes from the refrigerator and switched on the television. There, a sheriff's posse was pursuing a covered wagon through a ford. At any moment, I was sure, the driver of the wagon would leap off into a bush and hide there while the posse, firing all the time, chased the empty wagon. But whether this actually happened I never found out for at that moment the telephone rang.

"Hello! Mr. Pemberton?"

"Speaking."

"Oh good morning! This is Mr. R. P. Mills' secretary. Burger & Co."

"Oh yes. Good morning."

"Mr. Mills is in conference right now but he asked me to call and ask if you'd had a good trip."

"Very good, thanks."

"And is your hotel room satisfactory?"

"Extremely."

"Oh good. I'll tell Mr. Mills that. He'll be pleased to hear. He wanted to know if you were busy for lunch today."

"No. Nothing special."

"Oh! Well, in that case would you care to lunch with him?"

"I'd be delighted."

"Oh good. Mr. Mills will be very pleased to hear that. Could you come here at a quarter of twelve? He'd like to have you meet Mr. Behrens and Mr. Lloyd too."

"I'd like to very much."

That took care of lunch. What about the evening? Should I go sight-seeing, swanning around the bright lights? Or a theatre or a concert? Or should I taste the elegant masculine delights of the Knickerbocker or Racquets Clubs?

A further possibility occurred to me and I picked up the telephone again.

R. P. Mills was a black-jawed stocky little man sitting behind an enormous and rather bare desk. He greeted me most cordially.

"Well, this is great. It's very good of you to find time to come down and see us. I appreciate it."

"It's very kind of you to ask me."

"Not at all. I wanted very much to meet you. Did you have a good trip?"

"Yes, very good."

"And your hotel room is satisfactory?"

"Most. It's air-conditioned."

He pushed a cigarette-box at me. "Smoke?"

"Thank you." I took one and lit it.

"Lucky man. My doctor's made me give it up. I really ought to give the whole thing up. Retire. But how can I?" We both shrugged at the impossibility. "You know you look quite a bit like your cousin."

"Oh, do you think so?" I said, discouraged.

"Oh yes. I would have known you were a Pemberton at once. You all look the same. Well, blood is thicker than water. All the world over." He clenched his fist and held it out for me to see. "A business is a unit of its own." He gave his fist a little shake. "And a family is a unit of its own." Another shake. "And when you get the two together in a family business, well, it's unbeatable. Like us here." He withdrew the fist.

"Ye-es," I said thinking of our overdraft. "The snag seems to me that the best men can't ever get to the top unless they're members of the family."

He gave me a pitying look. "You needn't worry about that. They are." He paused for a moment. "I hear you've been down in the West Indies, learning all about it."

"Yes, I have. For the last eighteen months."

"Starting right at the bottom, eh? Good boy, that's the way to do it. Start at the bottom, learn everybody else's job as well as they know it themselves. That's the way to get them to respect you."

I wondered how much Ingram or Pattison respected me.

"Oh yes," I said. "But what I can't ever find out is when you learn the job at the top. You'd think that was the hardest part."

He chuckled. "Oh, you needn't worry about that, though it's good to see you're so smart. You learn the stuff at the bottom and put your back into it, and the rest'll come easy." He sighed. "I wish I could make my boy see that."

"Oh?"

"Yes. He's meant to be coming into this firm, but he won't come. He's picked up a lot of crazy ideas, socialist stuff. Says he's had enough of hereditary privilege. I told him he'd get no privilege in this firm. He'd start right at the bottom and have to put his back into it like any of the clerks, but he still won't come. He's working as a carpenter down on the Lower East Side. Says he's more use to suffering mankind there. But he's a good carpenter. He made that table there."

"Did he indeed?" I fingered it appreciatively and then wiped away my finger marks with my handkerchief.

"Yes, Arp's a good boy, but he's very pig-headed. Always has been. And so I've got to stick around here, killing myself with work, waiting for him to change his mind. He'll do it in the end. He's a good boy. He's married a nice girl and she's calming him down. His mother was scared he'd go and marry a Chinese girl or something. But Binkie's a nice girl, good class. Maybe they'll have a baby soon. That'll shake him up."

"Yes, I expect it will."

"I certainly wish I could have you meet him. It might make all the difference if he could meet someone else who was starting at the bottom and putting his back into it. I wonder. Are you busy for dinner tonight?"

"Yes, I'm afraid I am."

"Oh! Oh, that's too bad. Well, could you come for a drink first?"

"Yes, thank you very much."

"Great! I'll have Arp and Binkie come up to meet you. If he'll come—that's the problem. Carol!"

His secretary appeared, a smart girl with a big red mouth and a shiny nose. "Yes, Mr. Mills?"

"See if you can get hold of R.P.M. Junior and his wife."

"Yes, Mr. Mills."

"You'll have to send the office boy down or something. Tell him I've got a young man here I particularly want him to meet and ask them to come and have a drink in the apartment around five o'clock tonight. Say it's specially important."

"Yes, Mr. Mills."

"And you'd better call Mrs. Mills too and tell her."

"Yes, Mr. Mills."

The girl went out.

"Smart girl," he said. "She'll get hold of Arp all right. I certainly hope he'll come. But even if he doesn't I'd like to have you meet my wife."

"I'd like to very much. Will your daughter be there?" The pretty daughter so admired by Justin.

"Gaby? No, she lives in Wilmington now she's married. I don't think she could get away."

"No. Did you say five o'clock?"

"Yes, but come earlier if you get thirsty. Netty will be at home. Come along now and meet the boys."

I was taken out and introduced to Mr. Lloyd and Mr. Behrens. I never quite discovered why it was so necessary to meet them, but I was able to reassure each of them separately that I had had a good trip and that my hotel room was satisfactory.

Outside in the narrow canyon of Pine Street we gasped in the sudden hot damp air.

"Bad weather for an old one like me," said Mills. "My doctor says I ought to go and live in the country. I've got a nice place up in Connecticut, but I only get there week-ends and sometimes not then. I'd like to have you up to see it."

"I'd like to very much, only I'm sailing tomorrow night."

"Too bad. Well, another time."

We crossed what must have been the bottom end of Broadway and plunged into another skyscraper. Halfway up we emerged into what was evidently a luncheon club. It was also clearly meant to be an English club. The décor was vaguely Tudor, the members sat in Windsor chairs round one long refectory table, there were Spy cartoons on the walls. On a side table were copies of Wisden and such journals as the *Eton College Chronicle* and the *Household Brigade Magazine*. I wondered if Justin was a member. Almost certainly.

Mills gave me a large dry martini which was almost pure gin. "Lucky man!" he said. "My doctor won't let me touch alcohol now. And I really need it to get through the amount of work I have to do."

"I expect you're pretty busy," I said.

"Busy! I'm up at six every morning and I do a couple of hours' work before getting to the office at nine sharp. And often I have to work evenings and week-ends too. My doctor says I've got to ease up, but how can I?"

I mumbled sympathetically.

"What would you like to eat?" he asked. "What about roast beef and Yorkshire pudding? It's good here. Make you feel just like home."

"Just like home," I said.

I took the subway uptown and staggered round the big stores looking for a present for Diana. It took quite a while but I found what I wanted in the end. A nightdress, very full and short, barely covering the hips; it was blue, with white lace and black bows. To be worn underneath it was a pair of very brief briefs, also with lace and black bows. It was a sexy, appetizing garment and I gazed at it admiringly till I almost felt a fetish about it. My thoughts, centered completely on Diana, were a reassurance to me, a cauterizing of an uneasy conscience. I was gratified too by the shocking price I had to pay.

I overslept and I did not reach the Mills' apartment till six o'clock. I was aware of being far from immaculate; my suit was creased, my face was flushed and marked by the pillow. I was also an hour late, although it seemed to me that six was a good hour to start drinking. Everyone was already assembled and R. P. Mills came forward to greet me.

"Hello! Come on in. We were beginning to think you must have forgotten the address."

I apologized humbly and was introduced to Mrs. Mills.

"How do you do, Mr. Pemberton. You must be the only person in New York who isn't minding this heat."

I assured her that the West Indies weren't nearly as hot, but she didn't hear me. She was already asking about my trip and my hotel room.

"And this," said Mills, "is R. P. Mills Junior. Mrs. R. P. Mills Junior, Mr. H. Pemberton."

We shook hands. I had expected Arp to come in his working clothes, with sawdust in his hair, scruffy and defiant; but he was a good deal more immaculate than I in a well-pressed and well-fitting suit, a dark tie and a white shirt. I couldn't see any sawdust, even under his nails. Binkie was also in a fashionable well-pressed frock, a plain girl with a heavily lip-sticked mouth and a shiny nose.

I made the routine conversation, where I was staying, how sorry I was I was not staying longer, how it wasn't so much the heat as the humidity, what a good lunch Mr. Mills had given me. At one stage Binkie was called over to talk to her parents-in-law, and I was left alone, deliberately I thought, with Arp.

"Your father was telling me about you," I said. "I saw the table you'd made in his office. I wish I could do things like that."

Arp ignored this. "My father's just given me a bellyful about you too. You seem to be his fair-haired boy at the moment."

"Oh, do I?"

"Yes. So that's why I came, to see what the sucker looks like."

"Sucker?"

"Well, aren't you lapping up all this corn about family businesses and starting at the bottom?"

"It's just what I've been doing for the last eighteen months," I said. I wasn't liking Arp very much.

"And do you really think that you were doing a lot of good to others doing that?"

"Well, perhaps not to others. But to myself. It'll be a great help to me later."

"Will it?" Arp looked sourly at me. "I can think of a lot of things which would be of more help. Anyway, it's a lot of hooey."

"How do you mean?"

"This pretending to start at the bottom. Everyone knows that you're going to jump the line in a year or two's time because you're the President's son or nephew or something. You don't start anywhere near the bottom. It's just pretense. If you really did want to start at the bottom, you ought to go into some business where you have no influence and work your way up in that. Then you can be pleased with yourself if you get to the top—if you really think getting to the top is a worthwhile activity."

I decided the moment had come to counter-attack.

"Is that why you won't come into Burgers?" I asked. "Because of having to start at the bottom?"

His eyes narrowed. "I couldn't care less about tops and bottoms.

In my profession there aren't any tops and bottoms. There's only work to be done."

"But don't you think it's rather a pity to break the succession?" I said, astonished to hear myself saying it. "Your father says it's run father to son for four generations. That must be pretty unique."

"So I should hope. If everyone just did exactly what his father did, we shouldn't get very far, should we? Yes, think of it, Daddy and Grand-daddy and Great-grand-daddy and Great-great-grand-daddy all sitting in the same plush President's chair. Do you think that's anything to be proud of? I want to sit on a somewhat harder bench."

"But it'll be a pity if the firm folds up just because of you, won't it?"

"It'll be a world-shattering loss," he sneered. "Burgers! General Agents. Selling what they didn't make and buying what they don't use. Parasites! No use to anyone."

"They're a lot of use to us," I said. I was glad his father wasn't listening.

"Well, maybe parasites do have some purpose in the insect world. I wouldn't know. But that doesn't stop me feeling that there are higher forms of life."

We left it at that. I didn't say any more to him except good-bye. Nor did I get a word with Binkie. For the rest of the time, Mrs. Mills spoke to us. Before the irresistible onrush of his wife's garrulousness, even R. P. Mills fell silent.

I wasn't quite sure where to take Fiona. I didn't know what taboos the smarter restaurants might have against her and while I had spotted a Chinese restaurant not far away, I felt that that would be the last place in New York where she would want to go. In the end I left it to her.

"It depends how busting out with dollars you are."

"Trickling very sluggishly."

"Let's go down to the Village then. I shared an apartment down there for a few months once. I'd like to see it again."

We took a Fifth Avenue bus down to Washington Square and mingled with the evening strollers.

"You're horribly over-dressed," I said. "Why aren't you in a shirt and jeans?"

She laughed her musical laugh. "Too conspicuous uptown. People stare at me enough as it is. And for that matter why aren't you wearing shorts? And your coat and tie!"

I removed them and we merged indistinctly into the crowd. I took her arm; a slight feeling of prudery prevented me putting an arm round her waist like other couples. We paused for a moment to watch a game of chess on one of the big permanent tables and then strolled on.

"My apartment was over there," she said pointing down a street, "across Sixth Avenue. But there's a restaurant here where we went quite a lot."

In the air was a babel of languages unknown to me. People sat on every doorstep and on the fire escapes which hung down the outsides of houses like creepers; they stared at us incuriously. The restaurant was crowded and incredibly noisy. A juke-box blared in the corner.

"What would you like to drink?" I asked when we had jostled our way to the bar.

"I think I'd like a long screwdriver on the rocks, please."

"Heavens!" The barman seemed to understand. "I think I'll stick to a martini."

We sipped our drinks—Fiona's turned out to be nothing more alarming than vodka, orange juice and ice—and I surveyed the scene. On one side was a party expostulating violently in Italian. On the other a solitary young man in rimless glasses, a T-shirt and shorts which, as he leaned across the counter, seemed to conceal concave buttocks. Beyond him were two Negroes, flamboyantly shirted, who were arguing heatedly about the knee of someone called Campanella. One girl in particular attracted my attention. She too was in a T-shirt and Bermuda shorts and she carried a book under her arm; her fair hair was in a horse's tail and her face (pretty) was the greasiest I have ever seen. As I watched she went up to a man who shook his head and turned away. The second man she tried spoke briefly to her before he too turned away. I reviewed in my mind the great courtesans of history and literature—mostly of literature—and concluded that the trappings and the technique had changed drastically, not perhaps for greater success.

The girl was now talking to the hollow young man next to me and he at least bought her a drink. She put her book down on the counter and picked up her drink, talking all the time. I can never see anyone carrying or reading a book without wanting to know what it is and so I lowered my head towards the counter till I could read the title. It was Donne's *Devotions*.

The young man was gazing at me with curiosity. I straightened up again.

"Well, how are you liking New York?" asked Fiona.

"Oh, I haven't had time to get to grips with it yet. I'm still seeing it through the eyes of Dos Passos." Fiona frowned in some perplexity. "He wrote a book about New York," I explained. "So my viewpoint's a bit distorted, though I don't expect it's as odd as my idea of the deep South."

"You haven't done any sight-seeing yet?"

"Not really. What ought I to see?"

"They run tours around the city. You ought to go on one of them. They'll show you everything, Central Park, Radio City, Empire State Building. You may even get Chinatown at night." She was looking sideways at me.

"I've got to go there," I said. "I can't wait."

"I wish I had an opium pipe," she remarked. "But then I don't even smoke tobacco."

"You're terribly disappointing. I can't find anything sinister about you. Where do we eat? Through there?"

The Negroes were arguing now about whether Campanella was a better catcher than Yogi Berra. The girl with the greasy face had moved on to a fourth man to whom she was talking agitatedly. She glanced up at me as we squeezed by her.

"Personally," she was saying, "I find the Art of Fugue more satisfying."

For a blinding moment I stared into the colorless eyes of her who found the Art of Fugue satisfying, and I realized I had misjudged her calling completely.

"Were you like that when you lived here?" I asked.

"Pretty well," Fiona admitted.

"Did you talk all the time about Donne and the Art of Fugue?"

"Donne?" She was evidently searching in the depths of memory for some clue. "Oh, you mean the man who is always quoted at the beginning of every novel?"

I smiled. "Yes, him."

"No, I never read him. I don't read a lot. I'm not an intellectual, you know, though I try to keep up."

"What are your interests?"

"Chiefly at the moment my job. Housekeeping for Daddy, keeping the home running smoothly. He's very keen on that. But anyway that's what I'm interested in—cooking, sewing, domestic stuff generally. Pretty dull, I'm afraid," she added with a rueful smile.

"Far from it. Some young man's going to be very grateful for it." I paused. "Is there a young man?"

She shook her head. "No, I'm afraid not."

"Oughtn't there to be?"

"I'd like there to be, of course. But it isn't very easy for people like us. I mean I've really got to marry a West Indian Chinese and I haven't found one I like yet. I don't want to marry any old laundry proprietor just because he's Chinese. I know I don't seem frightfully well educated, but it would break Daddy's heart if I dropped too low. If I could find a doctor or a lawyer, and he was nice too—but it's so cold-blooded looking for the right race first, and the professional standing next and the actual person last of all."

"Must he be Chinese?"

"Oh, I think so. It's so difficult once you start mixing races. Neither family ever quite accepts the other. I don't feel as if I could cope with it."

"What about this big city?" I asked. "There are probably thousands of nice young men here who would fill your bill."

"Maybe. But what am I to do? Buy my opium pipe and go down to Chinatown?"

The vichyssoise was cold and savory in my mouth and I was enjoying myself. Fiona too seemed to be forgetting her romantic problems and her eyes were beginning to sparkle. I filled up her glass again.

"Anyway," I said, "I don't quite share his views about having to work down in the slums, but otherwise he said just the things I went about saying myself when my cousin first started putting the screws on me."

"Well, I suppose young men often feel like that. They want to strike out on their own, not just follow in father's footsteps."

"Yes, but we ought to have been blood-brothers. In fact I couldn't stand him. I found myself defending all the things I disbelieve in, trotting out all the stuff that was used on me. I thought him conceited and surly and wanting to break his father's heart out of sheer cussedness."

"He doesn't sound a bit like your blood-brother."

"I should hope not. He's so unpleasant that I think he'd lose all his firm's good will if he came into it. He's probably much better carpentering in the Lower East Side, wherever that is. No, the thing that really needled me was that here was another young man who wanted to strike out on his own, and he's had the guts to stick to it. I hadn't."

There was a pause.

"I didn't realize," she said quietly. "Didn't you always want to be a planter?"

"Oh Lord, no. I wanted to be a publisher or a literary journalist. It wasn't just that I wanted to go my own way and get away from father's footsteps. It really was the life I wanted, my sort of world. Books have always meant a great deal to me."

"Did you try it?"

"Yes, I worked on a literary magazine for some time. I loved it. But there wasn't a lot of cash in it, and my wife was having twins, and I felt I ought to look to the future a bit more." I smiled deliberately. "It seemed to me that a paterfamilias of such splendor ought to have something more solid behind him. So I came back to the fold."

She looked at me sympathetically. "I'm sorry," she said simply.

"Yes, it was a blow. No fatted calf either. However, there it was."

She smiled into her soup. "It must have been hard. Still, you were obviously quite right."

I didn't say anything. She threw me a quick glance. "I daresay your friend Arp will do just the same when he's a bit older—especially if he has some children."

"I wonder," I said slowly. "I'm not sure. He struck me as tough."

"The part I couldn't have borne," said Fiona, "was the separation. If I'd been your wife—or you. No, that's wrong. I could have borne it if I'd had to. It does seem wrong though. Families are so terribly important; they're meant to be together. But the having to come out and live in Natividad, that wouldn't have worried me at all."

"Well, of course not! It's your home."

"Even if it wasn't! What's wrong with the place? I think it's nice. It's warm and beautiful and friendly and its troubles are no worse than anywhere else's. Probably a good deal better."

That wasn't a bit what Walker had said to me, and he had lived there longer than Fiona. But then he wasn't young and romantic. It was never his home. It was never mine either.

I said: "It isn't till you get away, till you come somewhere like this that you realize what you've been missing. It's the civilized intellectual life I want. The cultural life. I like coming into a strange pub and hearing a girl talking about Donne and the Art of Fugue. In Natividad all the women ever talk about is themselves."

Fiona lowered her head. "Touché!" she murmured.

"Oh, I didn't mean you."

"I think you did in a way." She raised her head and looked me in the eyes. "Hugo, I'm not nearly as clever as you. I haven't read nearly as much; I'm a pretty ordinary person. I haven't any right to say this to you."

"Go on."

"Well—" she hesitated, feeling for words—"this bothering about where we live and how we live and what other people talk about, I don't think it really matters. I don't think that's what we're here for."

"What do you think we're here for?"

"I think we're here to do our job. To do our best."

That was almost what Arp had said to me; yet he and Fiona were arguing in opposite directions.

"But surely it matters what work we do? Suppose we are asked to do something we aren't fitted for?"

"Well, of course it depends on the circumstances and who asks you. But, generally, I don't think it matters in the least what you do so long as you do it well."

"Ye-es." I thought for a moment. "What about yourself? Supposing you were asked to do something that you dreaded, something like——"

"Accounts," she volunteered, "my private horror."

"All right, accounts, in somewhere like the Antarctic." It was getting a little improbable.

"I can think of places I should dislike even more," she said. "Even if I was pressed to marry the wrong man as well, I should put up with it as best I could. I should try and make a go of it."

"You wouldn't fight it?"

"No. Why? I don't think one should fight one's personal destiny. There are so many other things more worth fighting."

"You give me furiously to think," I said.

"I'm sorry. I didn't mean to be so priggish or pompous. It's my——" She paused irresolute.

"Your oriental fatalism coming out."

She smiled. "Now then, Hugo!"

It is perhaps a revelation of my own mind that while half my attention had been absorbed in her philosophic disputation, the other half was considering her thick eyelids like rolled venetian blinds above newly-polished windows, her flat nose, her full lips and startlingly red lipstick. I felt a twinge, an echo of the grinding I had known when I first started to get serious about Diana; and that brought an immediate reaction, a counter-twinge.

There must have been a little silence between us, though I had not noticed it.

"Tell me about your twins," Fiona said. "I'm sure they must be sweet."

Next day I went sight-seeing, though they were hardly the sights Fiona had suggested. I went to three bookshops and browsed for hours, my faculties stimulated by the infinite variety of creative endeavor, sensibility, entertainment, by the hours of sheer pleasure represented by those thousands of books. In the end I bought a copy of the *Saturday Review*, two recent best-sellers, and some older books which I had somehow missed reading before: *Tortilla Flat, Death Comes for the Archbishop, In This Our Life*. Between them they cost so much that I had to lunch cheaply at an Automat.

In the afternoon I went to the Museum of Modern Art, the Frick and the Metropolitan Museum. I returned to my hotel with enormous aching feet, drunk with the splendor of Rubens, Renoir and Gauguin. I am not normally a museum or gallery maniac, but at that moment I was thirsty for civilized beauty, just as I was hungry for love.

5

I HADN'T GOT a cabin to myself and by the time I went to bed my companion was only a mound of bedclothes. His name, according to the suitcase I kicked on entering, was Warner; he had taken over most of the wardrobe and chest of drawers for his clothes; his false teeth stood in a glass above the basin. He was, I deduced, inconsiderate and no longer young. All the same I had no wish to wake him and I went mousily to bed in the near darkness of my reading light, scrabbling in my suitcase for my night things and putting on odd pajamas in the process.

None of my last three nights had been the sort recommended for, say, convalescents and I was tired. As I stretched before turning on my side, I could feel the throb of the engines through the bunk. I was just wondering whether we were out of sight of land, when I fell asleep. Two hours later all the cabin lights were turned on and I awoke with a sickening jerk. My companion, a bulky figure in gaping pajamas, was bumbling about, looking for his slippers.

I almost asked him what was the matter but I decided not to bother. He went out leaving all the lights on. I wondered whether to get up and turn them out, but laziness and politeness prevented me. I was shamming sleep, when he returned and went sluggishly and clatteringly back to bed. He seemed to be asleep immediately.

I am one of those people who cannot easily go to sleep again if they are once awakened. I lay for hours listening to his breathing, which was deep enough to irritate me and not quite stertorous enough to justify me in throwing a shoe at him. I had, so it seemed, just fallen asleep again, when all the lights went on and he was hunting for his slippers again.

This time I shammed sleep throughout, wondering if the purser could find me another cabin. What had Justin said his name was? Oldham? Oldfield? Perhaps the contact might be useful after all.

I had just struggled back to sleep for the third time when I was awakened by a bell shrilling through the cabin. The lights went on again and with bleary furious eyes I saw Warner sitting on the edge of his bed stretching.

He switched off the alarm bell. "That's it, boy," he said. "There she goes again. Start of another day."

"Do you realize," I said, "that it's only five o'clock?"

"Six o'clock, boy, six o'clock. Clocks were put ahead an hour last night. Ah, caught you on that, did I, boy? Yes, six o'clock, God's own time. Best time of the day six o'clock in the morning. Always get up then, rain or shine, summer or winter. That's the way to take all the tricks. You don't let anybody get ahead of you if you get up early."

I thought of asking who was trying to get ahead of him on this ship, but it didn't seem worth it.

"That little alarm clock wakes me every morning at the same time. Sundays too. Wonderful little clock. Got it in Switzerland years ago, keeps great time. Maybe it loses a couple of minutes a week. Yes, boy, it's a wonderful little clock. Always wakes me up. Six o'clock every morning."

Perhaps the barber's shop had ear-plugs. But it would be much better to change my cabin. Perhaps in the meantime he'd drop dead.

"Plenty of time for you, boy." His voice had changed and I realized he must have put in his false teeth. "You just turn over and go to sleep again. Yes, boy, you turn right over and don't pay any attention to me. I guess you need more sleep than me, though I reckon you had a pretty good night. Every time I looked up in the night, there you were fast asleep like a little baby."

I grunted. Perhaps I would die myself.

"I slept pretty well myself. Always do on a ship. They say they're a kind of rest cure, don't they?"

I opened an eye. He was standing, naked and bulging, before the wash basin. I turned quickly towards the wall and pulled the bedclothes over my ears.

"Yes, boy, it's great to be going to England again. Finest country in the world after the States. My great-grandmother came from England. My mother's grandmother. She came from King's Lynn, Norfolk. Do you know King's Lynn?"

I grunted.

"Always go back there. Nobody left now, but I like to see the old place. Feel it's kind of another home to me. No, my home's in Chicago. Yes, boy, Chicago. Do you know that Chicago's the third largest city in the world in size? Yes, sir, it is, the third largest in size. They say it's the windy city, but I know places just as windy. Yes, boy, Chicago's a great city. You ought to come and see it. We come and see London and Paris. You ought to come and see Chicago. Did I say it was the third largest city in the world in size?"

I grunted.

"Well, I'm wrong. It's the third largest city in population. Yes, boy, in population. Los Angeles is the third largest city in size, but Chicago is the third largest in population. First New York, second London, third Chicago. Yes, boy, that's the way it is."

He developed this theme while he dressed and I have never known a man to dress so slowly. Indeed at one moment I decided he must have abandoned the project. But at last I heard:

"Well, boy, up on deck for a breath of God's own fresh air. You just turn over and go to sleep again. Plenty of time, boy. How many times around that deck for a mile?"

"Eight," I said, very loud and clear.

"Eight times is it, boy? Eight times around the deck for one mile? That's for me. That's it, boy. Eight times around the deck. But not for you, boy. You just pop back asleep again, eh boy?"

He went out leaving on all the lights. I don't think he could have been more than once around, and indeed from his figure I hardly expected more. He was back depressingly soon.

"Well, had a nice nap? Not much of a day, boy. Thick fog outside. Always get a fog here. It's the Labrador current meeting the warm current from Florida, that's what makes the fog. Yes, boy, always get a fog here, any time of year. I was here once in November . . ."

He sat down and enlarged on the subject. Physical geography was clearly of all-consuming interest to him. Finally he looked at the wonderful little alarm clock and announced that breakfast must just be starting.

"Well, be seeing you, boy. Don't lie there too long or you'll miss your breakfast. Never want to do that. It's pretty important in life to have a good breakfast, eh, boy."

I was standing before the wash basin, thinking morosely about shaving, when he returned.

"That's better, boy, that's much better. That's what I call a breakfast. Coffee, orange juice, pop-crispies, ham and eggs, and waffles and syrup. Ah! You'd better hurry up, eh boy, or you won't get any. It'll all be gone if you don't hurry up."

"Breakfast goes on till ten o'clock," I said sourly.

He didn't answer. He had taken out his teeth and was rinsing them under the tap.

I was still in a filthy temper after breakfast and this was not improved by the size of the queue at the purser's office. But the temper began to clear when I went on deck. Fiona was standing leaning over the rail, staring into the fog. She was wearing a coral-colored sweater with a deep collar, and Bermuda shorts. I had an almost irresistible desire to pat her on the bottom as I approached. I buried my hands firmly in my trouser pockets.

"Oh, hullo! How are you?"

"Bloody," I said, "like the weather. Do you realize that this is due to a hot current meeting a cold one and that it always happens?"

"The weather," she asked, "or your temper?"

"Both probably, but I haven't quite worked it out yet."

I waved at the sea. "According to the hymn writers, Heaven is meant to be like that."

"Heaven?"

"Yes. A glassy sea. You spend your time casting down your crown around it."

"Oh!" She contemplated the scene. "Oh dear!"

"Almost I persuade you to be a Buddhist?" I asked, looking at her.

"Almost you do," she laughed. I liked her laugh with its own unusual lilt. I realized that I was playing for it deliberately.

"Well, what shall we do today?"

"What is there to do?"

"Plenty. First round of the deck-quoits. First round of the ping-pong. Boat drill practice. Beef tea and tombola in the Jungle Café. Film Show. Bridge drive in the Carlton card-room. Hostess-conducted tour of the shopping arcade. Grand get-together dance in the Ritz Ballroom. Tea and sewing-bee in the Palm Court Verand—shall I go on?"

"Please don't. Suggest something practical."

"What about a bathe?"

"A bathe?" She wrinkled up her nose at the fog. "Today?"

"Why not? Rumor has it that there's a pool somewhere in the bowels of the ship and according to the notice-board the water temperature's 74. I think it's just what I need after the night I've just had." It would be nice too to see Fiona in a bathing suit.

"Oh, all right," she said. "Give us an appetite."

"Can I speak to Mr. Oldfield?" I asked.

"Mr. Oldfield?" One of the deputy assistant pursers looked at me with some surprise. "I'm afraid I don't know the name, sir. Have you consulted the passenger list? Or perhaps the Chief Steward's Office, on the other side of this archway?"

"Mr. Oldfield is not a passenger," I said icily. "He is the Purser."

The man rounded his eyes. "Oh no, sir," he simpered. "Mr. Carpenter is the Purser."

"Oh! What is Mr. Oldfield then?"

The man shrugged indifferently. Then he said, "One moment please," and went away to consult another assistant purser. I saw them talking, shooting me glances of deep suspicion. Then he came back.

"Mr. Oldfield used to be the Purser, sir. He transferred to another ship last year."

"Oh dear."

"If it is a personal matter, we could arrange to forward a letter to him, sir. Or perhaps I can help you."

The woman behind me in the queue was fidgeting restlessly.

"I'm sure you can," I said winningly. "I only want to know if I can change my cabin."

The man's face set. "I'm afraid it's quite impossible, sir. All berths on the ship are taken. There is a notice to that effect on the notice-board on the Lower Promenade Deck."

"Yes, but isn't there——"

"I'm afraid I can't help you, sir. Yes, madam?"

The woman said: "I'm afraid I was going to ask the same thing. Is there any possibility of——"

"I'm afraid not, madam. All berths are taken."

"Oh. Oh dear! But——"

"I'm sorry, madam."

"Let's find something called the Coconut Grove Bar and have a drink," I suggested.

"Make us feel quite like home," said Fiona.

The bar, when we finally tracked it down, had a vague décor of palm branches—date-palms, though, not coconuts—superimposed on the usual gilt and buff. Over a drink I told Fiona about Mr. Warner and my rebuff at the Purser's Office.

"Oh, poor Hugo!" she said sympathetically. "I do feel for you."

"And the barber's shop hasn't got any ear-plugs either."

"I can lend you some cotton-wool, if that would help."

"Thank you. I think it might. But the real object of the exercise is to avoid sitting next to him at meals. Where we sit at lunch today, we shall sit for the whole of the rest of the trip. The problem is whether we go in first or last."

"I should think in the middle of the throng and be quick on the draw. But he may not be at your table at all."

"Oh, he is," I said gloomily. "I know that already. By the way, where are you sitting?"

"Oh, I'm at a little table tucked behind a pillar. We're a nice crowd, judging from breakfast. Two blacks, one Indian, two Japanese, one unidentified as yet, probably Filipino, and me."

I stared at her. "You mean . . ."

She smiled. "Yes, all the niggers together. Little Harlem."

"Good God! But they can't do that! You mean, we're all white and you're not allowed to sit at the same table as us?"

"Oh, it's not deliberate. It just happened to be the only seat free when I checked in with the Chief Steward."

"Quite a coincidence!"

"Oh yes. That's how it always works. I'm used to it."

"God Almighty!" I said. "It makes one bloody angry."

She gave a little laugh. "Relax, Hugo. It isn't worth making a fuss about."

"Well, I think it is, even if you don't. I know! I'll come and sit at your table, and let them sort that one out."

"Oh please!" She was serious now. "Please, Hugo, don't. Don't make a row. It isn't worth it."

"But why shouldn't I come and sit at your table? I'd much rather talk to you than to Warner."

"Oh please don't. I don't mind a bit, so why should you? I haven't got to know the others very well yet, but I expect they're charming. They're first class passengers, too. Probably they're bishops or ambassadors or something." She paused and looked at me earnestly. "Please, Hugo, don't make a fuss. I'm quite conspicuous enough already without that."

I grunted sullenly, unconvinced.

"White man go home," she said.

I looked up startled. She was watching me intently, a gentle smile hovering on her mouth. I relaxed and smiled back.

"I think it's too bad of you," I said. "You let me get all worked up and hot under the collar about the way you're treated and race relations in general, and then you tell me to forget it and laugh it off. It isn't fair."

"I'm sorry. I didn't mean to. I just thought it might amuse you. I wish I'd never mentioned it, but I thought you'd find out anyway. Really, Hugo, it doesn't matter to me, at least not here. It would be a different story in Natividad, but here——There are even compensations."

"Such as?"

"I get a cabin to myself."

I stared at her. "Do you, by jove! Almost you persuade me to put on disguise."

She laughed at that and I saw, with another little tight pull at my solar plexus, that what I had said had given her pleasure. I signaled for another lot of drinks. They were duty-free and enticingly cheap.

"There is one thing you could do for me," she said slowly, "that is if you wouldn't mind?"

"Of course. Anything you like. Even introduce you to my cabin companion."

"Oh, I wouldn't ask you to do that. No, it's——" She broke off and gave a little shake of her head.

"Well? What is it? Bicycle with you in the gym?"

She smiled and shook her head. "No, it doesn't matter at all. It was just an idea and——"

"Oh come on, spout! You've got me all worked up again. Speak and I will do your bidding."

"No, it's nothing. I wish I hadn't mentioned it. It was only an idle thought."

I was thoroughly curious now. "You can't get away with it a second time. Come on now."

"No, Hugo, please not. I'm so sorry. It's just that I'm talking too much this morning."

We went on like that for another ten minutes, but she wouldn't budge. I felt rather irritated.

I succeeded in not sitting next to Warner. Instead I found myself beside a young man with puffy eyes, his sole distinguishing feature. Beyond him were two girls, red-mouthed and shiny-nosed in the prevailing fashion, who were about to do eleven European capitals in six weeks. Beyond them was a tall shaggy middle-aged man who seemed familiar, though I spent some time at that first lunch in trying in vain to place him. Next to him was Warner and between Warner and me was an American couple I secretly named the Dodsworths. I never found out their real name, or, for that matter, the names of the others; and I don't suppose they ever discovered mine.

For the most of that meal, and the ones that followed, I talked, or rather listened, to Mrs. Dodsworth, who, though she had a great deal to tell me about her past and future life, proved more sympathetic than I had first thought. I had little converse with the young man on my left, except for:

"Is this the first time you've traveled on this ship?"

"Yeah."

"But you've been across the Atlantic before?"

"No."

"Oh I see. Do you live all the time in America?"

"No."

"Oh, you move about a bit then?"

"No."

"Oh. Which is your home town?"

"Toronto."

I suppose it served me right, but I couldn't help feeling that some part of the gift of speech had been denied him. But what a nice man to share a cabin with!

The capital-collecting girls, however, were compensatingly enthusiastic, questioning me across the Canadian about various picturesque ceremonies which they wanted badly to see and of which I was almost totally ignorant. Warner was talking to the shaggy man (What was his name? Where had I seen him before?) who kept nodding heavily, whether in agreement or weariness I could not determine. Mr. Dodsworth was rather left out in the cold.

In the big mirror I finally located Fiona's nigger heaven. She was sitting between a Japanese and a Negro, facing half towards me. She was talking intently to the Japanese. I watched her for some time, long enough to surprise Mrs. Dodsworth, but I never saw even the ghost of a smile.

Beyond the marble pillars that flanked the entrance of the Ritz Ballroom I could hear the wail of Louie Gerard and his band. Everyone seemed to be going in and I was just joining them when I noticed Fiona. She was standing by the notice-board outside, talking intently to the Japanese.

I went up to her. "Coming to the dance?"

"Oh hullo!" She gave a quick nervous glance at the Jap. "I don't know. Yes, I mean, I suppose so."

The Jap took her hand and gave a formal bow. "Well, good night, Miss McDougall. I have enjoyed this talk very much. Till tomorrow then." He gave me a formal bow. "Good night, sir."

"Good night," I said with a gracious nod. I thought he had a high silly voice.

We went into the ballroom.

"Isn't your friend coming too?" I asked, pretty generously I thought.

"Mr. Koso? How can he? You've taken his girl." She smiled at me.

I felt rather good. "You mean it's you or nothing? Is he so far gone."

"Oh no. He's very formal and correct. But there's no one else for him to dance with. At least there's the black lady at our table, but I don't expect he'd want that. He wouldn't dare ask a white girl."

"I wouldn't have thought you and a Jap really had so much reason to be so pally."

"No, you wouldn't, would you," she said reasonably.

"Anyway, stop worrying about him and concentrate on me."

We stepped on to the floor and I took her in my arms. She was very light and smooth on her feet and we danced well together. I noticed a lot of people watching us and I wondered what they were thinking.

"You do realize, don't you, that I shan't sleep a wink tonight unless you tell me what it was you wanted me to do for you?"

She glanced up at me. "Oh, it wasn't anything. Only this."

"This?"

"Yes. To dance with me, with everyone here."

"Well, of course I was going to. But why didn't you ask me?"

"I didn't see how I could, when I got down to it. It's not the sort of a question a girl really can ask, particularly——"

"You mean I mightn't have wanted to?"

"Well, I can think of some people who mightn't have. Some people don't like associating in public with a yellow girl. The last time I did this trip nobody danced with me the whole voyage."

"Good God! Well, you needn't worry this time. I've spotted several wolfish glances resting on you."

"Oh yes, I get those all right. But dancing with everyone present is a different matter."

The music stopped and we stood apart, clapping perfunctorily. "Were you afraid I might disown you in public, then?" I asked.

"No, not really. That was why I started to ask you before I lost my nerve. People do, you know."

We started to dance again. "Do what?"

"Disown you in public. They're awfully nice when you meet them in a passage or somewhere and then they look straight through you ten minutes later in the bar or the ballroom. One woman was perfectly charming to me everywhere and then I found she was complaining furiously to the steward at having to share a bathroom with me."

"Dirty. Might catch something," I said bitterly.

"Yes, I suppose so. And yet I can't really blame her. I'm sharing a bathroom with the black lady at the moment and I'm not enjoying it very much. Though I'd never complain to anyone, of course."

"Fiona, tell me one thing. When you hoped I'd dance with you tonight, was it just to give a public exhibition of our, well, association?"

She looked at me intently. "Oh dear! Yes, I suppose it was that. And it would serve me right if you walked straight off the floor and left me standing here." She paused and took her arm away from my back. "But I didn't ask you, did I? I stopped myself in time."

I held her tighter and I could feel the shape of her bosom through my jacket.

"No, I asked you, for the sheer pleasure of it. No ulterior motive."

"I know, and thank you. That's what makes it so nice."

I looked down into her face and wondered just how every feature differed from an Anglo-Saxon face and why it still added up to a pretty girl. "I couldn't care less what anybody thinks, whether anybody watches us or not. They can all go off to bed for all I care."

"Except the band."

"Yes, except the band." One thought was nagging at me and I went on at it again. "Just supposing I was Chinese too, and not white, would you enjoy dancing with me more, or less? Or wouldn't it make any difference?"

The answer was a little unexpected.

"Oh, I think I'd like it even more," she said slowly and thoughtfully. "You see, there might be a future in it for us."

The next dance was an Excuse Me and we sat it out. I knew from dances in Natividad that there is no greater humiliation for a girl than still to have the same partner at the end. After what Fiona had told me I did not feel like risking it.

We sat on high stools at the bar and I ordered drinks. Next to us was the dour Canadian. Not knowing his name I couldn't introduce him, so I said vaguely, "Good party, this," which gave him an opening if he wanted one. He simply answered "Yes."

I found I had left my wallet in my other coat and I went down to my cabin to fetch it. When I came back, I was surprised to find Fiona dancing with the Canadian. Evidently the thaw set in suddenly in northern climates.

They were dancing one of those silly shipboard dances where you keep your hands behind your back and hold an orange between your two foreheads. The Canadian was concentrating like anything, but

Fiona was giggling so much that I felt sure they couldn't last long. Somehow it seemed terribly pathetic and sad.

They dropped the orange about half a minute later and left the floor, Fiona laughing apologetically and the Canadian frowning with annoyance. I was overwhelmed with sudden pity for her. Poor little girl, I thought, with her three swains, Mr. Koso, the scowling Canadian and me, a married man. And, at the end of the line, the hope of a Chinese dentist in Port Catalan who might, with luck, be nice as well.

She climbed on to the stool beside me and between giggles told me all about it.

"Gatoff!" I said suddenly.

She started. "Me? Why?" She slid to the ground and stood looking at me with apprehensive eyes.

"Nicholas Gatoff," I said. "Sorry, nothing to do with you. Just a name I've been trying to remember all day. He sits at my table, next to Mr. Warner as a matter of fact. I knew I'd seen him before somewhere."

Fiona had climbed on to the stool again. "Ought I to know about him?" she asked.

"Oh, I don't think so. He's editor, or was, of a magazine called *Vista.*"

"Oh. I don't think I've met it."

"Haven't you? It's a monthly that deals with current affairs, literature, the arts, that sort of thing. It's quite influential."

"You knew him before, then?"

"Well, just. I've met him."

We clapped politely as bottles of champagne were presented to the couple who had held their orange longest. Louie Gerard and his boys blared out again and I led Fiona back on to the floor. As I held her, I thought Gatoff; poor girl, so pretty, so gay, so hopeless; Gatoff, I wonder.

I stalked Gatoff for two days before the exact opportunity occurred. He was sitting in the Palm Court Verandah ("a nice place to meet your friends with magnificent sea views") drinking a pink gin. With careful timing I wandered through and greeted him.

"Good morning," he said. "I wish these clouds would clear away. Too cold to sit on deck, I think." He waved at a chair. "Won't you join me?"

I accepted and we talked about the weather and about Warner, from whom we were both suffering a good deal on this subject. At last I said with careful casualness, "I think we met at the Salters' cocktail party a couple of years ago, didn't we?"

"The Salters? Oh yes, that was it. I knew we'd met somewhere," he said politely. Clearly he didn't remember me from Adam.

"Lady Salter's good fun, isn't she? Always gives good parties."

"Yes. Seems to know everyone. Never know who you'll meet there, though I wish she'd organize her drinks a bit better. Let's see, you were . . . ?"

It seemed too late to tell him my name. "I was working for the *Literary Digest*," I said.

"Oh, that heap." He looked at me and went quickly on, ruffling his long grey hair with his hand: "I was sorry when it folded up. It hadn't a chance of course. Run on quite the wrong lines. But I'm always sorry to see anything like that fold up. There are few enough serious literary journals in all conscience."

I resisted, by the skin of my teeth, the temptation to come loyally to the defense of my old paper. That was all past history now.

"It was fun while it lasted," I said.

He sipped his drink. I thought he had offered me one, but he was doing nothing about it. I wondered if it would be rude to order one for myself.

"What are you doing now?" he asked.

I told him.

"Ho, I should think there's a bit more cash in that, isn't there?" he said, staring unconcernedly at the magnificent sea views.

"A little. But in other ways it's less appealing." I didn't want to pitch it too strong.

"Oh, I don't know. Travel's a great experience. What did you think of Jamaica?"

I explained that I had hardly been off our own sugar plantation.

"What's the feeling like there about us—the British? Do they want to kick us out?"

"I don't think so. On the whole they're pretty loyal. Of course there are dissatisfied elements. You may wake up and find 'White Man Go Home' painted on the outside of the house. But it's only a small minority who do that sort of thing."

"Is that what they say?"

"Yes. The funny part is that, apart from a few aboriginal Caribs who have mostly died out, the whites have been in the West Indies far longer than any other race."

He didn't find it very funny. "Of course you get that sort of thing everywhere now. It's a symptom of the times. And very infectious."

"Oh yes. But I have a feeling that we deserve a bit of it too."

That brought his attention round to me with a jerk. His eyes stopped contemplating the sea views and the rest of the verandah. He seemed to stop waiting for someone more interesting to come and talk to him.

"Deserve it?"

"Yes." This was coming off nicely. "I don't think we shoulder the white man's burden quite as we should."

His eyes were on my face. "How do you mean?"

"Well, you remember how Curzon defined it: 'The Almighty has placed your hand on the greatest of His ploughs . . . that somewhere you have left a dawn of intellectual enlightenment where it did not exist before.' That doesn't appeal much today. We only want a good time, sport, cheap drink, lots of servants, low taxes. We couldn't care less about intellectual enlightenment."

"Yes," Gatoff said slowly. "I see what you mean."

"I tried to do an analysis of the British colonial figure as seen in English novels."

"Starting with Kipling, I suppose?"

"Yes, and *Sanders of the River*. The real white man's burden stuff. Send us Sanders or two battalions."

"Nowadays they just have to send the battalions, eh?"

"Yes. And then after that you got the stuffy rigid Poona lot—people like E. M. Forster's. And the emphasis on sport. And then Maugham and the white man starting to go to seed, though we'd already had a bit of that from Conrad. And then you come on to the moderns, Graham Greene, Waugh, Hanley, where the white man does very little except drink too much, sleep with other people's wives and boss up the blacks. I've been trying to write an essay on it," I added carefully.

Gatoff unfortunately ignored my last remark. "A picture of decline and fall you think? It's a bit out chronologically, but it's an idea. You think that the decline is responsible for all the present troubles?"

"Oh no. But I think it coincides. If you plotted the two graphs, I think they might correlate."

"Yes, possibly. But I wonder how far we can trust our novelists. They use a bit of imagination, you know. I wonder if anyone like Sanders really existed?"

"I don't know about him, but I think the contemporary picture's pretty accurate from what I've seen."

He nodded and turned back to the sea views. "But you say your troubles aren't as bad as other places?"

"Oh no. We're nothing like Africa or Cyprus or places like that. But it's there all the same."

He nodded again and this time there was a long pause. He seemed to be looking for someone else to talk to and I realized I'd failed. I wondered if I should go away and find that drink.

"What was the run today?" he asked suddenly.

"Five. Five-three-five."

He pursed his lips. "I always take three. It's never once turned up all the days I've been on ships. The amount those seamen's orphans, or whatever they are, must have made out of me!"

I said sympathetically, "I was on nought."

He looked at me for a moment. "Nought, were you?" He pursed his lips again—they were thick and fleshy—and shook his head. We relapsed into silence.

"That essay of yours, might I see it sometime?"

I was startled and most gratified. "Yes, of course. It's in my suitcase. When would you like it?"

"Well, now, of course," he said irritably. "While it's in my mind."

I belted down to my cabin and rummaged in the suitcase under my bunk for *From Sanders to Scobie*. I remembered that it was supposed to be unfinished, and I detached the last page. I couldn't wait for the lift and ran up the stairs, arriving back in the verandah in a nonchalant panting stroll.

Gatoff was lighting a cigarette and he took my manuscript without a word, laying it flat on the glass-topped table and reading it bending over the table so that the shadow of his head came in the light. He sucked in great gulps of smoke, each time with a little "pah" of his lips.

I hate having something I've written read in front of me. I lit a cigarette myself and stared resolutely at the sea. At least, I thought, my name is on the top. He will have got that.

I stole a glance at him. He had stopped reading and was staring like me into space.

"What about Jingle?" he said.

"Jingle?"

"Yes. In *Pickwick*. He ended in Demerara where they were going to make a man of him. One can hardly think of him shouldering the white man's burden, but according to you he ought to have been at that time."

"Oh, that's what I call the Colonial Fallacy," I said. "It keeps cropping up right through. Authors use the colonies as a dumping ground and reformatory for semi-villains. Even Simenon has done it and he's usually so realistic. A colony would be the last place to send those sorts of characters; they'd go completely to the bad in no time."

Gatoff nodded and went on reading. One page later the two girls from our table looked through the window.

"Hello!" they said. "We've both just been knocked out of the shuffleboard."

We both rose. "Come on in and drown your sorrows," said Gatoff.

They came and joined us and I ordered a round of drinks. They were nice girls and I didn't grudge them their cokes; but I wished them just then at the far end of the ship. One of them talked to Gatoff about ship sports, the other asked me about Trooping the Color and the Ceremony of the Keys at the Tower. Presently Warner and the Dodsworths joined us and it all got very merry.

My manuscript still lay on the table completely forgotten. I noticed that it was acquiring wet rings from the glasses stood on it. I retrieved it surreptitiously while the others were moving towards lunch, wiped it carefully and put it back in my cabin. I had thought that my encounter with Gatoff might, in my mother's phrase, perhaps have been Meant. But evidently not.

I talked to Gatoff several times during the next two days, but we neither of us mentioned my essay or the white man's burden. I don't recollect those days with any great pleasure. I was finding it increasingly difficult to be civil to Warner or the Canadian or even Mrs. Dodsworth. I suppose it was the broken nights catching up on me. There was Fiona, of course, and she was as delectable as ever. But I was making a deliberate effort to spend less time with her, ever since the night when I had whiled away some silent hours by a detailed consideration of the possibilities suggested by her having a single cabin. We still danced and drank together; we exchanged our London addresses and I promised to introduce her to Diana. But it wasn't the same. I left her, with a good deal of self-admiration, more and more to Mr. Koso and the Canadian and even to Warner, who told her a lot about Chicago that was new to her. The weather was cool and cloudy. I both longed for and dreaded our arrival at Southampton.

On the last afternoon I was on deck, bracing myself for the farewell dinner that night with its speeches and funny hats, when I was aware of Gatoff beside me. He looked shaggier than ever, the wind blowing his long hair away from his head like a plume of smoke.

"No land in sight yet," I said conversationally.

"About your essay," he said abruptly.

"Yes?"

"Would you like to finish it and send it along to my office? We might just be able to use it."

Ah, this was more like it. "Yes, certainly."

"Of course I can't promise anything. We always have far more stuff that we can use and I don't know what they mayn't have collected while I've been away. But I'd like to see it again."

"Yes, of course I'll do that. Thank you very much."

He pursed his lips and walked a yard away. Then he turned round and said, "Did you say you'd done some reviewing?"

"Yes," I said. I hadn't said it, but no matter.

He nodded and walked away.

The thing that really puzzled me was why I wasn't more pleased. I'd just brought off the coup I'd been plotting so carefully. I looked like getting my toe inside that particular door again and it was work I could quite well do in my spare time from the London office. Everything else was good too. Home at last to my wife, my children, to civilization, to a nice job in the City, to a rise in salary.

It was like one of those summer days when the sky is too blue to be real and everything is so brilliant and close and clear, and some dreary old weatherwise countryman tells you that it will be raining before night.

Part Two

1

I HAD BEEN wondering where Diana would meet me and I had watched the notice-boards on the ship and in the Ocean Terminal for a message from her. There had been nothing from her and I had quite made up my mind that I should find her waiting for me at home. Indeed, what would she do with the children if she sallied out to meet me?

I jumped quite a bit when I spotted her standing about a yard away from me at the barrier at Waterloo. For a fraction of a second I did not recognize her. She was so much more beautiful, so much more elegant, so much slimmer than I had remembered. As she stared up the platform for me, she was like an advertisement for spring fashions, posed and fetching. She was in a gray frock whose simplicity was designed not to deceive anybody for a moment; her face with its straight cheeks and slanting cheek-bones was very carefully made-up; as always she was bare-headed and her auburn hair looked as if it had come straight from the hair-dresser. Tall, slender, incredibly beautiful and, I suddenly remembered, mine.

"Hullo, stranger!" I said.

She turned slowly, a little bewildered by the hurrying crowds, and for a second her eyes rested on me, unrecognizing. Then they suddenly dilated.

"Hugo! Oh! I was looking for you up the platform," she added irrelevantly.

We kissed, too close now to be able to see each other any more. Someone banged into me and said "Sorry."

"We're holding things up," I said. We moved towards the taxis, shooting little sideways glances at each other like a very young and infatuated couple.

"You aren't nearly as sunburnt as I was expecting," she said. "I was imagining you looking like, oh, one of those men——"

"Smoking pipes and wearing topees in that advertisement. Sorry to let you down, but I don't possess either and I didn't get much chance to go out of doors lately. But you," I said, "you're straight out of an advertisement. *Vogue,* I think."

"Not *Woman Today?*"

I considered it. "No, I think *Vogue.*"

"I'm not sure that I can have you making unfavorable comparisons about the old school mag."

In the taxi I took her in my arms and kissed her properly. As I kissed her I thought, This is what I've been waiting for all these months and now it's here at last. Afterwards I realized that I hadn't noticed the actual kiss very much. That was a bit disappointing and it seemed specially important that I should know, so I kissed her again. Her lips were harder than I'd remembered.

It was a peculiar sensation, holding her there and kissing her, like going back to a house you've known very well as a child, a school, say, or your grandparents' house; you know by habit where the door handles and light switches are, you can find them in the dark without looking, and everything is the same. And yet it's all different. You'd forgotten lots of it and how it smelt and the way the buhl clock ticked. And some of it's new. It was like that, kissing Diana. I kissed her automatically, by habit, our mouths as always sideways, my hand pressing the back of her head towards me. It was utterly familiar and routine, and yet it was like kissing a stranger.

"Oh darling, it's been so long," she murmured. "I didn't think these last weeks would ever go."

"Me too." I was sitting very close to her, my arm tightly round her. It felt like taking a girl home from a night-club.

"I haven't been kissed in a taxi since we were engaged," she said.

"Good. I mean, we haven't been in taxis much since then, have we?"

She gave a short laugh. "No. And anyway why kiss in a stuffy taxi stinking of leather and stale cigar smoke when home is nicer?"

"I can think of several reasons," I said and I kissed her again.

"Oh darling, it's so wonderful to have you back. I've missed you so much."

"Yes, so have I."

"Have you really? I'd half hoped you might have been consoling yourself with some dusky beauty. What was her name, Tonga something?"

"Tondelayo. Well, I did consider it, but black beauty didn't really appeal when it came to the point. And those Indian women with their whiny voices, oh no! Of course most of the estate wives would have taken off their clothes and rolled at my feet if I'd even winked, but I didn't really fancy them either. Anyway I was living in a total glare of publicity. You've no idea what it's like being a Pemberton out there. Every time I blew my nose it was reported in the *Natividad Chronicle.* Absolutely no opportunities for a bit of discreet slap-and-tickle."

Diana made a moue. "It's terribly disappointing for me, darling. I've been imagining you soaking whisky and seducing the missionary's wife like anything."

"We hadn't got a missionary. The place is sort of Christian already. Darling, you've been reading too much Maugham."

She sighed. "Well, it's nice not to have to share you with anyone else."

"And what about you? You're the one who has had the opportunities."

"Opportunities? Me? Darling, with two tiny tots, a girl hardly has time to clean her teeth. Every time I slip into the bathroom for one second they come and call me."

"How are they?"

Diana gave a happy secret smile. "Oh, they're adorable. Simply heaven. They stagger about the place, clapping and tumbling over. Siegmund is very solemn and steady. He hasn't got on very far with his talking yet. I'm afraid he may grow up a bit pompous if we don't watch out. Sieglinde's quite different. Never stops talking, bullies poor Siegmund terribly."

I laughed. "I expect he'll get his own back some day."

The twins' real names were Mark and Jane, but the nicknames, given them while they were still on the way, had stuck. I sometimes wondered what Freudian complexes they might not develop, if they had not grown out of them by the time they started to go to the opera.

"And what's the next move?" Diana asked.

I squeezed her. "You're so much more beautiful than I'd remembered, and I've suddenly remembered too that you're mine. Can't you guess?" My hand closed over her small breast.

She gave me her little sideways glance. "Yours indeed. I'm glad you're not disappointed, sir. I'm not either. I've got a tall very distinguished husband, a tough hard-bitten planter. Oh so glamorous! You can't think what pit-a-pats it gives me, though I would like you to be more sunburnt. You wouldn't like to try some grease-paint, I suppose?"

"It would come off on you."

"Well, that would be a fair revenge for my lipstick. No, darling, I was really trying to be businesslike and practical. I mean, what happens next? What's Justin cooking for you?"

"Oh nothing frightful," I answered easily. "In fact, three weeks' holiday to be exact. And then a spell in the London office finding out what they all do there." I paused.

"And then what?" This was it.

"Well, I don't know exactly. It's one of the things I've got to talk to Justin about. I imagine I'll take over some of his work in the London office. That's always been the idea. That's what all this training in the colony has been in aid of."

"You won't have to go out there again for some time, will you?"

"Oh no. I shouldn't think before next winter. Justin's going this winter and it'll be my turn the one after. That's eighteen months off. We'll both be going then. Sort of state visit. You won't mind that, will you?"

"I'd be fascinated. I'd love to see it, even though you haven't really enticed me with your descriptions of it. But we wouldn't have to stay too long, would we?"

"Oh no, certainly not. Two or three months at most, that's all Justin ever does. Rather nice in the middle of the winter."

Diana smiled happily. "Very nice. This is the life for me. Makes me feel like a film star or someone."

There was a pile of letters waiting for me in the flat. I picked them up and started to go through them when I realized that it was perhaps not the most delirious way of home-coming. I put them back and went into the nursery. Siegmund was sitting on the floor, painting earnestly great gaudy shapes on a sheet of cartridge paper. Sieglinde was trotting about, chattering. In the background stood a blond girl of about twenty whom I didn't know. I took her to be a new, though unexpectedly young, daily cleaner.

Sieglinde rushed up to me, put her thumb in her mouth and frowned. "Mummy," she said at last.

"No, I'm Daddy," I explained. "I haven't seen you for a long time."

"Where Mummy?"

"She'll be here any moment. But what about a kiss for me?"

I gathered her up and kissed her. She let forth a bellow of rage and kicked me in the tummy. Gingerly I put her down again. At once she stopped bellowing and ran to the blond girl.

"Mummy!"

"No, darling," said the girl in a foreign accent. "I'm not Mummy. And look, this is your Daddy home at last after being so long away."

"Mum-mee!"

I squatted on my haunches, bringing me to near her level. "Are you glad to see me?" I asked, for lack of anything better to say.

Sieglinde turned on me and poured out all her grievances. "'Linde want pint 'Mund got pint won't let 'Linde pint 'Linde want pint." There was more in this vein. She turned, plunged at Siegmund and wrested the paint-brush from his pudgy grip. He gave one bellow of misery, stopped abruptly and calmly picked up another brush. Then he began, in intense concentration, to draw wavy lines of almost solid blue paint across his earlier pattern. Sieglinde watched him for a moment, enthralled. Then mortification overcame her. She shouted, "'Linde want pint 'Mund not got to pint," and snatched away the second brush. Siegmund repeated his usual routine, but this time there was no replacement brush to hand and his fingers fumbled unsteadily across the wet paints and then were wiped across his face and blouse. He howled.

The blond girl said crossly to Sieglinde: "No, darling, you must not take away his paint-brush when he is painting. Look, now you have made him cry."

Sieglinde dropped the brushes to the floor and began to howl too. I wondered what fatherly action was required of me.

"Heavens, what is going on?" said Diana entering. She crouched and hugged Sieglinde. "Darling, what's the matter?"

Sieglinde tried to say something, I could guess what quite easily, but she was choking with sobs and couldn't get a word out. Her face was scarlet.

Diana moved on to Siegmund. "Darling, what's the—what have you got on yourself? Paint! Look, all over your blouse and your face. AND YOUR KNICKERS TOO! Berta, what have they been up to?"

The hubbub was terrific. I roared out a snappy synopsis of events to date, giving the impression that Sieglinde was largely to blame.

"But it's her paint-box," said Diana. "He should never have had it. Berta, why did you let him get hold of it?"

The girl pouted. "He wanted to paint. She never wants to paint, except to take it away from him."

"That's nothing to do with it. I've told you before to keep their toys separate. And I particularly wanted them to be good and smart when their Daddy came home. You'd better——"

I felt that nursery rows were unsuitable for welcoming fathers and I slid silently out and down to the living-room.

Diana came down a couple of minutes later.

"Sorry about that, darling." She sighed. "It's always like that with children. You get all worked up about how sweet they are and how you're looking forward to seeing them again and hugging them, and then they throw a scene like that. They do it every time. They never miss. And it isn't only ours—they all do it. God, what a life!" She sat down wearily. "Oh well, only another fifteen years."

"They may not be all joy then," I observed. "Isn't that supposed to be the difficult age?"

"What age isn't, from nought to a hundred? They may break our hearts then, but at least they won't make so much noise."

"Oh, you never know. They may go about singing. But, for the moment, wouldn't the answer be to give Siegmund a paint-box too?"

"Oh, he's got one somewhere, but he doesn't take any interest in it. He only wants Sieglinde's things. And Berta spoils him."

"I've brought them some presents," I said. "Shall I unpack them now? It might restore peace."

Diana gave me her sideways look. "How sweet of you, darling. But let's wait till after tea. Let them cool down first. I couldn't face another scene just yet."

I was a bit damped by that. I wondered if Diana had guessed that there was one for her too.

"How come Sieglinde's so cockney?" I asked. "She can't have got that from you or that girl Berta?"

"Oh, I believe children usually are at some stage or other. It's to do with the shape of their mouths. And of course they pick it up a bit from Mrs. Kerridge."

"Oh, she's still here, is she?" I thought for a moment. "Then who's Berta?"

"She's a Swiss girl I got in to look after the children, to see us over this bit. I didn't think you'd want me to be too tied to the children just now. No one realizes quite what a tie they are."

"I do. I remember before I went away. But do you think we can afford all this?"

"She's quite cheap. Only three pounds a week and her keep. It's not like having an old-fashioned nanny. I thought it was worth it for the moment. And if we're going to go away somewhere——"

That started a new train of thought. "Would you like to go away somewhere?"

She looked at me eagerly. "It's what we promised ourselves, isn't it?"

Before I went out to Natividad we had promised ourselves a second honeymoon to celebrate my return. It was about the only happy thought that had occurred to either of us at that time, a little idyll in a waste of bickering and nerve-grating and demoralized hanging about.

"We'll be like that film," I said, "with the wise old judge and the couple on the verge of divorce."

She smiled. "So we shall. But anyway I would love to see it all again, and bathe in the moonlight, and eat canelloni in the Piccolo Paradiso, and drink wine and lie in the sun and do nothing at all and have you around."

"Me too. When do you want to go?"

"Oh darling, I can't wait. Just as soon as you can arrange it."

"Of course. I'd better get on the blower to Cooks before they shut."

As I sat by the telephone dialing, Diana came and stroked my hair.

"Darling, I've saved a bit out of the housekeeping, if you think this is too much for us. I mean if you can't manage it."

"Clever girl!" I reached up and stroked her hand. "But it's all right, at least I think so. I've saved up a bit for it too."

Diana kissed the top of my head. "Oh, it is lovely having you home. We will have fun, won't we?"

"Hullo!" I said abruptly. "Continental travel, please. Of course we will, darling. Hullo, is that continental travel?"

"Justin rang this morning," Diana said. "He wanted you to ring him when you got here."

"And you've only just remembered. Naughty!"

"Well, I thought I and the children came first. No need to rush round groveling to him the minute you get home."

"I don't grovel to him. But he is my chairman, you know."

"Do I not! And he holds our fates in the palm of his hand. All the less reason for kow-towing to him."

"Darling, one telephone call is hardly kow-towing to him. There may be something urgent."

"He only wants us to go and have a drink with him tonight. I said you could probably manage it, but I would be putting the children to bed."

"But won't Berta do that?"

Diana said grimly: "Darling, if you think I'm going to spend this red-letter day talking to Justin, you're much mistaken. Watching him gloating over the loving couple he has so kindly allowed to be re-united again. Go yourself, if you think you must, but leave me out of it."

I thought of several things to say, but I didn't say any of them. On the whole it seemed to me that Diana was right.

"I think I'd better go," I said. "I don't want to rub him up the wrong way just at this moment. But we could meet somewhere afterwards and have some dinner. How about that?"

Diana smiled that odd half-hidden smile of hers. "Oh, lovely, darling, that would be a treat. But I don't want to run you into huge expense. There is food here if you'd rather eat in."

"I think we might stand ourselves this for once. Could you meet me at the Excelsior at half-past seven? I'll come straight on from Justin."

"You'll need a nice dinner after that," said Diana. "Don't let him bully you too much."

Justin had already left his office but his secretary, Miss Yorke, was still there.

"Oh, Mr. Hugo, hullo! We'd been wondering if you'd arrived."

"Oh, yes. Just got in a few minutes ago. How's everything?"

"Oh, not too bad, considering. Very busy you know, just at the moment. Did you have a good trip?"

"Yes, very nice. A bit hot in New York."

"Still, I don't expect you noticed that after the colony, did you? The Major left about half an hour ago. He left a message to say, if you rang, would you meet him for a drink at White's at half-past six. I gather that Mrs. Pemberton can't come."

"No, that's right. She'll be bathing the children."

Miss Yorke gave a motherly chuckle. "And how did you find them? I expect they must have been very excited to see you."

"Oh yes, they were indeed. All right, Miss Yorke, thank you. White's at half-past six then. I shall be coming in to work with you quite soon, you know."

"Oh will you, Mr. Hugo? That'll be very nice for us."

Berta brought in the children after tea, clean, calm and smiling. They were formally introduced to me. I sat one on each knee and told them who I was. Siegmund had Diana's auburn hair, and Sieglinde had a faint look of my mother, but otherwise I looked in vain for any resemblance.

"Dad-dad," said Siegmund at last, after much coaxing. His sister, however, was less easily convinced.

"She's just showing off," said Diana. "She knows you're her Daddy perfectly well. I've been preparing her for this reunion for weeks."

Sieglinde, bored, slid off my knee and shouted, "Kack! Kack!" at Diana.

"No, darling, not tonight. You've got Daddy to talk to today."

"Kack, kack, Mummy. Want kack."

This time Sieglinde won and after a bit of readjustment Diana had a child on either side of her on the sofa while she read them Jack the Giant-killer out of an enormous picture book. Siegmund sat silent, concentrating furiously. Sieglinde talked ceaselessly, repeating what Diana was saying, including the frequent "Don't wriggle" or "Don't suck your thumb." Seeing the three of them close together like that did something to me.

I slipped out unnoticed and returned with the toys I had bought them in Port Catalan. When the story was finished, I produced them. The twins fell on them wolfishly.

"You must say thank you to Daddy," Diana said to Sieglinde.

Sieglinde ignored this.

"Darling, I told you to say thank you to Daddy."

Sieglinde gave her a baleful glare and went on trying to unwrap the parcel.

Diana pulled away the parcel. "Darling, you won't get the present unless you say thank you to Daddy."

Siegmund, who had been gazing raptly at the outside of his parcel, now looked up and saw to his horror that he was not the only one with a present. He burst into roars of mortification. Sieglinde noticed his present, grabbed at it, missed and began to howl. We were off again.

I resolved the situation with what I thought a master-stroke worthy of Solomon himself. I changed their presents over; this satisfied their self-esteem sufficiently for them to dare show the required amount of gratitude. When I left them, Sieglinde was talking hard to a model aeroplane which made quite a realistic buzz in reply, and Siegmund was gazing in dumb wonder at a doll which, according to the immodest label, 'winks, flirts, sleeps, wets'.

In the tube, on my way to White's, I was aware of the pain in my cheek-bones, hard and insistent. So many of my meetings with Justin, though superficially jocular, had been either ominous or downright unpleasant, and this one might be no exception. I told myself that there was no reason to think our meeting tonight would be anything but social. Indeed it would have been far more ominous if he had not wanted to see me. And there might even be good news, a rise, a directorship. Perhaps, if there were a favorable opening, I might raise the matter, ask for a little light to be shed on my whole future in the firm.

On second thoughts I decided against it. The prospects might not be as favorable as I hoped and had given Diana to understand. I had no wish to be blighted on the eve of my second honeymoon. Besides, tonight's meeting was in a club and Justin never talked business there. The business meetings, those gruesome jovial chats, always took place in his flat. Tonight would be social, nothing more. But the ache was still there in my cheeks and my thoughts couldn't move it.

To distract my mind, I picked up a discarded copy of a weekly paper whose prime purpose seemed to be to titillate the lascivious. The whole of the front showed a girl in a meagre bathing suit and a wedding veil getting out of a Daimler. It is hardly necessary to quote the caption, but what astonished me was the length of her legs. But then Diana's were pretty long too, and every bit as good. Indeed Diana could very well have stood in for the girl, if her bust had been better. I wished Diana would put on a little more weight, whatever it did to her waist and hips. I didn't like girls to be too thin. Fiona, now, was much plumper. She would have looked rather good, stepping out of the Daimler, and she might have had an even more disturbing effect on the readers of the paper.

I turned over and read a long shaggy dog story about a hippopotamus-sexer and a man who scraped a penny on a wall. I thought, Oh I do hope there's no bad news tonight.

Justin had given me drinks in White's so often that the place felt like home. The porter knew my name without my saying it and told me that Justin was in the bar. He hardly needed to say it.

I heard Justin's high slow voice, before I saw him.

"Hullo!" I said.

He turned slowly and surveyed me without surprise. "Good evening, Hugo," he said. He stretched out the thumb and forefinger of his right hand as if he were a gardener about to squeeze a greenfly off a rosebud. I did the same and our fingertips touched briefly. It was our usual salutation, a concession to the custom of shaking hands without the obscenity of excessive fleshy contact.

I sometimes thought that Justin's arm was the most characteristic part of him. The dark gray sleeve, tailored by Huntsman, had, at his instance, a cuff and two buttons only. Beyond was the correct inch of white silk cuff, made to measure by New and Lingwood. Unseen, except when he took his coat off to play billiards, was a gold cufflink, made out of his intertwined initials by Cartier. Half-seen was the black face and eighteen-carat rim of his watch, worn on the inside of his wrist; it had been made to his exact specification by Patek Philippe and gave all sorts of information like the phases of the moon and the times of high tide off Shoeburyness. Beyond, on his little finger, was a signet ring, again probably from Cartier; and, at the end, his finger-nails professionally manicured every week by Maurice. The whole effect was deliberately that of elegant costliness and it was perhaps a pity that on meeting he always reminded me of a bored camel.

"What will you drink?" Tonight his voice was almost falsetto.

"Can I have a champagne cocktail?" I said. "I'm celebrating tonight."

"Of course you are!" Justin didn't sound quite as genial as he might. I thought, If you're a bit short, you can always hock your watch. "A champagne cocktail, please, George," Justin said to the barman, "and two more large whiskies."

While Justin was paying for them, I glanced at my watch and concentrated on the other members standing near me. It was a private game I always played whenever Justin bought me a drink at the bar of White's. I would count the number of times I could overhear the word 'furlong' during a timed minute. Tonight it was only three, but I had once got nine.

"Here's your tipple, Hugo," said Justin. He turned to a big bald man with a military moustache beside him. "Charles, meet a cousin just home from the West Indies. Brigadier Hope-Gordon. Go on with your story, Charles." Justin nudged me. "Listen to this, Hugo."

"Well, anyway," said Brigadier Hope-Gordon, "this man was scratching up and down the wall with a penny and I said to him, 'What the hell are you?' And he said, 'I'm a hippopotamus-sexer.'"

"A what?" said Justin.

"A hippopotamus-sexer. So I said, 'What the hell's that?' And he said, 'It's a man what tells the sexes of unborn hippopotami.' And I said, 'That's very interesting, but why are you scratching on a wall with a penny?' And he said, 'Well, you see, sir, the other's only a part time job.'"

He gulped down his whisky. I grinned politely. Justin whinnied with delight.

"Well, I must be off," said Brigadier Hope-Gordon. "I see my guest approaching." He nodded to us and strolled away.

"Bye-bye," said Justin. "Priceless fellow, that," he said to me confidentially. "You never want to believe a word he says. He's full of stories like that. Don't know where he gets them all from. He's Lehmann's, you know, the discount people."

I nodded appreciatively.

"Well, what's it feel like to be home?"

"Very nice."

"Absence make the heart any fonder? I expect Diana and the kids were glad to see you."

Justin always said 'kids'. I remembered my mother saying: "It's so odd having one member of the family a class below all the others. Dear Daisy would have been so surprised. I suppose he gets it from all those barmen and jockeys."

"Oh yes, they were," I said.

He asked me what sort of a trip I'd had and how I'd found New York, a city he was accustomed to admire above all others. I found it difficult to work out a satisfactory answer, since I had no good report to give of the gay crowd in the Racquets Club, the Moselle in the Knickerbocker, the beauty of Miss Mills or the humor of Oldfield the Purser. I concentrated instead on Burgers, the hospitality of R. P. Mills and the English club where he had given me lunch. Justin, of course, had been there, though he didn't seem to be a member.

"I think an up-town club is more useful for people like us. You're usually lunching with someone else when you're downtown. I wonder if I oughtn't to put you down for the Knickerbocker."

"Would I use it a lot?" I asked intrigued.

"Oh well, you never know. It's a useful thing to have behind you. We'll think about it."

He moved off into the billiards room. I followed with aching cheeks. This was the moment.

"Hugo," said Justin, lowering himself, with a caution that was new to me, into a black leather armchair, "I've been thinking a good deal about your London clubs."

I gave a sigh of relief. I knew just where we were.

"Yes?"

"Well, frankly, I think it's time you were put down for this place. It's time you had a good club and I think this would be much the best one for your purposes. You hear all the inside stuff here long before it gets anywhere else."

"What sort of inside stuff?"

"Oh, political, Stock Exchange, racing, general stuff. It gives me a terrific advantage, I know. To say nothing of Charles's stories." He gave a reminiscent smile. "He can second you, now you've met him."

Justin leaned over and pressed the bell for the steward.

"Of course you really want two clubs, to ring the changes. Perhaps Brooks's or the St. James's as well. We'll have to think about that. You're still a member of the Guards, aren't you?"

"Yes. An overseas member."

"Good, better hang on to that. It's somewhere to take Diana. I expect she'll insist on your going on with that. But you really need another one, somewhere you can take a bounder to lunch when you wouldn't want to bring him here. We'll have to think about that too. And a dining-club's nice. I might put you down for Pratt's. You get some amusing evenings there. And I suppose you'll want somewhere to swim and play squash. You'll have to choose one of those for yourself. I can't help you there, at least not directly. And of course you'll have to have the West India, though I don't expect you'll ever use it."

I have telescoped the homily a good deal. It lasted a good half hour and I knew I could always stretch it to an hour or more with an odd question like "What about Boodle's?" I had heard it several times before, and, as Justin's homilies went, it was pretty harmless. I very much preferred it to the one on the mystique of family businesses.

I said rather ingeniously: "Yes, I see I need most of these. But I'm not sure if I can afford all the subscriptions."

Justin brushed that one away. "Oh, I don't think you'll need to worry about that. We shall be paying you a bit more in future."

This was the answer I had been hoping for and I began to feel rather good. Another nice thought had occurred to me. If Justin thought it necessary for me to have so many London clubs, he must be meaning me to spend most of my future time there.

The steward was hovering before us.

"You were drinking a martini, weren't you, Hugo? A martini and a large whisky and soda please."

"And that's all there was to it," I said. "I'm to get a rise and I'm to join about twenty-five exclusive West End clubs."

"Did he say how big a rise?" asked Diana.

"No, but I think it ought to be quite substantial. He's always made this cast-iron difference between learning the job and actually doing it. He admits that he's been paying me rather little the past two years."

"Does he now! Jolly dee of him." Diana swallowed a mouthful of duck. She didn't seem to be enjoying her dinner as much as I'd hoped. "A shilling a week, do you think?"

I said: "I'm getting five hundred now and I think he ought to raise me to about eight hundred. That's what Stevens gets and I think I ought to be more or less level with him. Things are dearer in London than in the colony."

"Well, I'll believe it when I see it. Will there be anything over for the housekeeping, do you think, or will you have to spend it all on your clubs?"

I smiled. "Most of it, I expect, but there may be a bit over for you."

"And I shan't see much of you in the evenings either, with you trudging from one to the other. Oh well, I suppose it's something to be married to the second-best clubman in London."

She wasn't smiling, but I chuckled. "By the way, he's leaving a card for us at the Travelers in Paris."

Diana looked surprised. "But didn't you tell him we were flying to Rome?"

"Yes, but he couldn't seem to understand. He said he'd better do it all the same, just in case."

"Just in case what? In case our plane crashes into the Eiffel Tower?"

I shrugged my shoulders.

Diana leaned forward. "Darling, don't let's talk about Justin any more tonight. You know how he gives me the creeps."

I poured her out another glass of champagne. It was Moet non-vintage and rather good. We talked about ourselves, and then about the children.

"They seem very sweet," I said.

"Oh yes, they're enchanting. I love playing with them and showing them things." She paused. "What I'm not so keen on is bathing them and feeding them and dressing them and undressing them and getting up in the middle of the night to see what they're shouting about. You can't think what a help it is to have someone else to do all that for me at the moment."

"I can imagine it. But I thought mothers were meant to like that sort of thing. Isn't it supposed to do something to them?"

"True mothers go into ecstasy when their child is sick over them," Diana said grimly. "Sorry, darling, but if you wanted that, you've married the wrong girl."

She was looking seriously at me and I gazed for a moment into her chocolate eyes. "I don't think I did, you know."

She smiled her secret smile and dropped her eyes. "Thank you," she said very simply.

"By the way, what do we do with them while we're away?"

"Oh, they'll be all right. Berta will be there."

I demurred. "But we can hardly leave them all alone for over a fortnight with a comparative stranger. Wouldn't it be better to send them down to my mother at South Meon? I know she'd love to have them."

"Oh, I don't think it's really worth it," said Diana. "All that long journey and the packing. Children always travel with twelve times their own weight in luggage; it's somebody or other's law."

I smiled wanly and persevered. "But it would be so nice for them down there at the moment. Be a change from London. They can rampage round the garden. Besides my mother would like it. She's always saying she'd like to see more of them."

Diana began to look a bit mulish. "Well, if it comes to that, it's even longer since Daddy saw them. I'm sure he'd love to have them."

"But that's an even longer journey," I protested. "And what on earth would he do with them? Pat them on the head and send them back again."

Diana's father was a retired barrister, now Chairman of Quarter Sessions, and he lived by himself in the Peak District.

Diana wouldn't give way and I saw one of our old-style arguments developing. "Of course it's sweet of your mother," she said, "but I'm not sure that she'd really want them on her hands all the time."

"She'll have Berta."

"She may not take to Berta."

"Look," I said firmly, "I don't frankly like the idea of leaving them all alone with Berta. You can't really know what she's like if you've only had her a few days. And I really think that my mother will be very hurt if they don't go down to South Meon. You know how easily these things cause offense. And it's not as if we had to go ourselves."

Diana stared into her champagne glass for a long while without speaking. "All right," she said at last, "it does seem the answer, doesn't it, if you think it'll be all right. Perhaps we ought to ring her up tonight."

I didn't bat an eyelid. "I must do that anyway," I said.

I still don't know why Diana suddenly gave in, whether it was a strategic withdrawal, or a genuine change of mind, or a desire not to have a row on our first night, or the champagne, or just love. I felt suddenly very warm and loving towards her myself.

"Let's go home," I said.

I got through to my mother just before the cheap period ended, and she said all the things I expected her to say: How lovely to hear my voice again and was it lovely to be back; how thrilled Diana must be and did the twins recognize me; had I had a good trip back and was the ship as luxurious as it used to be; how right we were to go off on our own to Italy and she would adore to have the children, and Berta too; if they could come on the two-twenty-seven tomorrow, she would meet them in Petersfield; she was sure we would have a simply lovely honeymoon and we would remember, wouldn't we, that she wanted more than two grandchildren; and her fondest love and blessings for Diana and me.

I rang off in nine minutes, just as the third lot of pips were going, with a hot ear and a feeling of embarrassment. I suppose it was all those weeks I spent on Signals courses in the army, but I have never overcome my conviction that telephones require terse laconic messages rather than a prolonged and rather expensive flood of intimate affection, better conveyed in a letter.

I reported the conversation to Diana, who said, "Good, that's all right then," and came over and kissed me. I kissed her back very hard, running my tongue round the inside of her lips, and holding her slender body very tight. Surely she hadn't been quite so thin before I went away; perhaps that was the babies.

"I've got something for you too," I said.

"Ooh!"

I went and fetched the nightdress I had bought her in New York, and she unpacked it with the same glee as Sieglinde, also without saying thank you. She held it up, a puzzled expression on her face as she worked out what it was.

"Oh darling, it's lovely! Heavenly! Oh, what fun! Oh, you are sweet to me." She held it against her and pea-cocked in front of the glass, swaying her hips professionally. "Darling, do you think they're pajamas or a nightdress?"

"That's something we've got to work out," I said. "But I take it the general purpose is clear to you."

"Crystal clear." She came and kissed me lightly. "Thank you so much, darling, you are nice to me. They'll be fun for Italy."

"Fun tonight too."

"Better keep them for Italy." She suddenly dropped her eyes. "Oh darling, I'm so sorry. I was praying that you'd be stuck in a fog for a couple of days or something."

Of course it wasn't her fault, and I was cross with myself for feeling so disappointed at her. Then, as my expectancy dropped away, I was aware of feeling very tired and, in a way, rather relieved.

"Never mind," I said reassuringly, "I think I'm too tired to be very amusing tonight. It seems ages since I had a really good night's sleep."

Diana tucked my arm in hers and moved towards the bedroom. "Let's go and have one now," she said.

I got into bed while she was still in the bathroom. I lay flat on my back and lit a last cigarette. I watched the smoke drifting up towards the ceiling and I tried to get my bearings. Diana came in, looking about fifteen in dark red pajamas and no makeup. She sat on my bed, took the cigarette out of my mouth, kissed me, and put it back again.

"Glad to be home?"

"Mmm."

"It's nice having a man around again. Having razors and things all over the bathroom and smoke in the bedroom."

I took the cigarette out. "Do you hate it very much?" She never smoked in the bedroom.

"Oh no, darling, because it means you. It proves I'm not a grass widow any more."

There was a long silence. She watched me and I still stared through the smoke at the ceiling.

"What's ticking over under all that hair?" she asked softly.

I glanced at her for one short flash. "I was wondering what usually happens when a married couple lose a bit out of the middle of their marriage. How do they make contact again?"

"Aren't we making contact?"

"Yes, I think so. But are we going on where we left off and pretending that I've never been away? Or do we go back to nought and start getting to know each other all over again?"

"I don't know. But, darling, I still love you as much as ever."

I flashed another glance at her. "You're sweet. But love's nothing to do with it. You can love someone without knowing them very well."

"Well, which are we doing, starting again or going on where we left off?"

I let out a great lungful of smoke. "I don't know yet. I'll let you know when I do."

2

THE NEXT DAY was pretty hectic. Diana was busy getting the children ready to go to South Meon and I was in a whirl of air tickets and currency and wondering whether we dared go without getting a reply to our telegram about rooms. I also posted off *From Sanders to Scobie* to Gatoff.

Diana had been most interested in this development. She had read my essay with care and approval.

"Darling, it's frightfully good. No wonder he liked it. But if we're really as awful as that, it does make me glad that I haven't got to live in your little home-from-home."

"Yes, indeed. Do you think the covering letter's all right?"

"Excellent, I thought. He sounds a bit absent-minded, so it's just as well to remind him."

"I don't expect he'll print it," I said gloomily.

"Well, he might. You've got him interested and that's three-quarters of the battle. But what about this reviewing? That's what really interests me. Did he say what sort of thing it would be, books or plays?"

"He said nothing beyond that one sentence. He didn't promise anything. I don't think we should count on it."

"Oh no, but it would be nice if it came off. I should think it would be books, if anything. I'd love to be married to a critic. One of the most feared and fearless of our contemporary reviewers. Darling!" She kissed my cheek. "Would you be able to do it as well as your office work?"

"Oh, I expect so. I don't imagine there'd be as much as all that. It might mean an occasional spot of midnight oil."

"Supposing your two masters happen to clash? Supposing you're meant to review a new play on a night when you're scheduled to do a club crawl with Justin?"

Those clubs seemed to have got her badly. I laughed. "And supposing the same night the children had whooping cough and you had flu and Berta was raped and the fuses blew and the drains blocked up? Darling!" I kissed her.

I posted my essay to *Vista* and when we returned from Italy I found a printed patience card thanking me for sending my work, which was having the editor's immediate attention. And that's all there has ever been. I sometimes wonder if Gatoff has lost it or whether he gives it his immediate attention afresh each day.

By the afternoon post there was a letter from Justin.

Dear Hugo,

It was very pleasant to see you again last night and I must thank you for providing such an agreeable interlude. You will be interested to know that I received by the morning mail a letter from Walker in which he speaks highly of your work while in the colony. Apparently some plantfields of yours have yielded about five tons to the acre. This is good news and I hope means that you will make the grade when you start to learn our work here in London.

About the salary rise I mentioned, I shall now have no hesitation in giving you this, and I am telling Hodges to pay you at the rate of £550 a year, as from July the 27th when you start work here.

I am writing to the Travelers today. Have a good holiday and don't eat too much spaghetti.

Yours ever,
Justin P.

I gave the letter to Diana. "It wasn't five tons," I said. "It was five point seven tons and it's the record for the colony." I rubbed my cheek-bones viciously and they felt a bit better.

Diana read the letter with a grim face and then dropped it on the table with a little flick of her fingers.

"I shall eat as much spaghetti as ever I please," she said.

That night we caught the night plane to Rome, that trying journey that dumps you out in the Via Nazionale at half-past three in the morning, when the station isn't open yet. But all our weariness fell away later in the day at the sight of Vesuvius across the Bay and the blue cone of Epomeo rising from the blue sea into the blue sky.

"Darling, it's just as lovely as ever," Diana said breathlessly.

It was all much the same as when we had last seen it: baying tourists in tight bright shorts, and local women in deep mourning, and local men walking about the streets of Porto d'Ischia in striped flannel pajamas, and withered oleander blossoms on the pavements and shrieking children, and thin tired horses straining to pull the carriages with their little frilly canopies up the hill to Casamicciola, and Vespas, and the mountains on the mainland which only came like ghosts in the afternoon, and the dust, and the blinding light and the cobalt sea. Our hotel was a converted Spanish villa and our bedroom had a high painted ceiling. But it was a different room. It is only by the different layout of the furniture that I can remember which honeymoon was which.

"Here we are back again," I said. "*Wein, weib und gesang.* Live, love and laugh." And that was pretty well all we did.

We lived. We wandered through the streets and bought gay straw receptacles whose purpose still remains obscure. We took a bus to the far side of the island and climbed Epomeo, and the view was so goldy-misty that we could not even see Capri, and the sun set while we were still on the mountain, and we floundered helplessly through vineyards in the dark before we got back to street lights. We ate figs and cactus fruit and ice-cream while waiting for buses. We drank Lachryma Christi in the open air café in the Piazza di Bagni. We water-skied at San Montano. We ate prodigious amounts of pasta and I hoped that Diana would put on a little more weight. We swam slowly and lethargically. Above all we sunbathed. We lay for hours on the sand, frying ourselves to a rich caramel, and smelling sweetly of sun-oil, the scent of which is to me the supreme aphrodisiac.

"At last I'm going to get my sunburned planter," said Diana. "If I bought you a pipe, would you smoke it?"

And I would mumble something, reluctant to break off my own contemplation of Diana. How long and slender her legs were, stretching the warm golden distance from her coral-and-white striped shorts to her straw sandals. Sometimes I would marvel that anyone so slim could ever have produced two children. But usually I wouldn't remember about that, and I would just think that she was a young beautiful girl and that she was mine.

We loved. At last the American nightdress came into its own and the cherub on the ceiling (if it was a cherub; we argued a good deal about it) would have seen us as a twin-headed, many limbed hydra furiously writhing, discreetly, bridally veiled with mosquito net. Loving Diana was an exciting business, for she had the capacity to resist and provoke at once, to cause me to summon all my strength and rude vigor to subdue her. Each time behind our mutual passion—and it was mutual—was the faint tart taste of rape, no less mouth-watering for being synthetic. There was, I suppose, very little tenderness in our love-making. Afterwards I would feel the same solid triumph one feels after winning a hard game of squash against an old adversary who usually wins.

Looking back, I think that the violence of our love and my intense though fluctuating possessiveness was due not only to the mixture of our two characters but to the events of our engagement. The first time I had asked her to marry me—or, more precisely in the modern idiom, asked her if she would like us to get engaged—she had turned me down. She was very nice and gentle about it, but she was quite firm. No reason was given and I spent a lot of time trying to soothe my sore pride by inventing possible explanations. However, we continued to see each other, to lunch and drink together. Twice I sounded her with phrases like "Be careful or you'll get proposed to again," and each time I got a negative, though gay, response.

And then, one evening, I suddenly realized that she was asking to be asked again. Ideally, I suppose, the man refuses to be drawn at this stage. The pleasure of 'too-lating' or 'if-onlying' or 'she-who-will-notting' is not easily resisted. Indeed for a fraction of a second I toyed with the idea, but she was looking very lovely and I wanted her badly, and a few seconds later we were formally engaged.

But all through our engagement I couldn't get over the feeling that it was too good to last. She never said why she had changed her mind and I did not want to press her. Had the other man let her down? Had she decided that a career could be combined with marriage? Had she decided that she was in love with me after all? I never found out. But every time I saw her, I half expected her to break it off. Each time the wedding arrangements got a little further advanced, I would think, It looks as if she does mean to go through with it. When we finally emerged from the church, my chief feeling was not love or pride but astonishment.

I never referred to it. Diana only mentioned it once, and then obliquely. She said: "Darling, I was a mean puss to you at the beginning. You're welcome to take it out of me however you please." And I had answered very solemnly:

"The snag is that I've left my horsewhip behind. I thought it too heavy to bring by air. It's got a solid silver handle." In other words, we followed our usual custom and laughed it off.

We laughed a lot, too, this second time in Ischia. Indeed I recall our happy helpless giggling even more vividly than anything else. In particular we resuscitated Patrick. This dated back to a week-end we spent with a godfather of Diana's who had a golden retriever called Patrick and who spoke directly to no one else in the house.

I explained to Diana that this was a variation of an army Signals method known as 'Through me' procedure and its advantages struck us forcibly. For the next year or so we were often accompanied by a large imaginary golden retriever, through whom we conversed. Later, during that rather sour demoralized period when Diana was grappling with diapers and I was waiting for Justin to send me out to Natividad, Patrick went into abeyance, or perhaps more correctly, into quarantine. But now he was with us again. At breakfast I would snap my fingers several times in the approved manner and say:

"Patrick! Patrick! Patrick! Sit! Sit! Sit! I said, Sit, Patrick! Sit! There, that's a good boy! That's a good boysie! There's a good dog then! Patrick, do you think Auntie Di would like to go bathing? Do you think she would? Do you? Do you? Do you? Do you, Patrick? Do you think she'd like it? Do you? Good boysie!"

And Diana would snap her fingers and begin, "Good old Patrick, come to Auntie Di." Repetition was the essence of "Through Patrick" procedure, and indeed of all conversation with dogs.

On the beach we would send Patrick bounding into the sea to fetch imaginary sticks we hurled in. We would dodge neatly aside as he came and shook himself dry all over us. The faces of our neighbors at moments like these never failed to delight us.

In Rome, on the way home, Patrick attracted similar attention. We stunned into silence the English party in the open-air restaurant in the Piazza Navona by our discovery that Patrick had a secret passion for *zabaione*. We sent him bounding into the Trevi fountain to retrieve some of those coins and when he came out to our shouts of applause he shook himself dry beside us so violently that the man standing beside us moved hastily away. I also photographed one of the touts photographing one of the tourists throwing in his coin. This, strangely, made him very angry, though I assured him, in my queer Italian, that it was specially lucky and I gave him a penny to throw in for himself; this he threw, probably most unluckily, into the gutter.

But there were times when we were serious sight-seers and Patrick was left behind. We admired the Tritone fountain, we tried and failed to find the spot in the Piazza San Pietro where the double colonnade turns into a single line. We ate orange water ices at Doney's. We traveled, solitary memorable travelers, in the splendid caverns of the Metropolitana. We stood silent before the Phidias and Praxiteles statues on the Quirinale. We wondered whether we were allowed to lie on the floor of the Sistine Chapel. We walked up and down the Raphael Loggia and Diana said to me as we stood in a cloud of American tourists, "We've got to be civilized about this thing, Winthrop." She said it in a loud, tight, clipped voice, her Bette Davis voice. And, later, in the same loud clipped voice I said, gesturing vaguely at the huge floodlit mass of the Colosseum towering above us, "It's no use, Imogen, this thing is bigger than either of us."

Live, love and laugh. That was the line and we both stuck rigidly to it. I thought we were starting our married life all over again, but I wasn't sure and I never mentioned it. Deliberately, I kept my mind away from the problem. It never occurred to me to bring out my various, ingeniously suppressed, dark thoughts about Justin and my future; just as it never occurred to me that Diana herself might be concealing something from me.

We had several pale green effusions from South Meon. My mother hoped that we were having a really lovely holiday, darlings, which would give us wonderful memories to last us the rest of our lives. They were having marvelous weather really, all things considered, and the children were enjoying themselves enormously. She had thought they looked a bit peaky when they first arrived, but they had quite thrown this off now. Jane laughed and shrieked from morning till night, the little sweetheart, and was sometimes even a little naughty!! Mark was blossoming out a lot but she thought he seemed to have much less life than Jane and she wondered if he had been getting enough green vegetables. Indeed, both children weren't nearly as regular as she would have liked, but she was giving them magnesia regularly and they were much better than they were. She had shown them the hole in the rhododendron and they had had great games there, just as I used to, did I remember? They had spent a most enjoyable afternoon in Winchester, getting the children more underclothes and socks which they seemed to need badly. And on Friday they were going into Portsmouth for the whole day to buy them all their winter clothes, so much better to buy them now before the prices went up and she knew Diana wouldn't want to be bothered with it. She thought it would be so nice to have the children really nicely dressed, they were such pretty little darlings.

She wasn't very happy about Berta, she didn't seem to be very clean somehow, she always seemed very sulky when spoken to or when given advice by someone who, after all, knew a good deal more about looking after children than she did. She thought there was something to be said for the good old-fashioned nanny after all, though of course Diana did it beautifully too and it would frankly be a great relief to her when Diana had charge of them again as she hardly liked to leave them alone with Berta. But she mustn't worry us with all this domestic stuff when we were on holiday, but she thought we would like to know how the children were and how . . .

The end of our honeymoon occurred at about half-past three in the morning at Ciampino airport, as we sat waiting for the London plane. The effects of the Frascati and the Aurun we had drunk for dinner had worn off and I was feeling rather bloody. The future, it seemed to me, could well be rosier.

"Darling," said Diana, "are you going to try and get Justin to give you a bigger rise, or are you going to leave it for the moment?"

The gaiety and the laughter floated away. The shades of the prison-house were closing in fast.

"Well, I thought I'd give myself a week or so to get dug in and see how the land lies, and then tackle him again. Unless, of course, a suitable moment crops up earlier."

Diana nodded. "I only meant that I think we'll manage all right, if you'd rather let it go for the moment. I mean, it would have been nice to have a bigger rise, and we shall need it in the end, but, well, even another fifty pounds helps. That's a pound a week."

"Yes. Just about pay the milkman."

"I don't want you to have to start by asking for more money, if you've got more important things on hand."

"We'll have to see. You don't usually get things out of Justin simply by asking for them. And it puts one in rather a weak position for other things."

"That's what I thought. As long as the bigger things materialize all right. And as long as it comes in the end."

I said reluctantly: "I suppose we shall have to do a bit of budgeting and see how we're going. Later, when we've settled in."

"Yes."

"About Berta, how do we stand there? How much notice do we have to give her, or don't we have to give her any?"

There was an unexpected silence. I glanced at Diana. She was staring straight ahead of her with rather a strained look about the set of her jaw.

I put my hand on hers. "I'm sorry, darling," I said. "I know how you hate looking after the children yourself. I'd let you have a nanny if we could possibly afford it."

"Hugo." She hardly ever called me by my name. "We've got to keep Berta a little longer. You see, I've got a job."

"A job?"

"Yes. At *Woman Today,* in the fiction department. Not my old job, but it's quite good. Acting as assistant to the fiction editor."

I hadn't got any reason to have that ache in my cheek-bones. No reason at all. "When did all this happen?" I asked.

"Oh, about a month ago. Well, nearly two months now."

"And that's when you got Berta?"

"Yes. I had to get someone."

I looked at her. "But why didn't you tell me all this before?"

She gave me an odd scared little glance and smiled. I think it was nerves and not amusement.

"I meant to, but somehow it didn't crop up and I never got around to it. I was afraid you mightn't like it and I didn't really want to have it all out on your first night back. Or really out here."

She was quite right, I didn't like it very much and it irked me that she could know how I should feel. But I wasn't in a very strong position myself. I had been dodging issues too.

"It's only temporary," she said. "It happened quite by chance. I happened to run into Maureen Blow in the street. The editor's secretary. I knew her very well, of course. Didn't you meet her too? She was talking to me on the stairs when you came to collect me one day. And she was at our wedding."

"I can't quite recall her."

"Well, anyway, it doesn't matter. But it was funny running into her again, and she asked all my news, and I suppose that's when she thought of it. She rang me the next day and asked if I could possibly help them out. Julia Longworth, the assistant fiction editor, had gone off to have a baby, and then suddenly Joan Carr asked for three months to go and nurse her mother who's dying, and so poor Miss Webster was left high and dry. And so they asked me if I'd come and hold the fort for a bit. It really did seem indicated. I mean they'd always been very good to me, and it seemed only right that I should help them out when they were up the creek. Besides, I thought it might make the time pass a bit quicker. And it did too."

"Yes, I see. But I don't know that I quite fancy the idea of leaving the children alone all day with Berta. How much longer will you be doing it?"

"Oh, only another month or so. One of them should be back by then. And Berta's not too bad, you know. She's fond of the children and she had a very good reference. I was afraid your mother wouldn't take to her, but——"

"If it's for another whole month, perhaps we ought to get a proper nanny."

She frowned. "I'm not sure that they're quite as wonderful nowadays as your mother thinks. And I believe they can be rather tiresome. They've got such lavish ideas about staff and things. They cost more too."

"They are paying you for this work, I take it?"

"Ten pounds a week. It more than covers Berta and the extra I'm having to give Mrs. Kerridge for cooking lunch. But even so it seems to melt away, there never seems to be anything over. I seem to have to take a lot of taxis."

I didn't like it very much. I still didn't like the thought of the children being left all day with Berta and Mrs. Kerridge. And I suppose I didn't like the thought that Diana needed so badly the extra cash she was earning.

"What are your hours?" I asked.

"Ten till six."

"You can't see much of the children then, before they go to sleep."

"Oh, I'm always back in time to kiss them good night, unless there's a crisis or a hold-up on the underground, or something."

I felt I was being a bit too much of a cross-examining counsel. "But apart from all this, you like it, do you?" I asked more amiably.

"Yes, I do. I really do rather enjoy it. Well, you know what magazines are like. I was getting in a terrible rut."

Another thought occurred to me. "Was this why you didn't write to me that last month in Natividad?"

She looked puzzled. "Not write to you? Darling, I've always written to you."

"Not that last month."

"Perhaps they didn't reach you in time. Or perhaps I thought they wouldn't. You know I don't always write on the same days every week like a schoolgirl writing home. I write to you when I want to, when I've got something to say. It's much nicer."

"And you didn't want to tell me about the job?"

"Well—not really in a letter. I thought it would keep till we met." She glanced at me anxiously. "Darling, are you cross with me about this job? I—I was afraid you might be. It's only temporary, you know."

"Of course I'm not cross. Why should I be? Am I such a crosspatch? You couldn't do anything else. The only thing I do wish—"

I was about to reproach her for keeping things from me, but at that moment the loudspeaker announced our plane, and I never said it. Perhaps it was just as well.

3

I HAD ONLY once been to the London office of Wright, Pemberton & Co., Ltd., to collect some papers before sailing, and then I had not been admitted beyond the waiting-room. Justin always preferred to see me in his flat or one of his clubs.

I went up to the third floor. No one was about. I rang the bell marked "Inquiries" and waited. Nothing happened. In my keenness I was the first to arrive and I stood for a moment irresolute. Then I tried the door, found it open and went in.

I had asked to be allowed to work in the office, during those six months between my joining the firm and sailing for Natividad. It had seemed to me that, whatever I did, it must be of more value than kicking my heels at home. But Justin had absolutely refused—refused with a violence that had startled me. It would give me and everyone else quite the wrong idea if I were to start at that end, it was out of the question, the statutory starting place was in the cane-field and no variation could be permitted.

And now I had arrived. I prowled about, poking my nose through doors and wondering what went on. Then it occurred to me that it would not look very good for me to be discovered snooping on my first day, and I retired to the waiting-room and read an old number of the *West India Committee Circular*.

"Ah, Mr. Hugo, welcome to the office," said Pratt, the office manager, a grey wizened man who had been with the firm for over thirty years. "Come to be put through the hoop, eh?"

It had been a school maxim that all human faces could be classified under three headings: horse-faced, mouse-faced or apple-cheeked. Pratt was indisputably mouse-faced.

He introduced me to the rest of the outer office staff. "Mr. Hugo, this is Jolly who does the shipping."

"Yes, of course, we've met before." Mouse-faced again, with stupefying halitosis. I hadn't remembered that; perhaps it was new.

"And Lord, who does our insurance."

"How do you do." Yet another mouse-face.

"A had the honor to meet you and your wafe," said Lord, articulating with fanatical zeal. "At your wedding."

"Oh yes, of course, so you did." We had invited most of the office staff.

"And Miss Lumley." Mouse-faced again, yellow sweater, no bust. "Miss George." Almost apple-cheeked, greying hair, no bust. "Miss Slade, who runs the switchboard." Mouse-faced again, lovely lustrous henna, green sweater, a staggering, unbelievable bust. "And Greta, the office girl." Horse-faced, bouncing puppy-fat, orange lipstick almost reaching to her nose.

"How do you do."

Pratt went on, "The Major said we were to put your desk there." He pointed to a small typist's desk wedged between Miss Lumley and the switchboard. I should be sitting in my own light and anyone coming in at the door would almost fall over me. I gazed at it with distaste. It was hardly an incitement to megalomania.

"Where are all the rest?" I asked.

"Mr. Hodges has got the next two rooms for his staff. He's the accountant, you know."

"Yes, yes," I said testily.

"Mr. Phillimore and his sales side are on the other side of the passage. The boardroom is opposite them. The Major is through the door at the end."

"Perhaps I ought to go and see him," I said, "before I start work."

"He isn't in yet." Pratt pointed to an unlit red bulb on the wall. "That light goes on when he is in his office."

The next hour passed very slowly. I was shown where the Gents was. I was given a small piece of soap, a small towel and a cup. Jolly alone got out a heap of papers and settled down to work. Pratt asked me a few questions about Natividad which he had always wanted to visit, and then, his polite conversation exhausted, he turned to the *Daily Telegraph* and read it with great care. Miss Lumley opened a lot of letters, Miss George went out of the room, Miss Slade did something obscure to her finger-nails, Greta asked me if I took sugar in my tea. Lord embarked on what I can only describe as a cultural tour of the room.

"Pardon me, Miss Slade, but A wondered if you are going to the ballet tonate."

"Well, I hadn't thought of it," said Miss Slade hopefully. "Are you?"

"Alas, no, Miss Slade. A wish A was. It's the Swedish ballet, you know. At the Royal Festival Hall. They say it's most worthwhale."

He moved on to Pratt. "Pardon me, Mr. Pratt, but did you view the play on Tee Vee last night?"

"Er? Huh? Yes, I watched some of it. Silly, I thought it. If I'd been by myself I'd have switched it off. But we had company in."

"Oh dear, what a pity! It sounded as if it mate have been going to be good. Such a promising adea! A read about it in the *Radio Tames.*"

With a sinking heart I saw him approaching me.

"Pardon me, Mr. Hugo, but did A gather that you were a literary man?"

"Well, I worked for a time on a literary magazine, if that's what you mean."

Lord swallowed. He had an enormous Adam's-apple. "A was wondering if you admire the novels of Virginia Woolf, sir."

That shook me. "Well, yes I do. I don't enjoy them very much, but I can't help admiring them. I'm thinking of things like *The Waves.* Why, don't you?"

Lord took a deep breath. "Whailst A do not enjoy her stale, she has brought a new damension into the technique of Henry James and James Joyce."

I began to get a bit fed up with this. "Oh yes, she certainly did that. At least if it wasn't her, it was someone else. The trouble was that in the process so many other dimensions got squeezed out. I think that's why she's so little read these days. It's all extrovert stuff nowadays. Do you read her a lot?"

He swallowed. "No, sir. A don't hardly at all."

I went on remorselessly. "And Dorothy Richardson too, she's not much appreciated nowadays, is she?"

He swallowed again, said, "No, sir," and went back to his desk. I looked round the office, but no one else seemed to find it at all unusual.

Once the novelty had worn off I got rather bored, and to occupy myself I began to make a list of points about Malmaison on which I had strong views. Later I could work them into a careful memorandum for Justin, as Walker had suggested. I jotted them down as they came into my mind: the basic wage in the factory, the urinal, the loco-line extension, the new Barbados seedling, the possible use of wheelbarrows instead of old sugar bags for shifting earth, the simplification of the monthly costing abstracts, better promotion prospects for overseers. That was more than enough for my first bombardment, so I didn't put down the need for a third head pan-boiler, the growing tendency of everyone to treat Sunday as an ordinary working day, the general emphasis on cane tonnage rather than on juice purity, and the refusal of everyone, except perhaps Walker, to listen to suggestions from anyone who had been less than ten years in the colony. The last point was unlikely to win favor with Justin and had better be left out altogether.

The red light went on an hour later. Pratt picked up the letters he had been reading, divided them into three heaps and gave a heap each to Jolly and Lord.

"What goes on?" I asked.

"This is the morning's mail," Pratt explained rather unnecessarily. "I go through it and I give the insurance ones to Mr. Lord to deal with and the shipping ones to Mr. Jolly."

"What about the others?"

"Those are mainly from machinery manufacturers. I shall acknowledge them all today, of course, and then send copies of them out to Mr. Ingram for his decision. They'll go out on Friday. Miss Lumley!"

He indicated the letters. She came across and took them. Not a word passed.

He evidently saw that I was unimpressed, for he put down the *Daily Telegraph* which he had picked up again and said: "We work in fits and starts here in this office, Mr. Hugo. Some days we're so rushed we hardly know what to do. I've been here till seven o'clock in the evenings sometimes. But at other times, of course, it's a bit quieter. Like today, so far. Thursday's always a busy day. We get the colony mail in that day, and we try and get the answers off, if we possibly can. But there's so much, it sometimes has to wait till Friday. And that's a great nuisance. Always so many other things to do on a Friday."

His hand moved to the edge of the newspaper, and then stopped. "How do they manage it in the Port Catalan office? Mr. Stevens, he's right on top of it all, I bet. We're good friends. I expect they're kept pretty busy, aren't they?"

"Oh yes," I said, "they're busy too. But—" I glanced meaningfully at the red light.

"Oh yes, the Major's in now. I'll tell him you're here."

He picked up the little intercom telephone and after a lot of obscure wagglings, said: "Miss Yorke? Oh, good morning. How are you keeping this fine day? Are you? Oh good. Well, I hope you enjoy it.

Look, will you tell the Major that Mr. Hugo's here and would like to see him."

There was a long pause. Miss Lumley clattered away on her typewriter. I stared intently at Greta without seeing her, and rubbed my cheek-bones hard. If I could, I was going to have the showdown with Justin here and now. I wasn't going to wait a week or two. I wanted to know now, today, just what my future was, and where and when and how much. It was mostly my present feeling of extreme futility that made me change my mind; but I think now that what Diana had said to me at the Rome airport had something to do with it too. I had got to stop messing about and find out just where I was heading, before the whole thing drifted too far to leeward.

"Oh, thank you, Miss Yorke." He turned to me. "The Major will ring when he's ready for you." He half picked up the paper, and then said, "Yes, last time old Stevens was over here, we had a rare good time. . . ."

It was another fifty minutes before Justin sent for me, and by then I was almost past my resolution. Miss Yorke was waiting in the passage for me, and ushered me through into Justin's office, murmuring: "Good morning, Mr. Hugo, finding your way around all right? The Major's in here." She pushed me in and shut the door behind me.

I had never been in Justin's sanctum before and it was pretty startling. To begin with, there was no desk. There was a sofa on one side of the fireplace, and two big armchairs were on the other, all in brown leather. Between them was a small glass-topped table with a blue Venetian glass ash-tray, a Ronson table lighter, a silver cigarette-box and one cardboard file. The rest of the room was filled with other chairs, occasional tables, a rather good bureau between the windows, some glass-fronted bookcases, standard lamps, a drinks cabinet, and a side table against the wall with newspapers and periodicals, both business and society, arranged like a dentist's waiting-room, and no doubt for the same purpose. There was a big vase of zinnias; an Algernon Newton hung over the mantelpiece. The only purely business equipment in the room was a low table half-hidden behind the sofa with two telephones, an intercom loudspeaker and a tape-recorder. The whole place was evidently meant to be a gentleman's living-room rather than an office. It was like the hero's rooms in a Buchan or Dornford Yates novel; one glanced instinctively for the polo cups or the crossed oars. But Justin had never been much of a sportsman, though he talked knowledgeably about it.

He was sitting on the sofa and waved me to the armchair opposite.

"Ah, good morning, Hugo. Have a good holiday? You're looking pretty fit."

"Yes, very good, thank you."

"You're a lucky boy. Wish I could get away for one, though I hope to snatch a long week-end at Le Touquet over the Bank Holiday."

This was a familiar gambit. Justin, being indispensable and overworked, could never take a proper holiday, and so he would snatch a week-end in Paris or Monte Carlo, or squeeze in the inside of a week (which usually meant ten days to a fortnight) in Madeira or St. Moritz. With his usual long week-ends at Sunningdale or Bray, his odd days off for racing, it totted up to a couple of months or more.

"Diana and the kids well?"

"Yes, thank you. Blooming."

The formalities dispensed with, we turned to business. Justin took a cigarette from the box and lit it. He didn't offer one to me.

"Well now, Hugo." His voice had moved up half an octave. "You're here to do a spot of hard work, you know. You mustn't think that now you're in the London office, you can sit back and take it easy."

"I never thought that," I murmured.

"I mean, this isn't just a way of giving you a paid holiday in this country. You've got to put your back into it properly."

"Of course. I want to be as much help as I can. In fact, I've got several ideas about the Natividad end to put up to you."

He looked at me blankly.

"Shall I put them up to you in a memorandum?"

"Oh! Oh yes, I suppose so." He frowned. "Keep it short, though. The typists are pretty busy." He smoothed out the frown, cleared his throat and said:

"Well now, Hugo, I've given a great deal of thought to your training here, and I have decided that you must work in each department in turn. I want you to start in the outer office and do a couple of months there, working under Pratt, Jolly and Lord, each in turn. And I really mean work, not just looking over their shoulders while they work. Take the thing over and do it yourself. I want you to know as much about shipping invoices and bills of lading as Jolly. It's very important that. And the same with insurance and purchasing. Do it yourself, it's the only way. I want you to do the job of everyone in this office."

Including yourself? I wondered. "Yes," I said.

"And then, after that, you go on and work under Hodges. And again I want you to do all the actual work yourself. Actually keep the cash book, write up the invoices, post the ledgers yourself, and if you can't get the figures out, stay all night till you have. I want you to go through the whole thing right up to Trial Balance."

"I did that in the Port Catalan office," I said.

"Well, you can do it again here. All right?"

I nodded resignedly. I had been expecting something like this. "And then?"

"After that? We'll have to see how you get on. Probably a spell under Phillimore."

"Yes. I should imagine that's pretty important."

"Well, not really, I do most of the selling myself in here. It's rather complicated now with quotas and some of the markets tied and some free. Phillimore only just watches it all and collects the stuff for me to decide on. Still, you may as well learn the procedure and see how it all works. We won't spend very long on that."

I leaned forward, feeling a little sick. "And after that?"

Justin stubbed out his cigarette in the beautiful big blue ash-tray. "Office hours," he said, "are from nine-thirty to five-thirty. I don't keep them exactly myself, because I usually take work home with me. But I think you'd better, just to show you mean business. And you'll take your turn coming in Saturday mornings. Lunch, you can have an hour for that. I think most of the staff use the A.B.C. down the street or that little café opposite. I don't think you'd better use those. As a member of the family it might be awkward. But there are plenty of good little eating-houses about. Later on I suppose you'll want to join the City University. I think it's the best lunch in the City."

For a moment I was afraid that we were in for a dose of clubs again, but he stood up and said: "Well, I think that's all. Keep at it, because there's a lot for you to learn here. They're pretty hard-pressed in that outer office. I'm going to have to give Pratt a whole-time assistant, but for the moment you're that assistant, you see? I'm going to tell him to work you as hard as he likes."

I should have smiled at that, but I was too screwed-up.

"Well, good luck! Don't hesitate to come and ask me if there's anything you want to know."

I was standing facing him. "There is one thing," I said doggedly.

"Oh yes, that reminds me," he said. "I've got a small job for you to do. The bank have got in a bit of a flap about things, and are coming here for a meeting on Thursday. They would choose Thursday, day before the Bank Holiday, but still, we're in debt to them, as I dare-say you know, so we've got to co-operate and keep them sweet."

I said brightly: "Oh yes, Walker said something about it. They want to drop the overdraft."

Justin frowned. "Walker shouldn't have said anything about it to you. It's not very important. We're over the limit, but then this is the time of year when you might expect that. They know that we're pretty sound financially. We made a good profit last year." He shrugged the whole problem off.

"I can never quite follow how we can make a profit and at the same time push the overdraft twenty thousand over its top limit," I said. I rather hoped it would annoy Justin.

"It's the difference between the Profit and Loss account and the Crop account," he said with weary patience, as if he were explaining something to a dense housemaid. "You'll find out about all that in due course. We trade, we make a profit, we declare a dividend. We also need money to finance our present operations, and that we have to borrow. It doesn't really matter whether we borrow it from the bank or from one of these investment companies or from the public. It's really better from the bank, because we can repay it when we don't need it. We don't have to keep it lying idle."

"But don't we always need it?" I asked. There had been worries about the overdraft for as long as I could remember.

Justin looked at me steadily. "The part that concerns you is this: The bank aren't nearly as concerned about the overdraft as they are about conditions in the colony, labor and so forth. I want to call you in during this meeting, as you are the person most recently out there. Give your picture of things out there, reassure them that everything's all right."

"I don't feel very reassured about it myself. Both Walker and Stevens think that there's going to be a strike."

"Well, there's no need to say that," he said sharply. "Use your brains. And anyway we've had strikes before and survived them." He suddenly relaxed and went on more reasonably: "No, the line is that this fellow Ramnarine is just a flash in the pan and that the other fellow, what's his name, the Sugar Workers' Union chap—"

"Maraj Singh."

"Yes, him. Say what a good level-headed chap he is, and how there are bound to be teething troubles at this stage, and, well, you know the form. At least," he added, "you ought to by now. If you don't we'll have to send you out to the colony again."

I nodded and said: "No, I think I've got it. Tell the truth but dwell on the bright side. Brim over with confidence."

Justin smiled and gave my arm a little pat. "That's the stuff," he said. "Quite a good line to take anyway."

The telephone rang. Justin picked it up and answered. He always lowered his voice when telephoning.

"Yes? Oh, good morning, Charles. Very well indeed. And you? She did well, didn't she? What? Well, that's quite a thought. Just a moment, Charles."

He covered the mouthpiece and said to me, "Better cut back to your work, Hugo, and get on with it." I hesitated, my decision to force a showdown hanging fire. "You've got a lot still to learn, you know. No time to waste."

As I went out, he was saying, "Well, Charles, we'd better have lunch."

I hadn't quite realized that I should be home before Diana and I felt a little forlorn and unwelcomed. There was so much I wanted to beef about and I felt, perhaps unreasonably, irritated at having to cope with Berta and the children all alone.

The nursery was in total disorder. The tables, chairs and floor were covered with clothes and toys and unwashed tea things and spilt milk. The radio blared at maximum volume. Both children were on the floor, absorbed in some obscure diversion. Berta was sitting stodgily, knitting.

"God, what a row!" I said, pointing at the radio.

Berta smiled at me and went on knitting.

I grabbed both children and hauled them protesting loudly to the living-room. There I sat them on the sofa, one on either side of me, and said, "Once upon a time."

Both children instantaneously froze into rapt immobility, gazing intently at the floor. I felt very fatherly and rather heroic at filling the gap so resourcefully.

I found story-spinning on the spur of the moment surprisingly difficult and perhaps my plot was too complicated, or perhaps too simple, or too much of a woman's story. After a minute or so Siegmund began to wriggle with increasing violence, till he slipped like a fish from my grasp, and was gone. Sieglinde shrieked, wriggled free of my distracted hug and followed. I found them back on the nursery floor.

I was a little piqued. "Berta, what time do they go to bed?" I asked.

She knitted and smiled serenely. Then she looked at the cuckoo clock. "Perhaps now." She put down her knitting and clapped sharply. We all jumped. "Bedtime, darlings. Stop playing, bedtime now."

Immediately there was uproar drowning the radio. "Oh no! No! No bed! Want play. Want Mummy! No bed. Want Mummy."

"No, bedtime, darlings," said Berta, beginning to gather up the strewn garments. "No more play. Play tomorrow. Now quickly into bed and perhaps Mummy come and kiss you good night."

Diana returned, looking elegant and professional and rather tired, just in time to tuck the twins in.

"Have you had a lovely time, darlings?" she asked. "Did Daddy play with you?"

"No," said Sieglinde briefly.

"I tried to tell them a story," I said, "but it seemed to lack popular appeal."

"Too bad. I'm sure Daddy told you a lovely story. Lucky Sieglinde to have such a kind Daddy. Perhaps tomorrow he'll tell you another one, all about how Creepymouse was naughty and got into Sieglinde's bed and she thought he was one of her toes."

I had to admit to myself that this particular plot had not occurred to me and I was uncertain how far it could be developed.

The child was immediately immobile and rapt. Then when no story came she said: "Tell now. Tell Keepymou in 'Linde's bed and very naughty and has adventures. Tell! Tell!"

"No, darling, tomorrow. Got to go to sleep now. Now what do you say before you go to sleep?"

If I hadn't been feeling so cross I might have felt a good deal of pleasure and family pride at the way Diana went through the final rites. But why the hell couldn't she get home earlier? And how was I expected to know who Creepymouse was?

"Darling, he's a little sugar white mouse in her last Christmas stocking."

"He must be pretty moldy by now."

"Oh, he's long since gone, but the memory lingers on. He's always frightfully naughty—that's what they really love, his not drinking his milk or spreading butter all over everything. Dreary stuff like that. Give it a nice moral twist at the end, and tickle their legs as you tell it. They can take it for hours on end."

"I think *belles-lettres* are more in my line," I said drily.

Diana flumped on the sofa. "I only discovered it by trial and error. It didn't come naturally to me either."

I said, not looking at her, "You wouldn't like to come home a bit earlier and do it yourself, would you?" There was no response, so I went on: "They were calling for you this evening. It can't be much fun for them only seeing you for a couple of minutes before they go to sleep."

"Sorry, I was held up this evening," she said wearily. "Miss Webster called me in just as I was leaving, and I had to wait hours at Holborn. I'm usually home well before this. And I do see a bit of them in the morning."

"It can't be more than a minute or two then and everyone's rushing about. I used to have a whole hour of my mother's undivided attention every evening before going to bed."

Diana gave a sigh. "I know, darling, so did I. But things don't seem to work that way any more. And when I was looking after the children myself, I didn't have a moment to play with them at all. I don't know why. By the time I'd get through all the chores, the day was gone. But I will try to be home earlier, really I will, darling. Miss Webster's always quite good about letting me go, only tonight was a bit of a flap." She got off the sofa and came to me. "How was the office?"

"Unspeakable," I said sourly. "A long lecture from Justin about not slacking and putting my shoulder to the wheel—"

"What! After all you did in that colony!"

"Oh, I suppose he thought it wouldn't do any harm to spout it all again. And then I did a shipping list. That really is breath-taking. You make sure that there are enough copies of the Bill of Lading, and shipping invoices, and consignment notes, and insurance certificates, and copy them all out and make sure they all correspond. Then felt I like some watcher of the skies, when it begins to rain."

"Bad as that?" Diana said sympathetically. "Well, thank God you haven't got to do that sort of stuff for ever."

"Yes, I suppose so. And nobody in that Outer Office does a damn thing except Jolly, the shipping man, and even he doesn't now I've arrived. Pratt, the manager, spent the whole day doing letters, which were only brief acknowledgments. But he was making quite a good headway with the crossword by the time I left. And now he's got to have a permanent assistant because he's so hard worked. God! when I think how they have to slave away at Malmaison, it really makes me sick."

"Oh, it's that sort of office, is it? Just what I would have expected from Justin."

I stood with my back to the fireplace and made an expansive gesture. "I don't think it's only Justin, I think it's a basic property of all offices. They're like vegetables, they've got to grow or die. You don't need to do anything once you've planted the seed of organic growth.

The office doesn't need to do anything; it is enough that it exists. You start with one secretary, and time and nature do all the rest. One day you suddenly find there's a girl manning the switchboard, and then another one buying stationery and stamps, and then a clerk to pay them both and keep the accounts, and then more accountants to get out the stuff for the auditors, and typists for them. And before the leaves start to fall you find that you've got a full-scale typing pool, and a maintenance staff, and a welfare department, and a board of directors, and a canteen, and a transport manager, and a publicity department, and a records filing staff, and someone to produce the office dramatic society's Christmas performance of *Charley's Aunt*. And there's no reason why anyone should ever find out that the office doesn't in fact do anything."

Diana kissed me. "Darling, I believe you've made a discovery like Newton and his apple. But I assure you, it's not like that on *Woman Today*. We're short-handed and very hard-pressed. And be pleased for my sake, I may be going to have quite a triumph. I think I may have found a new author."

"Oh really? Who?"

"Someone called Doreen Peabody. No idea who she is. She just sent us a story out of the blue and I thought it might well make a very good serial for us. That was before we went to Ischia, and today Miss Webster told me she quite agreed and had passed it on to the editor. It'll be a terrific feather in my cap."

"In Miss Peabody's too, I expect. Unless she turns out to be someone already famous in disguise."

Diana seemed slightly deflated. "I don't think so," she said slowly. "It came from Salford. And it was very fresh and charming. It stood out a mile from the tired old hackwork and the amateurish stuff. I really think our readers will love it—if we do it."

"Oh good," I said vaguely.

"Sorry, I'm boring you," she said quickly.

"Not a bit. I shall read it with pleasure."

Diana looked at me hard and then turned the chocolate eyes away. "I know it isn't the highest form of literature," she said sadly. "This woman isn't going to be the new Colette. But it's quite a thing to pick out someone who can write at all."

"Of course."

"Darling, there's a bottle of gin and some Noilly Prat in the cupboard and some ice in the fridge. Would you like to blend them artistically?"

"Do you think we can afford to drink martinis?"

"Well, this lot's paid for already, and I think we need it."

She looked crumpled and tired, and her face had her disappointed-little-girl look. Even after all the spaghetti, she was still too thin for me.

"All right," I said. "We'll drink Miss Peabody's health."

Some time in the dark hours we were both awakened by one, or perhaps both, of the children howling. I am a very light sleeper and was awake at the first whimper; Diana took a little longer to stir. She gave a low groan.

"What's the matter, d'you suppose?" I asked.

"Oh, one of them had a nightmare, I suppose. Or wind. Or just woke up and got bored."

We lay for a moment listening. The screams were getting short and tight. It only seemed to be one of them, so far. Diana turned on her side.

"Aren't you going to go and see what it is?" I asked.

"Berta will cope," she murmured sleepily. "She'll come in if it's anything urgent."

"But, darling—"

Diana grunted. "I got up not once but several times in the night for months when they first started teething. Berta can do it now. It's what we pay her for, isn't it?"

The screams went on interminably. I thought I could hear the child giving little short panting chokes between each bout, but I think it must have been my imagination. They were too far away for that.

"Berta isn't having much effect," I said. "We'll have them both going in a moment. Listen! That's the other one now, isn't it?"

Diana gave another groan and switched on her bedside light. She pulled herself to her feet, fumbled for her dressing-gown and slippers and went out. Her face was swollen with sleep. The noise was much louder when the door was open and then it stopped. Presently Diana returned carrying Siegmund, scarlet and tear-stained.

"I've brought you a young man who's bored and wants to go to a night-club," she said in a low caressing voice. "There, there!" she went on patting his back rhythmically, "are you wanting bright lights and lots of champagne? Daddy's own little boy. But you've got to go back to sleep again, you know. Now, you wouldn't be sick down me, would you?"

Siegmund was giving occasional burps and sobs, but he gazed at the room over Diana's shoulder with placid interest.

"Give him to me," I said.

Diana came round and put my son into my arms. He lay there, cradled, gazing up at me with watery contemplative eyes. Then he gave an enormous yawn.

"What's the matter with you?" I said, imitating Diana's caressing voice. "What are your plans for the rest of the night?"

He put his first two fingers into his mouth and sucked furiously. He closed his eyes. His body felt warm and damp from his exertions.

"I think he's gone to sleep on me," I said.

Diana smiled. "It's your hypnotic eyes, darling. I'd better put him back before he wakes again."

When she came back, I asked her, "Didn't Sieglinde wake?"

"Dead to the world. She likes her beauty sleep. Mummy's own little girl!"

She made a wry mouth and got back into bed.

"And what about Berta? What was she doing?"

"Hogging it. Fast asleep, snoring hard, mouth wide open. Rather obscene."

"But how could she sleep through that?"

"I don't know," said Diana wearily. "Good peasant stock, I suppose. Used to sleeping in with the cows."

She turned out the light, and I heard her tossing for a long time. Then she was still and I heard her breathing regularly. There were sounds of traffic outside, and the light was coming in round the ends of the curtains. In an hour and a half I would have to get up.

4

The colony mail came in on Thursday morning, and the outer office staff fell on it like the Israelites finding manna. Pratt was positively triumphant as if he had devised the air-mail service himself. However, apart from reading and nodding sagely over it, no action was taken on it, and the letters were passed through to Justin and vanished from our ken.

We all went back to our usual occupations. Lord made his culture-conversational round of the office, which apparently was part of the routine. After the first morning I was left out of this, to my relief; I much preferred the shipping lists. However, I was not left out of two new gambits of his, Beautiful Thoughts and puns. When I grumbled that I was still sitting in my own light, he said with earnest optimism, "Well, sir, lafe is full of little shadows, but the sunshane makes them all." It was very hard to bear and my self-control was stretched to its limit when he later said, "Greta, lake to be snappy and faind me some rubber bands?" This was quite beyond Greta, but Miss Slade said with bright coyness, "Oh, Mr. Lord, you are a scream." I gazed stonily at them both.

In due course Pratt gave a deep sigh, folded up the *Daily Telegraph* and said in a loud, important voice, "Miss Lumley, are you ready for the colony letters?"

There were three letters to be written, I gathered, one each to Stevens, Ingram and Hughes. But they were in answer, not to their letters received today, but to the ones that had arrived a week before. Pratt dictated well, loudly, slowly and coherently, but his text was sadly lacking in drama. I gave up working on my lists and listened, as he clearly wanted.

"We thank you for the information contained in paragraph 4 of your letter and we are passing this on to the manufacturers. We will inform you of their reply in due course. With regard to the point you raised in paragraph 5, we attach herewith a copy of a letter we have received from Archdale Robertson & Co., Ltd. Perhaps you would advise us in due course how you wish us to answer this letter. We thank you for the information contained in paragraph 6 which we have duly noted. With regard . . ."

Behind me I heard Lord say, "Well, Miss Slade, they say it's the dullest hour before the yawn."

And Miss Slade replied encouragingly, "Oh, Mr. Lord, you are dreadful."

I wondered if any of them knew about the meeting with the bank, and, if they did, whether they cared.

Justin had given me no idea of the time of day he would want me and no summons had arrived by the time I went to lunch. I lunched off a Cornish pasty in a pub, for I had not yet found anywhere both within bounds and my means—means which I suspected were a good deal slenderer than Pratt's or Lord's or Jolly's. It wasn't a very satisfying lunch, and I was feeling pretty low by the time the call finally came at half-past three.

Miss Yorke, as usual, met me in the passage.

"They're in the boardroom," she said, as if it was some cozy piece of gossip.

I smiled at her and went in.

I had never been in the boardroom before and my impression was of fumed oak, and tobacco smoke, and the portrait of my grandfather which I hadn't seen for years, hanging over the mantelpiece. Justin was sitting at the head of the table, and on his right was a big red-faced man I recognized as Sir Arthur Graham. Beside him was Hodges, apparently taking minutes. On the other side of the table were three men, presumably from the bank. The one next to Justin was speaking as I came in. He was rather bald—mouse-faced, probably, but it was difficult to tell under his horn-rimmed glasses.

Everyone glanced at me as I came in, but nobody made any move, or paid any further attention to me, and I remained standing inside the door, waiting.

The bald man was saying, "I trust you understand that we have no desire to cause any embarrassment or difficulty. We have had a long and happy association with this firm, but at the moment, as you know, we are not quite our own masters."

The two men nodded in agreement.

"As you know, we have been ordered to reduce the volume of our credit. But, even apart from that, we think that two hundred thousand is rather a lot to have tied up in one rather uncertain business—politically uncertain, that is."

"How much are we overdrawn at the moment?" asked Sir Arthur, sucking at a pipe which was making noises like the bath water running away.

"About two hundred and thirty thousand," said Justin. He was fidgeting with his pencils, and I thought he looked a bit rattled.

The man next to the bald man said, "Two hundred and thirty-three thousand last Monday." He was a dark little man—rat-faced, I thought.

Sir Arthur's pipe gave an especially pronounced gurgle. The bald man glanced at him with faint distaste and said: "Well, of course we want it brought down to the limit as soon as that can be conveniently arranged. And then, later, we must try and find a way to bring it down to a maximum of one hundred and fifty thousand. I think that would meet our requirements."

Justin gave a little cough and said: "Of course it always is high at this time of year when we're not grinding. It'll come down as soon as the crop gets under way."

"But will it come down enough?" asked the rat-faced man. "It didn't come down much last year, or the year before."

"We had an unusually high maintenance account those years," Justin explained.

Sir Arthur had evidently cleared his pipe blockage by blowing through it. "Well, what suggestions on how we do it?" he asked, exuding smoke like an erupting volcano. "Sell out the whole thing?"

"No, no, of course not," said the bald man smoothly. "But we thought that it would be just on matters of this sort that Mr. Nelson would be of assistance to you."

"Quite so," said Justin a little bleakly.

"For example," said the rat-faced man, "it might be necessary to reduce the dividend for a few years until the overdraft is down to its new level."

This seemed to produce a minor sensation. Justin glanced at Hodges and me anxiously and said, "I hardly think that would bring in more than the odd thousand or two."

The rat-faced one, Mr. Nelson I presumed, said, "Still, it would be a move in the right direction."

Justin drew some lines on his blotting paper, and staring at them, said: "Gentlemen, it has been my special pride since I have been chairman of this company that we have maintained both our profits and dividends at a level higher than they ever reached in my predecessors' time. Isn't that so, Hodges?"

"Yes, sir," said Hodges like a soldier.

"That is something none of my predecessors managed to do, and in view of the difficult world conditions and inflationary trends generally, I regard it as a duty to the company and to our shareholders to maintain, if not actually to increase this level. It would be a great blow to our prestige, here and in the colony, if we were to reduce our dividend now. In any event I do not think a dividend of eight per cent. is unreasonable. There is considerable risk involved in having capital invested in a business which is specially vulnerable to political upheavals or world depressions or droughts and things."

"Mr. Chairman, that is precisely our feeling too," said the bald man with smooth triumph. Justin bit his lip in annoyance.

Sir Arthur knocked out his pipe like a chairman rapping for order. Everyone looked at him.

"Not a financier myself," he said, "but it beats me how we've run up this overdraft as well as making good profits." He fumbled with some papers. "Says here, 'Net profit before tax, thirty-six thousand, four hundred and twenty-two—'"

Justin interrupted him. "Gentlemen, perhaps we could leave this matter over till later. I have another suggestion, which I think might be preferable. It may be possible for us to raise additional capital outside. I was talking tentatively to Lehmann's the other day and they might be willing to help us. Perhaps I could discuss it with Mr. Nelson some other time."

Nelson gazed at him suspiciously.

"I know Lehmann's pretty well," Justin went on. "Brigadier Hope-Gordon is an able fellow, and most reasonable."

"I'm all against cutting the dividend," said Sir Arthur. "Everything else is going up these days."

"Well, anyway," said Justin, "perhaps we could leave all that for the moment and pass on to the next item. I see my cousin has arrived."

The bald man nodded. Justin turned to me with an almost audible sigh. "This is my cousin, Hugo Pemberton."

Sir Arthur glanced up and said gruffly, "Hullo, Hugo, how's your mother?"

"This is Mr. Hildyard of the Bank." Justin introduced me to the bald man. "Mr. Nelson, who is coming to join our board and give us the advantage of his experience in financial matters." I shook hands with the rat-faced man. "And Mr. er, Webb."

"Webber," said the third man, pumping my hand vigorously.

Hodges fetched a chair for me and placed it at the far end of the table, so that I was facing Justin, and over his head my grandfather in his high stiff collar.

"My cousin has just been spending eighteen months in Natividad," said Justin, as if they all didn't know already. "Learning every side of the business from the bottom up." He gave a slightly strained smile. I wondered for a moment if that mightn't have been a joke misfired.

"Good boy!" said Sir Arthur. "That's the only way." He was carrying out complicated mining operations in his pipe, involving the sharp end of a latch-key and a lot of blowing.

"We turned him into quite a planter," Justin went on jovially. "What did those fields of yours yield?"

"Five point seven tons of sugar to the acre," I said.

"That's a record for the West Indies," said Justin.

It was a record for the colony, not for the West Indies, but I wasn't going to contradict him.

The bald man leaned forward and looked at me. "It's good to hear that you got on so well," he said. "Did you like it out there?"

"Oh yes, very much indeed." God forgive me, I thought. You too, Grandpa.

"Did you have any opportunity to study political and social conditions there?"

"Oh yes. You can't help it, you live with them the whole time."

"And what opinion did you form?"

I had thought that one out in advance. "Well, of course, this is a transitional period and there's bound to be a certain amount of unrest, but I don't think things are anything like as bad as they are in some other colonies—or as they are sometimes painted," I added.

"But mightn't they become so, Mr. Pemberton?" Nelson asked.

"I don't see why they need," I answered, bravely I thought.

Hildyard, the bald man, turned to Justin. "Mr. Chairman, we have had a most disquieting report from our branch manager in Port Catalan, Mr. Cornish. I daresay you know him."

"Oh yes, indeed. Know Cornish well."

"Well, he has reported to us that this new pirate union, the Natividad Labor League, is gaining a large following among the sugar workers. He is of the opinion that this strike which is threatened for the new crop may very easily paralyze the whole sugar industry."

"Oh, I think Cornish is taking too pessimistic a view," said Justin. "We've been threatened with these strikes before. They don't usually come off, and if they do, they never last long. After the out-of-crop break, most of the laborers are too hard up to be able to strike for more than a day or two."

"Unless this new union finances them," said Nelson.

"I think you'll find, when it comes to a showdown, that their loyalty is to their established union, which has done so much for them. The Sugar Workers' Union." He looked down the long table at me meaningfully. "Hugo, as a fresh pair of eyes in the colony, would you like to give us your picture of it all? Be quite frank, don't pull your punches. Tell us what you really think."

I knew that this was the nodal point, but I felt quite calm and assured. I had thought out in my bath exactly what I was going to say and I gave them a somewhat tendentious report with great confidence and sincerity. Sober realism, quiet optimism, shrewd analysis of trends and causes, a complete mastery of detailed and sometimes not quite relevant facts. I dropped in a few impressive local names which I was sure no one else would know.

I must have spoken for nearly fifteen minutes, and I thought it was a pretty good speech. Everyone listened with close attention except Sir Arthur who was refilling his pipe and kept zipping and unzipping his pouch. Hodges, taking it down frantically, stopped me twice, once for a name and once to tell me to go slower. Justin looked much happier and gazed at me with benign approval.

When I finished, there was a short stunned silence. Then Sir Arthur struck a match and said, "That's good to hear," through the dense blue clouds.

Hildyard said, "It's certainly most encouraging."

"That's what we think," said Justin with quiet triumph. I was feeling rather pleased with myself. I'd probably done myself a bit of good, as well as the firm. "And, of course," Justin was saying, "my cousin has actually been living on an estate at Malmaison. He hasn't just been wandering round the Port Catalan cocktail parties." He didn't say "like Cornish," but he might have. "He's had a chance to get to know the laborers themselves out in the fields. And that's what he thinks, and I must say I share his view."

"And may I say, Mr. Chairman," said Webber, butting in for the first time, "that we consider one of our prime functions to be to assist all sound commercial enterprises in these backward territories?"

Both Hildyard and Nelson glared at him, and he subsided.

"Well, Mr. Chairman, we must just hope for the best," said Hildyard. "I must say, to be perfectly frank with you, that one of the chief factors which encourage us about your position generally, is the very high opinion we have of your man out there, Walker. I've met him once or twice and formed a great regard for his knowledge and capabilities. I know that Mr. Cornish shares that opinion."

"Oh, Walker's first class," said Justin casually. "I suppose he knows more about that island than anybody else in the world. He's really got it taped."

"Like to meet him," said Sir Arthur, tactlessly I thought, for they were co-directors.

"Mr. Chairman," said Nelson with pointed slowness, "what will be the position when Walker retires?"

Since my speech, Justin seemed much more relaxed. He slumped half sideways in his chair and he had stopped fidgeting with his pencils. His language, I noticed, was no longer so formal.

"Well, I don't think we need worry about that at the moment," he said cheerfully. "He's good for a long time yet."

"Apparently," said Nelson, "he has hinted lately, just something he said which reached Mr. Cornish, that he might soon be retiring."

"Oh that!" said Justin easily. "He's always talking about coming home and buying a cottage in Yorkshire, has been as long as I remember. But it's only a pipe dream. He knows really that he won't. Why, he'd be bored stiff. He's a big man out in Natividad—in some ways bigger than the Governor—he wouldn't want to start being a nobody over here." Justin made an expressive gesture with his hands. "I think, you know, that Cornish has got hold of the wrong bit of gossip there."

It was very neatly done and the bank people all looked a little peeved. I kept my mouth shut.

After a moment Nelson said: "All the same he is not in his first youth. I am wondering what set-up you envisage when he comes to retire."

"Well, we've got this chap Reynolds," said Justin. "He's been twenty-four years on a sugar estate in India. He knows practically all there is to know about coolie labor, and that sort of thing. He's out there now understudying Walker. I thought him a good type, didn't you, Hugo?"

"Oh yes." It wasn't actually a lie to call him a good type, was it? And anyway what did one more matter? "He's quite—er—an expert on his subject."

"He'll be taking over more and more of the routine estate work from Walker," Justin explained. And then he added, quite casually, almost as an afterthought, "And then my cousin will be out there most of the time too."

That woke me up all right. I stopped congratulating myself and patting myself on the back for having made such a good impression on everyone, and stared hard at Justin. He gave me an engaging, reassuring smile, and turned to Hildyard.

"As you know, I take the view that the fountain-head of the whole business is in the colony, in Natividad itself. I don't believe in trying to run all the detailed side of a business like this from an office four thousand miles away. I don't know if you've ever been in the offices of the Natividad Sugar Company, our rivals?"

He smiled inquiringly. Hildyard grunted.

"Well, they've got a staff of hundreds. Floor after floor of them, all drinking tea and writing memos to each other. Well, that's just the sort of set-up I'm trying to avoid. That's why I've just got a compact little office here with a small staff, most of them in consequence rather hardworked. Of course, I've got to be here myself for a lot of the time, to be near the brokers and the ministry and the other head offices. It's my tactical command post."

He gave a positive grin as if he had made an uproarious joke. Sir Arthur nodded and said, "Very sound."

"The rest of this office," Justin went on, "well, it's just a registered address and an agency. The headquarters of the company, the main H.Q., is in Natividad. And that's why I've decided that from now on there will always be a member of the family in residence in the island. This just wasn't possible when there was only myself, but now that there are two of us, I think we owe it to the company and to the colony itself—and to you yourselves, gentlemen—to have a—an arrangement like that."

Hildyard nodded slowly. "Speaking without time for reflection," he said, "I think that is a most important and useful suggestion. I know my colleagues will be very interested in it."

Justin was well away now. I saw the glint in his eye.

"You see, gentlemen, one of the advantages of a small family business like ourselves is that we are a family first and foremost, even before we are a business. And the people in Natividad know that. They know us personally, and they respect us. They feel they can come to us for help." He gave a deprecatory shrug. "They call me 'Big Father' or even 'Big Daddy.'"

"Brrhm!" grunted Sir Arthur, embarrassed.

"It's a very special relationship, one which I treasure and which I think has a special importance in the development of these—er—backward territories. Finlays, you know, they've got a couple of estates out there, they are very much the same sort of firm, and have very much the same sort of ideals and methods as I have. I hear young John Finlay is out there at the moment, going through exactly the same program I laid down for Hugo. And I think that the work we do in the small"—he gave another deprecating shrug, beautifully and effectively timed—"family businesses is perhaps of greater value to the future welfare of the colony and its commercial prosperity than these huge corporations like the N.S.C., where everything is impersonal and cut-and-dried. We may not have the capital they have, we have to borrow rather heavily from our friends"—a warm ingratiating smile to Hildyard on this word—"in order to finance our various schemes for increasing production and welfare and so forth. But I think we are very important, family businesses like ours, to the future of the colony. And I think it would be frankly a tragedy if we were squeezed out, or had to amalgamate with one of these big corporations merely because of a shortage of working capital. It's one of my pet ideals, gentlemen. You must forgive me if I sound a little *empressé*. But it's an ideal for which I, and my predecessors, and other members of the family have made considerable sacrifices; and for which we shall continue to make sacrifices."

Perorating nobly, he sat back in his chair and eyed us. This was the stuff. I knew it almost by heart. I hoped that he wouldn't absent-mindedly call for a double whisky and soda, or start telling them what clubs they ought to join.

There was a slightly awkward pause. Sir Arthur said, "It's a grand thing, a family business," and blew through his pipe. Apparently it was blocked up again.

Hildyard said: "I think we must all have a lot of sympathy with your ideals, Mr. Chairman, and I assure you the bank will do nothing to try to frustrate them. We merely want to be reassured that everything is going as well as it possibly can, and to afford you such help as lies within our power."

I was hoping that the bit about my spending most of my time in the colony was a red herring, one more of those tendentious half-truths that we had gaily scattered through the meeting. With luck I might hear no more about it.

Nelson was looking at me closely, and then he turned to Justin. "Mr. Chairman, exactly what post do you have in mind for your cousin?"

"Well, of course," said Justin, "at the moment he's learning our work here in London, such as it is."

"I meant later on. Will he be joining us on the board, for instance?"

There was a pause. Hildyard said: "I think that would be a very happy appointment. It would strengthen board meetings in Natividad, which—" He gave a little smile. "They are a little thin on the ground when you yourself are not in the colony, Mr. Chairman."

Justin looked at me expressionlessly and then at his finger-nails. I wondered if he was expecting me to say something, so I said, "I should be very happy to serve in any capacity I can." It struck me as a good, noncommittal, modest way of saying that I wanted to be made a director as soon as possible.

"This is rather a domestic affair," said Justin, "and might I ask you gentlemen to leave the matter to my discretion? My cousin will, of course, be a full member of the board in due course. That is what I have been training him for, for the last eighteen months. But I think perhaps it might be a mistake to rush things at the moment. He is still a very young man and this fact is well known to people in the colony. I think it would in fact give him added prestige if he were to have a few more years' experience before being appointed to the board of this company."

I watched Justin's mouth, as he spoke, that large mouth with the self-indulgent lips. Camel-faced more than horse-faced. I watched him like an incompetent and apprehensive small schoolboy watching his house captain.

"The sort of set-up I had in mind," Justin went on, "I haven't had a chance yet to work out the details, but the rough idea was that my cousin might possibly, after his return to the colony, be appointed a local alternate director. There are provisions for such a position in our articles."

Hildyard nodded learnedly, as if he knew the articles well.

"He would not be a full member of the board, but he would represent me in Natividad, at meetings which I may not be able, for one reason or another, to attend. Something like that. It would mean that there would always be three directors present, myself or my cousin, Walker and Muir, who, as you know, used to be in charge of our Port Catalan office and now lives in Barbados. He still keeps in close touch with our affairs and flies over for meetings. He is a most valuable member of our board."

"That sounds quite a workable arrangement," said Hildyard judicially. He turned to Nelson. "Don't you agree?"

"Of course it's only a rough idea," said Justin modestly. "It's just the lines on which I am thinking."

In other words, I thought, you're going to wriggle out of it.

"When you say 'represent you,' Mr. Chairman," said Nelson, whose thirst for practical detail was apparently limitless, "do you mean that he would take the chair in your absence?"

Perhaps ferret-faced rather than rat-faced. I wondered if Justin would like having him as a director, nagging for precise details when he was meant to be satisfied with wooly platitudes.

"Oh no, by no means," said Justin hurriedly. "Walker will continue to preside in my absence."

"If I might make a suggestion, Mr. Chairman," broke in Webber, who seemed to have recovered his initiative, "perhaps Mr. Walker might be appointed a joint managing director. That would give him the requisite seniority over Mr. Pemberton here."

"He has that anyhow," said Justin. "The details, as I say, will have to be worked out in due course. I just mentioned the broad idea in case it might commend itself to you."

"Would Mr. Pemberton be an alternate member of the London board?" asked Nelson.

Justin looked at him with contempt. "No, not yet awhile. He will be a local alternate director, operating in Natividad, which, as I said before, is the fountain-head of the business." He paused and I thought for a moment that we might be going to get it all over again. "The London board," he went on, "is the full board of directors of the company. Myself, as chairman, Sir Arthur Graham, who as you know is a man of very wide experience over a large field and whose practical advice is so valuable to us." He bowed towards Sir Arthur, who grunted and banged on his ash-tray with his pipe. "And Mrs. Wright, of course, when she feels able to come. And Walker and Muir when they are over here."

There was a moment's pause. "And Mr. Nelson," said Hildyard. "Yes, yes," said Justin hastily, "of course. I am confident Mr. Nelson is going to be of the greatest assistance to us. A most valuable member."

Nelson let these blandishments flow past him. "Will your cousin work at Malmaison or in the Port Catalan office?" he asked.

"We-ell," said Justin, with an exaggerated shrug, "I don't think we can come to any definite decisions at the moment. I suppose he might divide his time between the two."

Sir Arthur nodded and grunted and soon everyone else was nodding and grunting too. I sat and stared at Justin, but I couldn't see any glint of triumph. You twister! I thought. You double-faced, two-timing twister! I play your game, I say all the things you want me to say, and then you drop this on me out of the blue when the bank people are here and I can't answer back. And what about all the time when you let me think I was going to get a permanent job in the London office? You can't pretend that I imagined it all myself.

You know you deliberately led me up the garden path, you twisting bastard!

My cheek-bones ached and I rubbed them viciously. Sometimes I thought it might be sinus, but it only came at times like this.

Justin was saying to the bank people: "My cousin has got an awful lot to learn here in a short time. If nobody else wants to ask him anything, perhaps we could let him go back to it now."

I didn't make any effort with the shipping lists that afternoon. I just stared out of the window and thought about life. Greta brought me a cup of tea and I sipped it slowly. I suppose it was tea; it might have been soup for all I noticed.

Pratt had his crossword half hidden under a file. He said: "Well, Mr. Hugo, just got those letters finished off. I always feel safer when they're off my chest."

I was glad to think that safety could be bought so cheaply. Miss Lumley and Miss George were banging away on their typewriters. Lord said: "Not much sugar in the tea today, Greta. Do A have to lump it?"

Miss Slade said, "Oh, Mr. Lord!"

I suddenly thought, why should Justin get away with it? I might have been outmanœuvred, but I wasn't beaten yet. If he thought he could stampede me into going and living in that hot little colony as simply as that, he had another think coming.

I got up quickly and went out, clumsily knocking Jolly's arm in the process. He was just writing some figures and swore at me, biting back his words when he saw it was me. His breath smelt worse than ever. I found Miss Yorke in her little cubby-hole.

"Is the Major free?" I asked.

"Oh no, Mr. Hugo, they're still at it. I've just taken them in some tea."

"Well, when he's got rid of them, would you tell him that I'd like a word with him?"

"Yes, certainly. I'll give you a buzz."

By twenty-past five there had still been no buzz and I went back to Miss Yorke.

"I'm terribly sorry," she said, "but the Major had to rush for his plane. He wasn't sure he'd catch it as it was. He hardly had time to sign his letters."

"When did he go?"

"About half an hour ago."

You too? I thought. But of course you're on his side too.

I looked at her reproachfully. She pulled her fingers awkwardly and then picked up an envelope. "He left this note for you," she said, giving it to me.

"Oh thanks." I put the letter in my pocket. I wasn't going to read it in front of her. "By the way," I asked, "that memorandum I wrote for the Major, about the estate and the factory, did he ever read it?"

"Oh yes. I've got it here now."

She went back into her cubby-hole and returned with the paper. I had been rather proud of it—terse, tactful, constructive and neatly typed by myself. As I took it, I saw that Justin had initialed it and penciled underneath "No Action."

Miss Yorke was watching me. When I glanced at her, I caught the glint of satisfaction in her eye.

"I'd better keep it in the file in case he wants to see it again," she said smoothly.

She took it from my unresisting fingers. I nodded and walked away without speaking. No Action. I smiled to myself. Of course I had been asking for that, hadn't I?

I went into the Gents and read Justin's letter. It was on the grand *From the Chairman's Office* paper, but in his own spidery handwriting, every letter separated from the next one.

Dear Hugo,

That was a fine performance on your part. Just what the doctor ordered. You seem to have made a big hit with them, which should come in handy some time. *Merci mille fois.* Sorry not to have time to say it in person, but I am dashing helter-skelter for *le rouge et le noir*. Wish me luck!

By the way, Charles Hope-Gordon says he would be delighted to second you for White's. He says he was much taken with you that evening. So you seem to be winning friends all round the place!

Why not come and have a drink at the flat when I get back on Wednesday evening? Sixish. Unless you've got anything else on.

Yours in haste,

Justin P.

I put the letter back in my pocket. "I hope zero comes up every time," I said as I emerged.

"Hope what, Mr. Hugo?" said Pratt who was standing just outside.

"Hope for a break," I said.

5

DIANA WAS LATER than ever that night and once more I had to grapple with the twins by myself. This time it went better; I was beginning to know the tricks. I refused to let them go on playing with each other's toys, I silenced their protests, I sat them on the sofa and told them to stop scrambling on top of each other, I tickled their legs and described to them at staggering length the domestic and exceedingly mundane adventures of Creepymouse. Several cantos later I gave the story an abrupt moral twist, the twins each a sweet, ignored their wails for more, and packed them off to Berta and bed.

I was feeling pretty whacked. It had been a trying day, and Creepymouse had taken my last reserves of strength. I made myself a very large martini and thought savagely about life. I was wanting badly someone to whom I could really blow my top off about Justin, and I was cross with Diana for not being available. I thought I would ring her at her office and chivvy her, in case she hadn't yet left.

I picked up the telephone and dialed the number. While I waited for someone to answer, I remembered I didn't know if Diana had reverted to her maiden name or not. I put the receiver down again. It wasn't the real reason, of course. The real reason was that I knew I wasn't going to be able to beef about Justin to Diana after all. It wasn't possible within our relationship. I knew what I wanted from Diana—her love, her passion, her submission, her laughter, her loyalty, her admiration. I didn't want her sympathy.

My mother might have filled the bill, but I didn't think I could take her particular brand of sympathy either, the brisk, make-the-best-of-a-bad-job brand. And she might so easily miss the point altogether. Anyway she was sixty miles away.

And then I thought of someone who would know exactly what I wanted and from whom I could take it so easily. It was high time too that I did something about my promise to keep in touch. I rang Information and asked for the telephone number of Fiona's flat.

As I listened to the ringing tone and waited for her to answer, I felt again that strange sick feeling that I remembered from my courting days; from my schooldays too, that uneatable lunch before the first round of the football cup. There was no answer. I checked the number with Information, left it a quarter of an hour and tried again. There was still no answer. She'd probably gone away for the weekend, I thought grimly. Like Justin. I felt very let down, and cross with myself for having counted on it.

Diana was still not home by the time the children were in bed, so I tucked them in and kissed them good night myself.

"Where Mummy?"

"I expect Mummy's been kept at the office. You go to sleep and she'll be here in the morning."

"Want Mummy say good night."

"Got Daddy tonight. Good night, sleep well and don't talk to each other."

I went back to the living-room, mixed myself another drink and settled down to wait for Diana. It was too bad of her, I thought, after saying she would make a point of being home earlier. The children might as well not have a mother at all. It was enough to make them into maladjusted retarded delinquents. I don't know how long I went on brooding in this vein; I kept on with it because the alternative train of thought, about Justin and my future, was even less appealing. Indeed, there is something rather satisfying about grinding over and over a grievance, like rubbing a chilblain.

I had finished my drink and was thinking about a third when Diana returned, clutching a bulging brief-case.

"Sorry I'm so late," she panted. "The editor had a pow-wow just as I was ready to leave, and one can't cut those. Ooh! I've run most of the way from Gloucester Road. Darling, I'm dying for a drink. Could you possibly mix me one while I go and kiss the children good night?"

I went to the drink tray. "The children are asleep," I said coldly. "Don't go in and wake them up."

Diana stopped on her way to the door. "Oh! Oh dear, is it as late as that? Did you tuck them in?"

"Yes."

She flumped on to the sofa and curled up her legs. "Oh well, make a change for them to have you. They have me every night. What did you do with them?"

I said wearily: "I told them about Creepymouse getting up very early in the morning to go down and catch the milkman and tell him not to leave any milk that day so that he needn't— You don't want me to tell it to you too, do you?"

Diana laughed. "No, darling, but it sounds absolutely perfect. I'm sure they loved it." I handed her a drink and took one more myself. Diana took a big gulp, sighed and said, "Ah, that's better."

I took mine and sat down on the arm of the chair opposite her.

"Actually," she went on, "the pow-wow tonight was rather exciting. The editor quite agrees with us about Miss Peabody's serial and we're going to buy it and do it for eight weeks starting on the 4th of November. I'm to edit it myself, as it's my baby, so to speak. I'm everyone's blue-eyed girl." She looked as pleased as Punch.

"Good," I said indifferently. I waited a moment and then I said with deliberate care, "One would almost think Miss Peabody mattered more to you than your children."

There was a dead silence for about fifteen seconds. Diana stayed absolutely rigid, not seeming even to breathe. There was an odd look on her face, the look she would have had, I suddenly thought, if I had slapped her hard. And indeed that was more or less what I had done. I don't know if it was the gin, or whether I had been more than half over my indignation before I made my crack, but I felt a sharp pang of compunction. She looked so very young and defenseless, sitting curled up there. "Sorry," I said, "I didn't quite mean that."

She looked at me steadily. "I think you did, you know. At least, you may not have meant to say it, but you think it." She looked away and took a deep breath. "I think maybe you're right in a way."

I sipped my drink and said nothing. I wished I hadn't said what I had, and I was also glad.

"I'm not really much use as a wife and mother," she said, rather sadly. "Perhaps we did wrong to get married."

"Oh steady!" I said hastily.

"No, darling, I mean it. And yet I don't. I know I seem a pretty hard-boiled career girl, but that's only half of me, you know. I think I'd have been awfully unhappy if there hadn't been any more than that."

She sipped her drink thoughtfully. I kept quiet. I thought I saw at last why she had been so hesitant about marrying me.

"I do try to be a good wife," she said with a wan little smile. "I mean, I'm a much better cook than I was, and I do darn your socks and—and we do have fun together, don't we?"

"Lots of it. I've no complaints."

"No, it's the children. Perhaps we oughtn't to have had them so soon. Perhaps we ought to have waited a bit longer."

"God send-a them a-we," I murmured reminiscently.

"What's that?" She paused, and then when I didn't say any more, she went on: "I know I don't seem very motherly, but I did want children, and I do love them. The thing about children is that they're a long term project. I'm looking forward tremendously to having a teen-age daughter and a schoolboy son. I want to see Siegmund in Pop, looking like that photograph of you; and I want to see Sieglinde tearing about in a flurry getting ready for a dance."

It occurred to me that both these visions would be pretty expensive to achieve, but I didn't interrupt.

"It's just babies that I don't get so thrilled about."

"I think they're pets," I said.

"Oh yes, they're sweet, and we've got a specially sweet pair. But, you know, they're very rarely quite as sweet as you keep thinking they're going to be. They're such appalling egoists." She frowned. "I've often thought, all these great children-lovers, the people who really go to town on it and declare that they love having a heap of children romping around them, and telling them stories, and never happier and—well, you know the type."

"Oh yes. What about them?"

"Well, they're usually bachelors."

I chewed that one over. "I think you're on to something there."

"It's very easy to adore all children in the abstract. I do it without any trouble. And then it's such a let-down when you get home and find they're being naughty or playing you up or bad-tempered. It's unfair to the children, I suppose; one shouldn't build up such dream images of them. They're just people like anyone else, sometimes nice, sometimes trying or boring. Age doesn't come into it."

"Look," I said, "don't give the matter another thought. I'm sorry I said what I did. It just slipped out. Forget it and let me give you another drink."

She handed over her glass. "But I am thinking about it. I suppose if you've got the real kitten-licking instinct, you like them just because they're small. That's obviously the bit that's missing in me, and I can't see how to acquire it. But I will try, darling, I really will. I'll be home on time if I have to leave everything unfinished on press night. Perhaps Miss Webster would let me work from nine-thirty till five-thirty. That would give me an extra half hour at home."

I poured out her drink and then snapped my fingers several times.

"Patrick!" I said sharply. "Patrick! Patrick, here! Here, sir! Here, good dog! Good boysie-woysie! Would you like to take this drink to Auntie Di? Would you? Would you? Would you do that? And tell her not to worry. Tell her she's doing fine. Tell her she's a sweetie-pie." I squatted down on my haunches and stroked his head. "Tell her she's your Uncle Hugo's blue-eyed—brown-eyed—girl too. And, Patrick, tell her not to worry. Tell her that Uncle Hugo only said it because he was in a filthy temper. He's spent the day doing shipping lists three feet from a man who apparently eats garlic for breakfast. You'd never do that, would you, Patrick? You'd rather have a nice dog biscuit, wouldn't you, Patrick? And then Uncle Hugo comes home and finds that Auntie Di has had a lovely day discovering unknown authors and he's so plain jealous that he loses his temper and is beastly to her. Tell her he's very sorry. Will you do that, Patrick? Will you? And will you lick her face just to show it's all right really? Good Patrick!"

I glanced at Diana, and saw to my horror that she was crying. I had never seen her cry before, even when I was leaving her for the West Indies.

"Quick, Patrick!" I commanded. "You're needed. Go and lick her face quickly!"

On Saturday I went down to South Meon to see my mother. Diana and I had had a bit of an argument about this too. We had all been invited for the Bank Holiday week-end, and as I hadn't yet seen my mother since my return, I was keen to go. Diana evidently wasn't. She said it would only unsettle the twins to cart them off down there again so soon, and she didn't want Berta to go again. Nor could she face the thought of taking them and leaving Berta behind; she had had a pretty tiring week one way and another, and how was she to cope with the children's feeding and dressing and bed-time and be bright and punctual for meals with my mother? I suggested leaving Berta and the twins in London and going ourselves. Diana said she didn't like to leave them all alone with Berta, especially after the episode of Siegmund's nightmare. I forbore to point out that earlier she had been prepared to leave them alone with Berta while we went off to Italy; and Diana repaid the compliment by not pointing out that it was silly to reproach her for not seeing more of the children and the next moment to take her away from them. So in the end I went by myself leaving her to divide her time between Creepymouse and Miss Peabody.

The train was crowded, but it was a perfect day and the Meon

Valley, that loveliest part of Hampshire, was green and shining in the sun. My mother's family had lived there for generations, and if my roots were anywhere outside central London, they were in South Meon. I looked at the beeches and the downs and the thatched villages and the pub where I had spent some pleasant evenings, and I hated the thought of Natividad more than ever.

My mother embraced me fondly, told me I had put on weight and wasn't I brown, and did I know I was playing cricket for the village and they did so hope I'd be able to play and she thought it was such a good thing to do. And so, instead of the leisured drink on the lawn and lunch, I had to bolt down hurried mouthfuls in intervals of routing out white flannels and boots.

Our village ground was green and lovingly tended, and round it were elms and oaks in dark midsummer green. Above us was the blue and white English sky. The pavilion smelt of leather and bat-oil. Our opponents, from Chawton, another village further up the valley, were old adversaries. Everything was quite perfect, like an advertisement for beer or National Savings.

I batted number three, as befitted an honored Vice-President, and I hoped fervently that I might not disgrace myself. My hopes were not completely fulfilled. The Chawton fast bowler was a tall blond young man and I never saw his first ball at all. It hit the top of my pads and shot off like a bullet to the boundary for four leg-byes. The umpire was Joe Black from the Home Farm; he grinned at me and signaled four runs; I grinned back. However, he could do nothing to save me from my second ball, which removed my middle stump, again without my seeing it. I loped back to the pavilion with a wry grin, deeply thankful that I hadn't got hurt, and spent the next couple of hours sitting on a very hard bench and gossiping with the rest of the team about television personalities, a topic on which, after my long stay in Natividad, I was sadly ill-informed.

After an enormous meal of cheese sandwiches, ham sandwiches, sticky buns and very strong tea, I sallied forth to take more exercise. Once again I was largely frustrated. Only three balls came my way. Two of them stung my hand intolerably. The third was a catch, my brief potential moment of glory. The Chawton batsman, a young man with prematurely grey hair, was hitting the ball as if he hated it, until a mis-hit sent a dolly catch into my hands. I took the ball on the end of my middle finger and dropped the catch with a bitten-back cry of agony. The grey-haired man went on to make seventy-one and win the match.

My sympathies were with the regular member of the side, whose place I had usurped, but the rest of the spectators must have had a lovely afternoon.

South Meon House was, I always thought, perfect; a small Queen Anne manor house with a pediment over the front door and long slender windows. The dining-room was perhaps the best room in it, green and gold, molding round the ceiling, the pictures on the walls that my great-grandfather had collected, and the long view across the valley to Old Winchester Hill. On a summer evening, you just wanted to sit there and let it all soak in.

I didn't want to talk much now, even though there was in theory so much to tell my mother; and I was dazed and sleepy, partly from the long day in the sun and the hectic start that morning, and partly from the three pints of bitter I had had in the pub after the match in a belated attempt to recover goodwill.

Bella, the dog, was also lethargic. She lay on the floor, swollen and introspective, and watched me blearily. She wasn't such gay company as Patrick.

"I hope they won't be too hideous," said my mother. "But it wasn't a very auspicious cross. Mrs. Mason let her out when she shouldn't."

"What will you do with them?"

"I'd like to keep one, if there's a pretty one. Or perhaps two. You know, it's company. And Joe Black said something about wanting one. And perhaps Mason or Mrs. Gregory. . . ."

My mother was a fountain of liveliness. She had changed into a dinner frock, even though she had had to cook and lay the dinner herself. She chatted brightly and copiously about local affairs, the opinions of Mason the gardener, and what a sound man he was, so much sounder than his wife who was a bit of a whiner, the iniquities of the government and Russia. She said what heaven it had been having the twins down there and couldn't they come more often, it had done them so much good, though she hadn't cared at all for that Berta girl, so surly. We covered a lot of topics, but she never asked about Natividad, or, for that matter, about Italy, and I was rather glad she didn't.

Somehow we started talking about the house itself. She looked down at the carpet and said: "I'm going to have to have a new carpet next year. Do you know this one is twenty-one years old?"

"It must be. I can't remember any other one."

"No. Nineteen-thirty-five it was. Lasted well, hasn't it, better than the stair carpet. That's got to be replaced next year too. It's almost through. Oh dear, what a year it's going to be! It's high time I had the drawing-room redecorated. It's looking terribly shabby."

"I thought it looked all right."

"That's only a man's view. A lick of fresh paint makes such a difference and it's so easy. And the drawing-room's so important. It's one's shop window."

"Yes. But it would need more than a lick." My mother always used words like "lick," "hop," "handful" to minimize her larger undertakings. I hesitated for a moment and then said: "You won't launch out into too much expense, will you? I think the dividend may well be cut this year."

She looked sharply at me. "And that'll mean less income for me?"

"Yes, I'm afraid so."

"Just for one year or for longer? And by how much?"

I shook my head. "I don't know."

"Well, how can I budget when I don't know how much I'm going to get? What's the matter? Have we had a bad crop?"

I told her about the bank and the overdraft and Mr. Nelson.

"Really, these banks!" said my mother irritably. "They make one wild. I've had a tiresome letter from the bank manager in Petersfield asking me to repay my overdraft. And I've banked there for forty years, but never a word of thanks. Oh dear, I suppose I shall have to sell something." Her eyes wandered sorrowfully round the dining-room pictures.

"I didn't know you had an overdraft."

"Since last year. First time since your grandfather first gave me a dress allowance." She gave a deep sigh. "I don't know what to do. Everything costs so much nowadays. I cut down and cut down and it still doesn't make any difference. Finish the wine, darling. It's rather good, don't you think? Only nine shillings a bottle."

"Very nice."

"But when I think of how we used to eat and drink. The dinner parties we gave. And we had the Chester Square house as well as this one, and servants at both ends. And there was supposed to be a slump in sugar at the time too. It's all very odd."

"Yes, it's the new age," I said, rather sententiously.

"Well, I don't like it. But, seriously, Hugo, what am I to do? I've got rid of all the staff—the cook, the maids, the chauffeur. I've only got Mason and I must have a gardener. The place would be a jungle in no time without one. And Mrs. Mason, she comes in for a couple of hours in the morning to help with the scrubbing. And sometimes Mrs.

Heath for the odd half-day. That's not really the height of extravagance, is it?"

I smiled. "It doesn't sound it." I suspected that it was another of her "licks" or "handfuls."

She sighed again. "I suppose it's rather silly for an old woman like me to go on living in a house this size."

I gave a secret sigh. I knew this one well. It was the end of every mention of finance.

"I often think that I should move out of here. I hear poor Mrs. Woodward is ill and isn't likely to recover. I might buy her cottage, when she does. I could just manage it nicely by myself."

"Oh hardly," I protested. "It's got no sanitation or anything. You couldn't live there."

"Oh, I could make it very nice. And then you and Diana could have this place. You ought to have it anyway. It would be just right for you, especially when your family's a bit bigger. And the children could come down and have tea with Grannie." She smiled at the picture.

Of course it was preposterous. How did she think I could afford it, if she couldn't? Or did she think that I got the same salary as Justin or my father? Anyway, she didn't mean any of it. It was her defence-mechanism against the thought of moving. She wanted to be reassured that, though the skies might fall, though Wright, Pemberton & Co., Ltd., might go into liquidation, she would never have to leave. She had been born in the house, she had spent all her girlhood there, she had been married from it, and a year later she had been back there again as its owner and mistress. She had borne me there, and she wanted to die there and be buried in the village churchyard with her ancestors and her husband. And so she offered to move out every time I came down.

I smiled fondly at her. "Of course not. Things aren't as bad as that yet. And we couldn't possibly manage this house. Anyway, I have to be in Mincing Lane at half-past nine every morning."

"Well, you could go up in the train. People do."

"Not all the way from here. It would take hours and cost a fortune."

"Well then, let Diana and the children stay down here. Lovely for the children in the summer, and all the riding and everything, and nice for Diana too. And you could give up that dreadful flat, which I'm sure costs you far too much, and move into digs, and come down for week-ends. Lovely for everyone."

"But I don't want to live in digs and only see Diana once a week.

Besides, I don't think Diana would like living down here. She's a town girl."

I knew immediately that it was a mistake to say that. My mother didn't miss. "I sometimes think that it would do her a world of good to rusticate quietly for a bit in the country."

As we were washing up afterwards, I said, "I should like to go to church tomorrow." The thought had occurred to me as I was coming down in the train; I thought it might help a bit.

"Of course," said my mother. "You're reading the lessons."

"Oh, am I?"

"Yes, didn't I tell you? I met Phil Gregory in the street and told him you were coming down, and he asked me if you would. I said I was sure you would. And they want us to go in for drinks afterwards. Around twelve."

That cut out my embryonic idea of staying for the late Communion and I couldn't face the thought of the early one. But I rather liked reading the lessons. It was a chore that sometimes fell on me when I was down, and it made me feel rooted and squirearchic.

The rest of the evening we spent in the usual way trying to find out what the lessons were. No one could remember where the lectionary was, and when it was finally located, no one could remember which Sunday after Trinity we had got to. Finally we had to ring up the Rector and get it from him. Then we argued about whether it was the Revised or the Amended Lectionary, and whether it was Table A or Table B.

"Do you remember what it was last Sunday?"

My mother shook her head. "I wasn't listening very carefully. Could it have been Esdras?"

"Not unless something very odd had happened. A Saint's Day or something."

There was no doubt that religion was a complicated business. Finally we settled for the Maccabees and St. Luke. Then we started on another search for a Bible with an Apocrypha, this time in vain.

"Well, I shall just have to do it unseen. Let's hope they didn't do too much begetting."

"Don't worry, darling. I'm sure they'll like it whatever you read. Have a good sleep. You'll like being back in your old room, won't you? Breakfast whenever you feel like it."

When Diana and I came down to South Meon together, we slept in the guest bedroom, but I liked being back in my own room. It was in here that I had spent nights of school holidays and Long Leaves and army leaves. It had been my main base from the moment when I left the night nursery until I went up to Oxford. And though it had since been completely redecorated and now had that impersonal spare bedroom look, yet the shape of the room was the same, and the shape of the trees outside was the same.

My sleepy feeling had worn off during the hunt for the Maccabees, and I lay for a long time in the darkness, staring at the pale outline of the window, and thinking of all that had happened to me since this had been my own room. On the whole I wasn't very satisfied with my progress. And then I started wondering if Siegmund would ever have this room as his very own. That seemed improbable, and in a way I was sorry. But I didn't really want to live down here all the time, quite apart from the problem of earning a living, and apart too from Diana's certain reaction to such a plan. Would I ever be able to afford to keep it as a holiday and week-end home? Perhaps, if the firm did very well and I got a big enough salary. That was just pie in the sky, and in the meantime I was being asked to kick my heels in Natividad. I shied away quickly from that thought. I should never get to sleep once I started on that.

Anyway, this was my mother's home and she would stay here till she died. That was definite. But was it? Supposing the dividends failed altogether? Supposing the firm went into liquidation? What would happen to the house then? And to my mother? And to me? And to Diana and the children?

I switched on the light and began to read *Jean Santeuil.* I must have fallen asleep over it, for the bedside light was still on when the birds woke me at five in the morning.

I got to the church early to have an advance peep at the Maccabees. They seemed fairly straightforward, if a little dull. But St. Luke was about Christmas, and on second thoughts this struck me as inappropriate in August. I decided that I must have misread it and that it must really be St. Mark. This provided a passage about a man sick of the palsy, which I thought suitable.

I had meant to pray hard, but I was heavily distracted. How the Gregorys' little boy had grown and who were those girls with Mrs. Barbour? Nieces, my mother whispered, but she wasn't sure, they might be stepnieces. And who was the man singing bass in the choir? And would the Rector slide from one Creed into the other, as he had been known to do? And did his false teeth fit any better?

And then there were my lessons. I boldly walked up to the Lectern during the Gloria of the Venite, and then found I had to stand there, conspicuous and sheepish, while they sang a psalm. I read the Maccabees doggedly, and gave the congregation an extra ten verses to help refurbish my ego. And I was nearly caught again in the second lesson; I only just remembered in time that the Te Deum has no Gloria.

But the hymns were jolly. The Rector gave us a sad and hackneyed sermon on the hydrogen bomb, which failed to comfort me much, and I came out, smiling to my friends, chatting about the cricket match with the Gregorys, and with my problems still round my neck like an albatross. I might have shown the flag but I had made no contact whatsoever with God.

I got back to London late on Sunday night. Diana was curled up on the sofa looking quite staggeringly pretty, and surrounded by Doreen Peabody's manuscript. I kissed her, intending a light greeting, but it turned into something rather more sensual. She was wearing the green frock she had been photographed in, and which cunningly seemed to give her a larger bust than she really had. She was smiling her sideways secret smile and her eyes were shining. I knew she was longing to be loved, and instinctively I played for time, spinning out the moment of desire.

"Had a nice time, darling?"

"Very nice," I said, lighting a cigarette. "It was lovely down there. I played cricket for the village and I made four runs against a very fast bowler."

"My great big he-man!"

"And I read the lessons in church and drank three pints of beer in the pub."

She raised her eyebrows. "The rustic life as she is lived. How was your mother?"

"Oh, in good form. She made me a steak béarnaise."

"I've done that for you in my time. Don't you remember?"

"Indeed I do. It was excellent. You must do it again some time soon."

"Darling, it takes ten years off my life each time. But if you want it, you shall have it. Did your mother say anything about the children?"

"Only what you'd think. They'd had a wonderful time and she didn't like Berta. Oh, she suggested we all go and live there, and she'd move out into a cottage in the village."

"Oh that!" Diana wrinkled her nose. "I hope you scotched that."

"Well, more or less. I said it was quite beyond our means."

"Even it if wasn't, it's the last place where I'd want to live. I mean it's lovely for the odd week-ends, but for all the time! I think children brought up in the country are much stupider than ones brought up in cities. I don't want mine to get doggy and horsy."

"What about Patrick?"

"Exactly. He's quite enough. But you won't bury me in the far prairie, will you, darling? Not a pavement for miles around. I should loathe it."

I laughed, but I didn't comment. Instead I said: "What about you? What have you been doing?"

She told me with some pride. She had spent practically all her waking hours with the twins, I suppose in a fit of remorse, she had played with them and taken them out and told them stories and helped bath them, and it seemed to have been quite a success.

"Not much time for Miss Peabody, but I'm getting on with her now." She patted the typescript. "It's going well. I think we may have a record fan-mail for it."

"Oh good." I picked up Chapter One and read aloud, "'The sleet was teeming down as the tired bony horses dragged the Carlisle coach up Scraw Fell.'" I looked up. "Love and revenge in the Lakes? Hugh Walpole stuff? Lots of beatings?"

She laughed. "None. It's a sort of cross between *Jane Eyre* and *Far from the Madding Crowd.*"

"Gosh! Oh well, they say mongrels have great vitality." I sat down and started to read. Diana leaned across and flipped away the chapter. I was hoping she would.

"You can't start it tonight, darling. You've got all day tomorrow to read it. Besides . . ." she hesitated and then said, "there's something I've got to tell you—or ask you, rather."

"Constance Holme!" I exclaimed.

"What?"

"I've been trying to think of her name. The woman who wrote this sort of book."

"Oh, did she? Oh!"

I seemed to have put Diana off her stroke. "Well, ask away."

She was looking at me with a strained sideways look. "It's sort of arising out of this book. It's the magazine. They want me to stay on permanently."

For a flaring second we looked each other in the eye.

"But I thought——"

Diana looked down and began to fumble with the buckle of her belt. "Yes, I know. It was only temporary. But now Julia Longworth has written to say she isn't coming back at all. And I suppose I'm in their good books at the moment."

"Is she the one who was having a baby?"

Diana shot me a quick glance. "Yes," she admitted. "It's quite an honor really and a good job, assistant fiction editor. And the way's wide open for me to be fiction editor in due course, when Miss Webster moves on or up. I'd love that, hobnobbing with authors and publishers and agents."

"What did you say to them?"

"Nothing. I said I'd ask you."

There was a long silence. I lit a fresh cigarette from the stub of my old one, mainly in order to stop myself snapping "Nonsense! Out of the question!" She was my wife and I mustn't, must not allow myself to become jealous. It wouldn't make my work less dreary if she turned down the sort of job I longed for. Anyway, it was only a woman's magazine.

"You don't like it very much?"

"Frankly I don't. But you want to take it?" I tried to keep a rasp out of my voice, but it kept slipping in.

"Oh yes, it's right up my street." She paused for a moment and fidgeted with her buckle again. "You know, darling, when I was doing nothing except look after the children, I was fast going completely to seed. They aren't the most stimulating or intellectual of companions and—well, we won't go into that again. But I was turning into a complete cabbage. I went to one cocktail party and I was absolutely shocked by myself. I was getting just like all those girls I despise so much, people I was at school with, who were so bright and up-and-coming, and are now complete cabbages, only able to talk about how much their babies weigh. Ugh. No other interest in life at all. And then I was offered this job and it really did seem indicated. You've no idea how it's bucked me up. I should have been pretty dreary company for you, if you'd come back two months earlier." She paused and added, "I don't think I could bear to have to go to seed again."

I said: "People don't usually call raising a family, going to seed. It's one of the main objects of life, for women anyway." Diana didn't say anything, so I went on: "Look at it from the children's point of view. It's not working very well at the moment, is it?"

"I know. I'll try to organize it better, really I will. I'll leave the office at half-past five sharp and I'll take a taxi home. They're going to pay me another hundred a year, so I can afford that. We'll get rid of Berta and get a proper nanny."

Unless I got a rise, she would be earning more than I. But I mustn't let that affect the matter either. I must try to be fair all around.

"They still won't see very much of you."

"They'll have me in the evenings and at week-ends. I didn't see very much more of my own mother, and that worked out all right."

I wondered if it had, but I didn't say so. Instead I said, "I think it's important for small children to spend a lot of time with their mother."

"I'm not sure that I agree," said Diana flatly. "I'm not sure that it's a good idea that the person who's around all the time, the person they spend their time resisting, should be their mother. I think the mother should be someone rather special who does interesting and exciting things with them, not just the person who goes on repeating, 'Hurry up, stop playing about and drink your milk.'"

"But will you get the time to do interesting and exciting things as well as this job? Will you have the energy?" I shook my head with pontifical gloom. "I don't see how anyone can serve two masters like that."

The argument was getting more forthright and heated. At last we were digging down into fundamental attitudes.

"Masters! But the children aren't my masters," she said with some indignation. "If it was a question of looking after you, it would be quite another matter. But not children."

"They're pretty important all the same. I think they're entitled to your best time. After all, they're the rising generation."

"Oh God, that one!" exclaimed Diana. "Nothing is too good for children because the future is theirs. But it isn't, you know, because they're going to have children too in time. I think it's dreadful. We're told we've got to sacrifice ourselves for the next generation, give up all our interests and contacts because the next generation are entitled to all our time and energy. And then they grow up and leave you and you're left high and dry. And it's all been wasted, because the children start having to sacrifice themselves for their children before they have started to do anything, and so on ad infinitum. It's awful, makes us just like ants or bees, just existing to produce another generation, never getting any for'arder."

"But people do, you know. We do make progress."

"Only men and unmarried women. I think it's time the married women lent a hand too. Perhaps the world might be a better place if they did."

I smiled. "You make this job sound terribly cosmic," I observed.

She flushed. "Sorry, darling. I didn't mean to ride my hobbyhorse at you."

There was a long pause. I stood up and leant on the mantelpiece staring into the unlit gas fire as if I were looking into great glowing caverns of coal.

"Do you really want the job so badly?" I asked.

I heard her breathe deeply behind me. "Yes, I do. I think I could manage it and still see quite a bit of the children."

"It isn't that I want you to vegetate completely. You haven't got to ram every mouthful into their mouths. But I do want you to be *there,* in the background, available. If you were to do this work at home—would that be possible?"

"Only on the odd afternoon. They'd want me in the office most of the time, for conferences and things. It's a whole time job, this."

"If only it were a few years later," I said. "I wouldn't mind later on when the children start going to school."

"The job'll be gone by then."

"Perhaps there'll be others."

There was a short silence.

"So the answer is no?" Her voice was low and diffident.

"I'm afraid so," I said. "I can't see how you can take on this job at the moment. I haven't liked the idea of the temporary job very much."

"No, I thought you hadn't." Once again there was a short pause. "Darling!"

I turned and found her standing behind me. I hadn't heard her get up.

She spoke deliberately and slowly. "This is very important to both of us. Can I have it absolutely straight? Are you . . ." she hesitated and then went on, "are you forbidding me, as my husband, to take this job, even though I think I can manage it all right? I mean, are you bringing out the big stick? Marriage vows and all that?"

I caught the note of desperation in her voice and it stopped me answering immediately. Her face was a couple of inches below mine and very close. The chocolate eyes were serious and wide, and the skin was so very smooth over her slanting cheek-bones.

I knew then that I couldn't do it to her. She was me and I was Justin, and I was squeezing her in the good old family manner. Who was I to turn the heat on her, to lecture her about sacrifices and her duty? Any moment I should start advising her to join the Ladies' Carlton.

"No, I'm not," I said very gently. "If you really think you can manage it all, all right. Go ahead."

She gave a little gasp and pressed her cheek against my lapel.

My face was in her hair. "Oh darling!" she mumbled. "You're so nice to me it almost hurts."

I put my arm round her and kissed the top of her head and said nothing.

She looked up. "I really will try to get it properly organized. I really will. Promise. I'll see about getting a nanny on Tuesday."

"I'm sure you will. What about when we have to go out to Natividad?" This was an aspect of the problem that I had deliberately kept out of the argument. It was rather a red-herring, and only tentative, and I didn't want to talk about it anyway. But now I felt I had to mention it.

Diana took it in her stride. "Oh, I expect they'll give me leave, if it isn't for too long."

"And supposing it is for quite a spell?"

"Don't!" she shuddered. "Let's jump that ditch when we come to it. You said it wouldn't be for eighteen months, didn't you?"

"Yes, I think I did."

"Well, let's not worry now. I may have been sacked by then."

I let it go at that. I didn't want to start another storm, now that we were back in calm water. I had given way in order to make her happy; why spoil my big gesture?

We stood like that for quite a long time. "You're very nice, you know," she said. "I'm not sure that I'm quite nice enough for you. But I'll try to be."

"Supposing I had put my foot down and hadn't let you, what would have happened? What would you have done?" I hadn't meant to ask it, but curiosity got the better of me.

She looked at me sideways, teasingly. "Oh darling, that's not a very fair question, is it? You should have tried it, if you really wanted to find out."

Her eyes were half-closed and almost hidden under the long lashes. Her mouth had its little secret smile. I watched her in close expectancy. I saw the tip of her tongue between her lips, sensual and tempting.

But, for the first time, the old magic didn't work. I dropped my arm and went across to the cupboard to find myself a drink.

Part Three

1

On Wednesday morning a mysterious parcel arrived with the letters at breakfast. Both Diana and I gazed at it with the intrigued mystification that such things always arouse. Bulldog Drummond, I recollected, invariably drowned unexpected parcels in the bath in case they might contain poisonous spiders. Perhaps it was fortunate that I did not follow his example, for the parcel, when unpacked, proved to contain three new novels and a laconic note from Gatoff asking me to review them.

I passed the note to Diana without comment and I saw the little flare of pleasure in her eyes as she read it.

"Oh, darling," she said, "isn't this just what the doctor ordered!"

"Very nice. I thought he'd forgotten me completely."

"Evidently not. Just shows what a great impression you must have made on him." She gave me her special smile. "I like being married to a literary critic. That's the man I married. I knew you'd come back to it in the end. I knew it."

"I didn't."

"Oh yes, you did. Hence Mr. Gatoff now. You did it a-purpose."

I gave way and laughed. "So I did. And it worked too. Though three swallows hardly make a summer. God, I must rush."

"Me too."

She called good-bye to the children, shouted something at Berta, and gazed at herself briefly in the hall mirror. "Mrs. Hugo Pemberton," she murmured, "wife of the well-known literary critic, said today at her Kensington flat—" She paused.

"Well, what did she say?"

"She said, 'Oh what a nice day it is and how I like it when nice things happen.' "

She took my arm and squeezed it and we walked out of the house together. "Three swallows can make a summer, you know," she said. "At least they can begin one. Three cuckoos certainly do."

I squeezed her arm back. I was feeling pretty bucked too.

"By the way," I remarked as we got into the train at Gloucester Road station, one pleasant thought leading rather obscurely to another, "there's a girl from Natividad in London at the moment. We ought to do something about her. She's the daughter of Finlays' local senior director and I think she's rather at a loose end here. We came over on the ship together, and I said we'd ask her in for a drink or a meal or something."

Diana glanced at me. "Pretty?"

"Oh yes. Quite pretty."

She smiled her private smile. "Then of course we must ask her. It's good for you to be surrounded by beauty. Shall we have her to dinner? I could give her my famous grilled chop."

"Oh, I think a drink would do. Then she'd be able to see the children before they go to sleep. She wants to meet them specially."

"Fine! Let me know which night it is and I'll make sure they've got clean faces."

I rang up Fiona in my lunch hour and once again I was aware of the twinge of expectancy as I waited for her to answer. This time she was at home, and I smiled as I heard her unusual voice again. I caught sight of the smile in the mirror over the coin-box, vacuous and rather idiotic, and I wiped it quickly off my face.

"Hullo! Fiona? It's Hugo Pemberton here."

"Oh hullo! How are you?"

"Fine. I've been trying to get hold of you for some time, but you've been away."

"Yes, I was week-ending with the Finlays in Gloucestershire. And before that I was in France."

"Oh, how nice!"

She told me about her holiday in France. I told her about Ischia. We cooed inanely at each other. I invited her for the following evening. She accepted with a laugh. I laughed back. Goodness knows what we were laughing about. I suppose it was the contagion of high spirits, studio-audience laughter.

The somewhat incongruous combination of Fiona and Gatoff lasted me through the whole day, and I didn't feel the ache in my cheek-bones until I was actually in the lift going up to Justin's flat. I had come up in that lift so many times to learn my fate, and here I was doing it yet again. Even the musty smell of the corridor seemed full of foreboding and I felt rather sick.

Justin himself answered my ring. Behind him was standing a dark tubby little man.

"Ah, Hugo!"

"Am I early?" I asked. "I came straight from the office."

"Not a bit. I've only just got in myself," he added, perhaps a little defensively. "This is Dr. Schwartz. Ernst, meet a cousin."

I greeted the man who gave a little bouncing bow.

Justin said: "Hugo, would you like to go along into the living-room? I'll be with you in a moment."

He and the Doctor went into his bedroom. This too had happened before. Justin was always having courses of injections from obscure German doctors. I never knew what it was all for, or why it always seemed to be a different doctor.

Justin's living-room was furnished in his own individual style—'taste' is perhaps too strong a word—and was as full as his office was empty. Antique cabinets stood beside modern sectional bookcases. On the mantelpiece Georgian silver candlesticks blended with a French tortoise-shell clock, glassy Zeiss barometers and thermometers and colored photographs of Justin in fancy-dress. There was an attractive collection of Berdam glass in an illuminated alcove, adorned, as they say, with light. On the lemon walls were mock Utrillos and over the mantelpiece a mock Jan Steen (surely it must have been mock; I had never given Justin the pleasure of telling me) full of obscene allusions that Justin loved to point out. The Epstein bronze head stood on the window sill, and the green marble abstraction, something between a vegetable and a human thigh, was on the bookcase. On the television console was an acquisition that was new to me: a black wire maquette, possibly a honeycomb or a badly damaged harrow, mounted on rough stone and labelled 'Geoffrey'.

Pottering on, I turned to Justin's rather fine collection of art books, and pulled out at random the volume on Piero della Francesca. Here I had a shock, for inside the magnificent jacket I found, not Italian pictures, but photographs of nude female bodies. I looked at them with interest and, I may confess, some pleasure; the girls were all much plumper than Diana. But it was a considerable surprise. I had not thought Justin was so interested in that sex.

Through the door I heard Justin saying good-bye to Dr. Schwartz and I replaced the book between Tintoretto and Dufy. I wondered what lay behind their splendid jackets: *Sex Practices of Ancient India? A History of Flogging?*

"Sorry about that," said Justin coming quietly into the room. "Have you given yourself a drink?"

"Not yet."

"Well, let's go to it, then." He rummaged about for ice in the Chinese lacquered refrigerator.

"How was Le Touquet?" I asked politely.

"Oh, wonderful. A break like that does one a world of good. Gets one out of oneself. I was feeling very low before."

He worked away at the frosted glass-and-silver martini-mixer. "I made twenty pounds," he said, his back towards me. "Every time I stood on a five, it worked."

"Oh good."

He handed me a drink. "Salut!"

I couldn't bring myself to say Salut! back, so I merely sipped my martini and said, "Very nice." There was no doubt about it; Justin, whatever his other shortcomings, could make a perfect martini.

I indicated Geoffrey. "That's new, isn't it?"

"Not especially. I got it about a year ago from Gimpel's. I think it's rather good."

I nodded portentously. "Ye-es."

"You really feel that you know him inside out. It's a complete analytical portrait."

"Who was Geoffrey?"

He shrugged. "Oh, *quelconque*."

We could have gone on talking about Geoffrey and Le Touquet all night, so I thought I'd better kick off before we got side-tracked any further. I took a big gulp at my drink and said:

"I was glad that meeting with the bank went off so well."

"Yes, it was quite a success, that. You did very well for us. I think they took to you in a big way. They were certainly much more amenable to my various suggestions afterwards."

"Oh good," I said again. I sat down in an early Victorian armchair and helped myself to a cigarette from an inlaid box. My hands weren't quite as steady as I liked. I glanced up and saw that Justin was watching me closely. "That bit about my spending most of my time in the colony, was that for the bank's benefit, or is that the plan?"

"Oh, that's the plan," he said cheerily. He didn't seem to want to sit down. "I wish I'd had the chance to talk it over with you first."

"Because I don't like it very much."

"Oh, don't you? Well, all work's a bit annoying, isn't it? By the way, I'm afraid I've got some bad news for you."

I pressed my thumb and forefinger down over my cheek-bone and breathed deeply. My forehead was damp.

"I've had the articles looked up," he went on, "and I was wrong. There isn't any provision for a local alternate director. I made a mistake about that."

Like hell you did, I thought.

"We'll just have to appoint you a local attorney until the time comes for you to become a director."

"Oh," I said rather blankly. I always thought Justin might wriggle out of it. "But weren't the bank rather expecting it?"

"I've talked to Nelson about it. I told him frankly that I'd made a mistake and that there was no provision for the post. I also said I didn't think this was a very good moment for monkeying about with the articles. He agreed. He said he didn't think it mattered what the job was called as long as you were out there doing it."

"I'm not at all sure that I want it. I've had enough of that colony."

"Oh, come, come, it's not so bad. Anyway, it's the place where all the work's done. That's where you've got to be from now on, whether the countryside appeals to you or not."

I said rather desperately, "But you said in the beginning, when I first went out to Natividad, that I'd be coming to work in the London office with you, after I'd done my tour out there."

"Well, so you are," he said smoothly. "You're there now."

"No, I mean permanently. Like you."

"Did I say that?"

"Yes, you did. At least, that was the distinct impression you gave me."

"I don't remember it now. But I may have done. The point is, things change the whole time. One must be flexible in one's arrangements. I'm very keen to build up the Natividad end as against the London end. In the set-up as I'm seeing it now, I honestly don't think there'll be anything for you to do in the London office."

"What about sugar sales?"

"We've already got Phillimore doing that. He doesn't need any help."

"Or what about helping you? Walker said you would have plenty for me to do here."

"Walker knows nothing about this side of the business," he said sharply. "It's high level stuff, above his head. Above yours, too, anyway at the moment. I don't need any help, and, frankly, I don't think you could give it to me, even if I did."

"But I thought that was what I was being trained for."

"So it was. That's why I want you to be in the colony where you can be of most help to me."

And the further you can keep me from the chairman's office and the boardroom, the happier you'll be, I thought.

"Of course, as it will be your second tour, you'll be able to have Diana and the kids out there with you. I think you'll find that'll make all the difference to your liking the place. And they'll love it, I know. The sun and bathing and tennis and cocktail parties. After all, you enjoyed yourself pretty well out there, whatever you say now." He straddled before the unlit fire. "You know I quite envy you. That's where all the interesting things are going on."

"I've had enough of the place," I said. "I'm sick of it. It's the last place I want to settle in."

He was like a Victorian father admonishing his ne'er-do-well son. I could almost see his frock coat.

"You know, Hugo, we can't all do as we want in this life. I didn't want to come back from Le Touquet, but I had to come. We all have to make sacrifices, if this firm is going to go on and prosper."

"But why is it always me that has to make the sacrifices?"

"It isn't," he said curtly. "I make them too. I could be earning double or treble what I get from the firm elsewhere in the City. And I haven't had time for a proper holiday for years. I could have a wonderful time if I hadn't got the responsibility of running this firm on my back. Walker too. He's often had to give up quite large parts of his leave when I thought it necessary. He's always done it quite willingly."

Oh, has he? I thought. I remembered what he had said to me that last night at Malmaison.

"How long do you mean me to go out for?"

"Oh, permanently. Three years and then three months' leave. And then another three years. Just like the others."

"Three years is too long."

He was breathing deeply and I saw he was getting angry. "It's the statutory period. I let you get away with eighteen months last time because I didn't want to be harsh with you and you were married. But I can't do it again. It would cause bad feeling all round if you had preferential treatment. Everybody else does three years at a stretch out there. Nobody else complains."

"What exactly am I to do out there?" I asked after a moment.

He gestured airily as if he were offering me the whole world. "You'll find there's plenty to do. Give a hand to Stevens and Hughes when they need it. Walker too, if he's pressed. Keep an eye on things generally."

In other words, nothing. Show the family flag, kick my heels and bide my time.

I finished my drink and said sullenly, "Supposing I won't go?"

He looked at me intently and then he said with deliberate nonchalance: "I'm afraid I've got no other job to offer you. It's that or nothing."

At least I now knew exactly where I stood, but I felt no better. My last straw of hope had gone. There was a silence. I heard the clock ticking on the mantelpiece and a taxi changing gear outside in St. James's Street.

"You seem to me to be a bit mixed-up about it all. You seem to think that the world or the firm or someone owes you a living. In this firm you've got to work where there's work to be done. If you expect me to create a sinecure for you here in London, just because you happen to like living in London, you're making a mistake."

But you don't mind creating a sinecure for me out there, I thought.

"If I'd known all this at the beginning," I muttered, "if you'd told me sooner, I'd never have come in in the first place."

"I couldn't tell at that time. Indeed I hoped then that there might have been room for you in the London office. But conditions have changed, that's all. They're always changing. I now think it is very important for us to have a member of the family out there almost the whole time. You know how these local politicians keep talking about absentee proprietors." He stared at the picture on the opposite wall and stuck out his chin aggressively. "Look, Hugo, you've got to get this thing straight. We're not a large firm, though we're a very honored and respected one. If we don't all put our shoulders to the wheel, we're not going to keep going." The last words came out briskly like the command Quick March. "When old Samuel Pemberton first went out to Natividad in 1795 . . ."

I sat back and took it all, the whole works, great-grandpapa's pioneering efforts, the expansion under grandpapa, the achievements of the next generation, Justin's own modest but important contributions, the special love and respect in which we were held, our superiority over the other sugar firms, the mystique of the family business, the whole boiling works.

I'd sometimes spent a pleasant bath thinking out the reply to that well-worn speech: our grumbling underpaid staff, our comparative inefficiency, our labor troubles, our lack of modern equipment, our die-hard distrust of new ideas, our critical lack of working capital and high-level imagination. But I couldn't spout it now. There never seemed to be an appropriate moment. Once more I bottled it up.

"Can I have another drink?" I asked.

"By all means." He went to the marquetry table and started fiddling with the martini-mixer again. "I must say," he said over his shoulder, "it hadn't occurred to me that you wouldn't be willing to fall in with my plans for you. I've given them a great deal of thought, and I must assure you that they are in the best interests of the firm, and the family, even if they don't happen to suit your own personal inclinations. How old are you?"

"Twenty-eight."

"Well, I think it's time you grew up a bit, woke up to your own responsibilities. What d'you really want to do? Go back to that journalist stuff you were doing before, eh?"

I said nothing.

"That didn't bring you in very much, did it? Not enough to keep a wife and two children, was it? And, of course, if anything were to happen to the firm, I mean if we had to wind up, you'd have to support your mother too. Had you thought of that?"

Arp was right, I thought. You oughtn't to mix families and business together. You shouldn't have to have what was a purely business position complicated by your mother's personal problems. If only her income came from some other source, where no action or decision of mine could affect them!

"I should be all right," Justin went on, turning round with the drinks in his hands. "I can get other and better jobs in the City whenever I like. But you—and your mother——"

"I expect I could get another job too," I said defiantly.

"Could you? Have you tried?"

"No. But there are lots of jobs about at the moment."

"Labor Exchange jobs. Sweeping a factory floor or cleaning railway engines, if you want that." He gave me my drink. "I don't think you'd find it very easy to get an executive job with any prospects or future. Most firms have already got their young men lined up as trainees. You're a bit old to start that again. You'd be right behind them all, even if they wanted you. And it's not as if you had any technical qualifications."

"My degree."

"That isn't worth much these days. You've only got to read the advertisements in *The Times* columns to see that. Of course you might find something. But I think you'd be damned lucky and it would probably be a dead-end job. It's time you took a pull at yourself, Hugo. You're not an undergraduate any more, able to mill around from one thing to another as the whim takes you. You've got to steady down and do a job of work. Salut!"

He sipped his drink. I had already started mine.

"I'm offering you a good job, an interesting job doing responsible and important work, helping the firm through a rather difficult period. You'll be chairman when the time comes for me to hand over. And in the meantime you'll be paid a good salary."

"How good?"

"Seven hundred a year."

"That's not so much. Stevens gets eight hundred."

"I know, but I can't let you jump over his head. At least not yet. Later on, perhaps. I think seven hundred's a very fair offer, and of course it goes further out there."

There was another short silence. Suddenly he seemed to relax. "Well, anyway, Hugo, think about it. Don't rush into any violent decisions. You've got plenty of time, you'll be here for another three or four months. Think about it all. Look around for another job if you like, as long as it doesn't interfere with your work in the office. And do think about it from the firm's point of view, from the family's point of view. Think what your father would have wanted you to do. And think of your boy coming after you. You don't want to spoil it for him, do you?"

"Would it spoil it if I went and did something else?"

"I hope not," he said genially. "But, you know, the bank is expecting you to go out there and be on the spot. And they've got us very much where they want us at the moment."

He patted me on the shoulder, an unbearably patronizing pat. "You think it over quietly, Hugo. Talk to Diana about it. Talk to your mother."

But they were the last two people whose views I wanted at that time. Quite apart from my own personal difficulty in baring my troubles to either of them, there is never much point in talking a thing over with someone whose views you know so well in advance. My mother would be sure that I ought to do the best thing for the firm, as my father had always done; and after all it wouldn't be for ever. She had always liked Natividad on her brief, regal visits. She would think that Justin was, on the whole, probably right, and she would imply, even if she did not actually say, that it would be no bad idea to remove Diana as far as possible from the bright lights and fleshpots of London.

Diana, conversely, would beseech me to follow my own bent and to stop making sacrifices for an effete and probably moribund undertaking; to stop being bullied by Justin and to go my own way. We would manage somehow, she would be sure, brushing off rather too easily the enormous amount of managing which would have to be done.

Fiona's view too I also knew in advance, but she, unlike the others, was a person with whom it might be possible to talk things over. She at least had the capacity for sympathy, the comprehension that there was a dilemma and that there was no easy answer to it. But, of course, I had no chance to talk the matter over with her either when she came to have a drink the following day.

She was as pretty as ever in golden shantung and it was rather amusing to see her beside Diana, both so attractive and so utterly different. Fiona was a good deal shorter and rounder; by comparison she might have seemed dumpy, but in fact it was she who made Diana seem like an elegant rail.

We took her in to say good night to the children. The twins were looking particularly fetching, as if they had only just stopped blowing trumpets on top of little clouds. Fiona was duly fetched. I had had a strange sublimated hope that her own innate motherliness, her soft femininity might have drawn some special response from the children; that the whole visit might serve as a mild object lesson for Diana. But in fact the children, after a brief flash of curiosity, turned their attention back on to themselves. In due course we left Diana to it and I took Fiona down to the living-room for a drink.

"Oh, but they're delicious," she said. "What a pair of darlings!"

"What amuses me is that they're so different. Sieglinde's a complete egotist and never stops talking for a moment about herself, while Siegmund's the strong silent type, very serious and intense. I hope he gets a sense of humor later on."

"Didn't you say their names were Mark and Jane?"

I explained about their nicknames, but I don't think she followed very well and I was still holding forth to her about Wotan and Siegfried when Diana came back.

After that we made the usual drink conversation. How beautiful Provence was. Italy must have been lovely too. It was tiresome the way people in Paris would keep asking her about Indo-China. No, she hadn't yet been to Scotland, but she was going in September and was busy learning her reels. We wished we could go too. What a nice flat we had. She had been lucky to find a furnished flat near Sloane Square, of course much too big for her by herself, but her father was due in a fortnight or so. We must come round and see them. John Finlay was in hospital in Port Catalan with amoebic dysentery; hadn't I heard? Wasn't it dreadful about all this strike agitation? What a pity my wife hadn't been able to come out with me, but she was sure to enjoy it out there. Had we been to any plays? She had seen *Kismet* twice. And it really had been so nice seeing me again and meeting my wife and really she must be going now.

Somehow it was all rather disappointing, though I still don't know what I really looked for. But, all the same, I was sorry when she started to go and I contrived to delay her departure by pressing a last drink on her.

"Pretty girl," said Diana when I returned from seeing Fiona to the street. "But why didn't you tell me she was Chinese?"

"Didn't I?"

"No, darling, you didn't. I think you might have warned me. It's a bit startling if you're not expecting it."

"I suppose so," I said carelessly. "You get so used to it in the colony that one just takes it for granted."

Diana was watching me out of the corner of her eye, with her little secret smile and the tip of her tongue between her teeth. I knew she didn't believe me and I felt irritated with her.

"Anyway she was sweet," Diana went on. "I like to meet your dusky girl-friends, darling."

"Chinese aren't dusky."

"No, but you know what I mean. I expect she'd be great fun for a man."

"Really? In what way?"

"Oh, the usual way. I know Chinese are supposed to be awfully good at that sort of thing, aren't they? Or is it Indians?"

"I haven't the faintest idea." I saw that Diana was still laughing at me and I went on rather stiffly, "If you're implying that I've been having an affair with that girl, you're very much mistaken."

"Oh, but why not? It seems the obvious thing for you to do all alone out there—console yourself with a pretty little thing like that."

I said: "I had neither the opportunity nor the desire. In fact I only really met her on the way home."

"Oh, what a pity. Still, she's all alone now in a flat that's much too big for her. You must pop off and see her on your way home. It's the obvious thing to do. Fun anyway."

I stared at Diana. "Really, what things you suggest!"

"But, darling, I want you to have everything that's nice. I wouldn't mind a bit, really I wouldn't."

"Wouldn't you?"

"No, but if she's got any special tricks, you would pass them on to me, wouldn't you? I mean, a girl's got to learn somehow. You wouldn't keep them from me, would you?"

The whole conversation struck me as being in poorish taste.

"You don't need to learn anything," I said. "You're fine as it is. And anyway I've no intention of starting an affair with Fiona. Why should I want to, with a pretty wife to come home to?"

"Oh, am I? Am I as pretty as Fiona?"

"Just as pretty."

She chuckled to herself and smoothed out her dress, stroking herself sensuously. "Am I really? I think my waist and hips are better. My legs too. But I must say I envy her her bust." She caught my eye and grinned openly. "Nice gow."

Gow is a technical term used in the book trade to describe the cleavage between a woman's breasts. We had always delighted in it, and somehow the old joke made everything all right between us again. I relaxed and laughed back at her.

"Lovely gow," I said.

2

THE NEXT THREE weeks were, I see now, a kind of marking time. Not that life was stationary; we had plenty to occupy our time. But it was movement without advance, and the events can be recorded quite briefly.

Diana accepted her permanent post on the magazine and, except on press nights, she was usually home before me, bringing with her a despatch case full of manuscripts. We also spent our spare time in interviewing a series of grim professional nannies, all of whom expressed dissatisfaction at the meagreness of our domestic help. We engaged the first one who seemed to find us bearable and Berta was given a month's notice, news which she took with her usual blank impassivity. My mother came up to London for the day and left a note saying she hadn't realized that we would *both* be out all day and was sorry to have missed us and why didn't we send the children down again to her at South Meon, as they seemed a bit forlorn to her though had brightened up on her arrival.

At the office things went on in their usual well-oiled way. I stopped doing shipping and was transferred to insurance under Lord. And though I felt a good deal of personal relief at being able to sit farther from Jolly, the work was as monotonous as shipping, and there was far less of it. The important decisions, such as whether this year we could afford to take out the consequential loss policy that the underwriters were always pressing on us, were dealt with by Justin himself. We merely had the routine workmen's compensation claims to pass on.

We lived in a little world of our own and it seemed very far from Natividad. I often wondered what was going on out there. What was happening to Walker and Reynolds and Ingram and Hughes and Ramnarine? Justin doubtless was in touch, but no breath of their doings reached us in our little hermetically-sealed office. We could have been manufacturers of tinned soup or hot-water-bottles for all the difference it would have made. I had plenty of time on my hands to stare out of the window and meditate on my own problems.

And I didn't only meditate. Justin had told me to look around for another job and I took him at his word. I got in touch with Derek Martell who had run the *Literary Digest* and whom I hadn't seen since then. I asked him about possible openings, but when I finally got him down to the point, he wasn't very encouraging.

"Frankly, Hugo, I'd stick to your present job, if I were you. You can do this other stuff in your spare time, if you've got any."

I said it didn't look as if that would now be possible.

"Too bad. I'm sorry."

"What about publishing?" I asked. I thought that was right up my street.

"Not so easy as you might think. Everybody nowadays wants to be a publisher—that is if they don't want to be a land agent or an antique dealer. I gather there are queues of bright young men outside all publishing houses."

"Oh. What about magazines?"

"Much the same, I think. And television especially. I think, Hugo, you're a bit late now for that particular band-wagon. Though, as a matter of fact, I'm looking for a job of that sort myself at the moment."

"Oh, are you?"

"Yes. But I'll keep an eye open in case there might be anything for you too. I'll let you know. But for heaven's sake don't count on it—you know what these things are."

Rather discouraged I began to think of less glamorous jobs. I took to studying the Situations Vacant column in *The Times*. The vacancies were mostly for engineers in Rhodesia, but four seemed possible and I applied. Of the four, two didn't answer, one sent a circular letter thanking me for my application, and one, only one, summoned me to an interview.

I attended at the specified time, having taken time off to go to the dentist. The interview was conducted in a dark little office by a man of about forty whom I discovered to be an Old Etonian like myself. This, I thought, was promising. The Old School Tie should ensure a job for the boy. At last my costly education was going to show a practical return.

But it didn't work quite like that. The man cross-examined me in great detail about my football prowess, perhaps the least impressive part of my school career. It wasn't possible to take refuge in confident vagueness when confronted with questions like "Which years did you play in your House Side?" It all seemed to have little direct bearing on the business in hand, and I began to realize that my interviewer was the sort of Etonian who would never have spoken to me, if we had been there together. I was not really surprised when I didn't get the job.

I wondered sometimes if I were not trying too high. I could, for instance, become a bus-conductor at nine pounds a week. Posters reminding me of this faced me every time I traveled by bus. Nine pounds was less than Diana was getting, but it was something, and it would let me stay in London. I could carry on in my spare time with my true career, my literary journalism, my reviews for Gatoff (for I saw myself already one of his regular reviewers). And then I would think of the twins, and how they were going to be educated and what they would think of having a bus-conductor for a father. And my mother at South Meon. And then the whole thing would seem more hopeless than ever, and I would think about something else, usually Fiona.

I read the three novels from Gatoff in the evenings after dinner, while Diana was immersed in her own scripts. They were all novels of sensibility, beautifully observed and written, evoking moods and scenes, and moving very slowly towards sad and frayed endings. Diana looked at one of them and thought nothing of it, but I reflected that Gatoff himself, who had been in the midst of the Bloomsbury-Thirties group, might think very differently. In the end I wrote a notice, which, though objective and appraising, was evasively sympathetic. It looked rather well in type and Diana was delighted.

"Just like old times," she said. "I knew you'd get back to it in the end, darling. I knew it. Oh, isn't everything going splendidly?"

I made an incomprehensible noise.

"It takes me straight back to our courting days, before Justin came barging in, mucking everything up. Do you remember those articles you did for *Woman Today*?"

"Do I not!" I recalled my first sight of Diana, smiling efficiently across her heaped desk. "Just think what would have happened if I'd sent them to *Woman's Own* instead."

It may seem rather pusillanimous of me to have spent so many hours thinking about Justin's offer, without reaching any decision. But I was, subconsciously I suppose, waiting for some event to happen, which might give me a lead and precipitate things one way or the other. In this I was right. The event occurred on the late afternoon of Wednesday the 27th of August.

It had been the usual dreary office day and I was getting ready to go home. I had my bowler hat in my hand and the crook of my faultlessly rolled umbrella over my arm. I was just about to say "Good night all" when Greta came in and said: "There's a man to see you, Mr. Pemberton. In the waiting-room."

"To see me?" This was most unusual.

"Yes, sir. I didn't get his name."

I put down my hat and umbrella and went along the passage to the waiting-room. There I found McDonald, the overseer who had played snooker every night with Campbell and who had got the Portuguese girl into trouble. He was standing, staring at nothing in particular, and he looked short and insignificant in his tight, too bright blue suit and his too brightly striped tie.

"Hullo!" I said cheerfully. "I didn't know you were back."

"Oh, hullo, er, yes, I got back last week."

"Really? How was that?" Politeness demanded that I should ask, though I could guess the answer easily.

"I got married, so I had to leave."

"I'm sorry," I said. "We're a bit strict about that."

"You are that." His Scots accent had got overlaid with a thin veneer of Natividadian sing-song. "I had to marry her. It wouldn't have been right else."

I nodded. "Well, in the end I don't expect you'll regret it."

"I hope not. Of course it's a wee bit difficult at the moment. But, man, I was glad to get away from that colony. I wouldna have wanted to live there all my life, even though it's Silvia's home."

"Where are you living at the moment?"

"With my parents. In Greenock. The trouble is it's not a very big house and it's a bit, well, awkward in some ways. My mother's a wee bit upset at our getting married out there. And, ye see, Silvia's a Catholic. My mother keeps saying what's wrong with a Scots girl. She can't seem to realize that it's all done now."

"I expect she'll get used to it," I said. "Things will sort themselves out in the end."

"Oh yes, they will that," he said with sudden cheerfulness. "Silvia will soon make some friends in Scotland. Ye see, her father didna want her to go so far from home. But she'll be all right. It'll be easier when she's had the baby and we've got a place of our own."

I couldn't help admiring him for looking so determinedly on the bright side. How was he going to get a place of his own? And how would the baby make things any easier?

"Have you got a job?" I asked.

"Well, no, not just at the moment. But I'm looking around. I've got my eye on one or two. It's that that I've come to see you about."

I felt apprehensive, but I smiled encouragingly.

"I was wondering if ye'd give me a testimonial."

"Me? I don't think I'm quite in a position to do that. Why don't you ask my cousin? He's the man to do it."

"Yes, but he won't."

"Won't?"

"No. He says I broke my contract deliberately, and that's the end as far as he is concerned."

I bit my lip. Dear, kind, generous Justin!

"I think I'll need a testimonial for another job, and I thought maybe if ye could give me one, that would look all right. Ye're one of the family and ye knew me out there."

I thought of Silvia weeping in a cold grey house in Greenock. "All right," I said.

I led him into the outer office, which was now empty, and sat down at Miss Lumley's typewriter. I took off the cover and rolled a sheet of the firm's writing-paper into the machine.

"To whom it may concern."

"Man, you type fast," McDonald exclaimed.

I smiled. "I was a journalist before ever I was an overseer."

I stared at Justin's name on the writing-paper, and I thought of what he had done to this boy's life, to Silvia's, to Diana's, to mine; and, in revenge for it all, I gave McDonald a staggeringly good testimonial. I signed it with a flourish.

"All right?" I asked, handing it to him.

"Man! I say, thanks very much. This ought to do the trick."

"I hope it may help. And do let me know if there's anything else I can do."

I immediately wished I hadn't said that, and I had a moment's fear that he might try to borrow money off me. But he didn't. Instead he said:

"Maybe we could go round the corner and have a rum together. Like the old days."

"I'm afraid I can't," I said. "I've got some things here I've still got to clear up. Then I've got to dash straight home." I didn't want to get involved in a drinking session which neither he nor I could afford. I wanted him to go before he told me any more about his family.

"Not even time for a quickie? Oh well, another time, maybe."

I saw him out to the lift, where he thanked me once more, and then I went back into the office. I would give him ten minutes to get clear of the neighborhood, and then I would go myself.

I put the cover back on Miss Lumley's typewriter and sat down at a desk. I stared at the plain deal top. McDonald was in a mess, I was in a mess, and it was all the doing of Justin—of Justin and women and babies.

I was sitting at Lord's desk and the drawer was slightly open. I tried to shut it, but something inside the drawer was jammed. Idly I opened the drawer to ease the obstruction, which I found to be a book clumsily pushed behind a packet of envelopes. I glanced, as always, at the outside of the book. On the cover was a picture of a young man addressing what looked like a small business conference. He was speaking passionately, possibly describing a vision he was seeing through the window, and everyone appeared spellbound. The title of the book, I read with a sudden lifting of the heart, was *Win Power, Popularity With Brighter Talk.*

I fell on the book greedily. *During every conversation,* I read, *ask yourself "Will this talk seem worthwhile tomorrow?" If the answer is "No," change the subject. The worthwhile subjects (known for convenience as WW subjects) are history, philosophy, art, science and literature. If your partner cannot discuss any of these, you may, as a last resort, fall back on his own occupation. Each day make a point of discussing one of the five WW subjects with each person in your office/shift/shop.*

I decided we had got off pretty light, considering. I turned on a few pages. *When meeting someone in the street, do not say, "Bit warmer today, isn't it." This is not a WW conversation. Say instead, "Are you going to the organ recital/ballet/discussion group tonight?" Never lose an opportunity to start a WW conversation. For example, if you are asked to switch on the light, take the opportunity to mention some interesting facts about the lives of Faraday/Watt/Ampère (see Appendix for these).*

Very light indeed, I thought, turning on again. *Use humor freely in your conversation. Exaggerate. Make a list of ludicrous adjectives and comparisons and learn it by heart. Do not be afraid of puns (see Appendix for a list of these). Every day practice telling a funny story in front of the mirror.*

How to tell a funny story:

(1) *Always tell it as if it were your own personal experience.*

(2) *Speak a little faster and louder than you normally do, to attract attention.*

(3) *When you reach the climax of the story, slow down to emphasize it.*

(4) *Wait for someone else to laugh first before you join in.*

(5) *If nobody laughs, give a wry smile and say "I thought it was rather amusing."*

(6) *Ask yourself why the story failed. Practice it again that night before a mirror.*

I was debating whether to copy this out and send it to Brigadier Hope-Gordon at White's, when the telephone rang suddenly in the empty office, making me jump. I walked across to the switchboard, still carrying the book, flicked down the lever and answered.

"Is that Wright Pemberton?"

"Yes."

"Western Union Cablegrams here. We have a cablegram for you. Will there be anyone to receive it if we deliver it now?"

"Better read it out to me," I said, "and I'll take it down. Hang on a moment."

I thought I hadn't better write the cable down on the back of Lord's book so I found a memo pad and pencil.

"All right. Fire ahead."

The girl dictated slowly: "RITPEMBER LONDON DEEPLY REGRET WALKER DIED EARLY THIS MORNING HEART ATTACK FUNERAL THURSDAY ALLSAINTS PORTCATALAN FOURPM STOP ARRANGING WREATHS FROM CHAIRMAN DIRECTORS MRS. PEMBERTON HUGO PEMBERTON ETFAMILY PHILLIMORE PRATT HODGES LONDON OFFICE STAFF STEVENS."

"Shall I read it through again?"

"No, I've got it, thank you."

"Would you like a confirmatory copy?"

"Oh yes, please. Tomorrow morning will do."

I rang off and sat staring at the message, unable properly to take it in. Walker was dead. Walker, who carried the whole firm on his back. Walker, my friend and ally. Walker, who thought he had wasted his life in Natividad. Walker, who wanted to retire to a little cottage in Yorkshire. It wasn't possible, and yet, in another way, it wasn't so unexpected. He had seemed ill that last night in the colony. And what, I wondered, are we all going to do now? What happens next?

Dazed and shocked I read the message through again, and then my eye wandered down to the other page before me. *Do not say*

"I don't like the novels of Virginia Woolf." Your partner may admire them strongly and will look down on you for your lack of taste. Say instead, "Whilst I do not enjoy her style, she has brought a new dimension into the technique of Henry James and James Joyce." And Walker was dead, and wreaths were being arranged.

Justin must be told at once. I got up and walked along the passage, but his office was empty. The whole place was deserted. I came back to the switchboard, looked up the number of his flat and dialed it. The ringing tone throbbed into my ear. *If you forget a name while making an introduction, do not mumble or leave the couple to introduce themselves. Say instead loudly and clearly, "May I introduce Miss Roberta Partridge/Mr. Guy Biddulph?" (memorize these names). When the person corrects you with his/her real name, say, "I'm so sorry. I met a very delightful/interesting lady/man of that name the other day and so, of course, I mixed you up." Thus you will avoid an embarrassing moment, and pay a charming compliment at the same time.* Justin was clearly not in his flat. He was probably in one of his clubs.

I rang up White's and was put through to the hall porter.

"Can you tell me if Major Pemberton is in the club?"

"I haven't seen him come in, sir."

"Could you make sure? It's very important."

"One moment, sir, if you please. Who is it calling?"

"Hugo Pemberton. His cousin."

Cultivate cheerfulness in your talk. If someone grumbles about life, compare his petty irritations with the vastness of the sky/the song of birds/the sound of great music. He will soon see how insignificant his own troubles are.

"No sir. I'm afraid Major Pemberton is not in the club at the moment. Shall I give him a message if he comes in?"

"Yes. Will you tell him I'm trying to get hold of him?"

I dialed the number of Brooks's.

"Could you tell me if Major Pemberton is in the club, please?"

"One moment, sir. What name shall I say?"

"Hugo Pemberton, his cousin. It's very important."

"Will you hold the line, sir?"

On Sunday mornings, instead of reading the newspapers at breakfast, read an extract from a motto calendar and memorize it. Discuss it over the meal with your family.

"No, I'm afraid Major Pemberton is not in the club, sir. Shall I leave a message that you called?"

"Yes, please."

Where do I try next? I wondered. The St. James's? The In and Out? The Beefsteak? Perhaps even the West India?

I plumped for the In and Out. "Can you please tell me if Major Pemberton is in the club? It's his cousin, Hugo Pemberton, speaking."

"One moment, sir, if you please."

Every day practice short WW conversations with imaginary partners, bringing in some fresh topic of cultural interest such as a book review, a new opera or art exhibition. Copy into a notebook—

"Hullo!"

Justin's voice startled me. "Oh, it's Hugo here."

"Yes, Hugo?"

He sounded irritated at my interruption. For a moment I almost enjoyed myself.

"A cable's just come through from the colony, saying that Walker died early this morning."

"Who?"

"Walker."

There was a short silence. "Where are you speaking from?"

"The office. The cable came in just as I was leaving."

"Have you got it there? Read it out to me."

I did so.

"I see."

Again there was a short silence. "It's terrible, isn't it?" I said, feeling something was called for.

"Yes. Have you told anyone else?"

"No. I got in touch with you first."

"Quite right. Well, thank you for ringing, Hugo." He sounded brisk and unmoved.

"Anything else you want me to do?"

"No, you cut along home now. I'll deal with it."

"All right," I said bleakly. "Good night."

As soon as the line was clear, I telephoned through a personal cable of condolence from myself to Molly Walker. Then I stood up, feeling about as wretched as I'd ever felt in my life. *Compare your petty irritations with the vastness of the sky/the song of birds/the sound of great music.*

"God Almighty!" I said aloud.

I put the book back in the drawer of Lord's desk and slammed it shut.

3

The children were asleep when I finally got home and Diana was curled up on the sofa with a heap of scripts beside her.

"Hullo, darling!" she said. She glanced at the clock.

I said: "Yes, I know I'm late. There was a bit of a flap at the office. A cable came in just as I was leaving. Walker died suddenly early this morning."

She looked up at me quickly, alert and serious. "Walker?"

"Yes. Our General Manager. You know, I wrote to you about him."

"Oh yes. I'm sorry. You liked him, didn't you?"

"Yes. He was the hell of a good man. Just about the only one we had."

She glanced again for a moment at the typewritten page before her and then put it on one side. "I'm sorry, darling. Is there anything we ought to do?"

"Not specially. I've cabled his widow, and they're arranging a wreath from us both."

She nodded. "Was he very old?"

"Somewhere in the late fifties. I didn't think he looked very fit when I last saw him."

"I suppose it was the climate. It makes me more than ever glad that you haven't got to live out there all your life."

She looked at the clock again. "Time I coped with the supper."

"Shall I come and peel some potatoes?"

"If you like. But there's no need. I can manage."

She went out to the kitchen. I found the gin bottle. There was only about one measure left in it; I poured it out, added a couple of drops of French, and followed Diana.

"There's only one drink left in the bottle," I said, "and unselfishness having no place in the home, I took it. But I'll give you a sip."

"Just a taste," she said, sipping and leaving a smear of lipstick on the glass. "Sorry."

She began pottering about with saucepans and frying-pans, slamming the fridge and lighting the oven. I started to scrape some not-very-new potatoes.

"About Walker," she remarked, "will it make a lot of difference?"

"To me personally, or to the firm?"

"I meant personally."

"I think it probably will," I said grimly. "He was the only person who really cut any ice with Justin, and he was on my side."

"Oh, was he?"

"Yes, he was." I glanced at Diana and then went on scraping. "He wasn't altogether for the eighteen months project. And he tried hard at one moment to get Justin to allow you to join me."

"But he didn't cut quite enough ice."

"No, but it was nice of him to try."

"Very nice."

"He said he'd write to Justin suggesting that I should be made a director."

She looked at me quickly. "Are you? How did Justin react to that?"

I sighed. "Oh, nothing doing for the moment. I don't know if Walker ever wrote the letter."

She went on cooking. I could see she wasn't particularly impressed, or, for that matter, more than politely sorry about Walker. She'd never met him. He was merely a name, the man I had worked under, the taskmaster, the head gaoler.

"It'll be a great blow to the firm," I said. "He'll be a very difficult man to replace. Everyone thought the world of him. Especially the bank."

"Bank? How did they come into it?"

"Well, we're having rather a tricky time with them at the moment. We're miles over the overdraft limit, and it's getting higher all the time. I think the real reason they've played along with us is because of their confidence in Walker. They thought he'd pull us round. So he might have."

"Oh dear," said Diana, still darting to and fro, setting little whirring clocks, fumbling for kettleholders. I finished scraping the potatoes and we put them into the pressure-cooker.

"They can't have been counting on him altogether," she said abstractedly. "I mean, he'd have retired some time. Who'll succeed him?"

"I don't know. The man who has been groomed for it is a man called Reynolds, his deputy. He hasn't been with us very long. He's spent most of his life in India. Justin found him and sent him out to us last year."

"Is he a good man?"

"Personally I think he's a complete fool."

"And Justin picked him and sent him out to you," said Diana drily. "Isn't that sweet! Oh well, as long as it's not you. Would you like to lay the table?"

We were both a bit silent and abstracted throughout supper, and by the end of the meal I had come to the conclusion that it was high time I told Diana everything. The fact that I knew already just what she would say didn't affect the matter. For her own sake, she must be put in the picture.

We cleared away and stacked the plates for Mrs. Kerridge to wash up the next morning, and then, back in the living-room, I took a cigarette and said through the spurt of the match-flare:

"Justin's turning the heat on me again."

Diana put down the typescript she had picked up. "That bloody man," she said. "What does he want now?"

"He wants us to go out and live in the colony."

"What, for ever?"

"More or less. Till he thinks of retiring. We'd get leave every three years, of course."

"Oh God!" she murmured. Her eyes met mine for the moment, and then she looked away. "Is this because of Walker's death?"

"Oh no. He sprang this on me about three weeks ago. He's been hatching it for a long time. I suppose, Walker being dead, he may alter the plan now, though I don't suppose it'll help much. I don't see how it can."

There was a silence. I puffed at my cigarette. Diana stared vacantly across the room. I thought for a moment she was going to reproach me for not telling her earlier.

"Really," she said, "Justin is the absolute rock bottom, isn't he? Why can't he leave us alone!"

I told her some more of the background, about the meeting with the bank and the talk in his flat. I repeated the stuff about the importance of the Natividad end and the fountain-head of the business.

"It's quite clear," she said. "He doesn't want you knocking about, treading on his tail. So he's sending you away as far as he can, like a remittance man."

"He says it's vital for a member of the family to be out there all the time from now on."

"Well, why doesn't he go and live there himself, then? It's no use, darling, you can't convince me. It's just a straightforward double-cross, and there's no other way of looking at it. He lures you into this god-forsaken firm with vague promises of a nice job in the City. And then when you've done all the tough part just as he wants, he goes back on everything."

"He says he never actually promised me a job in London. Not in so many words."

"Oh yes he did. I remember him saying it, that night at the Savoy. But that wouldn't worry him, not for a moment."

"He says conditions have changed in the last two years."

"Huh! I bet he had this in mind for you the whole time." There was another pause. She stared angrily across the room. She looked at that moment as hard as nails. "Supposing you refuse to go?"

"Out," I said. "He made that quite clear. It's this or nothing."

She tightened her lips. "You see he can make things clear enough when he wants to. What did you say?"

"I said I'd think it over. There's no harm in playing for time."

"Not if you're being paid. Did he say anything about that?"

"He'll put me up to seven hundred when we sail."

"Big of him. And where do I come in?"

"Oh, you're allowed to come with me this time. The children too."

"Oh good show! It would mean giving up my job, wouldn't it? Going back to being a cabbage-mother again."

"We'd have a nanny out there. A black one. Everyone has those. They're quite cheap."

"Well, what do I do then, apart from sleeping with you? Gossip and play bridge and go to cocktail parties?"

"Just about."

"If I give up my job," she said, "we shall be pretty hard up. You go up a hundred and fifty and I come down six hundred. Not very tempting, is it?"

"Things are cheaper out there. And we get a free house. And I should get regular rises."

"Of course," she said drily.

The room suddenly seemed chilly and I went and shut the window. When I turned round, Diana was standing up.

"Well?" she asked. "What have you decided?"

I came back to her and I saw that she was as tense as a coiled spring.

"I'm still stewing it over."

"Because, as far as I'm concerned, there's nothing to stew over. The answer is no, no, no. And let's make the break now. Tell Justin he can go to blazes. I'd like to tell him myself. Hugo, let's get clear of that phony little dictator before he does us any more harm."

"Yes, I thought you'd think that. And what do we do then?"

"Anything. Anything you like so long as it's in London. You'd get another job as easy as pie."

"I'm not sure. I'm twenty-eight, and people like to take their trainees a bit younger."

I told her about my talk with Derek Martell, my answers to the advertisements and my interview with the Old Etonian. Once again she refrained from commenting on the way I had kept her in the dark.

"Well, that's not the end of it," she said. "You haven't scraped the barrel yet. The country's meant to be teeming with jobs."

"Labor Exchange jobs," I explained.

"Well, take one of those."

"As a matter of fact, I did toy with the idea of becoming a bus-conductor."

For the first time that evening, she relaxed and smiled. "Oh, darling, you must do that. You'd be sweet as one. I'd come and travel on your bus and you could sell me a ticket. We'd dine out on it for years."

"Yes, it would be a good joke for a while. But it's not much of a career, is it?"

"Oh, I don't know. I expect you'd be promoted, become a supervisor or something. Anyway your real career would be doing reviews for Gatoff."

I said: "Yes, but supposing Gatoff doesn't give me any more to do. You seem very certain that he will."

"Of course I am!" she exclaimed. "And if not him, it'll be someone else. I know you'll get there in the end. I haven't lost faith in you, even if you have. But you've got, got to stay in London. You haven't a hope of getting anywhere if you go and bury yourself in that long-lost island."

"Not in the world of letters," I said, "but I'd get somewhere in the business world. I'd be a biggish man out there. In the end I'd be chairman of the firm."

"If you live that long. And if Justin doesn't marry and have any children."

"He won't," I said with a confidence I didn't quite feel. Piero della

Francesca had shaken me on that. "He doesn't approve of matrimony."

"Not for you, but he's exempt from his own principles. Anyway, he's quite good at changing his mind, isn't he?"

All the relaxation had gone again. She was taut and determined.

"He says it'll all come to me," I observed, "and then on to Siegmund."

"Supposing Siegmund doesn't want it. Look, Hugo, Justin's only forty-something now. He's going to be boss of this firm for another thirty years unless he gets struck by lightning. Siegmund is going to have to suffer under him too. Just like you, just like all of us. I don't think I can face it." She paused and then went on passionately: "Do you really want to be chairman so much? Even if it means waiting for thirty years in that colony? And then what? Supposing Siegmund has other interests. Are you going to force him to go into it too?"

"No, of course not."

"Then you'd have sacrificed yourself in vain, wouldn't you? Sold your birthright for a mess of pottage."

I almost said that the firm and the chairmanship was my birthright, but I didn't. It wasn't true anyway.

Diana said with cold deliberate anger, "When a woman sells herself for money, she's called a tart, not a noble sacrifice."

I shook my head wearily. I was beginning to be sorry that I'd let myself in for this.

I said: "If I became a bus-conductor, I hardly think we could afford to send Siegmund to Eton. Or to give Sieglinde that coming-out dance. Busmen don't do that sort of thing."

"Oh that!" She dismissed the thought. "That was only an idle dream. They can go to the local school and get scholarships. Do it themselves the hard way. Far better for them anyway. How would we educate them out in Natividad?"

"We'd send them home."

She nodded. "Oh yes, I remember girls at school like that. They had to stay at school all through the holidays because they had no home to go to."

"There's always South Meon," I said. It wasn't a very pacifying remark and I went on quickly: "And that's another thing. My mother's entire income comes from the firm. If it were to crash or anything, she'd be on us."

Diana took that one straight. She didn't even blink. "Why? She'd be paid off, wouldn't she? She could put her money into something else."

"If the firm were liquidated," I said, "there wouldn't be much left after paying off the overdraft."

"But, Hugo, I don't understand. Why should the firm go into liquidation just because you won't go and live in the colony? Are you so vital to it?"

"No, not really. It's just that the bank have got us by the short hairs and they're pretty keen that I should go out there. Apparently I made a good impression on them at that meeting."

"That was a big mistake," she said.

"I know. But how could I realize that at the time?" I paused and stubbed out my cigarette. "It's all a mess, a mix-up. If it was just a straightforward business offer, it would be quite easy, but it's all got so mixed up with personal responsibilities."

Diana bit her tongue and then said: "Honestly, Hugo, I don't think it's a bit complicated. If only you'd stop trying to sacrifice yourself to your mother or your children. Or to the ideals of your great-grandfather. Or to the future of your great-grandchildren. It's just what I said before about bees and ants. This is your life, nobody else's. For goodness' sake live it the way you want to live it. Follow your own bent. Do what you really want to do."

"Walker said pretty well the same thing that last night in the colony."

"Well, if his bent was for growing sugar, no doubt he was happy. Yours isn't. Oh Hugo!" She put her hands on my shoulders and looked earnestly at me. "Don't let yourself be bullied into doing this. We'll manage all right. We'd have managed before if you hadn't panicked and run off to Justin when I started the twins. And then we'd have been free of all this today."

I let that one slide. "It's a gamble," I said. "Supposing it doesn't come off. Supposing I don't really get anywhere with this journalism. Supposing I'm still just a bus-conductor in twenty years' time. Nothing more. Nothing in print anywhere."

She looked at me hard, and then dropped her arms and turned away. All the fire had suddenly gone.

"It would still have been worth trying," she said in a low voice. "And you'd still have me."

4

We didn't mention the subject again. We walked round and round it, delicately, softly, like cats, wary of precipitating another great argument. For myself I couldn't face the thought of going over it all again; for Diana, I suppose she was reluctant to prove to herself that for all her conviction and eloquence, she still hadn't convinced me. Our meals together, except when the children were present, tended to be silent, preoccupied affairs. When we did speak, we would discuss gravely and politely such safe subjects as Berta's departure, the arrival and character of Nanny Humphreys, the warm September weather—none of them, I fear, very worthwhile conversations. We didn't seem to laugh any more; it wasn't that we were sulking, but that nothing seemed to us sufficiently funny. It was less than two months since we had giggled helplessly and idiotically over Patrick in Italy.

Diana spent an increasing amount of her spare time reading scripts, and for some reason this irritated me.

"They really ought to give you an assistant, if you're as hard pressed as that," I commented.

She answered without raising her eyes from the page: "Oh, it's all right. I just like to keep ahead, that's all. Anyway, I've always liked reading after supper."

I wouldn't have felt nearly so irritated if she had been reading a printed book for her own pleasure, and I was cross with myself for being so unfair. Oh well, she'd have to give it all up if and when she went out to Natividad.

Despite her revised working hours, she still wasn't seeing all that more of the children. She'd have more time for that too in the colony. Or wouldn't she? Would there be some other interest there as well?

Adversity or difficulties are supposed to bring couples closer together. Why did they always seem to drive us further apart?

One other point struck me too. My feeling in Ischia that we had gone back to the beginning, that we were starting our marriage all over again, was an illusion induced by the place or the sun or the wine or what have you. It was quite clear now that we were going on just where we had left off. And I suppose that was only right. You can't ever really go back to the beginning, however much you'd like to.

In the office, at least in the outer office, things proceeded on their own lackadaisical way. Walker's death was discussed all through one morning and prompted Pratt to put in a sentence of sympathy in his next letter to Hughes. But otherwise it had not the slightest effect upon us. I presumed that Reynolds had taken over, but nobody seemed to know or care. I speculated too about the start of the new crop, now imminent. I asked Pratt:

"Do you know when grinding begins again?"

He looked at me in baffled alarm, rather as if I had asked him to form a French government.

"I don't know at all," he admitted. "I haven't heard. The Major or Mr. Phillimore would know."

"I wonder what's happening about the strike," I said.

That didn't ignite his interest either. "Oh, let's hope there won't be anything like that, Mr. Hugo." He slid back to his own personal occupations. I reflected that it was high time he retired.

However, I regarded Jolly and Lord with greater benevolence. Jolly's indigestion, or perhaps his teeth, seemed to have improved, and I now regarded Lord's beautiful thoughts, puns and cultural peregrinations almost with affection. I even asked him once if he would mind turning on the light, so that we might have a brief WW chat about the private life of Ampère. But I couldn't get him interested in political conditions in Natividad, although I tried. They were outside his terms of reference.

I could, I suppose, have gone and talked to Justin about the crop and the strike, but I knew what that would lead to. In my present vacillating state, I was fighting shy of Justin.

In the end it was he who sent for me; to be precise, at half-past eleven in the morning of Tuesday, September the 11th, nearly a fortnight after the death of Walker. I hadn't seen him once during that period.

He rang through on the house telephone and I went along to his office. Miss Yorke, like an ever watchful dog, met me in the passage outside. I gave a false and exaggerated smile, and rubbed my cheekbones hard. She gazed at me curiously.

Justin was standing with his back to the empty fireplace, clasping his imaginary frock-coat-tails. By the window stood another man, and when he turned I saw it was Nelson from the bank. On the second meeting he didn't seem quite so rat-faced and he gave me a friendly smile of recognition.

"Come in, Hugo," said Justin briefly. "You remember Mr. Nelson, don't you?"

"Indeed I do."

Justin waved me to a chair, picked up the silver cigarette-box and offered me one. Last time, I recalled, he had rather ostentatiously not offered me one. I speculated on that as I lit up.

"Well now, Hugo," he began, his voice suddenly taking on its falsetto note, "have you been thinking over that proposal I made you about your future?"

"Yes," I said, and waited.

"Well? Have you decided yet?"

"No, not yet. You told me not to hurry," I added as I saw the sarcasm forming on his lips.

"Oh, did I? Well, the picture's changed a lot since then. Since Walker's death to be exact. The firm is now a little weak on the ground out there."

That was one way of putting it. I wondered if Nelson was going to say anything.

I asked, "Who's the new General Manager?"

"Reynolds."

"He's actually been appointed?"

"Yes. I confirmed it by cable the day after Walker's death. We can't afford to have a vacuum out there at the moment. And, to be perfectly frank, I think he looks like making a prize balls-up of it all."

The sudden slang startled me. I looked at Nelson and caught a gleam of amusement in his eye.

"You don't feel much confidence in him, either, do you, Nelson?"

Nelson picked up a letter lying on the table beside him. He said: "I can't feel much confidence in a man who could write this letter. The whole thing's obviously gone completely to his head."

"Still, we don't want any mistakes just now," said Justin.

"What's the position at the moment?" I asked. "When do we start grinding?"

"Tomorrow. The two o'clock shift in theory. But, as you know, there've been these threats of strikes for the last few months, and now it's come to a head. The president of this new union, Dr. What's-his-name—"

"Dr. Marshall," I said.

"That's him. Big black fool. He's issued a proclamation calling on all sugar workers to strike from tomorrow morning. Ramnarine's been going up and down the estates agitating."

"So they are going on strike then?"

"It looks like it. Reynolds is confident that they'll all turn out as usual. He says he's dealt with this situation dozens of times before."

"I doubt that," I said.

Nelson intervened. "Mr. Cornish, our branch manager in Port Catalan, doesn't take nearly such a rosy view. He thinks there may well be a general strike on all the sugar estates for most of the autumn."

"Anyway," said Justin to me, "Reynolds has announced that he intends raising steam at six o'clock tomorrow morning, strike or no strike."

"But if there aren't any cane-cutters, there'll be nothing to grind."

"He's going to work the distillery. There's plenty of molasses. And he wants to burn up some of that excess bagasse. His idea is to carry on as if nothing unusual were happening, and when the laborers see the factory chimneys smoking, they'll see the whole strike's a flop and go back to work. He's gambling on getting cane into the yard by Friday morning."

"He'd better," I said. "The bagasse heap won't last for ever. But I should have thought it would all have the opposite effect, with men like Ramnarine about. Just enrage them."

Nelson nodded. "That's our view too."

"What about Ingram?" I asked. "After all, it's his factory."

"He works under the orders of the General Manager," said Justin formally.

"Worked," Nelson corrected him. "Mr. Ingram's resigned."

"Resigned!"

"Yes, he had a row with Reynolds," said Justin. "Told him he could stew in his own juice. He's left the estate already."

"Good God!" I exclaimed. "Then who's Chief Engineer?"

"Allen's running it at the moment."

"I say, we are batting our second eleven," I said feelingly.

Nelson said, "I wouldn't be surprised if we didn't lose some more of our staff, if Mr. Reynolds goes on like this." He tapped the letter.

"Well anyway," said Justin, "Reynolds has got to go. And the sooner, the better. This is where you come into it, Hugo."

"Me?" I had forgotten myself in my anxiety over the strike. Now I was right back in my wobbly rut, aching cheeks, wet palms, sick stomach, and all.

"Yes," said Justin, not looking at me and speaking with proconsular deliberation. "I'm offering you the post of General Manager of the company's estate in Natividad."

There was a momentary silence. I knocked the ash of my cigarette into the blue glass ash-tray. My hand was trembling.

"I want to fly you out there on the very first plane. Get rid of Reynolds and take over the thing yourself. I'll give you a letter for Reynolds. We'll pay him everything we owe him under his contract." He paused and looked at me. "Well?" he squeaked.

I stalled. "I'm not sure that I'm up to that job. I mean, I'm only twenty-eight."

Nelson came across the room and stood inside the semi-circle of armchairs in front of the fireplace.

"I don't think youth is necessarily a bar to an important post," he said. "Provided the experience is there. You've certainly got that."

Pitt was Prime Minister at twenty-four, I thought, but look what a time he had.

"Walker was only thirty-one when he was made General Manager," said Justin. "Well? What about it?"

"It's a bit sudden," I said.

"Oh nonsense. You've admitted yourself you've been thinking about it all for weeks. It's just that I'm now offering you a much bigger job than I first had in mind for you. You'll be made a director, of course."

He glanced at Nelson who nodded and said, "Certainly."

"And how long would this appointment be for?" I asked.

It was Nelson and not Justin who answered. "Indefinitely. It'll be a permanent appointment."

Justin, I could see, was a little nettled. He said: "Some people would give anything to be offered a post of this magnitude. They'd think it an honor. Especially at your age."

"Oh yes, I know. I'm just not sure if I'm up to it."

Nelson said gently: "We think you are. That's why we've offered it to you."

"I'm also not very keen on settling permanently in Natividad. Nor is my wife."

"To hear you talk, Hugo, anyone would think the place was the black hole of Calcutta. It's one of the best of the West Indian islands. People go there for holidays. I must say I thought you'd have jumped at the chance. Or are you still hankering to be a journalist?"

I recognized the sneer in his voice. I said nothing. I wasn't going to start all that again, especially with Nelson there.

Justin gave a sigh of suffering patience and walked across to the window. He stared down into the street and then said:

"Well, there it is, Hugo. Make up your mind. Take it or leave it. As I said before, there's no opening for you this end. It's out there that the work's got to be done. And if you won't do it, you'd better clear out straight away. There's no point in your hanging on learning the stuff here."

I sat there staring out of the window, trying to make up my mind. Beyond Justin's head I could see the sooty front of the building opposite. Even leaning forward, I couldn't see the sky. The vastness of the sky, the song of birds.

"What will you pay me?" I asked.

"We discussed that last time," said Justin curtly.

"Walker got about four thousand a year, didn't he?"

"He'd been with the firm forty years."

"I don't think we should be mean at this moment, Major," said Nelson quietly.

Justin turned round and regarded Nelson with surprise. "I wasn't aware of being mean. But what do you suggest?"

Nelson said, "I thought two thousand would be a reasonable salary for that work and that responsibility."

For a moment I thought Justin would explode, but he swallowed it down and said: "Well, you've got the whip hand financially. I think it's excessive, but if you think we can afford it——"

"I think it would be reasonable," said Nelson. "And there would be directors' fees too."

I tried to concentrate on the dilemma, but I remember thinking more that it was Nelson standing now with his back to the grate and Justin at the window. Had I just witnessed the swing in the balance of power? It gave me a little throb of reassurance. I felt confidence in Nelson.

"I hope very much that you will be able to take up this appointment," said Nelson giving me a very friendly look. "And so do my colleagues at the bank, Mr. Hildyard and Mr. Webber. We were considerably impressed by your grasp of the situation when you talked to us about Natividad at that meeting, and you would have our complete confidence."

I acknowledged the compliment with a smile. It was such an elaborate beginning that I felt sure he was leading up to something.

He sat down in the armchair beside me. "I think it would be a very great pity from every point of view if this firm were unable to continue in business. As you know, we have been a little anxious lately about the size of its overdraft with us, but we felt sure that the Major and Mr. Walker between them would in due course get things on to a sounder footing. Speaking frankly, I think I can mention to you that the reaction of my colleagues at the bank, especially Mr. Hildyard, to the news of Mr. Walker's death was rather disturbing."

"Disturbing?"

"Yes, to anyone who has the future of this firm at heart. I believe I am right in saying it would cause a good deal of hardship to your family as well as to the firm's employees if the company had to be wound up, either voluntarily or compulsorily. And confidentially I can tell you that we were discussing that very possibility last week."

Justin said from the window, "I'm not sure if we need go into all that now, do we, Nelson?"

Nelson gave him a brief glance and went on: "I was not myself one of those who shared the general view. Personally I have a great regard for these old-established family businesses. A man has an idea, raises a small amount of capital and starts the business in a modest way, visualizing its eventual expansion into a large and prosperous concern. And then his son takes up the idea and develops it and so on. And so at last, after several generations, the ambition of the original founder comes true. That's how all businesses are built up, even the banks. And that's what has happened to this company, even if it hasn't yet developed to any very great size."

He paused. Oh God, I thought, you too!

"Anyway," he went on, "I felt myself strongly that we should not fail you at this difficult moment, and I was able to persuade my colleagues to allow you your usual credit facilities, and even to raise these to three hundred thousand."

I looked at him in surprise. "You mean you're *raising* the overdraft limit?"

"I hope it won't be necessary to draw as heavily as that. But it's as well to have a margin, especially with this strike." He cleared his throat and fixed me with a steely gaze. The smile had for the moment gone. "This increased overdraft has been agreed provided that a certain amount of internal reorganization is carried out in the company. And it seemed to us, as well as to the Major, that it would be a very happy appointment if you succeeded Mr. Walker as General Manager—not only because of your experience in the colony and knowledge of the current situation, but also because of your being a member of the family, with all the psychological and political advantages that that would bring."

He cleared his throat again and turned on his smile again. "I hope you appreciate the position."

Oh yes, I appreciated it all right. Take the job and we'll go on backing you. Turn it down and we won't. It was as simple as that.

For a moment I felt a little throb of pleasure at my own significance. With one word I could crash the firm, I could break up Justin's little empire, I could put him out of a job. I looked across the room to where he was standing, still staring out of the window. I wondered whether he was seeing anything.

The moment passed and I knew I should be only giving myself very temporary and trivial satisfaction. Justin would walk into another job—he had plenty of contacts. It was I who would be hurt, I and my family.

"Can I think about it for a little?" I asked.

Justin spun round. "Heavens, how much more time do you want? I want you on the very first plane we can get you on."

"Even if it was only a few hours?" I pleaded. "It's a pretty big decision for me."

Nelson said to Justin, "We could book him a passage now, Major, and cancel it later if he decides not to go."

Justin nodded. "Yes. I'll get Jolly on to it straight away. I take it, Hugo, that you don't want Diana and the children out with you on the same flight. It would be easier if they followed you out by sea."

"Oh yes. No hurry for them. They've got a lot of packing and things to see to." Diana would have to give at least a month's notice to her magazine.

"When you get to Malmaison," Justin went on, "you'd better move back into your old bungalow. It's empty." In his mind I was already safely installed out there. "Then, when Mrs. Walker has left, you can move into the manager's house."

"That is, if I go. When do you want my final decision?"

Justin sighed and looked at the black and gold watch on the inside of his wrist. "Four o'clock at latest. No extension after that, Hugo. No more shilly-shallying. Let me know by then, one way or the other."

5

I LOOKED IN BRIEFLY at the outer office to collect my hat and umbrella and then I went down into the street. It was a fine September day with a pale blue sky and big silver-white clouds. I walked slowly along Cornhill, through the lunch-hour scurry of typists and clerks. Somewhere in one of these buildings around me there might be a job for me. Or again, there might not. I could hardly find one in the next four hours.

I crossed over by the Mansion House and walked along Queen Victoria Street to St. Paul's. I went inside and sat down and tried to think things out. After a few moments I noticed that there was a service going on; there was a compact congregation and a man was preaching earnestly about inflation and football pools. I listened for a few minutes, but it wasn't any help. Despairing of divine guidance, I came out and found a pub. I drank a large gin and French and ate a couple of sausage rolls.

I thought of getting hold of Diana and telling her the latest developments. She would probably be lunching at this moment in the little restaurant where she had always gone. It wasn't so very far away. But somehow I couldn't face that homily again. I might have felt differently if she could have even glimpsed the other side of the case.

I drank some more gin and ate a ham sandwich. Then I came out and caught an 11 bus. In the last summer sunshine, on the top deck, I passed down Fleet Street and the Strand, once my happy hunting grounds, Victoria and Pimlico and came at last to Sloane Square.

After a little searching I found the block of flats, square and modern, overlooking the Duke of York's Headquarters. The flat was on the fifth floor. Fiona herself, wearing a printed cotton overall, opened the door to me.

"Oh hullo! You've caught me in the middle of washing up lunch."

"I only came on the spur of the moment," I said. "If I'd thought of it sooner, I'd have taken you out to lunch."

I glanced out of the window at the parade ground with its demi-culverins and ack-ack guns.

She smiled at me. "Can I give you some coffee, or are you on your way to lunch somewhere?"

"No, I've had lunch. But I should love some coffee, if you're making it."

She went out and I looked round the room. I had the odd feeling that I had been in it before, but I couldn't think when. Its furnishing was strictly, almost puritanically, contemporary. Everything was built-in. The tables and armchairs had thin splayed legs. The sofa and armchairs had pale wooden arms and folk-weave upholstery in clear contrasting colors. The curtains were also in folk-weave, buff with lozenges of primary color at irregular intervals. Three of the walls were acid green. The fourth was salmon pink with an acid green alcove.

Suddenly I remembered where I'd seen it before: in the furnishing pages of *Woman Today*. Or if it wasn't this room, it was one exactly like it. No doubt Fiona admired it enormously.

She came back into the room with a tray of coffee things.

"That was quick work," I said.

She laughed. "My little espresso!"

I took a cup and sipped. "Blue Mountain," I said. "Delicious. But, heavens, how it takes one back to the colony."

"Yes, I can't drink anything else now." She paused and then said: "I'm going back to the colony fairly soon. Finlays are trying to get me a passage."

"Really? I thought you were going to be here for months."

"Well, I don't know when I'll get a passage. Daddy isn't coming at all this year."

"Because of the strike?"

She nodded. "He told me I could stay on as long as I like, but of course I want to get back to him as soon as possible."

"Oh dear! So no Scotland after all."

She smiled and shook her head. "Well, I may be able to fit it in before I go. I don't know. It all depends. If not, we may go next year. We shall be owed an extra month's leave by then."

Sugar! I thought. What a life!

Fiona said suddenly, "I was so sorry to hear about Mr. Walker."

"Yes, that was dreadful, wasn't it?"

"And so sudden. Daddy had been talking to him only two days before." The instantaneous, inevitable reaction to sudden death. "He'll be a great loss to you. Daddy thought a lot of him."

"I think everyone did." I hesitated for a moment and then I blurted it out. "They want me to take over his job."

Her eyes opened wide. "Oh Hugo! Congratulations! That's wonderful."

"Is it?"

Her eyes were shining with pleasure for me. Slowly the shine dulled. "But of course it is. I mean, it's awful about Mr. Walker, but it's wonderful for you." She looked at me curiously. "Why, don't you want it?"

"No," I said. "I've got to give an answer by four o'clock this afternoon and possibly fly out tomorrow, if they can get me on a plane."

"So soon? Long before me."

"It was only broken to me this morning," I said. "It's quite a decision to take."

"Why? I should have thought——" She broke off.

"It means settling permanently in the colony. Or at least for twenty or thirty years. That's the bit I'm shying at."

"But, Hugo, is it really so sudden? I've seen all the time that this was coming. So have you. We talked about it that night in Greenwich Village, do you remember? You had an idea that this was coming then, only you wouldn't admit it to yourself. Oh, not the top job, of course, no one could have foreseen that, but having to live in Natividad. That's why you kept talking about it."

"I was only talking generally," I said. "It was just a possibility which I was afraid of."

Fiona put down her coffee cup and looked at me seriously. "And I did my very best to persuade you that it was all right."

"I still don't like it. My roots are here in London. I want to write, I want to live among people who have the same ideas and interests as I have. I shan't find *them* in Natividad."

I suppose that was rather a rude thing to say, but she paid no attention.

"All that's only a side-line, isn't it? Very nice if you can have it too, but it's not the main thing. The job's the main thing. That's your real life."

"Is it? I don't know. I wish to God I did. The one thing I do know is that I don't want to spend the rest of my life in Natividad," I said doggedly. We looked at each other for a few desolate seconds and then I added, "You think I ought to go?"

"Oh, Hugo, it's not for me to advise you. It's a decision you've got to take for yourself. But you know what I think. I told you that night in New York. I don't think it matters very much where you live as long as you do your job."

"I remember."

She gave a deprecating laugh. "Of course I'm biased. I like Natividad. It's my home. I don't want to be surrounded by writers and intellectuals. The movie-house is good enough for me."

I smiled sympathetically.

"It would be nice to have you out there. You'd brighten us up a lot. Great asset to the place."

"Oh maybe! Three star tourist attraction." I paused and then said: "Another thing. Diana doesn't want to go at all. Her roots are right here."

"Oh, I see. That must be a complication. But wouldn't she be willing to uproot herself for you? I mean—" She broke off, frowning. "Of course not being married myself, I can't really speak."

"You'd go wherever your husband had to go?"

"But of course!"

I had spoken of Diana's opposition as a major complication. And so it was. But not at that moment. Just then Diana was only a name to me, an abstract factor, someone as intangible as Fiona's future husband.

"Anyway she may like it out there," said Fiona cheerfully. "The sun and the bathing make up for a lot. Mrs. O'Hara didn't like it when she first came out. She's settled down now like a Natividadian born and bred."

"I think that's what Diana is afraid of. And then there are the children. You've either got to educate them locally or send them home and lose them altogether."

Fiona nodded. "I know. That is a snag. Daddy missed me terribly when I went away to school. But, even so, is it so important beside the job?"

I put down my coffee cup and walked across to the window, staring down at the buses in the King's Road, the vigor and bustle of Chelsea. I was a little disappointed in Fiona. No more than Diana had she been able to see the other side of the argument. And she knew nothing of the other pressures, financial and personal, upon me. Without any idea of the possible consequences of my refusal, she was still sure that I should go—a distilled limpid sureness against which I had no defence.

I wasn't seeing the scarlet buses any more. I was seeing the manager's house and the factory chimneys and the whining rebellious laborers. I was seeing myself in khaki shorts and a white cotton tunic and Diana in a damp cotton frock telephoning to someone about a bridge party and the twins swollen with mosquito bites.

"It's a big job," I said, "and a tough job. But I don't want to go. Oh, I don't want to go!"

"Oh, Hugo, I am so sorry." Her voice was very close behind me. "So very sorry. I do understand. If only I could help."

I turned round. She was looking at me with a strange expression which I couldn't place. Gentle. Tender. Amused? No, not amused. The expression, I thought suddenly, of a mother watching her child.

"Is there anything I can do to make it easier?" she asked. "Anything?"

She stood there, looking at me, smiling. Then she dropped her head, meek and submissive, and waited.

I stepped forward and raised her face and kissed her. I began to tremble and shake, as if I had been standing too long on the high dive and the blue safe water suddenly seemed a long way below. Her face was very near to mine, but it seemed blurred and misty.

"It's all right, Hugo," she said quickly. "It's going to be all right. Don't worry."

I put my arms round her and kissed her again, forcing my tongue between her lips, between her teeth, into her warmth.

I pulled down the sheet and stroked her soft and creamy body. I remembered the moment on the ship when I had longed to touch and pat her, and I exulted in my absolute possession of her, patting and fondling her smooth gentle roundness.

"Darling, you are sweet," I said. "But if I'd known that it was the first time, I wouldn't have done it."

She glanced up at me anxiously. "Was I very bad?"

I smiled, at the same moment triumphant and conscience-stricken. "You were wonderful. But it's not the sort of thing a man likes to take from a girl except——"

She was lying face down, her black head pillowed on her arms, facing towards me. "I wanted you to have it. I wanted it to be you."

"I think I did too." I traced the line of her spine with my forefinger. "I love you," I said.

She raised herself on one elbow and put her palm over my mouth. "No, you mustn't say that," she said quickly.

I kissed her palm and then pushed it away. "Why not, if it's true?"

"But it isn't true. It mustn't be."

"Too late. It is." I looked at her fondly. "There are going to be compensations for life in Natividad."

She was sitting up now. "No. Not out there. We can't."

"Why not?"

She hesitated. "You can't. You've got—someone else."

I smiled at her delicacy in avoiding Diana's name. "She won't be coming out for some time yet. Perhaps not at all."

Fiona gazed at me anxiously. "But she must!"

"Perhaps it would make everything easier if she didn't."

"Oh, Hugo, no, no, no! You mustn't say that."

I ruffled her hair. "You're the one that matters. You're the one I want."

She shook her head and I dropped my hand. "This is only for today," she said. "Only because of the crisis. Because of what we're going through. We can't go on in Natividad. Everyone would know. Think how they'd talk."

"Who cares!"

"I do."

"We'll get it all fixed up properly. We'll get married. I can't lose you now."

Her face was screwed up, for a moment almost ugly in its anguish.

"Oh, no, Hugo! Can't you see? There's nothing in this for us. Nothing after today. I'm yellow and you're white. It would never work out. It would cause too much scandal."

"Need we worry about that?"

"Yes, we need. You're taking on a big job. You're giving up a lot for it. You've got to give me up too. If you're going to do it properly—and it's worth doing properly, isn't it?"

"Yes," I said sullenly. "It had better be."

"Well, then you've got to avoid getting mixed up with a Chinese girl."

"I've got mixed up already."

She smiled and shook her head. I felt as I had once felt as a child when I had been given someone else's toy to play with, and I thought I was being given it to keep. That familiar pang of disappointment seemed to have been recurring at intervals ever since.

"Oh please, darling!" I looked at her and I knew there was no hope. "Really no?"

"Definitely no. We're just ships that pass in the night."

"And bump each other in passing," I said drily. "Quite a collision!"

She put up her hand and stroked my cheek. "Oh, Hugo, don't be cross. What does time matter? What does it matter whether we do it once or a hundred or a million times? The fact that we've done it is what matters. That's what will last."

"And this is all there is to it?" I asked unhappily. "Just one hour?"

"Does time matter so much to you?"

"Yes, I'm afraid it does."

She looked at me very sweetly. "Well, till four o'clock then. Then you must go and ring up. You can do it from here."

I looked at the clock beside the bed. It was ten past three.

"Fifty minutes," I murmured. "Better than nothing."

Fiona smiled and lay down again. I leaned across and kissed her. I pressed her smooth sweet body to mine and her broad yellow face swam and grew distorted. My heart began to pound.

"Sweetheart! Angel!" I whispered, delighting in the pleasure of the moment. But this time, despite the blurring of my eyes, part of my mind remained clear, distractingly, annoyingly detached. I went through the movements of love in a daze of desire and speculation. Why was I doing this? Because I wanted her. Why did I want her? Because she was pretty. Because she was unusual. Because I found her rather touching and pitiful. Because she was so feminine and motherly. Because she hadn't got any of those go-getting, masculine qualities which often irritated me in Diana. None of them very good reasons, I recognized reluctantly. And, lovely though it was, it couldn't last. She was right about that. There was nothing in it sturdy enough to withstand the erosion of time.

I said bitterly, "The moment of truth."

"Mm?" Her eyes were closed and she was breathing fast like someone going under an anaesthetic. I loved her sadly and furiously and the aloof corner of my intellect observed us drily.

It was clear enough why I wanted her, but why did she want me? Why was she letting me have all this, if it was only for a moment? Was she in love with me? Or was it a gentler, more altruistic motive, loving-kindness? Because she knew I was unhappy. Because she wanted to help. Because she knew I wanted it.

Maybe. But in all the warm flood of loving-kindness, weren't there also a few gritty grains of self-gratification? She was pretty, and gay, and for all that lonely; I was young, and desirous, and white. And the alternative was the shadowy, anonymous figure of a West Indian Chinese dentist, who might with luck be nice as well.

Part Four

1

Stevens met me at Rawson airport in Natividad. He was the only person in the island who had been told the reason for my abrupt return.

"Hullo!" he said. He mopped his forehead and gave me his hard bony handshake. "Welcome back, Mr. Pemberton!"

I noticed the Mr. and the pungent aroma of deference. At least one person now knew what to call me.

"Too bad your having to cut short your leave so suddenly," he said. "Did you have a good trip?"

"Very good." I was tired and travel-stained and the aircraft engines still buzzed in my ears. I had managed to scrape off most of my beard in the plane, but I badly needed a bath and a change of clothes. My mouth tasted like an old boot and my head ached. "Very smooth and easy," I said.

The afternoon sun beat me down like a sledgehammer into the tarmac. I wished I had a pair of dark glasses with me.

Stevens took my despatch case and my blue overnight bag. He glanced up at the plane. "I didn't quite gather from the cable," he said, "if your wife was with you or whether she was coming later."

"Oh, she's coming out later on, after Christmas." After Christmas, after quarter day, after the summer. The echo crowed at me mockingly. I said quickly, "Things ought to have quietened down a bit by then."

"Oh yes, we must hope so."

As we got into the station-wagon, he said, "Do you want to go into Port Catalan or shall we go up to Malmaison?"

"Oh Malmaison, and let's get on with it. You can put me in the picture as we go."

"The picture isn't any too bright," he said as soon as we were clear of the airport.

"Cane-cutters not back yet?"

"Oh Lord, no. Not a sign of that. It's pretty well a general strike in the fields. I gather part of one of the shovel gangs tried to do some work yesterday and the cane-cutters held up the loco and pulled them off the train."

"Pulled?"

"Well, persuaded them anyway. I don't expect it was very difficult."

"What about the factory?"

"Well, we're distilling. That's about all."

"That's not on strike, then?"

Stevens said: "I gather about a quarter of the people have turned up. W.A. says he doesn't mind about the others not putting in an appearance. They'd only have to be paid and there'd be nothing for them to do except sit around and make trouble."

I was pretty unconvinced by Reynolds' theory. "I expect they're making plenty of trouble where they are now. What about the rest of the colony?"

"The N.S.C. aren't quite as badly off as we are. Hopkins says they've all got some cane-cutters working and are grinding for a few hours a day. Trafalgar is grinding all the time. Finlays are out, though. They've got a general strike."

"So it's really us and Finlays," I said. "The two small family businesses."

Stevens gave a wry smile. "I suppose they think they can hurt us more. The N.S.C. is a bit impregnable."

"What are Government doing about it all?" I asked.

"Falling over backwards trying not to take the side of the planters. Almost toppling off their fence. The Governor has appealed for law and order and a spirit of goodwill and hopes that all difficulties may soon be ironed out so that production of our staple export shall not be——"

"All right," I said, "I get the drift."

"However, several Leg. Ass. chaps have been going round spouting on the other tack. Strike now for your rights, the hour has struck, white man go home."

"Who in particular?"

"Oh, the usual crowd. Marshall, Abraham, Chee. And of course Ramnarine is with us a good deal."

"Bless his little heart! Any trespassing?"

Stevens laughed. "He's careful to keep on the road. You'd think the police could get him for loitering or obstruction or something."

"I expect they could if they felt like it. Or dared to. One can hardly blame them for not sticking their necks out when the A.G. will probably let them down. Look, what exactly do the strikers want?"

"Trouble."

"Oh yes. But what is the nominal reason? What are the great concessions they hope to wring from us?"

"Well, from some of the speeches, you'd think they wanted us to pack up and go home. But in the meantime they'll settle for higher wages for all unskilled men, a share-out of the land and free this that and the other. And almost as an afterthought they want recognition of the Labor League as sole representatives of the sugar workers, and the withdrawal of recognition from the Sugar Workers' Union."

"I should have thought that was the crux of the whole thing."

"Oh yes," said Stevens, "it is."

"And what's the S.W.U. doing?"

"Oh, appealing to everyone to go on working as usual and not to forsake the union which has done so much for them."

"It has, too."

"Yes, but nobody remembers that now. Maraj Singh was howled down when he tried to address a meeting at the saman tree. They pelted him."

"Hurt him?"

"He had to have his head stitched up."

"And ten years ago they were all behind him, weren't they?"

"Oh, to a man. But in those days he was probably the best agitator in the West Indies. He was the one who was promising them our canefields for their back-gardens."

"What about Port Catalan?" I asked. "Any trouble there?"

"No, not really. Everything much as usual. It hasn't yet turned into a racial issue. If it does, we may get some rioting and looting. But I don't think it will. It's taking a different line."

"At the moment," I said. "But nothing ever stays still, does it?"

We turned on to the Parkway and rattled along it at sixty.

"When do you think it'll end?" I asked.

"Oh, God knows! Till one side or the other gives way."

"Well, we can't give way. We might on wage claims, or conditions or hours of work. But not on recognition. We've got to stand up for the S.W.U. Once we give way we should be changing unions every year. We'd never get any proper labor relations."

"I agree," said Stevens. "Both the N.S.C. and Finlays take the same view. I was talking to McDougall only this morning. They're going to fight it out to the end. I must say," he added savagely, "our loyal laborers turning on their own union rather gets one, doesn't it. Maraj

Singh is very bitter about it. All his subscriptions have fallen and he's practically starving, I gather."

"While Ramnarine rolls in money, I suppose."

"I believe so. Though he still looks like a scarecrow."

"What about the strikers? How are they going to manage for money?"

His face puckered oddly. "Well, W.A. says they won't. That's what'll drive them back to work next week."

I could see he didn't share that view. I waited for him to go on.

"There's a rumor going around town that they're getting strike pay from somewhere."

"It's not really so very surprising, is it? I hardly think the Labor League would have staged this strike in such a lavish way if they couldn't finance it."

In Maidstone everything was quiet and shuttered, more against the heat, I thought, than against riots. It all looked horribly familiar—the rusty corrugated iron roofs, the peeling white houses, the stained-glass porches, the stumps of diseased coconut palms. Beyond Maidstone we reached the Malmaison boundary and the first cane-fields, some just springing, some partly grown, some in full arrow, fourteen-foot walls of purple and green.

"They look pretty good," Stevens said. "Nice and straight."

"They'll look even better when they're cut and loaded. As far as I remember we ought to be reaping this lot now."

"Will they spoil a lot if they're left?" Stevens had never been a planter.

"Not for a month or two. They're plant canes. Then they'll start to go off."

"By the way," he asked after a moment, "what's the position about W.A.?"

"Reynolds?"

"Yes. The Saheeb." He grinned, pulled out a soiled towel and mopped again. "What happens to him?"

I said: "I've got a letter to him from the Chairman. Relieving him. The idea is to get him off the estate as soon as he can get his stuff together. Tomorrow if he can do it."

"And then what? Fly him home?"

"Yes. You'd better try all the airlines. He can stay in Port Catalan till then. Put him up at the Royal."

Stevens nodded. "We ought to get him a flight in a day or two. What about his salary?"

"Let him draw what he wants for the journey. They'll settle all the rest in London office. They'll pay him off there."

He smiled. "Frankly, I don't think there'll be many people sorry to see him go." He shut his mouth suddenly with a little pop. I suppose he thought that wasn't the sort of thing he ought to say to me now.

There was a crowd of about two hundred gathered under the big saman tree: all men, with cutlasses and forks and long-handled shovels. I didn't like the look of it very much. The edge of the crowd straggled across the road and we had to slow down to avoid knocking into them. Under the saman tree, standing on something, I saw the chubby ragged figure of Ramnarine. He was off the road, trespassing.

As we slowed I heard his voice. Gone was the begging whine; instead was a hysterical high-pitched scream:

"They got all your land. They got all your money," he shouted. "You got to hit them now. You got to hit them hard. If you wait one day, if you wait one hour, then all gone. Thing finished, story done. You got to hit them now while they weak and you strong."

I peered across at him. The men on the edge of the crowd peered into the car. When they saw it was me, they shouted abusively and began to wave their shovels and cutlasses.

So much for their natural love and respect for the Pemberton family, I thought.

Ramnarine had evidently asked them a question for there was a great roar of "Yes!"

Stevens accelerated. "Did you hear what he was saying?" he asked.

"Yes. Charming, wasn't it? However, there's one good thing. At least we can get him now for trespass."

"Yes, maybe. But he'll have two hundred witnesses to swear that he never left the road."

"Where are the police?"

He shot me a glance. "W.A. told them to keep clear. He doesn't want them around."

"Why on earth not?"

"Says it would be interpreted as a sign of weakness."

"Good God!" I said. It seemed I had only just arrived in the nick of time.

We stopped in front of the estate office. I jumped out and went in.

"What about your bags?" Stevens asked, following me.

"Oh, leave them for the moment. Let's get this sorted out first."

In the outer office the clerks, mumbling over the endless costing abstracts, looked up at me, dumbfounded. I nodded curtly and walked quickly through into the General Manager's office. It was empty. I went on into Hughes's office next door. He looked up, sallow and hook-nosed, and jumped with surprise.

"Pemberton!" he exclaimed. "Well, man, what are you doing here? You're meant to be in England. Nobody told us you were coming back so soon."

"Well, I'm back."

He stood up and came round the desk to me. "Couldn't you get enough rum in England, you old sozzler? Or couldn't they just stand the sight of you at home? Did they send you back under guard, eh, Pemberton?"

I grinned feebly. In a way I didn't really dislike him.

"Back for a spot of hard work, eh? But, man! why didn't London office tell us you were on your way——"

"Where's Reynolds?" I asked.

He broke off abruptly, looking at me in a hurt way. "In his house, I should think. Asleep."

"Asleep!"

"Yes, he sleeps after lunch every day. He says he needs it. I think I do too."

I picked up Hughes's telephone. "Get me Mr. Reynolds," I said.

"Sorry, suh," said the soft sing-song voice of the operator. "We can't ring the Man'ger before four o'clock."

"Can't! Why not?"

"Man'ger's orders, suh. He not to be disturbed till four o'clock. Sorry, suh."

I kept my temper. It wasn't her fault. I turned to Stevens. "Look, go and rout him out, will you? Tell him I'll see him here in half an hour's time. Oh, and you'd better give him this letter too," I added, pulling it out of my pocket, "so that he's in the picture."

Stevens nodded. Hughes was gazing at me with an uncomprehending smile.

"What goes on?" he asked. "What's all this in aid of?"

"I'll tell you in a moment," I said.

I went back into the Manager's office and sat down at the desk—my own desk now. It was quite tidy. The blotting paper only had sweat marks on it; no ink. I rang up the police superintendent in Maidstone.

"Major Garnett speaking."

"Hullo, Major, it's Hugo Pemberton here. I'm speaking from Malmaison."

"Oh hullo! I didn't know you were back in the colony."

"I got back about five minutes ago," I said. "Can we have a detachment down here as soon as possible?"

"But Mr. Reynolds said he particularly didn't want any police on the estate."

"Mr. Reynolds isn't General Manager any more. I've taken it over and I want some police as soon as you can get them down here. There's a crowd at the saman tree and it looks a bit nasty." Garnett said nothing, so I went on: "They're waving cutlasses and Ramnarine's telling them to come and hit us hard. I think you'd better get someone here quickly."

"You think there may be a breach of the peace?"

"Full scale riot, if you ask me. Threat to law and order."

I could almost hear his indecision, his reluctance to take a step in which he would not necessarily be backed up.

"You're asking for this officially?" he asked at length.

"I'm asking as General Manager of this company. I want the police to come and protect life and property. And also to prevent Ramnarine trespassing on our land and inciting our laborers."

He sighed heavily. "All right, I'll send a section down. With rifles and fifty rounds?"

"Better send some tear-gas too." The police were great chaps for shooting at hostile crowds, and the colony had already quite enough massacres and martyrs to go on with.

I badly wanted a shower and to get out of my thick London suit. There would, I reckoned, be time before the police, or Reynolds, arrived, and I was sorely tempted. But I knew I ought really to go up to the factory and see what was going on there.

As I came out of the office, I was almost overcome by the sunlight and my own weariness. I leaned against the wooden wall and screwed up my eyes. Then I pulled myself together.

Mercifully the station-wagon was still there. As I drove up the road, I passed a group of overseers, Bolton, Williamson, Miller, Harvey, loafing, their hands buried in the pockets of their khaki shorts. I waved and they broke off and stared at me as I went by.

"Mr. Allen?" I asked the factory gate-keeper.

"Mornin', Man'ger," he said grinning. "Me real glad to see you back, Man'ger."

"Thank you." It was nice to find someone welcoming me, but how did he know I was the new Manager?

"Where Mr. Allen?"

"He upstairs in his office, Man'ger."

I went up and the clerks and draughtsmen in the Engineer's Office looked at me in astonishment. At least they didn't know why I was back. Allen was sitting on the edge of his table, staring glumly out of the window. The reflected light from the aluminum-painted roof of the sugar-house opposite lay like a scar across the room.

Allen said "Yes?" without turning round.

"Good afternoon, Allen," I said.

He spun round. "Good God! Well, old boy, what are you doing here? When did you get back?"

"This afternoon. I'm taking over from Reynolds."

He whistled. "You're the new manager?"

I nodded. Once the surprise had worn off he didn't look too pleased.

"Well, that's a quick one," he said. I wasn't sure exactly what was the quick one. "Fine, fine. Oh, and congratulations, of course."

"Thank you." We had never liked each other very much and I wasn't quite sure how to handle him. For the moment it would be best to keep to practical matters. "Tell me what's going on."

He told me. It was pretty well what Stevens had said.

"How's the bagasse holding out?" I asked.

"I think it'll last about another twenty-four hours. After that we burn wood, or shut down."

"Shut down," I said firmly. "We've got the week-end coming anyway."

"And do we stay shut down till we get some cane?"

"Yes. Too expensive burning wood just to make rum. Like to walk round with me?"

He had half taken a cigarette out of a packet. He pushed it back with incredible slowness and walked to the door. "Okay," he said, leaving out the 'old boy.' I wondered what he would call me now.

The factory was strangely silent without the roar of the knives and crushers. It was a little like a cathedral on a summer afternoon with a few sight-seers buzzing like flies. The main engine and the huge flywheel were immobile and deserted. I led the way to the boilers.

"Number Two Babcock and Number One Stirling," I commented. "Why do we need two boilers to run the distillery?"

Allen said: "W.A. wanted smoke coming from both chimneys. He thought it would impress the cane-cutters."

There was a group of men, mostly Negroes, standing outside the furnace doors—Raleigh, the foreman, a paler one called Hosannah whose father was reputed to have been an overseer and who I thought usually worked on the centrifugals. The others I knew by face but not by name.

"Mornin', Man'ger," they said. "We real glad to see you, Man'ger. We proper glad to have you back."

Raleigh said, "We are very pleased to know you are our new Man'ger."

"Thank you," I said. "Well, keep at it. There aren't so many of you around at the moment."

Their black sweaty faces stretched wide in grins.

"No, Man'ger, we go stay here. We work hard, Man'ger." The foreman touched his cap and we moved on. It was unbearably hot in front of the furnaces and my suit was clammy.

"They aren't all your ordinary firemen, are they?" I asked.

"No, they're from all over the place," said Allen, "from the curing and the machine shop and the bagging room." He added, "I wonder how they knew you were the new Manager."

"Their tom-toms work better than yours," I said.

Beyond the fifth boiler boys were shoveling bagasse on to the carrier from what remained of the heap.

"So that's all that's left of it," I said. It had been a fine mountain in June.

"Yes, doesn't take long to burn it up. Seems a waste, doesn't it, just for the distillery. J.B. blew his top so much that—"

"I know about Ingram," I said. "Better shut down one of the boilers straight away. The other one can keep going till two o'clock tomorrow."

Allen nodded. "I'll damp down the Stirling. It uses more fuel than the Babcock."

I was relieved. He seemed to be accepting my new authority without demur. I had expected resistance and prevarication. Perhaps he was still too startled. Or perhaps it was just that for the moment our views coincided.

One of the boys was looking up at me eagerly. I saw, with a sudden start of pleasure, that it was Jailall.

"Mornin', Man'ger," he said. "Me real glad to see you back again." He gave me an enormous grin.

"Thank you, Jailall. How are you liking this job?"

"Very much, Man'ger."

I'd hoped they might find him a better job. "Is this what he does all the time?" I asked Allen.

"He's only just started. He's been doing odd jobs out of crop. I suppose you want him back as a houseboy now?"

"I don't know. Do you want to come back to me, boy?"

"Oh yes, Man'ger, yes please, Man'ger."

I looked at Allen. "Oh yes," he said sourly, "he'll earn more money with you. But I can't let him go straight away. We haven't got another bagasse boy."

"You won't need one after tomorrow," I said. I nodded at Jailall and led the way behind the mill to the powerhouse in its steel grill box. The powerhouse was a mass of switchboards and cables and fuse-boxes; there was a steady hum from the two Mirrlees generators. In the middle, under the arc-lights, was a huge Negro in dark blue overalls. I couldn't recall his name.

"Good afternoon," I said. "Everything all right?"

"Yes, suh." For once there was no grin, no Man'ger, no word of welcome. He gazed at me with a dead black pan.

"Everything under control, Panama?" asked Allen.

"Yes, suh."

"Who's on after you?"

"Pemberton, suh."

I kept my face as dead as his. There were several Negro families on the estate called Pemberton, their forebears having adopted the name as a compliment to my forebears.

I said: "You'll have steam until two o'clock tomorrow afternoon. After that you'll have to switch over to the BTH. Will you tell Pemberton and the other one?"

"Yes, suh."

"That's one good thing about having steam up," said Allen, his hand resting on the cold silent BTH. "We save on the diesel."

As we came out of the powerhouse I said to Allen, "Is he a good man?"

"Panama? First class. Why?"

"I thought he seemed a bit surly."

"Oh no, he's all right. One of the people I can rely on. I've got my eye on him as a possible foreman."

"Oh really?" I glanced at my watch. "I'd like a quick look at the distillery before I have to get back to the office."

"Swijter's in the lab, if you want him," said Allen.

The distillery, like the pan-loft and the crystallizers, was under joint control. The chemist was responsible for its operation, the engineer for its mechanical efficiency. The result was a steady internecine war between the chemist and the engineer, who wrote each other rude notes and rarely spoke except to damn the field staff outside.

I went into the lab which was crowded with intelligent young Indians with nothing to do. Swijter sat at his desk reading something, probably the report of a technological congress.

We went through the usual astonished recognition scene.

"I'm just going to take a look at the stills. Like to come?"

"Yes, of course. And I am very much seduced by the news of your new post. That is the only good news we have just now."

He heaved himself out of his chair. He was rounder than ever and his white trousers were skin tight. Allen hadn't come into the lab and we found him staring intently and pointlessly at the lime pump. Facing us across the open space was the continuous-still, recently installed. It was some thirty feet high, with a ridiculous little aluminum roof like a paper cocked hat.

"Are you using the pot-stills too?" I asked.

"But yes, of course," said Swijter. "We have so much molasses. So much steam too."

We climbed up the ladder and went along the catwalk, looking down at the wash seething in the vats. Above them hung the heavy sickly smell of fermentation. Then we went up another ladder on to the platform of the continuous-still, Swijter gasping and mopping with the exertion.

"Where is Sookraj?" he asked. "He should be here."

"Perhaps he's on strike," said Allen drily.

"No, he came on shift. He must have gone to the lavatory. I tell these boys so, so many times they must not go away and leave the still. I will go and find him."

He looked angry and shame-faced, and bumbled away down the ladder. I tried not to notice the triumphant leer on Allen's face and I looked earnestly at the thermometer and at the sample jet—white, crystal clear and boiling. Then I followed Swijter down the ladder. It was a relief to get away from that stifling platform.

As I passed the molasses tank and started down the second ladder, I heard a ground-bass roaring and above it the sound of people shouting indistinguishably. Several people ran by below me, and the shouts grew louder. A young Indian appeared at the foot of the ladder; I recognized him as Baldeo Singh, the rum store clerk.

"Suh! Suh!" he yelled. "Quick, suh! Strikers, they in rum store. They drink-a the rum."

Swijter hurled himself down the last rungs and I followed as fast as I could.

"Christ!" said Allen behind me.

As I turned the corner of the rum store, I saw what was happening. The back gate, which should have been locked, was open wide and the mob of strikers was jostling and pushing in the doorway of the rum store. Swijter rushed into the mob shouting: "Go away! Go away! Forbidden to come here!"

Someone yelled: "Give us the rum. Rum!"

They all started up: "Rum! Rum!"

Swijter seized an Indian and pushed him roughly. "Go away!" he cried.

The Indian turned on him and hit him with his cutlass. Swijter dropped his arm and the scarlet stain began to seep through his white shirt. "Go away," he shouted.

I tore into the mob myself and surprisingly they let me through. I suppose they were so besotted by the thought of rum that they didn't recognize me. I barged my way into the rum store; the long low room was filled to suffocation. They were drinking rum out of pails, buckets, pannikins, cupped hands. In a few minutes they would be fighting drunk on neat overproof rum and the place would be a shambles.

The commissary was cowering in the corner.

"Come on!" I called. "Help me clear these people out of here."

He gazed up at me, too terrified to answer. I snatched a pail of rum from someone beside me and threw it on the floor. I must have hurt his mouth for he gave a cry of pain and put his fist into his mouth. The front of his shirt was stained with rum. Then he lashed out at me with his hand, wet with blood and saliva. I tried to duck but he caught me on the neck and knocked me back on someone else.

Already they were beginning to fight, snatching the pails and pannikins from each other. Cutlasses and shovels were raised. Somebody fell to the floor with a scream; somebody else fell over him. The hubbub and the stench were appalling.

There was only one man who had a hope of controlling that crowd and it might well be beyond him by now. "Ramnarine! Ramnarine!" I shouted.

Nobody heard my shouts in the noise. I looked around for him but I couldn't see him anywhere.

It could only be a matter of seconds before I was felled and disappeared underfoot. I bent double and charged for the door as hard as I could, for all the world as if I were ramming a rouge in the

Eton field game. I was below arm level and my impetus carried me through. Thin bodies gave before my shoulders and I was suddenly out of the rum-stinking shrieking gloom into the savage sunshine.

The rest of the mob were still outside, jostling at the door, howling for the rum. Tear-gas was the only hope now, I thought, and it had better be quick.

There was no sign of Swijter but I found Allen arguing fiercely and I thought rather uselessly with the rum store clerk.

"The police!" I said. "We've got to get them up here in double quick time. I'll ring from your office."

"The lab phone's nearer," he said.

A hand plucked at my sleeve. "Suh! Suh! Please, suh!" It was Jailall.

"Not now," I said. "Later."

As I moved off, he clutched at me desperately. "Man'ger, please suh! Please!"

Despite the urgency of the moment, something in the boy's voice made me stop. "Well, quick, what is it?"

"Mr. Panama in powerhouse he a bad man suh, I mean Man'ger."

I looked at him in puzzlement.

"What's all this?" said Allen.

"Man'ger, Man'ger, Panama he bad man. He friend of Ramnarine."

"Nonsense," said Allen. "Get back to your work, boy."

"Ramnarine in powerhouse now," screamed the boy. "With Panama. They turn out all of the lights, suh."

Both Allen and I glanced at the factory, Allen saw it before I did. "My God, the boiler-feed pumps!" he exclaimed.

The boiler-feed pumps were electrically driven. If they were switched off, the boilers would run dry and blow up.

Allen was already running across the yard to the factory. As I ran after him, I suddenly thought of the continuous-still cooling water pump.

Involuntarily I glanced up at the tall dark pile with its little shiny hat, looming above me. In that fraction of a second as I looked, the still exploded.

Jailall, his reactions a little swifter than mine, dragged me to the ground and threw himself half across me. I don't remember a bang, though there must have been a big roaring one. I remember the little cocked hat on top of the still lifted into the air as if plucked off by some great invisible hand, and the cloud of steam and the whizz and patter of fragments round me and the fine hot mist smelling revoltingly of low wines and someone shouting—possibly myself—and a sheet of flame that for one blinding fraction of a second dimmed the sun.

2

THE EXPLOSION MUST have put the fear of God into the rioters. I ran to the lab to call the police and when I got back to the distillery, they had all fled, all except a handful of drunks and three men, presumably injured, lying on the ground moaning. The drunks were in due course rounded up by the police, enormous grinning Negroes in dark blue uniforms, bristling with rifles and bandoliers. They seemed disappointed that they had arrived too late to do any shooting.

The back of my left hand was hurting. There was a red weal across it; I suppose it had been hit by a piece of hot aluminum. I thought I had better get it dressed before it blistered or got infected, and I went across to the dispensary. The three injured rioters were already there being treated. One of them greeted me drunkenly.

"Mornin', boss. Hullo, boss, mornin' boss. Boss, they proper hurt me, boss, me real frightened. Ow, boss. Mornin', boss."

I ignored him and went into the inner room with the nurse. My hand was bathed in bicarbonate of soda, and bound up; and the nurse reassured me that it would soon be all right but it must be dressed every day. He then looked at me sharply and suggested I sit down and have a cup of tea.

I smiled. Hot sweet tea—and this was certainly sweet—was the regulation treatment for shock. I didn't feel particularly shocked but I suddenly felt very, very tired. I had been rushing about, it seemed, for a long time. I was short of sleep, hungry and thirsty. It was pleasant to sit for ten minutes or so in that clean white room with its rows of bottles and its antiseptic smell and the yelling babies in the hospital beyond, and drink tea and smoke a cigarette. Less pleasant, though, to think about the damage to the factory and the future of the firm, already rocky enough without this; nor was I cheered by the results of my first day as General Manager, though I couldn't quite see that any of it was my fault. However, I was glad in the end to abandon my tea-cup and my dark broodings, and get back to work.

There was plenty to cope with. The police had duly cleared the rum-store and the compound, but the place was a shambles. Wood and aluminum and alcohol lay about in an air-raid tangle of disorder. The commissary was measuring the rum that remained in the puncheons. I thought of making some scathing remark about his craven attitude, but I bit back the words. No point in alienating the Customs and Excise at this moment. Swijter, his arm in a sling, was surveying the wrecked still. It was damaged, he said, beyond repair. The pot-stills were damaged too, but they could be put right in due course. But how could he produce good rum without the continuous-still? I tried to console him, asked after his arm and moved on into the factory.

Here the news was better. Allen reported that there was no material damage and he would be able to start grinding as soon as there was some cane in the yard. The sugar-house was hollow and echoing. A few workmen crept about, quiet-voiced and excited like servants in a house where there has just been a sudden death. I wondered where Panama was, and Ramnarine, and for that matter, Jailall. I had an idea that I owed a good deal to him.

My own burden of work lay in my office, the General Manager's office. I cabled to the London office reporting the riot and the explosion, and I got back by return an indecently hysterical cable from Justin. I sighed deeply, dispatched Stevens back to Port Catalan to hold the fort there, and got down to it.

For the next two days I hardly left the office, except for brief forays in search of sleep, food or gin. With the nagging persistence of falling leaves cables fluttered in from London office, it seemed, every few minutes, containing a mass of detailed, overlapping and often contradictory instructions. Clear distillery compound forthwith and prepare for arrival of Canadian engineer to advise on erection of new still. Do not touch distillery compound until after inspection by loss adjusters. Hold everything pending instructions from leading underwriters. Brokers report Aickmans appointed adjusters representatives flying out forthwith. Underwriters have appointed Petherick Frere Port of Spain Trinidad loss adjusters. Summers representative Petherick Frere arriving Tuesday meet airport book room Royal Port Catalan. McGuire and Hurst representatives Petherick Frere arriving Thursday will stay Directors House Malmaison. Cable estimated loss bonded rum. Cable bank statement. Cable report labor and strike position. Cable monthly expenditure figures. Cable weather report.

It struck me that on top of our other vicissitudes we were going to have a whacking great bill from the cable office. I wondered if this were Justin's reaction to the crisis, or whether it was always like this.

I had my delayed interview with Reynolds. It was a novel experience to be top dog and I was interested to find that it didn't give me the aching cheek-bones I was used to. I couldn't help admiring the unwavering jauntiness with which he carried off the scene.

I waved him to a chair but he perched instead on the edge of my desk and offered me a cigarette, just to make it quite clear that I was only his successor and not his superior.

"I'm sorry about all this," I said vaguely. "You got the Chairman's letter?"

"Yes, old boy, got it just before the balloon went up. Frankly it gave me a bit of a shock, but at least it let me out in the nick of time. It wasn't my responsibility after that, was it?"

He smiled happily at me as if he had just made some subtle unanswerable legal point.

I agreed. "No, I'd taken over by then."

"Bad luck starting off like that. And leaves you with lots of chaps hanging about with nothing to do. Take a tip from me, old boy, and make work for them to do. Keep 'em on the hop. Your coolie is all right as long as someone's bossing him up. Take that from me, I know what I'm talking about there."

"I daresay."

He scowled at the end of his cigarette. "Of course I know it's not your doing, but frankly I think it's hard on a chap. Promise him a job, confirm him in it, and then push him out before he's even had time to turn around. It's not the way I like being treated. If I'd known I was going to be treated like that I wouldn't have taken on the job in the first place."

I said, "But, of course, we didn't know, either. It was just the way things have turned out."

"I don't like being put in just to keep a seat warm for someone else," he said. I started to interrupt, but he held up his hand. "Oh, no hard feelings! There's nothing wrong with a bit of jobs-for-the-boys stuff. People should look after their own families. But it isn't so good when it does someone else down."

I wondered if Justin had suggested the job-for-the-boy line in his letter, or if Reynolds had thought it up for himself.

I said, "It was thought a good thing for political and psychological reasons to have a member of the family in this job at the moment."

He roared with laughter and slapped his knee. "That's a good one. I wish I had a cousin who'd think of things like that for me." The laugh stopped abruptly. "Mind you, I think your cousin's making a mistake. In a job like this you want a man with experience. Though you did pretty well when you were working under Walker and me here, you just haven't got the experience yet."

"I'm getting it quite fast," I said. "You're going to Port Catalan tomorrow, aren't you?" I couldn't take much more of him. Any moment he might suggest staying on to give me the benefit of his experience in these difficult times.

"Yes, I'm flying to Trinidad tomorrow evening and picking up the *Colombie* there."

I stood up and held out my hand. I wondered if I ought to give him a drink or dinner. "Well, best of luck!" I couldn't face it, perhaps Stevens would take him to lunch at the Country Club.

We shook hands. "Same to you," he answered with endearing warmth. "I expect you'll need it more than I shall."

I felt depressed. However a brighter aspect of the situation struck me, and I dashed off a cable to London office suggesting that, now Reynolds had gone, Ingram might be recalled from Barbados, where he was on holiday, and reappointed as chief engineer.

Justin's reply was a honey. "YOUR SUGGESTION RE INGRAM UNDER CONSIDERATION BUT MUST REMIND YOU ALL STAFF APPOINTMENTS EXCLUSIVE PREROGATIVE OF CHAIRMAN."

The only cable I got at this time that gave me any pleasure was one from Diana, asking anxiously how I was after the explosion. I replied fondly and reassuringly, but, even so, it was a laconic and rather tantalizing contact. I had had as yet no letter from her. Indeed I hardly could have unless she had written the same day as my departure, and she had never been a very punctilious correspondent. I was still pretty well in the dark about her plans and movements and, for that matter, about her general reaction to our future life.

I felt the inadequacy of our contact the more keenly because, despite the pressure of work, I was rather lonely. I had thought I was lonely enough before, during my apprenticeship, cut off from Diana, from the junior members of the staff by being a Pemberton and from the seniors by being junior. But now that I was actually at the top, it was even worse. I had long discussions about the factory damage with Allen and Swijter and Hughes, but that didn't fill the vacuum in my private life.

I went across to the club one night, officially to show the flag and be matey with the boys, and actually in search of company. But the club seemed emptier than it had before. Without the Ingrams no one had organized any bridge. Neither the Allens nor the Swijters were there. Overseers mooched about drinking rum and soda and looking through the old magazines. A few wives knitted together in the corner. The gramophone was silent and nobody talked very much. The shadow of the strike lay heavily on everyone's spirits, I could see, and the presence of the newly-promoted General Manager only added to the awkwardness. I decided that I would not come again except on special guest nights.

So when the day's work was done, I would go alone back to my house and sit among Walker's furniture and drink some whisky and have my hand bandaged by the sick-nurse and ask Jailall when his new baby was due. The broad acres of the big house seemed to echo forlornly under my footsteps. I had not been able to bring any books with me because of their weight and Walker apparently had kept none. Sometimes I fiddled with the radio, a luxurious mahogany affair with a bright green eye that winked and refocused itself hypnotically. I would try the BBC Overseas Programme, which was usually transmitting nonstop light music. Then I would switch to New York where with luck you might find a Chopin Prelude played by eight pianists at eight pianos. And then, all intellectual diversions failing, I would go back to work again and start grappling once more with figures and reports. Sometimes I read back through the old files. There was a certain wry pleasure in reading Walker's correspondence with Justin, especially when it concerned myself.

I would go early and silently to bed and write, in my pajamas, an instalment of my current letter to Diana. It was a surprisingly difficult thing to do. I didn't want to put her off the place too much before she even arrived. I would talk a bit about the factory and the strike and the postponed arrival of the loss adjusters from Trinidad. They can't have been very exciting letters to get.

After five days in the Malmaison office, I went down to Port Catalan for a couple of days. I had a twinge of pleasure as I drove away in the General Manager's big blue Buick behind Thomas, the General Manager's black chauffeur. But it was a pretty mild twinge, really.

The company owned a house in Queen Street. Stevens lived on the ground floor and the upper floor was a self-contained flat for the General Manager and visiting directors. Doris, the buxom black maid, gave me an enormous dinner, chuckling away to herself, and I ate it in solitary state.

I didn't sleep very well that night. The flat was hot and there was a lot of noise in the street outside. The smell of curry from the shabby hotel opposite wafted through my bedroom like sea-mist. I lay in the damp darkness and listened to the cocks, which seemed to crow all night.

God, what have I done to myself? I thought.

3

The next day was one long rush. I started off with a session with Stevens at the office; I sat majestically at Walker's huge desk and looked down the long wooden noisy room at the little table where I had sat a year before, learning about Trial Balances. This sort of thought occurred to me a good deal at this time. I suppose I was trying to reassure myself.

Then I drove down to see Mendoza, our solicitor. The big Buick almost filled Main Street from side to side and we moved very slowly, sounding our horn the whole time. I don't expect anyone heard it especially in the general hubbub.

Mendoza was an able and incredibly harassed man and I never felt entirely at ease in his presence, partly because I knew that he acted for every other reputable company in the colony. Out of the dozens of solicitors registered and practicing, he was the only one whose integrity was beyond question. In a dispute he usually found himself acting conscientiously for all parties.

I was a bit relieved to find that he was not also acting for Ramnarine. We discussed the ensuing legal proceedings. I was keen that these should be criminal and not civil as I had no wish to get the firm involved in a large bill for costs. Mendoza, perhaps understandably, did not share my enthusiasm for this view and pointed out that the Government were notoriously unwilling ever to prosecute anybody for anything; and did I want Ramnarine to get away scot-free? He also pointed out that the two other sugar companies were also interested and it might be as well to discuss the matter with them before giving him any final instructions. He didn't actually say that he was acting for them too, but I knew that was what he meant. We left it at that.

From Mendoza I went on to Galloway's and had myself measured for a new palm-beach suit. My tropical wardrobe, I had discovered, was sadly inadequate to my new stellar position and to the large number of meetings and parties I should henceforward be attending in Port Catalan.

I then walked across Main Street into Mannheim's and spent a little while buying a wrist-watch for Jailall. I had been pondering ways of rewarding his devotion and prompt action, which had saved both the factory and myself from more permanent damage and it seemed to me that a big bright shiny watch would fill the need nicely. I found one, which also told the date, for seventy-five dollars and took it away with me. It was nice having enough money at last.

I returned to the car and was driven royally to the interview I had been dreading all morning.

The bank's noble premises—classical in reinforced concrete, with a broad flight of steps—were in a fine position on the corner of Main Street and the Esplanade. Brief-case under arm, I sauntered nonchalantly up the steps and was ushered into Cornish's office without waiting. Cornish himself welcomed me at the door smiling genially.

He was a military looking little man in an immaculate white suit and a plain blue tie—the colony office uniform. I had met him once or twice before and was always startled by his accent. It was a secret and, so far, frustrated ambition of mine to hear him speak the words 'brown cow', but it is a difficult phrase to bring into a conversation, particularly into the sort of conversation we were going to have that morning.

"Well, it's nice to see you back," he said waving me to a chair and sitting down at his desk. I took a cigarette and said it was nice to be back.

The electric fans oscillated and droned. I removed a drop of sweat from my forehead with my little finger. Cornish made some remarks about my new job and what a happy appointment it was and what a loss Walker was and he was sure I'd be as much a success as Walker had been and anyway he wished me the very best of luck.

I replied modestly, though, I added, "I haven't made a very auspicious start, have I?"

"Well, I suppose there's nothing like having your troubles at the beginning and getting them over."

"Just so long as you do get them over."

He asked sympathetically about the explosion and the strike. I told him in some detail and he listened attentively.

"Of course, you know, we've got an interest in all this. We hold your deeds and insurance policies here. I was looking through them this morning."

"The loss adjusters are coming next week from Trinidad. They'll be wanting to see the policies."

Cornish nodded. "I'll have them ready. What do you personally think the damage amounts to?"

I hesitated. "Well, the chemist says the continuous-still is *kaput*, finished. The pot-stills need a little repairing but they can be put right quite easily. But you can't make good rum with a pot-still alone."

"Are you going to put up another continuous-still?"

"Oh yes, I think so. Just as soon as the damage figure is agreed. But, of course, it takes a bit of time."

He said, "Rum's a pretty important part of your output, isn't it?"

"Input too," I joked rather desperately.

He gave a wan smile.

"It's not our chief thing," I said, "but it's quite a profitable side-line."

He looked at me through half-closed eyes. "A blow, but not a fatal blow to your company, is that about it?"

"Just about."

"I hear the rioters looted the rum-store. That must have been quite a party."

"It was!"

"Do you think you lost a lot there?"

I said, "We reckon about three thousand proof gallons, a little under."

"They must have drunk a lot."

"They did themselves quite well. Some of them passed out. Most of the rum went on the floor and down the drain, though. They were smashing open the puncheons as fast as they could to get at it."

"What a waste!" he murmured.

"I know. It was matured stuff too. However, it was all insured, of course."

"Yes. Well, I suppose it's one way of selling your rum. Saves freight charges too and losses in transit."

It was my turn for the wan smile.

He asked, "What about the factory itself?"

"Oh, that's in pretty good order. We could start grinding tomorrow —if we had any cane."

Cornish nodded heavily. "This strike's an absolute sod, isn't it? I was afraid it was going to be worse than some people seemed to think. What's the position with you at the moment?"

I said, "A lot of the factory workers have come back. I think largely curiosity to see the damage. They do nothing much except sit around and draw their wages. And the shovel and weeding gangs are partly back, so we can do a bit of cultivation."

"Oh good."

"Yes, but we haven't got any cane-cutters. They're the people who are holding up grinding. It's all quite peaceful, though," I added. "No more riots or anything like that. The whole place is like a Sunday afternoon in London."

His wan smile. "I'm told it's the same at Finlays too. Oh well, we must be grateful that it isn't spreading."

I agreed. "The S.W.U. are doing what they can, telling people to go back to work. But they don't seem to cut much ice at the moment."

"So I've heard. It's this new union that's bitching things up, isn't it. Can't you turn any heat on your own cane-cutters? Threaten to sack them if they don't go back to work?"

"You can't really sack them," I said. "They're all casual laborers anyway. They turn up when they feel like it. They go from estate to estate as the mood takes them."

"So you've both settled down to siege warfare. Is that it? See which side starves the first?"

"Yes, I suppose so," I said, a little reluctant to put it that way.

"Well, I hope your funds last the longer."

"So do I," I said fervently.

There was a moment's pause. I was just going to speak when he said:

"I was a little surprised to discover that you don't carry a consequential loss policy."

I pressed my fingers against my cheek-bones. The skin was damp to touch.

Cornish went on, "You'd be happily placed now. They'd be paying you for all the time the factory was standing idle. And for all the time your distillery's out of action."

"I know," I said unhappily. "We've never carried that policy. Of course, it's often been mooted, but—"

But what? What was there to say? That Justin had done nothing because—because he didn't want to make innovations or because he was feeling indolent that day or because he damn well wasn't going to accept suggestions from someone else.

"You're a great firm for family traditions," Cornish observed drily. "The Major has talked to me about them several times. But still, it surprises me that we didn't insist upon it."

"I know. I expect you will now." I added, "I think we felt our insurance bill was already high enough. We were trying to avoid fresh commitments."

He nodded vaguely. "Still you've got the other insurance money coming in. That should help a bit."

This was the point I had been dreading all the way through.

"What's our balance at the moment?" I asked.

He had the figures at his finger-tips. "Two hundred and seventy-nine thousand," he said.

"Good God!" I murmured, shocked. "As high as that?"

"Yes, I'm afraid so. You've paid out some pretty big cheques lately. Income tax. A big one to Transport and Harbors. I suppose that was for freight. And you haven't had much coming in either."

"Well, you never do out of crop, unless you can sell some rum."

"The whole of the last crop's gone, has it?"

"Oh yes. Shipped and sold. And they've had some pretty big bills to meet in England too lately. Sugar bags. Fertilizers."

"Any big ones outstanding here?" he asked.

I thought for a moment. There was a big one for wharfage due any moment, but I thought we could stall on that for a bit.

"There's the ordinary wages and salary bills," I said. "They go on all the time."

He smiled. "All these factory people hanging about with nothing to do."

"Just so. But of course there are the monthly staff as well. Overseers, engineers."

"I mean," said Cornish, "do you think you're going to want to draw over the three hundred thousand?"

"Oh, I hope not! But it rather depends how long this strike lasts."

"How long does it take you to make and sell some sugar, once it's over?"

"We can start making it as soon as we get the first lot of cane in. But I don't know what the shipping position is. I'll try and persuade the Controller to get us space on the first ship available. You ought to get the money within forty-eight hours of its being unloaded in England."

"Yes, I see."

I went on with some show of enthusiasm. "We've got a nice little special contract for a thousand tons of Yellow Crystal. We make quite a bit on that."

He looked encouraging, so I asked: "What happens if we need to draw over the three hundred thousand?"

"I'd have to ask for fresh instructions from London."

"Do you think we'd get it?"

He shrugged his shoulders. "I don't know. Credit's a bit tight at the moment."

"I know Mr. Nelson's very keen to help us," I said dourly.

"Yes, I know he is. He's a nice chap, Nelson, isn't he? But this would be decided on a higher level."

"You don't know how they'd regard the matter?"

"No idea at all." We both looked blankly at each other. He went on, "Nobody wants to see you shut up shop, least of all us. We make a lot out of you."

"You certainly do," I said feelingly.

We both gave wan smiles, first me and then him.

"If it's only a question of tiding you over while the sugar is at sea," he said, "I don't think we'd be difficult over that. But, otherwise, I should think it would probably depend on how quickly the strike folds up."

I prodded away another trickle of sweat. "You mean if it goes on, we shall be up the creek without a paddle."

"Well, let's say without an outboard motor."

He smiled wanly. I bravely raised one in reply.

I went back to the flat in a rather sombre frame of mind and had a couple of large pink gins. Stevens came up and lunched with me in the Director's flat and Chuckling Doris served us one of her enormous meals. We talked business whenever she was not in the room and it was not a very gay occasion. Afterwards, sweating and comatose, we hauled ourselves downstairs and back through the heat of the day to the office.

The Estate Proprietors' Association held its meetings, I discovered with some surprise, in a shabby, hot little room above a shop. The only furniture was a plain table and hard wooden chairs, and the only decoration a cheap print of the Queen from which all the red had faded, pinned to the wall with thumb tacks.

It was my first experience of this powerful organization, of which I was now a member, and I had expected its premises to be more imposing. Stevens and I represented Pembertons; McDougall and

O'Hara, Finlays; and Grainger and Hopkins, the N.S.C. Everyone was very nice to me, congratulating me on my appointment, condoling about Walker and our labor troubles. I went on mechanically saying the right things and wondering if the meeting was ever going to start.

It was a bit of a shock seeing McDougall, but I thought his congratulations and condolences seemed especially warm and sincere. Once again I was aware of his eyes boring into me, appraising me. I suddenly wondered, with a sickening qualm, whether Fiona might have said anything in one of her letters. But surely not. I listened carefully for the remark with a double meaning, for the steely edge on the voice. Finally I took the bull by the horns.

"How's Fiona?" I asked.

"Very well, thank you. It was good of you to be so kind to her in England."

It seemed innocent enough. Admittedly he looked pretty inscrutable as he said it, but then Chinese always do. It isn't because they're actually being inscrutable, but the way their faces work, or rather don't work.

"Yes, we traveled across on the same ship together. We had dinner in New York and then she came and had a drink with us in London."

"It was very kind of you," he said again.

"I wish we could have done more for her. What a pity you couldn't come after all!"

"I know. It is always difficult getting away on leave. There is always some reason why you can't go at the last minute. You'll find that out in due course."

I laughed. "Oh dear, I hope not."

"Fiona liked your wife so much," he went on politely. "Will she be coming out soon? We're all looking forward to meeting her."

"Oh yes, she's coming," I said, quite easily. "As soon as she can get a passage. Has Fiona got one yet?" I put the question in a casual way, as if I were only asking out of politeness.

The inscrutable eyes remained fixed on me and I hadn't the faintest idea what he was thinking. "Yes, she sailed two days ago on the *Golfito*. She should be here quite soon."

I was totally unprepared for the sharp pang of excitement the words gave me. My loaded stomach heaved and turned over.

"So soon? It'll be nice to see her again. Nice for you to have her back," I added, squeezing the pleasure out of my voice.

It occurred to me that if Fiona had got a passage, Diana could have got one too. But even that thought didn't stop me feeling good just then.

The meeting got under way half an hour late. Grainger, the President of the Association, was in the chair, a tall bald man in a blue bow tie. He was not by reputation one of the more brilliant members of the N.S.C. staff and I suppose he was our President through sheer seniority.

We went through some of the longest minutes I have ever heard, and, slowly, laboriously they were adopted, proposed, seconded and signed. Then the secretary read out a letter from Molly Walker replying to the Association's formal letter of condolence, which had been sent last time. Somebody asked me where she was. I explained that she was now on her way back to England to be with her sons. Everyone grunted sympathetically.

The chairman then gave himself great pleasure in welcoming me to the Association and spoke eloquently of my surname and the high esteem in which it was held not only in the colony but throughout the West Indies. He expanded this theme for some time, and indeed, but for the deep booming voice, I almost thought it was Justin speaking. Somebody else followed, talking about my tender years and patting me metaphorically on the head.

Finally we got down to stern business. We agreed unanimously that we could not even consider the strikers' terms until the men were back at work. We also agreed unanimously that we couldn't consider the strikers' terms anyway as they were proposed by a union we did not recognize. We then proceeded to discuss the strikers' terms for over an hour. At times there were two or even three conversations going on at once. Grainger called it a useful exchange of views. Occasionally he listened attentively. The rest of the time he stared vacantly out of the window, probably thinking of the cocktail party he was giving that night and wondering whether he had ordered enough chicken patties and whether there was anyone else he ought to have asked.

In point of fact it was quite a useful exchange of views because we had to decide sometime what we were going to do about unskilled wages and, though it raised a lot of very big questions, individual ownership and farming of land. But, in the circumstances, it was hardly surprising that nothing was decided.

We then discussed the position of the two unions. Hopkins had a scheme for strengthening the S.W.U. by deducting the dues from the individual pay packets before they reached the laborers.

"How to be very, very unpopular," commented O'Hara.

"But we've got to do something," said Hopkins. "Otherwise the union will just fold up on us and we shall be left with Ramnarine and his boys."

McDougall said, "But if we make it clear that we are supporting the S.W.U. the laborers won't want anything more to do with it. They want a union which will fight us for them, not one that we're running ourselves."

I gazed across the table at McDougall and thought that only ten days ago, four thousand miles away I had seduced his daughter—or had she seduced me? I couldn't believe it.

"Hear, hear," said O'Hara.

"Well, what's the alternative?" Hopkins persevered. "Maraj Singh to go stumping round the colony calling them out on strike to back him?"

We didn't get anywhere with that discussion either, though it too had provided a useful exchange of views.

A lot of time had passed by and Grainger was becoming restive. So when I raised the question of legal action against Ramnarine, he said, "Have we time to discuss that now?"

O'Hara ignored him. "Obviously the man's got to be sued. Pembertons have suffered most. I don't know if you want to do it on your own?"

"Not a bit," I said. "We've all suffered from him to some degree or other. I think we ought to do this jointly."

"Agreed," said Hopkins. "But do what?"

"Well, do whatever's necessary," I said, "to make sure that criminal charges are brought against him for inciting to riot or breach of the peace or whatever is best."

"You'll never get it to court," said O'Hara. "You know what the A.G. is like."

"Well, if we keep booting along behind him," said Stevens, "we might."

"Nor will you get any damages that way."

I said, "We won't anyway. He's got no money."

"He's got pots of it," said O'Hara.

"Not officially. But I don't think it's a question of damages. We want him prosecuted and punished. Sent to prison under section whatever it is. Make an example of him, show people they can't get away with that sort of thing."

"Supposing he's acquitted?" asked Hopkins.

"How can he be?"

"Well, it depends on the jury. If they happen to be East Indians or members of his union or both, you'll never get him convicted. If it's a civil action, you won't have a jury."

Stevens asked, "Where is he at the moment anyway?"

"Lying low, I should think."

McDougall said, "I heard he was in Chelmsford and that he's hoping to stand in the by-election there."

I hadn't taken in properly that there was to be a by-election in Chelmsford.

"He'll probably get in," said Stevens.

I said, "I shouldn't think he'd like it much if charges were brought against him just when he's trying to show himself a respectable candidate for the Legislative Assembly."

"Oh, I don't know," said Hopkins. "He'll be speechifying away. He'll turn it to good account, show himself a sainted martyr."

"And if it's a civil action," said McDougall, "he'll be the little champion of the people fighting the big sugar companies that are trying to grind their faces in the dust."

"He'll be an even bigger hero if it's a criminal charge and he's acquitted or the charges are dropped."

I said, "But if he's convicted, I'm not so sure that he'll be such a martyr, at least not after the first day or two. I think he might find it quite a handicap. He wouldn't be able to cash in on the martyrdom line anyway if he's in the clink."

"Wouldn't he have to resign his seat if he was convicted?" McDougall asked.

No one seemed to know.

"He's got to get the seat first," I said.

Grainger made a maestro's gesture with his arm and looked at his watch.

"Gentlemen, I feel we ought to leave this matter over till next week. Time's getting very late."

So in the end we decided nothing, and I went back to the Director's flat and had a cold shower and changed into a dark suit. So Fiona was already at sea, was she. I looked thoughtfully at the big bed with the dropped net. And Ramnarine was in Chelmsford. And I was going to the Graingers' cocktail party. I should see there the whole of the upper crust of Port Catalan society from the Governor downwards. I should be welcomed and fondly greeted by every person in the room and I should go on repeating endlessly the same remarks about my job and Walker and the factory and the strike and life in England, over and over again like a gramophone record with a stuck needle. I thought of Williamson and began to sing "Give yourself a pat on the back."

4

I DROVE BACK TO Malmaison the next day, wondering if all my visits to Port Catalan were going to be like that and how many I was going to make in the next twenty years or so. I was back in time for lunch at eleven, and over a quick pink gin I presented Jailall with his wrist-watch. He gazed at it with popping eyes like a child looking at a Christmas tree.

"Oh boss! Oh Man'ger! For me? Oh Man'ger!"

"Yes, Jailall," I said. "For you." Surprise seemed to have robbed him of both speech and gratitude. "Well, you did very well when we had that trouble," I explained. "If you hadn't told me so quickly about Ramnarine being in the powerhouse, we might have had the boilers blow up. And if you hadn't pulled me away when the still went up, I'd have been much worse hurt."

He glanced at me briefly. "Yes, Man'ger."

He was holding the watch on to his wrist, staring at it with rapturous and for the moment totally guileless eyes.

"It must have cost much money, Man'ger."

I grinned at his reaction and put the glass to my lips again. At that moment an idea struck me and I put it down again without drinking.

"Jailall!"

"Yes, suh?" The child was swallowed up in the well-trained houseboy.

"Do you know how to get hold of Ramnarine?"

"Ramnarine, Man'ger?"

"Yes. Our friend."

"He no friend a-we, Man'ger. Ramnarine bad man."

"I'd like to see him," I said.

The boy looked puzzled. "You no want see Ramnarine, Man'ger. He bad man."

"But I do want to see him. Can you get a message to him?"

The mulish look spread across Jailall's face.

"Ramnarine no come here, Man'ger. He no come here a-we."

His eyes watched me closely. Deliberately I let my own eyes drop to the watch in his hand and then back to his face.

"No, not here," I said. "But he could meet me somewhere else. Well, boy?"

Jailall was all attention. "Yes, Man'ger," he mumbled.

"He could meet me on the Maidstone road, at the last canefield, by the cotton-tree. At six o'clock tonight."

The mulishness had faded from his face and was replaced by the ancient guile of his race.

"Six o'clock tonight, Man'ger?"

"Yes. Why not?" It would be getting dark then.

"Me go try, Man'ger."

"I hear he's at Chelmsford," I said. "You'll have to work fast, boy."

"Yes, Man'ger."

I stood up. I was a good head and shoulders taller than he was. I looked down at his black shiny hair and his immaculate white tunic and his bare flat brown feet. "You no say anything about this to nobody. See, boy? Not even Jehorah."

"No, Man'ger."

"If you tell anybody, me go cut your tail so hard you no sit down for a week."

An enormous grin burst across his face. "Yes, Man'ger."

"And now me go eat, boy."

In the office, after lunch I went through the back numbers of the *Natividad Chronicle* and read everything I could about the Chelmsford by-election. It had been caused by the death in harness of the Honorable David Moses, and though nomination papers were not yet in, there were already five candidates in the field, representing the little splinter parties that made up colonial political life. Ramnarine, if he stood, would be the sixth. I wondered what party he would represent. Probably he would form his own party for the occasion.

It seemed to me from the names that four of the five candidates already at work were Negroes and the Negro vote would be well and truly split. Unless a few more Indian candidates came into the field, Ramnarine should be in a strong position, especially with his union behind him. I tried to visualize Ramnarine in the Legislative Assembly. It was an intriguing thought. There was nothing like a few debates on the budget for sobering up a firebrand. He'd have to get himself a decent suit too. I wondered if he'd wear a top-hat for the State Opening. Quite likely, I thought.

There was a knock at the door and Hughes came in without waiting. He seemed a bit surprised to see me reading the newspapers.

"Sorry if I'm disturbing you," he said with elaborate irony. "I've brought the abstracts."

"Oh thanks."

They were huge sheets of blue paper covered in minute writing and figures. I glanced at them gloomily. They told you practically everything you could ever want to know about the cultivation of the estate—the cost of half-banking or fork-molding or sulphate of ammonia per square rod per week, compared with the month and the year before in every field on the estate. All the costs seemed to have gone up by a decimal, just as you might expect. I wondered what I was supposed to do with them.

"When were these finished?" I asked.

"Just now." He sang the words in the colony manner, the "now" being almost an octave below the "just."

"But they're the July abstracts," I pointed out. "It's almost October now."

"It always takes a couple of months to get them out," he said defensively. "The clerks have been working very hard on them. They have to be done in triplicate. Comparing and checking the copies takes a lot of time."

"It's not much use if they're always three months in arrears."

"But it's always been like that," said Hughes with finality. "I don't see how it can be any different unless I get some more clerks."

He was always wanting more and more clerks, building his empire.

"Or a simpler abstract," I said. "All right, leave them there. I'll go through them."

He put them down reluctantly and turned to go. I thought of asking him whether the Honorable David Moses had been a black or an Indian, and whether a member of the Assembly resigned his seat if he was sent to prison. But I didn't say anything. I didn't want to encourage Hughes to hang about my office gossiping, and I knew that Mrs. Hughes would spread everything I said round the estate.

I leaned back in my swivel chair and lit a cigarette. If only there was someone in the whole place I could talk things over with.

The mosquitoes were whining and the coconut palms were only black feathers against the sky when I reached the rendezvous. I had left Thomas and the Buick behind and I drove myself in the station-wagon. I stopped the wagon across the road from the cotton-tree and turned out all the lights. I sat there waiting, listening to the frogs croaking and the distant dogs howling. It was just six o'clock and there was no movement anywhere.

It took me a couple of minutes to realize that Ramnarine was standing under the cotton-tree, watching me. His dark skin and dark clothes merged into the shadow of the trunk. Only a faint flicker of his eyeballs gave him away.

I got out of the car and walked across till I was facing him. He stood watching me, motionless, as I came up. I was sure that if I had tried to hit him, he would have disappeared like a shadow before I could have landed a blow. I was just near enough to him to smell his breath, and very nasty it was.

"So you came, Ramnarine," I said very quietly.

His voice was low too. "Yes, boss. Me come."

There was a moment's pause. The mosquitoes stung my hand. I thought of suggesting that we have our talk in the station-wagon with the windows shut, but he might easily refuse to come with me. Besides, I was tactically well-placed standing before him, confronting him. The mosquitoes would have to be borne.

"You come to give me job, boss?" asked Ramnarine.

"No."

"You come to give me house, boss?"

"No." I added, "You won't be needing either a job or a house when you're in prison."

"Me in prison, boss? What for?"

"Causing a riot at the Malmaison factory. Trying to blow it up."

"Me never go near Malmaison factory."

"Plenty of people saw you, Ramnarine. You had a meeting at the saman tree first."

"They lie, boss, they lie." His tone was still quiet and subfusc. "Me in Chelmsford all day. Plenty-a people see me there. They swear before the judge me in Chelmsford all day."

"I have no doubt they will," I said, equally impassively. "But I think you'll be convicted all the same."

"No, boss. Me no think so."

"I think you will," I said solemnly. "Especially if the Chief Justice tries the case."

"You come to threaten me, boss?" There was just a touch of insolence in his voice now, and I felt I was making progress.

"I came to ask you a question, Ramnarine. When is the strike going to end?"

"Me no know, boss. The strike nothing a-do with me."

"You know lots of the strikers."

"Me know one two. Me tell-a them all time You go back a-work. You be good laborers. You work proper."

"You tell them that, do you?"

"Me tell them a-work hard, but they no listen a-me."

"Too bad," I said. "I hoped you had more influence with them."

"No, boss, me poor man. Me just laborer without job."

I asked him, "What were you doing that afternoon in Chelmsford when you weren't blowing up the Malmaison factory?"

"Me with friends, boss. Me got friends in Chelmsford."

"The ones you spent the whole day with?"

"Yes, boss."

"Getting ready to fight the by-election, were you?"

"By-election?"

"Yes. You ought to stand in Chelmsford, Ramnarine. Five black man candidates. No East Indian candidate. Lots of East Indians live there. You'll probably get in."

His eyeballs flickered as he blinked. It seemed to me that I was forcing the issue faster than he wanted.

"Me think so too," he admitted.

"You'd be good in Leg. Ass.," I said. "You'd be big man. Big man in all West Indies too."

"Yes, boss."

"Well, are you going to stand?"

"Me no know, boss."

"You'll have to decide soon."

There was a moment's silence. A mosquito stung the back of my neck. I slapped it away.

"Mosquitoes bad, boss?" They didn't seem to be bothering him.

"Not really. Why don't you stand at Chelmsford?"

A whine crept into his voice. "How can me, boss? Me go trial. Perhaps me go prison too."

I knew that the whine was, on this occasion, synthetic. But it didn't matter.

"Would that stop your standing?"

"Yes, boss. How me go fight election when me in court? How me go speak in Leg. Ass. when me in prison?"

"You'd have to resign your seat if you went to prison, wouldn't you? That's the law. Then there'd be another by-election."

The eyeballs flickered again. He seemed to know as little about that as I did.

"Me no know."

I said softly, "But if there were no trial and the charges were dropped, then you could fight your by-election."

There was a long pause. He regarded me impassively, without enthusiasm. I began to wonder if I was going to bring it off.

"No, boss."

My heart sank sharply. "Why not?"

"Me got no money, boss."

"You've got pots of money," I said.

"Oh no, boss, me poor man, me starving, me got nine pick'nie. No job, no house. How me go fight election with no money?"

I waited a moment to give my words emphasis, and then I said: "You could borrow the money, Ramnarine."

"Borrow? Who go lend-a money a-me?"

"The bank," I said.

"Bank no go lend money a-me."

"Well, they might—if I spoke to Mr. Cornish."

The eyeballs moved again. He said nothing.

"Banks are very secret," I said. "Only Mr. Cornish would ever know."

"How much they go lend-a-me?" he asked at last.

"Perhaps three thousand dollars."

He blinked again.

"That no enough, boss. Elections cost plenty money." He paused. "Five thousand dollars."

I said, "You know by law you are not allowed to spend more than three hundred dollars on an election campaign. You have to produce your accounts."

"Yes, boss," he said meekly. We both knew that every candidate in the colony cooked his election accounts.

"Perhaps they lend you four thousand dollars. Provided the strike comes to an end."

"Boss, me got no say in strike."

"No," I said. "Me got no say in bank, either. But me go try," I added. His pidgin English was infectious. I snapped out of it abruptly. "I hope all the task gangs and half the cane-cutting gangs will turn out for work on Monday. And all the cane-cutters on Tuesday. Strike over, story done. But it must happen by Tuesday. Wednesday will be too late."

"Boss, me got no say in strike," he repeated tonelessly.

"If the strike is over on Tuesday morning, then perhaps we hear no more about trial and prison. And perhaps the bank will lend you four thousand dollars."

There was a long pause. He stood there immobile like a cow on a dark night. I wondered if I had won or lost. I wanted to kick him, stamp on his bare toes, to get some reaction out of him.

"How me go pay back four thousand dollars?" he asked at last.

"That's up to you to work out with the bank. Pay it back out of your salary when you're a member of the Leg. Ass."

There was another faint flicker of white which might have been his few teeth bared in a smile.

"What will you call yourself when you are a member?" I asked.

"Just Ramnarine, boss."

"The Honorable Ramnarine," I murmured. "You ought to have two names. What was your father's name?"

"Ramdass."

"The Honorable Ramnarine Ramdass," I said.

"No, boss. All-a people call a-me Ramnarine. Me no want be Mr. Ramdass."

"You'd better take a first name then. Like all of us."

He said quietly, "Honorable Pemberton Ramnarine?"

I knew then that I had won. I turned and walked back to the station-wagon without another word. I took deep breaths of sweet warm fresh air. The backs of my hands were itching so that I could have screamed.

5

I WAS A GOOD deal on edge the next few days and I was aware that there were other reasons, besides the state of our overdraft, why it was important that the strike should end soon. Laborers who had turned out to work, the factory employees who had stayed loyal, were becoming demoralized, especially in the factory where there wasn't much to do except loaf about. It was a fertile breeding ground for all sorts of resentments and disaffections. The overseers too, were spending too much time hanging round the club and some of them were drinking too much. I told Pattison to find something for them all to do, but he was not a man of great creative imagination. Everyone, from myself down, was becoming nervy and irritable.

However, on the Monday morning, Allen telephoned me to say that the entire factory staff had turned out for work, even including Panama. What, he asked, was he to do with Panama? My first reaction was to tell him to sack the man forthwith, but on second thoughts I decided against it. I said the man was to be moved out of the powerhouse into some more menial work and that he was to be watched closely. Allen replied that it wasn't easy for him to find work in the factory for anyone, important or menial, until they got some cane. I told him to get cracking polishing the outside of the evaporators, and he rang off very puzzled.

I was relieved, though not surprised, when Pattison telephoned at lunch-time with the news that the cane-cutting gangs were back at half strength, and that all the other field-workers were back at work.

The next day there was a full turn-out of cane-cutters and the first carts arrived in the factory yard. We burnt wood to raise steam and began grinding on the six o'clock shift. I listened to the clatter of the knives and the roar of the crushers and watched the sweaty grins on the faces of the workmen. I saw the tired faces of the overseers riding home on their mules in the evening, and I thought it was cheap at four thousand dollars.

I went down to Port Catalan the following day, surf-riding gaily on my wave of success and badly wanting to celebrate in congenial company. As we got farther from Malmaison, my mind became less interested in the problems of sugar production and more in the fact that the *Golfito* was due to dock the following day. It struck me as highly auspicious that business should take me to Port Catalan just at that moment.

Whose cocktail party was it tomorrow night? I looked it up in my diary. The Cornishes. Fiona might easily be at that. I couldn't wait to see her again. I might take her out to dinner afterwards. We could bathe in the moonlight at Carib Bay. There didn't seem to be much of a moon, but starlight would be even more romantic. Perhaps later among the palm-trees—no, too many mosquitoes. One of the beach huts would be convenient, but a little cramped and unromantic. How discreet were the management of the Carib Bay Hotel? The VIP flat was the simplest but what would Stevens and Chuckling Doris think?

I reminded myself that the whole essence of romantic love had always lain in the overcoming of obstacles, and I laughed confidently to myself. If Fiona should prove reluctant, well, that was only another obstacle—not a very formidable one to a man who had just stopped the strike and saved the firm. Fiona would be pleased and proud of me. She'd want to celebrate too. Her lover and her blue-eyed boy. I wondered what she was doing at the moment. Bathing, probably.

I put my head back on the seat and spun down the Parkway in a giddy daze of masculinity. Never had the countryside seemed so beautiful.

Next day in Port Catalan I went once more on what I privately called my milk-round. First to Mendoza to tell him to drop all charges against Ramnarine and Panama.

"Of course it's not really up to us," he said. "It's up to the A.G."

"If we don't want to proceed any further," I pointed out, "I don't suppose he will. Couldn't you write him a private letter to say that now everyone's back at work we think it would be better to let bygones be bygones? Not exacerbate feelings by going over the whole thing again. You know the line."

Mendoza nodded. "I'll speak to him personally. I think that would be better. But you mean to take civil proceedings?"

"No. Not that either."

"What about the other companies? Are they dropping their charges too?"

"Oh, we discussed it at the last meeting of the E.P.A.," I said vaguely. "We're the ones who suffered most in the strike. It's really our move. I daresay we shall be discussing it again this afternoon," I added.

Mendoza sighed. "Well, let me know if there's any further change of plan, won't you?"

The wrist-watch could be left out of this milk-round, but I had another fitting of my suit at Galloway's and a little later again I was being ushered into Cornish's sanctum.

Cornish was his usual genial self, and this time I had no butterflies, no aching cheek-bones.

"Well, how are things?" he asked.

How now, brown cow? I thought. I said, "Fine."

"The strike folded up just nicely for you, didn't it?"

"Just what the bank manager ordered," I said happily. "I reckon that if production and shipping go according to plan, we won't even reach three hundred thousand. Especially if the insurance pay up properly."

"You'll have to keep back some of that for buying a new still, won't you?"

I grinned. "We won't have to pay for that just yet."

He pushed his cigarettes at me and said: "Wouldn't it be more comfortable for you, though, if you could stop living quite so near the overdraft limit?"

"It would indeed. But that's the next stage. First things first."

"Oh yes. I daresay Nelson will have some ideas about it."

"He should," I said. "That's rather what he's there for." I lit the cigarette and puffed through the smoke quite casually: "By the way, if a character called Ramnarine comes in here asking for an overdraft, we are prepared to guarantee it up to four thousand dollars."

Cornish looked me straight in the eyes.

"Oh I see," he said. "That's the way it goes, does it?"

I nodded. "I thought it was worth it at the price."

"How to reduce your overdraft. Guarantee someone else's." He laughed.

"An original piece of financing, I thought," I said. "And it worked."

We smoked for a few moments in silence.

"God, you young men!" he said. "I don't know where you get your ideas from. What'll people say when they hear about it? A fine old-established firm encouraging bribery and corruption."

I looked anxiously round in case we might be overheard. But the door was shut and the room empty except for us.

"Not a bit," I said cheerfully. "Ramnarine denies firmly that he has any connection with the strike. Naturally we believe him. He wants to fight a by-election but he has no funds. We think he has the makings of a fine statesman, so we are prepared, quite altruistically, to help him put his first foot on the ladder. Very public-spirited of us. It's just a coincidence about the strike ending. However," I added, "it would be just as well if nobody else knew about it. You know how people gossip."

Cornish laughed. "All right, I'll try and keep it close in here. Who else knows about it?"

"You, me and Ramnarine. He won't talk. He'd lose all his supporters if people knew he'd done a deal with us."

"Not unreasonably. Very well, I'll try and hush up your sordid little intrigue. Do you think he'll ever pay off the overdraft?"

"Oh, not for a moment. You can foreclose on the guarantee as soon as you like."

"I think we'd better run up a bit of interest first."

"Not too much, please. Four thousand dollars is already quite a lot."

He shook his head in mock despair. I suddenly wondered, for the first time, what Justin would say when he heard. Would he stop the four thousand dollars out of my salary? I quailed at the prospect. Perhaps I could hide the figure somewhere in the accounts. Somewhere in one of those costing abstracts.

"You're coming to our party tonight, aren't you?" Cornish asked.

"Yes. Looking forward to it very much."

"Good. See you then."

At the door I suddenly remembered something. "We've got a couple of loss adjusters arriving from Trinidad this afternoon. Would it be all right if I brought them along too? They'll be at a loose end otherwise, with Stevens and me both at your party."

"Of course. The more, the merrier. Which are they?"

"McGuire and Hurst. From Petherick Frere."

"Know the firm well. Not sure if I've met them. But bring them along. We'll liquor them up well. Perhaps then they won't adjust your loss too badly."

"That was my idea," I said, as I left for the E.P.A. meeting.

McDougall said, "As far as we're concerned, the strike's over. Everybody's back and we're grinding."

"So are we," I said.

Grainger nodded, seemed about to speak and then said nothing.

"I wonder why it folded up so abruptly," said McDougall. "Anybody know?"

His eyes rested on Stevens and me, calm and expressionless.

I shook my head. "No idea. I suppose they just ran out of funds."

"Must have," said Grainger. "That's the way these things always end."

"Yes," said McDougall, "but they usually peter out more gradually. Or else some form of agreement is reached. I've never known one to end quite in this way."

I said nothing. Hopkins said, "It was certainly a nice surprise."

I wanted to change the subject so I said, "I suppose, Mr. Chairman, we should discuss the strikers' demands, now they've gone back to work."

"Can't," he said. "Haven't been put up by the recognized union. I'm not going to deal with these pirate people."

"Are the S.W.U. doing anything?"

Nobody seemed to know. O'Hara said, "Maraj Singh usually bungs in some fantastic wage demand every year or so. I expect we'll be hearing from him soon."

"Unless we made our own offer first," I said.

That started them off and soon they were all explaining to me, as Walker had once done too, why it would be quite fatal. You couldn't start giving concessions to coolies without damaging the union's prestige and anyway there was no point in giving away money before you had to and anyway this was no time to start giving away money when we'd just had an expensive strike and anyway all claims would have to be carefully considered in the light of last year's accounts which were not yet complete and anyway the matter would have to be decided in London.

I thought of the seven cents an hour basic factory wage, but I kept my mouth shut. As the new boy I mustn't talk too much at these meetings, not to begin with.

In due course someone, Hopkins I think, raised the question of legal proceedings against Ramnarine. I had briefed Stevens to speak on that one.

He said, "Our view is that it would be wiser to let sleeping dogs lie and not give these people an opportunity of making political speeches in court."

Hopkins demurred. McDougall was inclined to agree. We argued about it in a desultory way. Then McDougall looked at his watch and said:

"Mr. Chairman, I wonder if you will excuse me. I have to meet my long lost daughter and her ship docks at five o'clock."

"Yes, of course."

He gathered up his papers, stood up and nodded at us.

"Remember me to her, will you?" I said, my heart pounding in my throat.

He smiled a quiet little smile. "Certainly."

Everybody else mumbled the same sort of thing. When he had gone, Stevens said, "Mr. Chairman, might I be allowed to leave too. I have to meet two insurance adjusters at Rawson."

"Of course," said Grainger. "In fact, I think we might as well adjourn this meeting till next time."

He looked, as before, immensely relieved. I felt relieved too, though I tried not to show it.

Cornish's cocktail party was exactly the same as Grainger's. The same sort of big bare room, the same pony whiskies, the same chicken patties, the same hired waiters, the same guests—with the addition this time of two loss adjusters and Fiona. My own conversational gramophone record, however, was a little different. Yes, it was a relief that the strike was over, no I supposed there was nothing like getting your troubles over at the beginning was there, could I introduce Mr. McGuire and Mr. Hurst who had come from Trinidad to look at our damage.

I spotted Fiona almost at once. She was standing in a corner at the far end talking to Mrs. O'Hara and Treadwell of Transport and Harbors. She was as pretty as ever though I hadn't remembered her being quite as plump as that. Perhaps they had fed her too well on the *Golfito* or perhaps her frock was too tight. It had the dropped waist which made her hips seem bigger and her legs shorter. Its cyclamen color was startling but unbecoming against her yellow skin.

I was hard put to it not to stare greedily at her and I felt that everyone in the room must be watching us. I slipped away from the loss adjusters and with a slow cocktail party rhythm I made my way up the room to her. It must have taken me half an hour to reach her. I congratulated myself on my tact and patience.

Then, suddenly, I was beside her.

"Hullo!" I said. I nodded and hulloed at Treadwell and Mrs. Roche who had replaced Mrs. O'Hara. Fiona too played her part beautifully. There was nothing in her behavior to suggest that she knew me better than any of the others. She told us about the *Golfito* and we talked about other ships and the strike and the weather. She asked after Diana. I said she was still in England. Treadwell said he was due for leave next year. Mrs. Roche said they were due the year after. I said what a pity it was that Fiona's father hadn't been able to get across and perhaps they'd have better luck next year. She giggled nicely at the three of us and agreed.

After a bit I began to despair of ever getting her alone to myself. As Treadwell wandered away Hopkins came up. But I managed it in the end. I said to Fiona, "Let's go and talk to your father," turning away from the others and nodding politely as I did so. I pushed her gently through the open door into the gallery beyond. There were other guests drinking and talking here too, but at least we were alone till one of them should come to join us.

"Lovely to see you again," I said. I stood close to her, smiling down into her eyes. She wasn't wearing any scent. It was darker out here than in the big room, but not dark enough to risk a kiss.

"Nice to see you too. I was so sorry to hear about your troubles. Are you all right?"

I reassured her and showed her my hand.

"I am so sorry," she said. "It must have been beastly. Still, there's nothing like getting your troubles over at the beginning."

I winced and crushed it immediately. "Serves me right for coming out to a place like this."

She took me up at once. "Oh you mustn't say that! You're a Natividadian now like the rest of us. Though it was a horrible way to start off."

"Never mind," I said. "Things are looking up. The strike's over and you're back."

She gave a little giggle and stared down into her glass.

"It was your doing," I said. "But for you I probably shouldn't be out here now."

She raised her head very slowly and looked at me. "Oh no, surely," she demurred. "It was so obviously the right thing for you. Anyone could see that."

I frowned a little. "It wasn't at all obvious to me, or to—" I broke off. I didn't want to bring Diana into this conversation.

"But surely," she said again. "You've got a big job out here. The sort of job anyone would want—particularly if they were young and ambitious."

I said nothing. She went on, "Daddy says you've made an excellent start."

"Very nice of him." I thought for a moment and then I decided I'd better have one more shot at trying to make her see my point. "I gave up a good deal to come out here."

"I don't see that. You're a much bigger man out here than you ever were in London." She was certainly frank.

"Even a castaway can be king of a desert island. But that doesn't mean it's a very satisfying life."

"But you're not a castaway," she pointed out, a trifle obviously. "I should have thought it was a very satisfying life to anyone with ambition."

I couldn't let it go this time. "Perhaps I haven't the right sort of ambition," I said.

"Are you still hankering for that writing stuff you were doing before? I thought you'd given that up."

I felt a little angry. I undressed her quickly in my mind's eye, but it wasn't a great success. "Well, I don't know, I feel that in the long run that sort of thing's more worth while. More WW," I added wryly.

"Pardon?"

"I mean, businesses come and go, but books go on for ever."

"But people may not read them. Everybody's got to eat sugar."

I said, "In a world crop of several million tons, the odd twenty thousand that Pemberton produces isn't going to matter much either way." I tried to keep the roughness out of my voice. "But Shakespeare does matter."

She took me up on that. "Were you going to be another Shakespeare?"

It was a bull's eye and I gritted my teeth. "Well, perhaps another Hazlitt."

"I don't know about Hazlitt. But if everybody went around writing books when they ought to be growing food to eat, we'd all get very hungry, wouldn't we."

"Yes, but I'm not everybody. Nor are you. We're each individuals, to do what we think best."

She giggled. "Well, this individual isn't ashamed to admit that she'd rather have sugar than Shakespeare. Or—who was it you said?"

"Hazlitt."

"Yes, him." She sipped her drink. A silence fell between us. It wasn't a bit the sort of conversation I'd wanted with her. I felt sidetracked and cross. If only I could get her away somewhere alone.

Hold her in my arms, kiss her, dominate her. Bask in her loving-kindness, her admiration. Forget about Pemberton and Shakespeare and Hazlitt.

Out of the corner of my eye I saw Grainger disengage himself from his group and for a hideous moment I thought he was going to join us.

"Look," I said, "don't let's argue about this now."

"Well, I didn't start it. I thought it was all over and done with."

"Anyway let's have some dinner afterwards. Would you like that?"

She said quickly, "Oh, but I can't. So sorry, I'd have loved to. But I must go home and give Daddy his dinner. I've got a job too, you know. And it's my first night home."

"Yes." I suppose I should have thought of that, but somehow I'd expected her to put me before anyone else.

"Well, another night, then. I've got to go back to Malmaison tomorrow, but I shall be in town again. We might go and have a starlight bathe at Carib Bay."

She giggled again. "That would be very nice. Wait till your wife comes out and then we must make up a party and do that."

She said the words in such a complete cocktail chatter voice that it took a second or two for her meaning to sink in. Hell hath no fury like a woman scorned but a man can be pretty angry too. And how could she talk about Diana! Then, more gently, perhaps being a Natividadian born and bred she couldn't see it was in poor taste.

Again we fell silent. She sipped her drink faster. "Where are you living at Malmaison?" she asked at last.

"In the Manager's House. In solitary splendor."

"Oh, I know. I went there once for your estate dance. That was in Mr. Walker's time."

"Yes, I expect it would be."

"Mrs. Walker was so nice, wasn't she. It must be very hard on her."

"Very hard. She's on her way home to be with her sons. They're at school in England."

"Are you living among her furniture, then?"

"Yes. She's left it here for the moment. She'll send for what she wants when she's found somewhere to live in England. I suppose we'll probably buy the rest off her."

"I see." She took a cashew nut from a passing waiter. "Will you be doing any other alterations?"

It was incredible, horrible. I was her first lover, I had deflowered her so recently, I had offered to marry her, to ditch Diana and share my life with her. She had given herself to me, without any strings attached. And now we were talking like this. When Grainger came up and started talking to us, when a loss adjuster drifted over and said, "I say, this is some party," we didn't need to alter the level of our conversation at all.

In due course Fiona and Grainger drifted back into the main room, smiling the regulation parting smile. I waited a few moments and then I took the loss adjuster up to Mrs. Cornish so that we could both tell her what a wonderful party it was. I found the other loss adjuster and introduced him to the Governor's wife. And then the first loss adjuster to the Governor, and the second to the Colonial Secretary, and them both to the wife of the Chief Justice.

I was fairly making the wheels whizz around. I fortified myself with several pony whiskies and chicken patties. The party was beginning to thin out. I saw Mendoza stop talking to the Attorney-General and, smiling correctly, look around for his wife. McDougall and Fiona seemed to have left already.

I collected the two loss adjusters and Stevens and we all thanked Mrs. Cornish again for her wonderful party. Then I took the three of them out to an expense account dinner at the Country Club and we all got hilariously, depressingly, anesthetizingly drunk. When I finally got to bed about three o'clock in the morning, the bed did backward somersaults under me, feet first.

6

I LEFT THE LOSS adjusters going through the insurance policies with Stevens and I went back alone to Malmaison. Never had the countryside seemed more dismal, and that wasn't wholly due to my hangover.

My vanity was smarting, an agonizing, comical and temporary complaint. Time was always an infallible healer. But even now, looking back, I think that Fiona's conduct was pretty riling. She had made it brutally, contemptuously clear that she wanted nothing further to do with me, that she wasn't in love with me, that she never had been, and that she didn't think a lot of me. How could any girl, I wondered sorely, with any warmth, any love in her, ignore so completely all that had passed between us such a short while before? At the great reunion with her lover, how could she bear to speak to him only in the refined, well-modulated tones of the bank manager's cocktail party. Did she know what she was doing? And did she care?

Her mind, her manner were different too, I made myself realize. The gentle humility, which I had found so touching in her, had gone, had been replaced now that she was back on her home ground, by something which was almost arrogance. Gone too was her ability to see the other side of the case—or had I always overestimated that? I looked back on our meetings in New York and London and decided that desire had distorted my powers of observation, if it had not made me blind. It left me mentally as well as physically disappointed and I felt lonelier than ever.

My head ached intolerably. I took off my dark glasses and polished them, but it didn't make things any brighter. I tried to doze, without much success. So I went on scratching at my hurt vanity as if it were a mosquito bite.

If she felt like that about me, why on earth had she ever let me go so far? Why had she given herself to me? Was it pity, regretted immediately afterwards? Vanity on her side? Simple lust? Curiosity about sex? Or was it, I wondered, something much more callous, the urge to demonstrate her power over me, the wish to show that, for all her intellectual limitations, she could make up my mind for me just by taking off her clothes? The bloody little bitch, I thought savagely. She deserved a good beating.

I began to feel a bit better. I now knew where I was on the map, and if it wasn't the place I hoped, at least it was nice to know for sure. As we got nearer to Malmaison I tried to think about the business problems ahead of me. But my mind shied off them. I began to think about Diana. At least she was honest. Or was she? I had been out in the colony for nearly three weeks and all I had had was that one cable asking how I was. Not a word about when she was coming out. It was more than inconsiderate, it was downright humiliating. Women, I thought, just out for all that they could get.

The first thing I saw when I entered my house was a letter from Diana lying on the hall table. I stifled a little qualm of remorse about my thoughts and read it over my pre-lunch pink gin. It was a long chatty affectionate letter. Diana wrote very good letters when she finally came to a boil.

She was still very anxious about my burn and was I quite sure I was all right? Exactly what had the doctor said? And how awful for me, coming back straight into the middle of all that. Really, what a place it was!

After a page or so of that she told me about her own doings. The twins were being the greatest fun and Sieglinde had suddenly started painting and was really doing it awfully well. Siegmund had remarked out of the blue that he didn't want to go to heaven as there would be too many stairs. Diana had told him not to be so lazy. It was easily his longest speech to date and showed that something was ticking inside. Nurse Humphreys (no Nanny for her!) was very reliable but an appalling talker and a fresh-air fiend. Both children had heavy colds, but she still insisted on taking them out for long walks in the park. She had had a row with Mrs. Kerridge who had walked straight out. Fortunately, by sheer luck, Diana had been able to find another woman the same day, and, touch wood, everything seemed all right at the moment. She had had no news from my mother, but supposed she was well. Justin had been his own inimitable self when he gave Diana the news of the explosion, but it had been nice of him to ring up at all. She was frantically busy at the office and thought she had found another good serial for them. Miss Peabody's opus was due to start in a fortnight's time and she was hoping for a record fan-mail. Yesterday she had rejected four hundred short stories by just skimming through the first couple of pages and then after she was in bed at night she had had such compunction for all the poor authors and the hours they had spent on their ewe lambs that she had got up and read the whole lot through from end to end. It had taken her the whole of the rest of the night and she had still turned down the lot, but at least her conscience was clear, though she felt a bit whacked now. A parcel of six more novels had arrived from *Vista.* She had rung up Gatoff and asked if she should send them out to me, but he had said no, send them back to him.

The last sentence turned the knife in the wound. So Gatoff had liked my reviews enough to want me to do more. If I had stayed in London, I might have become one of his regular contributors. And from there—but the books had been sent back and I was a sugar estate manager. I had never even seen my reviews in print.

I left most of my lunch uneaten and went upstairs to lie down. But I couldn't sleep and after half an hour I put on my shoes and went across to the factory. I watched the cane going through the mill and the evaporators boiling and the centrifugals spinning. It cheered me up a bit. If you stood near enough to the crushers, the noise could deaden your thoughts a little.

We were grinding well with only about 8% stoppages, but despite that we were producing well under a hundred tons of sugar a day. I went into the lab and looked through the figures with Swijter. The extraction was 105%; it was a permanent mystery to me why it was always over a hundred. The Boiling House Efficiency was 98.4. The Pol was 10.2, the Brix 17.1. The Absolute Juice Loss % Fibre was 48.37. I tried to remember the difference between Mixed Juice, Normal Juice and Absolute Juice but, for all my months in the lab, it had gone from me. I thought of asking Swijter, but there was no real point in confessing my ignorance. I would look it up sometime in Noel Deerr. It didn't really matter anyway.

The Purity was only 68. I pointed at the figure.

"It is always the same after the stop," said Swijter. "The purity is low, it is the rain, there is too much water. The cane is old too."

"Not too old. But you're right about the purity. That's what's wrong with us. These Indian canes are no damn good. All fibre and no sucrose." I pointed to another figure. "Look at that Java cane. Purity 83. That's the stuff."

"Java cane is a good cane," said Swijter proudly.

"I think the new Barbados seedling is even better."

He looked at me sharply. "Perhaps. Have we much more Indian cane to come?"

"We have indeed. Practically the whole crop. Everyone else loves it. So strong, so tough. It doesn't mind droughts or rats or frog-hoppers or weeds. Grinds well, plenty of bagasse for the factory."

"But what is the use of that," asked Swijter, "when it makes no sugar?"

I walked back through the blinding sunshine to the office and there, the crowning glory, I found two letters from Justin. At least it was the same letter twice. Correspondence with London office was always conducted in duplicate in case the plane might crash. As both copies always seemed to travel together, it never struck me that this had much advantage.

I slumped down into my chair and read the letter through. It was on Justin's special writing-paper and written in the quaint language that Chairmen of Pembertons always had used when writing to their General Managers.

> My dear sir,
>
> 1. My last letter CH 114 was despatched on September 24th. Since then I have sent you cables 714, 715, and 716 and have received your letter HP 2 and your cables 118 and 119.
>
> 2. I was pleased to hear that you have sustained no serious injury in the accident at Malmaison Central Factory and hope that you are now completely restored to health. I was sorry that you were not able to prevent serious damage occurring to the distillery but I am sure you took such action as you could. I need not tell you how heavy a blow this is to me and to. . . .

I looked out of the window at the white compound and the green and purple canes beyond. Yes, I had done everything I could and if there was no need to remind me, why write half a page about it. I skipped and read on.

> 3. Please instruct Allen and Swijter to send me detailed signed reports on the state of the factory forthwith. I am anxious too to have a cultivation report from yourself. The costing abstracts for July have not yet been received in this office. Kindly expedite these. Also let me have a detailed expenditure analysis for the out of crop period. . . .

What out of crop period? I wondered. Including or excluding the strike?

4. I am more than a little concerned to hear that the strike is continuing and wish you to cable me full details of all developments. I cannot emphasize too strongly how important it is for the strike to be ended as soon as possible. At the same time you must not make any promises of concessions to the strikers while they remain out. I am in daily contact with Mr. Drewe of the N.S.C. and Mr. Finlay and I will keep you informed of our decisions regarding these labor troubles.

I had cabled Justin the day before yesterday telling him of the end of the strike. Perhaps I would soon be getting some of these much heralded decisions.

5. Our insurance brokers say that Ashmore, Wise and Garwood have been appointed loss adjusters and their representatives will be arriving in the colony the week after next. They will stay at the Directors House at Malmaison. Please give them every courtesy and assistance. I need not tell you how important it is to make a favorable impression on them. I will write you separately a little later showing how I wish you to present our case to them.

6. I have decided to re-appoint Ingram as Chief Engineer and have cabled him in Barbados asking him to return forthwith. I feel that at this difficult time Ingram's experience should be of the greatest value to you and I hope you will not hesitate to follow his advice. Please inform Allen and Swijter of my decision and make sure that his house is ready for his return.

7. You must understand my concern at having so young and inexperienced a General Manager in charge at this critical time. Indeed I can admit that my first reaction to the news was that I ought to fly out and take charge personally until the situation had resolved itself. However, I cannot easily relinquish my duties here at present and so I am forced to leave the immediate administration of affairs in your hands. I hope you will regard this as a measure of the confidence which I feel in you and that you will prove worthy of it.

Yours faithfully,
J. M. Pemberton
Chairman.

It made wonderfully little impression on me and that was rather gratifying. Indeed I felt a sense of liberation. Once Justin's letters really lost their stinging power, once my emotions became more controlled or more self-contained, I should be happier, more equable, more invulnerable. I seemed to be making progress in that direction.

I rang for Miss Athene, my secretary, and began to dictate a reply.

My dear sir,

1. My last letter HP 3 was despatched on September the 26th. Since then I have sent you cables 120, 121 and 122 and have received. . . .

That evening I read through Diana's letter again and quite coolly, dispassionately I wrote her a stern reply. She had said nothing, I pointed out, about her future plans and when she was coming out to join me. I told her about Mrs. Bolton who was always coming out in the next month or two and after six years had still not arrived. I was not going to be treated like that. Diana must make up her mind one way or the other. If she was coming out, she must get London office to get her a passage on the very next ship, and go on pressing them till they had done it. If she did not intend ever to come, she must say so plainly. We would know then where we were.

I sealed up the letter and left it for post. I felt the quiet strength of one who has just taken a brave decision and forced an issue. It seemed quite likely that this was my farewell to matrimony, but that might not be such a bad thing for either of us. In my toughness I was resolved to be decisive, no matter how painful a decision it might be. Indeed, it might be more attractive because of its painfulness.

But what about the twins? That would be almost too painful, even for me.

I came off it in the early hours of the morning. I found my letter still lying on the hall table and I tore it up without opening it. I sat down at a table in the cavernous room, with the factory hissing and thumping round the corner, and I wrote Diana the sort of letter she would be expecting, like hers, bright, chatty, affectionate. I wrote about my hand and the children and Nurse Humphreys and Justin and the strike and the loss adjusters. I wrote about everything except Ramnarine, which I thought wiser not to put on paper, and Fiona.

I ended with a paragraph which she wouldn't be expecting.

Life is pretty quiet at the moment for me and there is nothing on earth to do except work. It seems to me that there is no point in your rushing out here sooner than you need. You'll have had quite enough of the place by the time we're finished, and Jailall is looking after me like an anxious hen. Why not hang on in your job at least till your serial is finished and your successor properly trained? I expect the magazine would be glad of that too, wouldn't they?

I sent her and the twins my love, stuck up the envelope and left it lying on the table where the earlier letter had lain.

I had given her all the loopholes she wanted, I thought with a little glow of pride. I had saved both our faces too. Bolton and I would start an exclusive little club together. For husbands dangling on strings.

I went down the back-steps to the factory and walked around under the yellow arc-lights. The man whose job was to test the pH of the limed juice was fast asleep. In my magnanimity I let him off with a rude awakening.

Diana's reply came eight days later, eight days of worrying over loss adjustments and juice purities and expenditure analysis. I was drinking a whisky and soda in my house when Jailall brought in a cable.

Oh God, I thought, what does Justin want now?

I opened the envelope and read:

"THANKS YOURLET BUT SAILING WEDNESDAY COLOMBIE CUMTWINS EXCITED LOVE DIANA."

I suppose it is a measure of how little I understood Diana that her reply, so utterly characteristic of her, should have been, for me then, so utterly unexpected.

Part Five

1

I SAID, "Well, see you both later," to Hughes and walked back to the house, clutching as always my loaded despatch case. As I came into the enormous room I heard Diana telephoning.

"Well, it's awfully nice of you, I'd love to come, only . . . Yes, of course, I will, only I'm an absolute beginner at bridge . . . No, really, I only started on the ship coming out . . . Oh, no, I'm sure you're all frightfully good . . . Yes, yes of course . . . Oh no, really not, but I'd love to try if you think you could bear it. I mean I'd probably always revoke or something awful . . . Ha, ha, ha! Just a moment, I hear my husband coming in."

She covered the mouthpiece and said, "It's Mrs. Garnett. She wants me to go and play bridge tomorrow morning."

"Fine," I said. "That's the stuff."

"But, darling I'm still hopelessly bad. I hardly know the rules." She uncovered the receiver. "Hullo, Mrs. Garnett, yes, he says of course I'm to come. Yes, I'll look forward to it very much. It's so nice of you. . . ."

As she talked I put my arm across her shoulders and kissed her disengaged cheek, putting her a little off her stroke. Her cotton frock felt damp. I straightened up and looked across the room, where the twins were playing on the floor with a heap of bricks. Their faces were swollen with mosquito bites, angry and sore with persistent scratching.

"Hullo!" I said, going towards them. Then I stopped and looked down at myself. I was wearing a white tunic open at the neck, khaki shorts and yellow cotton stockings. And the twins were suffering from bites and Diana's frock was damp and she was telephoning about a bridge party. It was exactly as I had imagined it.

I patted the children but they didn't seem very pleased at the interruption, so I went back to Diana. She had just rung off.

"It's dreadful," she said. "I can't play at all and I know they'll all be furious with me."

"Not really. They'll be delighted to have you there, and anyway they won't dare be furious at you."

"Even if I do everything wrong?"

"Especially if you do. They'll love putting you right."

She pulled down the corners of her mouth. "We start at ten, stay for lunch, have a short rest there and then go on again till evening."

"Bridge is usually played in marathons out here. Pity to stop a good game in the middle."

She nodded grimly. "Just what Mrs. Garnett said. I can't make out, darling, when my partner bids three of something, do I have to say something to keep it open?"

"Depends which system you're playing."

"Oh!" She looked helplessly at me.

"I should try first one and then the other and see which goes down best." I paused, staring at her dismay and then I said gently, "Oh, don't worry darling. It doesn't really matter. Just relax and take it as it comes."

She smiled wanly. "All right. I just don't want to disgrace you."

"You couldn't do that if you tried."

She looked so pathetic, I kissed her again.

"No, but I might easily without trying." She held up a large sheet of paper. It was a list of all the white staff on the estate with penciled comments in Diana's own handwriting. "Allen, second engineer, dark, wiry, chip on his shoulder. Mrs. Allen, pregnant, won't like me. Ingram, chief engineer, tall, bad-tempered, able. Mrs. Ingram, plump, fair,? in love with Hugo."

"You won't lose that will you?" I said. "It would cause a sensation. Change hands for a lot of money in the market."

"I'll keep it under lock and key. Are all the overseers in order of seniority?"

"More or less. But it isn't like the army. Pattison is head overseer and next to him, Miller, the crop overseer. All the rest are really equal though some have been here longer than others. But that doesn't mean they'll get promoted first."

She nodded. "I don't have to be introduced in any special order? It isn't like the Queen meeting ambassadors?"

I laughed. "Well, it is a bit. But you can talk to whoever is nearest. They won't be lined up for inspection."

"But will they wait for me to talk first?"

"Not Mrs. Ingram or Mrs. Allen. And probably not the Swijters. But the rest probably will, apart from saying 'Pleased to meet you.'"

"What in particular am I to say?"

"Oh, I should make it as dull as you can. How lovely it is to be out here at last. What a nice club it is. Is it always as hot as this? That sort of thing."

"I see. And they'll all be there, will they? The whole lot?"

"They haven't been ordered to attend. But they'll all be there all right. They'll all want to meet you."

She glanced at the paper again and then down at herself. "Perhaps I ought to change before we go. You wouldn't think this dress was clean this morning, would you."

"It's fine. They'll all be just the same. It's all quite informal. I'm not going to change. No need for panic, darling. Relax, you're the Queen. You can't do anything wrong."

She looked at me anxiously. I put my arm round her again.

"I'll be there rooting beside you," I said. "Keeping you well supplied with gin. Like one now before we go?"

"Oh, yes please," she said.

Two hours later we were back for a late lunch.

"Not too bad?" I asked.

"No, not really. Some of those overseers are pretty heavy going. Williamson, Miller, Bolton. Very sticky."

"Not Pattison? Did you get a word out of him then?"

"Oh no. Not one. But I didn't expect to. The Swijters were nice, though. And Mrs. Allen was quite civil. Not a rude word."

"Well, I should hope not."

Diana said thoughtfully, "Ah, but how to keep her sweet. That'll be the challenge. By the way, darling, am I to get on Christian name terms with them?"

"Oh Lord, no. That wouldn't be at all proper. Give them a gentle snub if they start calling you Diana. I don't think they will, though. They'll get as far as Mrs. P or Mrs. H, and stick there."

Diana made a moue. "I wonder if I shall remember to answer to that."

We ate for a moment or two in silence and then I said, "We shall have to give a cocktail party for them all in a week or two."

"What, this lot all over again?"

I smiled grimly. "This lot all over again. Who else? That's estate life."

She sighed, and then pulled herself together. "All right, darling, I get it." She paused and then went on, "Mrs. Allen asked me to take the children around to play with hers. She's got a little boy the same age."

"Yes, I suppose she has."

"I mean, ought I to do it or would it be infra dig?"

I laughed. "Darling, protocol isn't as strict as that. Of course you can take them round. But I shouldn't get too involved with the Allens." I looked round to make sure Jailall wasn't in the room. "Apart from Laura Allen being a complete bitch, you'll rub the Ingrams up the wrong way."

She nodded. "Concealed protocol, I see. But I might take the children around once or twice. Fun for them to meet some other children. Might help to bring Siegmund out of his shell."

"Yes. Incidentally, I think we ought to drop their nicknames now we're out here. People might think it odd of us."

She looked at me quickly. "And that would matter?"

"Yes, it would a bit. We're very much on show."

She seemed drooped and sad. I thought, that's something else that's died between us. Our private jokes.

Diana murmured, "I see. Caesar's children as well as Caesar's wife. All right, darling."

I noticed suddenly how dark were the rings under her eyes. I found I couldn't eat any more lunch.

There was something surprising and touching in seeing Diana, for the first time, lost and out of her depth. But, of course, being Diana, it didn't last long. In a couple of weeks she had the whole place taped. I watched her at our cocktail party or with the other wives or playing tennis with the overseers in the evenings and I was impressed by the precision with which she found and held the right line.

The thing that really got her interest was my work. She asked me, and anyone else handy, endless questions about the business. She dressed in riding-breeches and shirt (and she certainly had the figure for them: she looked like a girl in a high-class western) and rode round the estate with Pattison and me, being shown every side of the cultivation. She went round the factory with Ingram and Swijter and insisted on having all the figures explained to her. I even discovered her reading Noel Deerr.

I regarded these activities indulgently and even a little tepidly. It wasn't usual for wives to take such an interest in the affairs of the firm, and I was a little put out at finding that in a few weeks she knew almost as much about the business as I did. Of course it was nice to see her so keen, but I was secretly waiting for the first flush of enthusiasm to die away. I hope, now, that I wasn't too patronizing to her, because I dropped all that the moment it dawned on me, rather belatedly, that at last I had, resoundingly, someone I could talk things over with.

I came back from the office one evening to find her deep in a book—not Noel Deerr but Culbertson on Bridge.

"That's what I call keen," I said. "I hear you're becoming an expert."

She laughed and put the book down. "Oh, hardly that. Still, I'm improving. It's only a question of putting your mind to it, like anything else. Actually I quite like it, only we do it for such hours at a stretch. But there are worse ways of killing time."

I clapped my hands for Jailall and drinks.

"Is there so much time to kill?" I asked.

"Well, yes, there is quite a lot. I mean, I've never had three servants and a nanny before. And they hardly seem to need any organizing."

"I'm sorry. What about the children?"

"Oh, I play with them morning and evening, but they don't fill in the day. I suppose they will more when they're older."

The drinks arrived and I gulped mine.

"There doesn't seem to be any welfare work I could do," she went on. "At least not without embarrassing people and stepping on their toes. Unless I was to start a local Girl Guide troop."

I laughed at that. There was something comic in the thought of Diana starting a Girl Guide troop, just to give herself something to do. She laughed back and then I suddenly saw that it wasn't funny.

"Poor darling!" I said.

I felt very warm and loving towards her—partly, no doubt the whisky, and partly her very red lipstick, her black and white cotton frock, her bare unstockinged heel where she had half kicked off her shoe. I leaned across and kissed her hard. I couldn't wait to get her to bed.

"Let's go and have a shower," I said.

"Don't you want another drink first?"

"It's not a drink I want. Or even really a shower." I kissed her again.

"What, now?"

I held her close. She felt very warm and alive.

"Darling, you do have lovely ideas. I suppose it's being in a hot country."

I picked her up and carried her upstairs. She weighed very little.

"Big strong man!" she said happily.

I think that the next half hour was the turning point in our marriage, at least in the things that really matter. For the first time the act of sex was part of something much bigger. We were at last indisputably and indissolubly part of each other. Diana was gentle and submissive, I was tender and completely besotted. It was easily the most intoxicating moment of my life.

Afterwards we lay in the dusky room and listened to the frogs and the hard-backs banging against the mosquito screens, and I knew that nothing was ever going to be the same after this. She lay in the crook of my arm and I could feel her breath against my chest. I thought hard about her.

I had brought her to this place, where she was bored and unhappy. I had taken my decision against her argument, and she had accepted it loyally. Not once had she gone over the old argument again or questioned the rightness of my decision. I had bent her to my will. Unless I was careful, I should break her too. She was playing so fair with me, and I wasn't sure I was playing fair with her. Portia is Brutus's harlot, not his wife, I thought uncomfortably. But, of course, there was no question now of playing with each other, fair or otherwise. We were one person.

Conscience-stung I stroked her thigh and kissed her hot cheek. She murmured sleepily in my arms.

We were pretty late for dinner by the time we had had our showers and dressed. I wondered if Jailall guessed why, or if he noticed Diana's flushed face and enormous eyes. Poor Jailall, it must have been very frustrating for him, with Jehorah eight months gone.

"The thing is," I said, "the factory's grinding as well as Ingram can remember. And the cane-cutters are working better than Pattison can remember—I suppose they're trying to make up for lost pay. But we aren't making much sugar. We've only hit the hundred tons a day once this crop."

"Juice purity?" asked Diana. We were sitting in the gallery after dinner.

"Yes. It's still below 80. This damn Indian cane."

"And there's nothing we can do about it?"

"Not a thing. It's all there, fully grown, waiting for us."

She nodded, absorbed. "Just grin and bear it then. At least we don't have to plant any more of the stuff, do we?"

I laughed hollowly. "That's what I thought. When I sent my planting program to Justin, I cut out all the Indian cane and put in the Barbados seedling instead."

"And?" She knew what was coming all right.

"Justin's put in the Indian cane again."

"Just what you'd expect," she said, wrinkling her nose as if there was a bad smell. "On what grounds?"

"Oh, the Barbados cane isn't fully proved yet. And the whole thing was fully gone into six years ago, and the Indian cane has fully lived up to expectations. The field staff and the engineers love it—of course they do. It's easy to grow, easy to grind. And anyway Justin says we can't keep chopping and changing every other year."

"Why can't we?"

"I know. We've got to go on sinking, dropping behind all the other firms, just because he won't take a suggestion from anybody. Do you know our production is below what it was twenty years ago?"

"You don't surprise me. Are the other firms in the same boat?"

"No, not so badly. They never fell for this Indian muck in the same way. Justin was sold it properly by some visiting agronomist—and he's always had a thing about India. You know, the Imperial crown and Durbars and polo and sahibs and wogs knowing their places. Hence Reynolds. Hence this cane."

She sighed. We were sitting in the same chairs Walker and I had sat in that last night when we had got so drunk and he had told me not to waste my life out here. Diana was sitting in Walker's chair. I pushed the memory quickly away.

She seemed in tune with my thoughts. "I begin to see what Walker went through," she said. "Poor man."

I said, "Yes, it broke him in the end. I suppose it killed him." I suddenly couldn't bear my chair any longer. I felt I was being imprisoned, suffocated, as Walker had been. I began to pace up and down the gallery.

I began to talk quickly. "There are so many things I want to do. I want to appoint a Factory Manager. It's ridiculous having the place under divided control. It would have to be Ingram—he's the senior and Swijter would work under him. I don't think he'd work under Swijter. And then Ingram would be responsible for the whole factory. He'd do it well too. And I must have a new Deputy Manager. Not Pattison, he isn't up to it. Miller might do it, he'd have to be promoted over Pattison's head. He might be called Field Manager to show that he hadn't any authority in the factory. And the office, I'd like to cut out all those awful, costing abstracts that waste so much of everyone's time. It's all covered anyway in the expenditure analyses. I could sack half the clerks—save some money there. And then we could afford to buy some wheelbarrows for the shovel gangs." I chuckled and went on: "We could go further and get a tractor and plough. We've got to start mechanizing our cultivation. It's ridiculous to go on sticking to laborers with forks and shovels just like the old days when they were slaves and couldn't strike. The other estates are starting to mechanize. We've got to do it too."

I broke off and looked at Diana. She was watching me as if her life depended on it.

"Well, let's do it," she said.

"How can we? Tractors cost money and we haven't got any money. We need a new evaporator too. Anyway," I added gloomily, "Justin will turn it all down on principle. I tried some of it on him in London."

"Yes, but everything's changed since then. You're the big man now. And wouldn't Mr. Nelson back you on this?"

"I don't know. He'd hardly go against Justin on a technical matter. And he's there to see we keep on the rails and bring down our overdraft, not to launch out into buying tractors."

"But wouldn't he see that it was essential to us in the long run?"

"Well, he might—when our overdraft's a bit lower. And if the thing's put to him properly."

There was a moment's pause. Then she too was standing up, talking.

"Darling, Nelson likes you, doesn't he? I mean, he'd support you on anything reasonable, wouldn't he?"

"Oh yes, I think he likes me. He put me into this job."

"Exactly. And you're responsible to him and the other directors for running this place properly. It's like appointing a general. He's put in to win the battle. He can pick his own men and do what he likes. He doesn't have to refer everything back to the War Office."

"Doesn't he? I thought they did nowadays."

She went on unperturbed. "Well anyway, I think it's sink or swim. Why can't you get on and do what you want and let Justin go to blazes?"

"Just ignore him?"

"Yes. Just don't tell him what you're doing. Don't send him any more of those planting programs and things."

"He'd be cabling for them soon enough."

"Well, let him. You can keep him quiet. Send him some nice wooly letters about the weather and how we're all pulling together and putting our shoulders to the wheel. Tell him all about the estate club. He'd love that."

I laughed. "He'd find out in the end. These things get out. And anyway he's talking of coming out after Christmas."

"Oh God! Is he really?" She looked aghast.

"He's due for a visit. But he may not come. He doesn't come regularly. It rather depends how cold a winter it is in England."

She relaxed. "Oh I see. Well, we can jump that when we come to it. But, darling, what can he do when he does find out? He can't dig up the cane again. It'll already be growing."

"He can sack me for insubordination," I said.

She looked at me steadily. "You know, I don't believe he'd do that now, even if he wanted to."

I said slowly, "No, I don't think so either."

It was an astounding thought, being impregnable.

"I don't think I could buy a tractor without him knowing," I said. "He'd see the order in London office. But we might do the rest. What do you say? Shall we chance it?"

She opened her mouth to speak and then shut it again. She watched me expectantly, smiling her little secret smile. I knew she was meaning that it was my decision. She was still flushed and bright-eyed, and very lovely despite the circles under her eyes. I let my eyes wander over her and I thought of ourselves together a couple of hours ago. It wasn't a very difficult decision to take.

I came close and put my arms round her. "There'll be no holding us now," I said.

The next day I appointed Ingram Factory Manager and abolished the costing abstracts and sacked seven clerks and made Miller Field Manager and told him to get on planting the Barbados cane and warned him to expect the arrival of six wheelbarrows. It caused a local sensation.

2

DURING THE NEXT few weeks we settled down into the routine of estate life. After all the comings and goings, the strikes and the innovations, the excitement of taking over the job, life seemed a bit flat. I told myself that the last four or five months had been pretty hectic and crisis-ridden for me, and I didn't want it to go on like that for the next twenty years, did I? Of course that was true enough, but it was also true that I had to a large extent been living on the kick my new-found power and position gave me. As the weeks went by, the drug became more familiar and less effective. Indeed, I had quite a reaction against it.

I got a bit introspective about myself and started wondering again whether I had taken the right decision in coming back here. It was coming home to me that the manager of a plantation doesn't really stand on the summit of imperial glory and that I was turning into a pompous tinpot little dictator, a potential Justin-type, an irrevocable misfit in the larger and greater world outside. I was becoming, not so slowly, just the sort of colonial planter Fiona had wanted me to be. The thought punctured a lot of my swollen grandeur and I thought back with shame on my heavy lectures to Diana on the proper behavior of a General Manager's wife. I remembered too that it was three months or more since I had even opened a book unconnected with sugar, and in a spasm of remorse I bought some Everyman classics next time I was in Port Catalan. There's nothing like *The Brothers Karamazov* for making you see that making sugar and controlling other men's lives isn't necessarily the highest activity of the human soul.

Not that I didn't have a certain amount of reason to be pleased with myself. The factory was grinding fairly well, the money was coming in, the overdraft was coming down steadily. My various reorganizations seemed to be working out and I heard a highly gratifying rumor that Finlays were thinking of something of the same sort for themselves. I was emboldened to carry on the work and reorganize the pan-boilers, the foremen and the gang drivers. But the things I really wanted to do needed money and that we hadn't got. I couldn't see how we were ever going to get it. It was, in the long view, a very depressing thought.

I was also unhappy about Diana. She very quickly became bored with bridge and the other wives, and her efforts to do some welfare work aroused only incredulity from the rest of the staff, instant hostility from the E.P.A. Welfare Officer and apathy from the laborers themselves. This might not necessarily have discouraged us, if Diana herself had not begun to lose her energy and enthusiasm. She was becoming very listless and tired, the circles deeper under her eyes, the cheeks white and hollow. She slept badly and only played with her food. She didn't seem to want to read or play tennis. Playing with the children exhausted her. She was still keen enough on my work and it seemed as if she were hoarding her strength for that. I wondered if she were really ill or, just as likely, pregnant. But she insisted that there was nothing wrong with her and there was no need to see a doctor.

"Are you quite sure?" I asked. "Wouldn't it be better to make sure?"

"No, really, I'm fine," she protested. "No need to fuss over me." I looked at her closely. "No, darling, it's not a baby, if that's what you think."

It was no surprise to me that she guessed my thoughts. Since our great reunion we were very much in tune. I took her hand and squeezed it.

"I'm sorry in a way," she said. "I mean in a way it would be nice to have another one. But—" she broke off and added heavily, "I don't think I could face it at the moment. All that sickness and everything. Perhaps later on, when I'm more used to this place."

She smiled wanly. I felt both disappointed and relieved. Six months ago I might have had harsh thoughts that it would be good for Diana to have some more children. But not any more.

I kissed her gently. "Perhaps it's hookworm," I said.

She laughed a little. "Really, darling, the ideas you have. I'm always so careful about not being barefoot." She made a wry face. "I'll go and see a doctor if it sets your mind at rest, but I'm sure there's nothing the matter. Except early rising—that never suited me."

"It's not so early now, not since I gave up going to Manager's Orders. I mean, not five o'clock any more."

"For this relief much thanks. But to me half-past six is still early rising."

"Perhaps we could make it quarter to seven," I said. "Don't you get a sleep in the afternoon?"

She sighed. "Oh, I try. But the telephone rings, or someone comes banging on the back door, begging."

"Surely Jailall sees them off."

"Oh yes. But the noise usually wakes me. Or else one of the children won't sleep. That was what it was today. Mark had a bash at Jane."

I smiled. "About time too. The male sex was getting very henpecked. High time he asserted himself."

"But not so much fun for the rest of us. I don't think it was his masculinity so much as the heat or constipation. We're none of us quite settled in yet. Oh, don't worry, darling, we'll be all right."

"Good," I said. "But do go and see a doctor just to set my mind at rest. Why not come down with me to Port Catalan tomorrow? Make a break for you. It's the Godsells' cocktail party, if you'd like to go to that."

She seemed to brighten. "All right. It would make a change, and there are some things I want to buy." She paused for a moment and then she counter-attacked. "What about you, darling? You don't seem so good lately."

"Me? Oh, I'm fine. Putting on weight like anything. Can't do up the top button of my shorts any more."

"Oh, that's just whisky and yams. Local cooking." She looked at me seriously. "No, I had the feeling you'd got something on your mind. Something big—and worrying."

I hesitated so long that it wasn't possible to deny it. I thought of pouring out all my misgivings about whether I had done right in taking the job and whether we were ever going to be really happy growing sugar. But that would have been sheer cruelty, scrubbing off all the scabs, reopening all the sores just as they were starting to heal. If Diana was resigned to her new life, the least I could do was not to unsettle her.

Instead I gave her my other worry to chew on.

"But I thought things were going well at the moment," she said.

"Oh, yes. From the short-term point of view, everything's fine. But it's not nearly so good on the long-term picture. Every cent we make at the moment is going into bringing down the overdraft, when it ought to be ploughed back into the estate. Both the N.S.C. and Finlays are pouring money into their estates. If we don't do it too, we shall just fall further and further behind till we go out altogether."

She nodded. "You mean the tractors and cultivators?"

"Oh yes. But the factory needs a lot of money spent on it too. And there are hundreds of little things like new irrigation pumps and pest-sprayers and the roads and the loco-line and trucks and wagons. The N.S.C. reckon that in three years time there won't be a cart or an ox left at Trafalgar. It'll all be railway wagons or half-tracks. For the laborers as well as for the cane. We've got to do that too, somehow."

"Can't we get the money from anywhere?"

"Not from the bank, at least not at the moment. They're on the opposite tack just now. Anyway I don't think they'd finance a major program like that. What we need is more capital."

"Well, can't we find that? What about these finance firms in the City?"

"Oh yes, Justin's always talking about trying them. But nothing ever comes of it."

"Perhaps he doesn't try very hard."

"Oh, easily not. I don't expect he likes the idea of someone else muscling in on his private firm. They'd want seats on the board and all sorts of tiresome things like that. But I may be wrong, he may have tried them without any luck. I don't suppose many people would fancy putting money into this colony at the moment, especially into such a small rocky firm."

"With a small rocky chairman."

"Quite. And if it were made into a public company, that would apply even more strongly." I shook my head. "I don't know, there may be something cooking we haven't been told about. I'll try and find out when he's out here."

Diana was frozen. "Justin? He's definitely coming, then?"

"Says he is. He hopes to snatch a brief Christmas holiday at St. Moritz and fly out here at the end of January."

"Pity it's got to be such a brief holiday," she said sarcastically. "What happens when he finds out all the things you've been doing here without telling him?"

"Sky-high explosion, I should think. I'll try and keep as much as I can from him, get him bogged down in a mass of reports and figures. We'll keep him well liquored up too—he always drinks pretty heavily out here. He'll spend a lot of time in the club here and in Port Catalan holding forth and standing rounds of drinks."

"Do we have to be there too?"

"Oh yes. We tag along in the background, laughing at all his jokes like good courtiers."

"I can't wait," she said. "But darling, he's bound to find out about some things. I mean, he may not spot the different cane, but he's bound to hear about Ingram and Miller and all those clerks. There'll be trouble then."

"Oh yes," I said. "I daresay there'll be a blazing row whenever he's not actually standing drinks in the club. This is going to be the test of strength. We foresaw that, didn't we? See if we really have enough backing to ride out the storm."

"I expect we shall. Rather fun to have a big showdown with Justin and win. I should enjoy that. But oh! how I hate rows." She sighed wearily. "Perhaps he'll be so angry he'll have a seizure. Better still, perhaps he'll break his ankle skiing and not come at all."

I smiled. "Yes, they can't stop us dreaming, can they?"

Christmas was coming to the colony. Across the narrow Port Catalan streets radios blared through open windows the same two carols over and over again, "Jingle Bells" and "I'm Dreaming of a White Christmas."

"It makes a change from 'Good King Wenceslaus,'" said Diana. "Or do we come on to that later?"

"Oh no, we stick on these two right through."

She said, "There's something rather sweet about these blacks and Indians mooning about white Christmases and sleigh bells, when they've never seen a snow-flake in their lives."

"They'd be terrified if they did," I said. "They'd think they were all going to catch colds and die. Like rain, only worse. No, I think it's one of the triumphs of the Anglo-Saxon race. Most of the world has a hot Christmas but we've managed to persuade them all that it ought to be cold and frosty. So they have to pretend it is. I suppose Dickens sold it to them."

"I think it's ridiculous," said Diana shortly. "Why can't they admit it's a hot country and leave it at that? All that cotton-wool in the drug-store windows. It means nothing here."

"'Hot ice and wondrous strange snow,'" I quoted dreamily. "It's becoming part of the folk-lore of the place, like jumbies and evil spirits and the weather always changing at the full moon."

Diana said, "Mrs. Hughes told me she always covers the mango trees in her garden with artificial icicles. Do I have to do that too?"

I laughed. "Not if you don't want to. But you have to give a present to every child on the estate."

"Grown-ups too?"

"No, only the children. The Walkers used to give a children's party, but I think we might skip that."

"I'll do it if you want me to." She looked a little anxious.

"No, we won't this year. We shan't really be able to. I'm told we're going to be asked to dinner at Government House on Christmas night, and we've got to go to that."

"Royal command?"

"Just about. There'll probably be about thirty of us there, and we'll all play Consequences afterwards. The real McCoy—five courses, hot soup, hot turkey, hot plum pudding, hot mince pies—"

"Don't!" she said faintly. "It makes me sweat to think of it." She paused, while I thought of Christmas trees and paper decorations and boisterous games and the women with great dark patches on the backs of their evening dresses. You sweat in a different place in the tropics, in the small of the back, not in the arm-pits.

Diana said dreamily, "What I'd like would be cold consommé and cold salmon and new potatoes and asparagus and raspberries and cream and iced coffee."

I picked up her nostalgia. "I know. In a marquee, with the plop of oars from the regatta on the river outside."

She shook her head sadly. "Why can't we ever have cold food out here?"

"Some people have tried it," I said. "But it never works. People won't eat it. They say it would give them colds in the stomach."

Diana snorted and then said, "I don't know, I daresay I couldn't eat it either if it came to the point."

I listened to the radio for a moment. "That sleigh ride ought to give you quite an appetite."

Diana made a wry face. We both listened to the radio till the song ended.

Diana went to see the doctor who told her there was nothing wrong with her and gave her an iron tonic. Then she took the car and went shopping while I did a morning's work in the town office. She picked me up later, and on our way to lunch we drove down the Esplanade with its columnar royal palms, across Queen's Square, white and dusty, encased by solemn mock-classical Government Buildings and along the road that led to Harbor Point. We stopped the car and walked out to the end of the jetty.

All round us was water—in the harbor still and glassy, the little boats, the shabby schooners, the lumpish freighters at the wharves, silent, deserted and immobile in the noon heat. Beyond the harbor wall was the Caribbean, shimmering and opalescent, the water faintly rippled by the trades. On the other side was the picturesqueness of Port Catalan, the palms, the sprinkled white dolls houses, the rusty corrugated roofs. In the distance were the green scrubby hills. It was like a travel poster, the sort they put up in agency windows in a sleeting January to lure you into taking an expensive cruise to the sun.

I looked out across the blue, blue sea trying to estimate the exact angle on which the next bit of land over the horizon would be Devonshire, seductive and possibly sleeting. I had worked out the angle on previous solitary expeditions. It was about two fingers' breadth to the right of the lighthouse, though I daresay I wasn't properly allowing for the curve of the earth or something. But it didn't really matter.

We stood for quite a while without speaking. Then I stole a glance at Diana. She was staring in the same direction as I had been and I knew she was thinking more or less the same thoughts, though perhaps less concerned with navigational angles. Below her black sunglasses her cheeks were white with the nausea of home sickness. And I wasn't helping much either.

We went on staring across the sea towards England. Anyone might have thought we were watching a ship-wreck.

Diana had been to one or two of the big Port Catalan cocktail parties when she first arrived. Enough to have succeeded in fitting some of the names and faces together, but not yet enough to know every single person in the room. The parties, the nearest thing the colony could produce to urban sophistication, seemed to bring out some of her old vitality. She talked eagerly and amusingly (though that may have been mainly politeness to her hosts) and there was a little color in her cheeks (though that may have been mainly artificial). The faces round her were still tolerably unfamiliar and she was not yet at my own stage of total ennui.

She was talking to Fiona and, momentarily disengaged from any conversation, I stood and watched them. Since getting my marching orders, I had deliberately kept as clear as possible of Fiona. When we did meet, I had been brief to the point of curtness. Sometimes I toyed with the idea of saying something really savage and hurting, but I knew it wouldn't work. She probably wouldn't understand it, for one thing.

I watched her now, remembering carefully what I had done to her, calling myself a regular Don Juan. She was just one of my sexual conquests, a scalp at my belt. But I don't think I really believed it for a moment. It was I who was the scalp at her belt and the proof of it that I was here tonight, a typical planter, staring at her across the room.

She and Diana seemed to have a lot to say to each other. I was puzzled and rather displeased. They had really nothing in common—except me. Were they talking about me? Surely not. Neither of them knew anything about my complicated personal relationship with the other. Probably only cocktail chit-chat. Perhaps Fiona was trying to turn Diana into the perfect planter's wife. That wasn't as odd a thought now as it once would have been. But I didn't like it. I didn't want Fiona barging in telling Diana just what a round peg in a round hole I now was. I had just decided to go across and break them up, when a voice stopped me.

"Good evening, Mr. Pemberton."

It was McDougall, smiling up at me. I greeted him and he said, nodding at the girls, "I see they're getting on very well. Fiona likes your wife so much."

"She likes Fiona," I said politely. "Though, of course, they haven't really seen very much of each other."

He was looking at me intently and I suddenly wondered if he knew.

He went on in the same toneless voice. "She liked your children too. It was so kind of you to look after her so well."

I looked him full in the eye. "It was nothing," I mumbled. "A pleasure."

"A pleasure for her too. Very much so."

I swallowed some whisky. He couldn't be going on like this over just one drink in our flat. He must mean—

I changed the subject quickly. "Diana hasn't been to one of these parties for some time. We're such country bumpkins down at Malmaison. Still, it's good to get away occasionally, isn't it?"

"You must bring her to town more often," he said courteously.

I looked round for some means of escape.

"Mr. Pemberton," he said tonelessly, "may I have a quiet word with you?"

I almost choked. "Yes, of course."

"It is a little public here. There is something I want to say to you, in private. Perhaps we could go out into the garden. I don't think we should be missed for a few minutes."

I knew what I was in for, and I rubbed my cheek-bones instinctively. I thought of refusing, but he was already leading the way across the gallery, down the steps into the garden. Dully, full of foreboding I followed him.

On the steps down it suddenly occurred to me that it was like a scene out of a thriller. The sinister inscrutable Chinese taking me out of the brilliant gathering into the dark deserted garden. Men would leap out of the bushes and take me . . . Would I be tortured? What would they do with my body? Hide it in a laundry vat? Or would I be rescued in the nick of time by a hero, a journalist, say, in search of a story?

The thought made me smile and suddenly I got all my self-confidence back. I was going to be given an almighty dressing-down. Well, I wouldn't stand for it. I wasn't a schoolboy. I'd tell him in return just what a little bitch his daughter was . . . Or he might threaten to tell Justin. Or ask for compensation, for damaging one of his assets. My daughter, my ducats.

McDougall walked away from the lighted house till we could barely see each other. Then he stopped abruptly.

"Mr. Pemberton, I wonder if you have heard recently from your cousin?"

I was astonished. "Yes. A couple of days ago."

"Did he say anything about the future of your firm?"

This was getting odder and odder. I looked at him, but he was only a faint silhouette. There would have been nothing to see anyway.

"Not especially. It was an ordinary business letter about the crop."

"I see." He paused and I waited for him to explain himself. "I sometimes wonder," he went on at last, "if the days of small family plantations aren't coming to an end. There was a time when this colony had sixteen sugar estates each with a separate owner. Now the N.S.C. owns nine, we own two, and you own one. The other four have gone out of cultivation. You are really the only one left of the small old firms."

"I know." I knew it all only too well.

"Things are very difficult for small firms these days. You have to be big to stand up to these strikes and difficulties. And you have to develop and mechanize. The hand methods we have all used for the last hundred years won't do any more."

I didn't interrupt. He might have been speaking my own thoughts.

"I imagine you have plans for developing your estate."

"Oh yes," I said quickly.

"I am sure of that. I gather you have been doing quite a lot of organizing since you took over at Malmaison. We have all been very interested in your experiments. We may copy some of them."

"Oh good," I murmured deprecatingly. "They're only fairly minor things."

"Exactly. For the big developments you need a lot of capital. I don't know, but I fancy that may be your problem. It is certainly one of ours, and we are twice your size."

I wasn't going to confirm or deny that to a rival, so I said nothing. He glanced round him.

"This is in confidence, of course," he said.

"Of course."

"As you know, as well as these sugar estates, we also have an oil company in Trinidad. That also needs development and capital and we cannot manage to do both. Now we have just had an offer for our oil company from one of the big oil concerns. A very substantial offer in cash. It seemed to our chairman—do you know Mr. Finlay?"

"I've met him. I know John, of course."

"Oh yes. John is much better. He is working in our London office now. He's not to come out here again for some time."

"Poor man," I said drily.

"Oh, Mr. Pemberton, how can you say that! You see, if we accept this offer from the oil company, we shall have plenty of capital for developing and rehabilitating our estates. And Mr. Finlay thought that if our company could amalgamate in some way with yours, there would be great advantages for both of us."

I took a deep breath of warm air. "Yes."

McDougall went on in his quiet unemphatic voice: "The capital would be available for the development of Malmaison too. And the three estates together in one economic unit would be a much stronger business, greater resources, more flexible. And there would be a saving in administrative expenses."

"That's so," I agreed.

"It seems to us a very good idea, but I don't know how it will seem to you. Your family have always been very keen on their family traditions in the business. Mr. Finlay is going to talk to Major Pemberton about it and see how he feels. But he first wanted me to sound you out privately and find out your views before we go any further."

For once I was in no doubt about my own views. I stared straight into the dark mass of his face.

"I'm very interested indeed," I said carefully. "In principle at any rate. Can you tell me a little more about this amalgamation?"

I told Diana about it that night in bed, lying on my back, naked, watching my cigarette smoke drifting up, disappearing through the white opaqueness of the lamp-lit mosquito net into the darkness beyond.

"They're suggesting a straightforward take-over," I said. "Of course it's all still very tentative and hush-hush. They want to buy out all our shareholders and take the firm over lock, stock and barrel. Run it in with their business."

"Why do they want us so much?" Diana asked.

"Oh, I think Finlays feel the same as I do. In this business you've got to expand or die. This is their way of expanding."

"But, even so, I wouldn't have thought we were a very attractive investment. Though we're better than we were, aren't we?"

"Oh yes. Six months ago I don't think Finlays would have given a thank-you for us."

"That's rather a compliment to you, darling, isn't it?"

"Yes, I suppose it is, in a way." I burrowed under the net and stubbed out my cigarette in the bedside ash-tray, saying quite casually, "If this amalgamation does go through, they want me to become their Estates Manager. Run their three estates as one economic unit."

"Oh darling!" Diana was up on one elbow, looking at me. "That would be a pretty big job, wouldn't it?"

"Three times my present one. I only hope I'm up to it."

"Of course you are. Oh, Hugo, I'm so proud of you. What did you say to him?"

"I said I was very interested. I couldn't say more at this stage." I fumbled for another cigarette and lit it. "I must say, it would solve a lot of problems if this thing does come off. We'd have all the capital we wanted and we could do things much more economically—share heavy equipment and stores between the three estates. Perhaps concentrate the distilling in one place. And we could move the staff from one to the other. They'd like that—give them a change and better hopes of promotion. Finlays mean to take over all our staff, or as much as they can absorb. They want to close our Port Catalan and London offices; that'll save a lot of overhead, if not on salaries. They want Stevens, of course."

Diana said with a laugh, "I can't think they want the London office staff, do they?"

I smiled back. "You'd hardly think so, but they may not find out about them till too late. I daresay they'll take on the best, Jolly, Hodges, Phillimore, and pension off the rest. They're taking on all our pensioners anyway."

"It all sounds too good to be true." She crossed her fingers and held them up. "Let's hope it comes off." She paused for a moment. "What are the snags?"

I snorted. "That's right, pour on the cold bath, wake me out of my pipe dream. No, darling, you're quite right. Two snags mainly. One is the price for the firm. McDougall said something about four hundred thousand, which wouldn't be at all bad if we hadn't got to pay back the overdraft out of it."

"Does McDougall know about our overdraft?"

"I don't know. He shouldn't, but I expect he does. We'll have to tell him anyway, before they make a firm offer. But that leaves a hundred and fifty thousand, partly in cash, partly in special new prefs, for the present ordinary and preference shareholders. Justin will get the lion's share, of course, and old Mrs. Wright will have quite a whack, mostly prefs."

"What'll your mother get?"

"I can't quite work it out, but I think about forty thousand, just under."

"Sounds a fortune to me."

"Yes, it would be to us. But it's less than she's got now. And in Gilt Edged stock it'll only bring in sixteen or seventeen hundred a year. That's five hundred less than she was getting before and she wasn't managing on that. Still, the new income would be more secure. That's something."

"Would she have to leave South Meon?"

"I don't know. Maybe. Or perhaps I could make up the difference to her out of my salary. I gathered they'd pay me pretty well what I asked, within reason."

Diana chuckled and put her hand on my shoulder. "Darling, you do make me feel important."

I moved my head and stroked her hand with my damp and stubbly cheek. She didn't seem to mind.

"Of course, it may work out better. That figure is only tentative. We may be able to push Finlays up a bit more on their offer. Or make some different arrangements about the overdraft. Perhaps Finlays might take on some of it and pay it off gradually out of Malmaison profits."

"Yes, why not? It doesn't seem to me as if the snag is so insuperable after all. I breathe again. What's the other snag?"

I crossed my knees and looked up at her. "The other snag," I said, "is that I don't think any of it's going to come off."

"Why shouldn't it?"

"Because of Justin. You don't think he's going to like this scheme, do you? And apart from being Chairman, he's got a controlling interest in the shares."

"Yes," said Diana slowly. She didn't look too disappointed and I thought she must have foreseen this all along. "You mean because of the family, and all that."

"Just so. He'll have to discuss it with us all, of course, but can't you just imagine the speeches we're going to get?" I did a falsetto imitation. " 'The great name of Pemberton has been and still is one of the most honored, most respected and most admired names in the long history of the island of Natividad and indeed in the proud story of the West Indies themselves and never, while I have the honor to be Chairman of this company, could I agree to a course which would expunge our name and our traditions from the whatever it is.' "

"Don't! You give me the willies. But couldn't it be got around? I mean, couldn't the name be kept on somewhere? And couldn't Justin be made to see that it would be worth while for the advantages?"

"What? Selling our birthright for filthy lucre? No, the real reason he won't like it is that, as far as I can make out, there won't be any place for him in the new set-up."

Diana stared at me. I nodded slowly.

"I gather he's been patronizing them all for so long," I went on, "that now they won't have him at any price. Not even as a sweetener for the deal. Of course McDougall didn't put it quite like that, but I think that was what he meant."

"So Justin would be right out on his ear?"

"Exactly."

Diana began to laugh, first quietly, then uncontrollably, writhing helplessly on the bed, the tears pouring down her cheeks. It was infectious and soon I was nearly as bad as she was, idiotic, crazy, mad as hatters. Chuckling Doris through the thin wooden partition must have thought we were tickling each other to death.

3

Bells jingling, dreaming of a white Christmas, hoping for merree and bright days, we dashed through the snow in our one-horse open sleigh. Everything ran exactly to form. The factory closed down for the holiday. Diana produced presents for all the white estate children, including the new Allen baby. I decorated the plastic Christmas tree with plastic icicles and lights. The twins gazed at it in starry rapture until Mark clouted Jane on the back of her head with part of an airport control tower. For this he was duly smacked and they were both still howling when we left for Port Catalan.

Dinner at Government House also went as expected. There were thirty-four of us with name cards and orders of seniority and a band and the Queen's health and funny paper hats and funny mottoes in crackers, and balloons which we burst by throwing the forks at them. After dinner we played, not Consequences, but charades. Mrs. Grainger turned out to be a fiend at amateur theatricals and gave us hell for being so sheepish in our parts. There was always a half hour wait between scenes while she rehearsed us vigorously outside. The next day we signed the Government House book as a mark of gratitude.

We returned to Malmaison for the resumption of grinding and then, in no time, we were back in Port Catalan for the New Year's Eve ball at the Police Barracks. We sang *Auld Lang Syne* and Diana was rather shaken to find herself kissed hard on the mouth by, so she said, seventy-two men, half of whom she did not know by name. I said I hoped she hadn't picked up thrush or pyorrhoea, but she said alcohol was a disinfectant. I had also kissed the twenty women nearest to me, many of them middle-aged and sagging and girlishly coy. One of the more enticing ones was, of course, Fiona. I was determined not to miss her. She turned away her mouth at the last minute and I caught her where she would have had a dimple.

"Happy New Year, Hugo," she said.

"Happy New Year, Fiona," I said.

There was really nothing more to say. I turned away and kissed Mrs. Grainger with ardor. The next day we signed the Government House book to mark the start of the New Year.

We had a nice Christmas letter from Justin. He would be at Suvretta House till the 25th of January and we could cable him there if there was anything really urgent. But, please, only if it was really urgent, as he was crying for mercy. He had had his nose to the grindstone now for so long that he really thought he owed it to himself to have a really good break away from it all and set himself up for all the work he would have to do when he visited Natividad. So would we please wish him lots of sun and snow. He would be arriving, if nothing unforeseen happened in the meantime, on the 4th of February and he looked forward to seeing us both again and to getting down to things with me. As a well-trained uncle-substitute he would be bringing presents for the children with him.

There was not a word about the take-over by Finlays.

At this time there arrived a packing-case containing six Swedish electric calculating machines, destined for the Malmaison office. God knows what they must have cost. I was furious and exploded to Diana:

"What a way to make sugar! What a way to spend our money! Not a new evaporator, not wheelbarrows, but calculators! Just right for the clerks I sacked to use in working out the abstracts I abolished. Justin, huh!"

She was more phlegmatic. "Just look on them as Christmas presents, darling. They're just what he'd love, nice and gadgety like his watch. And expensive too. Visitors will be terribly impressed. That'll be something, won't it?"

I was a bit mollified and in due course handed them out like Father Christmas to Stevens and Hughes and the clerks I hadn't sacked. I think they were a bit defeated by them, and I never saw any of them in use, but I kept one back for the General Manager's personal use and Diana used to play with it, making it click and whirr away as she divided 61437.906 into 14182973.119. It made rather a nice noise and in the end I got quite fond of it too.

Diana and I were beginning to feel rather like a pendulum, swinging rhythmically to and fro between Malmaison and Port Catalan. Early in the New Year we returned again to town for McDougall's cocktail party. In view of the possible take-over of the firm, it was important that we should both attend the party. I also liked Fiona to see Diana and me together.

They were standing shaking hands at the head of the stairs, as we shuffled upwards to them. First McDougall, grave and polite, then Fiona in a brand-new hair-style and a white frock which emphasized the color of her skin. Beyond was a young Chinese, a good four inches shorter than Fiona, with a square face and horn-rimmed glasses.

Fiona said to Diana, who was ahead of me, "May I introduce my fiancé, Dr. Lee-a-Chow. Darling, this is Mrs. Pemberton. Mr. Hugo Pemberton."

We congratulated them both warmly. Fiona only met my eyes for half a second, the flashed entreaty of a scared animal. Then she looked away.

"Thank you," she murmured with a nervous giggle.

I glanced back at McDougall. Between guests, he was watching me, beaming, looking like a cat with a saucer of cream.

"This is great news, very exciting," I said vaguely and went on into the room, taking a drink from the tray as I passed.

"How very exciting!" said someone beside me. "I'd no idea. Nobody had said anything about it." She sounded peeved.

"Who is he, do you know?" I asked.

Someone else said he thought he was the assistant vet at the Agricultural Experimental Station.

"Of course," I said. "I knew I'd seen him somewhere before."

So it was a vet. Not a doctor, not a dentist, not a laundry proprietor, but a vet. Young, educated, professional, Chinese, but was he nice too? I glanced over the heads at the three of them. Difficult to say. He looked inscrutable behind his glasses. Anyway, the thing was Fiona had found someone at last. Or—a thought struck me, sparked from their remembered expressions. Had McDougall found him for his daughter? Was McDougall marrying off his daughter quickly before she could commit any further indiscretions? Before she could get entangled with another married man? Before their new young lecherous Estates Manager joined their firm? I looked at them again, wondering.

I tried to remember what she had said to me that evening in New York so impossibly long ago. Even if she were being pressed to marry the wrong man, she'd put up with it because you shouldn't fight your destiny. Courageous self-denying words when spoken in the abstract across a dinner table after a couple of drinks. But when you meet it in the flesh, it makes you squirm.

The voices round me were purring with excitement. My dear, he doesn't look very exciting, does he. I should have thought she could have done better for herself, after all her father is a member of the Union Club. Oh, I don't know, I think he looks very nice. Yes, I heard he was very nice. But no one knows a thing about him, he can't cut much ice. They say he's very good with fallow pigs. Well, that should come in handy when. . . .

I looked across at Fiona, giggling shyly at someone's congratulations. Her young man beside her was giggling too. The young man whom perhaps she was being pressed to marry and who was dull and not a member of the Union Club and very nice and didn't cut much ice and was good with fallow pigs and was now being torn to pieces behind her back.

Poor Fiona, I thought. And then, remembering, No, not poor Fiona at all.

I didn't succeed in getting a word with McDougall until the party was actually breaking up. With only a brief moment available I got through the necessary preliminary congratulations as quickly as I could. He thanked me courteously. If I had had any part in his plans, he gave no sign.

"I hope they'll be very happy."

"Thank you. I'm sure they will."

I paused fractionally before changing the subject. "By the way, is there any more news of what we talked about last time?"

He looked at me in surprise. "But yes. I thought you would have heard. Did not Major Pemberton tell you?"

"No." I was torn between suspense and anger with Justin at having to find out about the future of our firm from an outsider.

McDougall kept me waiting a second or two longer. Then he said in a low voice, "Oh, he turned it down flat. He wouldn't hear of it. I hear he was very emphatic. Quite short."

The pain flooded into my cheek-bones. I rubbed them slowly, staring at McDougall in disappointment.

He shrugged his shoulders, a little miniature gesture. "I think it is a great pity. But there! Perhaps later on—"

He turned to another guest who was waiting to say good-bye. I walked away trembling.

I blew my top off to Diana on the way home.

"It's the absolute limit. The one thing that might have saved the firm and he goes and turns it down without a moment's thought.

Just thinking of himself and his own position. All his talk about sacrifices and doing your duty, and all he cares about is his own position and his suite at St. Moritz. He owes himself a good holiday. Christ!"

Diana met me more than half-way. "It makes one so bloody angry one could yell. Why doesn't someone stick a knife into him? Tie him up in a sack and throw him in the sea. I'd willingly do it myself. We might do it when he's out here. That's quite a thought." She broke off as I took the corner into Queen Street too fast. "Steady, darling. Let's keep ourselves in one piece. Of course, we knew Justin was going to do this, didn't we? I mean, you prophesied it."

"Yes, I know I did. But it doesn't make it any easier to bear. It's such a waste of a wonderful chance, and it won't come again. No, the bit that really riles me is that he did it all off his own bat without telling a soul. He'd no right to do that. On a big thing like this he ought to have consulted the other directors. And the shareholders. And he hasn't told anybody. Just slapped it down and hushed it up. I had to hear about it from McDougall. That was pretty shaming."

That angle didn't seem to rile Diana so much. "Hugo, when you say he'd no right to do that, do you mean it was illegal?"

"I don't know about illegal. I think it was improper and intolerably high-handed. But there's not much we can do about it. Even if we forced a show-down, he's still got the voting power to win. It would come to the same in the end. No, we'll just have to work on him when he comes out here and see if we get any change."

"Perhaps we could lecture him on putting the firm first and making sacrifices."

"I think we'd be more likely to succeed by flattery. Butter him up. Ugh!"

Diana said, "Maybe he'll get buried in an avalanche. That would solve everything."

"I don't think he skiis much. He prefers the fancy-dress parties and diamond balls."

We put the car away and went up to the flat. In the sudden light I saw the color in Diana's cheeks, the shine in her chocolate eyes, the refreshed vitality. Anger was very becoming to her. I sucked in my breath sharply as the thought of glad and total possession lifted me like spring. How could I ever have preferred Fiona, I wondered.

"Fancy Fiona springing that on us," I said.

"Well, it's quite a normal way of announcing an engagement," she said reasonably. "It's the sort of thing that happens to girls, you know."

"Yes, I suppose so. What did you make of him?"

"Oh, just what you'd expect. They'll suit each other fine."

"I thought he seemed a bit dull," I said.

"Well, that's all right. She's a dull girl."

I couldn't make up my mind whether to defend Fiona or agree.

Diana looked at me. "But very pretty," she remarked. "We've always thought that, haven't we."

"Yes, she is." I paused and then added, "I don't know, but I had a feeling that her heart isn't in this. I wondered if old man McDougall mightn't be marrying her off before she could get into trouble."

"Is she the sort of girl to get into trouble?"

"Oh, I daresay. With wolves like me around."

We grinned at each other. Doris came in and told us that dinner would be ready in a few minutes and would we like a next drink. Diana refused and, after a second, so did I. There was something I had to say to Diana alone.

"You knew about her and me, didn't you?"

"Of course, darling. I put you up to it, didn't I?"

"What I mean is, I took your advice and called in at her flat one day."

"You are a big bad wolf. Was it fun?"

"Yes, it was, rather."

"Better than with me?"

"More different. Not better. Just different."

Diana gave a little laugh. "I'm glad. We girls don't like to think we're all the same, you know. You must tell me all about it some time."

I asked, "Would you really like me to?"

"Yes." She sounded a trifle uncertain. "At least I think I would. But not now. I don't know. I always thought I would if this happened, but now I'm not so sure. Just tell me one thing. Were you with her when you decided—" She broke off.

"Yes," I said. I was defenseless now against anything she might give me.

"History is made lying down," she remarked in a voice I couldn't place. "Who was it who said that?"

"You. I don't know of anyone else."

That was all she said about it. I was deeply grateful for her forbearance.

"I'm sorry," I said. "But it's all over now. Really it is. Completely finished. I couldn't look at her any more now if I tried. Not any more."

She smiled. "You hadn't better unless you want a jealous vet after you. He might do some horrible things to you so do be careful. But I'm glad you had fun. I like things to be nice for you. I just didn't mean you to take it too seriously."

I said, "You're very nice, I didn't mean it to happen. At least, not in cold blood. It just—"

"Oh darling, for heaven's sake don't start feeling guilty about it. I'm not the jealous possessive type. Perhaps I ought to be; perhaps I'd be a more satisfactory person if I was. But, there it is; I'm not."

"You don't care then?"

"Of course I care, but I love you enough not to care too much. I want you to have everything you want and I'm not so vain as to think I can provide it all myself. At least I think I'm not."

There didn't seem to be any answer to that except humility, and that is a silent virtue.

Later I became aware of Diana laughing.

"What's so funny?"

She shook her head. "Really, so like a man! Now the whole thing's over and there's no reason why anybody should ever know about it, you have to blurt it all out to me."

I stared at her in concern. "Would you rather I hadn't?"

"Oh yes. No. I'm not sure. Part of me's glad and part's sorry."

"Which part's bigger?"

She came and put her arm round me. "That's something you can tell me one day. But not now."

"All right."

"You know, I don't think Fiona really deserves any more of our time. I like her and I'm sorry for her, but we've got other things on our plate now. Let's forget her, shall we?"

I nodded and gave her a little squeeze.

She said, "But there's someone I haven't forgotten for a moment. Your cousin Justin. There's someone I don't feel the least sorry for."

After dinner Diana said, "You know, darling, I don't think he ought to be allowed to get away with this."

"Oh, agreed. But what can we do? He's got complete control of the company."

"Well, is it so complete? I thought the bank had a big say nowadays. Oh, not direct control, but they could put on a lot of pressure, couldn't they, with our overdraft?"

"They put on enough to get me this job. But could they, or rather, would they put on enough to make Justin sell the firm? He may have consulted them anyway about the offer."

"I doubt it," said Diana. "If he didn't tell you, why should he tell them? The offer was probably made quietly over lunch somewhere and then Justin slipped off to St. Moritz saying nothing. Simple for him."

"They might have heard from Finlays. Don't see why they should, though."

"How do you think the bank would react to the offer?" she asked.

"Difficult to say. It's not really their affair so long as their overdraft is secure."

"I should have thought that was exactly why it was their affair. You thought Nelson was a sensible man, didn't you?"

"Yes. He's keen on small family businesses, though. He gave me the usual hand-out on that. And he wouldn't want to lose a customer. Though as they are Finlays' bankers too, he wouldn't really be losing us."

"He'd want to keep this estate going, wouldn't he?"

"Oh yes. That's everybody's chief aim, isn't it?"

"Is it Justin's, I wonder? I thought he only wanted to keep his name at the top. But, Hugo, do you think Nelson would understand how important this deal is to keeping us going? About the new capital and running everything more economically and efficiently."

I smiled. "I expect he would, if it was put to him like that."

"Well, can't we put it to him like that?"

I stared at her. "You mean write to him privately and tell him all about it and how we feel."

"Yes." She was still flushed and eager. "Say how vital this thing is to the future of this estate—not the company, but this estate. That's the part that really matters, isn't it? And how distressed we are that it was turned down without any discussion with anybody."

"Yes, we might. It would be rather going behind Justin's back, though." I paused. "No, I don't see why it should be. Justin being incommunicado in Switzerland, Nelson's the obvious person to get hold of."

"It sounds to me like our big chance. Darling, don't let's miss it. You can always tell Justin that you refrained from bothering him at his own request. Anyway, who cares what that man thinks?"

I laughed. "I rather care what Nelson thinks. It's always been a tradition that you never say or do anything which might weaken the bank's confidence in the firm. You always close your ranks when you deal with the bank."

"Well, I think it's high time they were taken into our confidence. What about starting a new tradition? You all close your ranks when you deal with Justin."

So we drafted the letter. It wasn't quite easy, as we might be telling Nelson stuff he knew already and it was important not to upset his confidence in me or in the business, just in case the deal never came off. We were both professional journalists, used to getting our thoughts down on paper, but even so it was a couple of hours before we got it right.

"Well, there it is," I said, when it was copied out, sealed and marked "Private and Confidential." "The big stick to stir up the muddy pool. I wonder what we shall raise."

"Usually you only raise a big stink," Diana said. "But even that would be something."

We waited anxiously for the first bubbles out of the mire, an anxious week of watching mails and wondering. When the answer finally arrived, it was not from Nelson at all. It was a cable from London office signed Ritpember, notifying me formally that a board meeting would be held in London at 11 a.m. on January the 26th, and it was specially requested that I should attend.

I gave it to Diana. "Quite a long way to go for a board meeting."

She read it wide-eyed. "What do you think's cooking?"

"God knows! But it must be something. They wouldn't drag me all that way just to discuss the reappointment of auditors. Nelson must have been bombarding Justin in St. Moritz with cables. Poor Justin, and him crying for mercy and owing himself a complete rest."

"Unless he hasn't been told anything. Could they have done it without him?"

"I don't know. I don't think so. The meeting's fixed for the day after his return."

"Very nice timing," said Diana. "Keep him on the hop and at the same time do him out of the kudos of having to cut short his holiday."

I said, "If I were him, I'd cut it short anyway and get things organized. Of course," I added, "we're only guessing that this is about the deal."

"It does look like it, doesn't it?"

"Yes. But there may be something quite new coming up that we know nothing about. Or it may be an old family custom. Bring all the directors home for a meeting on St. Someone-or-other's Day."

She gave me her special smile. "I bet there's something up and that we've started it. Darling, don't you think, frankly, that it means the bank are keen on the deal?"

"I think that's jumping to conclusions," I said cautiously. "We can't go as far as that."

"Well, it's what I think. But then I'm only a woman," she added drily. "You are going home for it, aren't you?"

I grinned. "What do you think? It's my first board meeting, I couldn't miss it. Maybe my last too."

Diana said, "Oh no. You'll go on the board of Finlays."

"You are beating the gun, aren't you?" I said laughing. Considering the appallingly serious issues involved, I felt lighthearted. Almost alarmingly frivolous. I put on a preoccupied face and went down to the office to ring Stevens and tell him to get me an air passage home.

He was a bit mystified. "I've just had Muir on the long distance blower from Barbados. He's in a terrible flap. Says his wife is ill with malaria and he's not at all well himself and he doesn't see at all how he can suddenly fly to England at a moment's notice. Such a thing has never happened before in all his years with the firm and he isn't due to go home till next year when he has leave and will be staying with his sister in Loughborough as he always does. And he doesn't see how he can possibly get away now at such short notice."

I laughed. "You seem to have had quite a long call from him." I reflected rapidly. Muir was quite out of touch with events and would be only a complete stooge at the meeting—Justin's stooge, probably. Would our urgent need for expansion and capital mean anything to him? I said, "Tell him not to worry. It was only a formality, informing him. I don't think he's really expected to go. Tell him it's only a routine meeting, but we'll keep him in touch if anything important does emerge."

"Okay. That should satisfy him. I'll get cracking on your passage now. Any particular route?"

"No. The quickest. The one you can get me on easiest."

"All right."

That afternoon there was another cable, this time a personal one. "THANKS YOURLET THINK IT MOST WORTHWHILE FOR YOU TO ATTEND MEETING HERE 26TH STOP HOPE YOU CAN COME REGARDS NELSON."

"A WW meeting," I murmured.

Diana chuckled without fully understanding the joke. "Something's definitely up," she said. "And he's obviously right on your side."

"Well, I don't know about obviously. But it's a friendly cable."

"Fancy spending another two shillings or whatever it is to say 'Regards'."

"I don't suppose he paid for it himself. I wonder what he means by worthwhile. Worth the time and the fare to London."

"I can only think of one thing that would be worth it."

"I don't really understand it," I said. "He can't force anything through against Justin's wishes. Justin's only got to call for a shareholders' meeting and he can vote us all down."

"Perhaps Nelson has persuaded him. Or brought pressure to bear on him in some way."

"What, in Switzerland?"

"Well, perhaps Justin wasn't so hard to persuade after all. Though that seems a bit unlikely. Anyway, Nelson thinks it important, whatever it is. We shall know soon enough. You will keep me in touch, won't you, darling? Send me a cable when you know what it's all about?"

"Yes, of course, but it'll have to be in code, or the whole colony will know all about it. Can you translate Bentley—or we could have some private code, some word to mean that it is about the deal."

"Patrick," said Diana. "Just send me Patrick. I'll understand."

"And if it looks like going through by any chance, I'll send Super-Patrick."

She laughed. "Of course. Oh, I do hope it is that, darling." She paused. "How long do you think you'll be away?"

"Goodness knows. Your guess is as good as mine. It entirely depends what goes on. It couldn't be less than a week by the time I've got there and had the various confabs and got back again. It may well be longer."

"Nice for you if it was."

"Oh, I don't know. I wouldn't want to be away too long, not at the moment. I'll have to make Ingram acting manager, but even so—" I broke off and added, "And then there's you too."

She smiled. "Oh darling! All this and me too! I'll be all right. Jailall will look after me."

"Yes, but—"

"It won't be the first time we've been parted by a few thousand miles, will it? As long as it's not for eighteen months."

I laughed. "It certainly won't be that. But there won't be much temptation to dally, if there's nothing going on. London in January isn't very attractive."

"Oh, don't you think so?" She gazed at me, her eyes solemn and wistful. "Give it my best love, won't you."

Part Six

1

IT WAS A raw winter afternoon at London airport and the thick suit which had been such a hot encumbrance in Port Catalan and Bermuda now seemed paper-thin. I shivered as we straggled across the tarmac to the buildings. I was getting to know the place well; it was the fourth time I had passed through those Airport Buildings in the last six months. I was under the impression that this particular journey showed a certain advance on the previous ones, but I was too cold to be sure.

Inside it was warmer. I paused at the bookstall on my way to the customs and surveyed the books and magazines. The books displayed had all been published since I had last been here. I suppose a gardener feels the same when he goes away for a spell and returns to find that all his roses have bloomed and faded and gone while he was away. I wondered if any of the novels displayed had been the ones Gatoff had sent me to review and Diana had returned to him.

I bought a copy of *Vista* and then the new issue of *Woman Today*. They made a fine pair together, incongruous and comic for anybody who didn't know their significance: the mind and the body, the male and the female, the obverse and the reverse, the eclectic and the popular, the inquiring and the reassuring. They lifted me with dizzy eye-pricking nostalgia straight back into the far-off, bickering, invigorating, exciting days when the world was our oyster. My present journey, I decided as I thawed out, was far from being an advance on its predecessors.

As I passed, I glanced at the notice-board where there are always messages for other travelers but never one for you. There was one for me. That yanked me back into the world of jockeying-for-position and business intrigues.

The message was not from Justin, as I expected, but from Nelson. Would I ring him up as soon as possible at either his office or his home number?

I rang him from a call-box at the airport. Nelson was not the man to waste more than a sentence on inquiring after my journey and where I was staying. He asked me to have a drink at his flat that evening. Feeling a certain amount of conspiratorial excitement, I accepted.

When I got to my hotel, it occurred to me that I ought to ring up Justin and report my safe arrival. He too would probably be wanting to give me a drink and do some lobbying. I could imagine the scene, the conversation perfectly. Probably in his flat. Now look here, Hugo, we've got to stand together as a family. Not let ourselves be pushed. I know I can rely on you. I would have to try and fit him in after Nelson, when I knew a bit more how the land lay. Possibly after dinner. If it could be helped, better not have dinner with him. Too long drawn out.

I talked to Miss Yorke. Ah, Mr. Hugo, no, the Major isn't in the office. Yes, he's back from Switzerland, got back an hour or two ago, had a wonderful time, lots of sun, still I expect you've been having lots of that too, haven't you, ha ha ha. Yes, I'll cable the colony and tell them you're safe and sound. Where are you staying, oh is that comfortable, oh good. Yes, the Major wants to see you. Could you come in half an hour before the meeting tomorrow. Yes, at half past ten. He wants to see you then. All right, Mr. Hugo, good-bye.

I rang off, rather riled at the peremptory summons. As a director and General Manager I didn't think I ought to be sent for like a schoolboy to the headmaster. And I felt that a half-hour before the meeting was hardly adequate for the big issue confronting us. And didn't ordinary civility demand that he speak to me himself? Oh yes, Mr. Hugo, the Major wants to see you as soon as possible. Could you please ring him at his flat? At White's? At the In and Out? At Brooks's? At the St. James's?

I felt pretty annoyed with Justin and then it occurred to me that he probably meant to annoy. It was probably deliberate. Treat his cocky young cousin in a contemptuous, off-hand way in case he was getting too big for his boots. So I stopped being annoyed. It was gratifying to find that I could turn off the emotion like a tap. While I was about it, I had better stop being cocky and filled with self-importance.

That being so, should I ring up Justin myself and be friendly? Would he be in his flat, and, if not, in which club? I found myself suddenly swimming in a flood of memories of the night of Walker's death. Slowly I surfaced, breathing deeply, and then I decided not to ring Justin. Why should I go chasing after him if he couldn't be bothered to talk to me? It was, after all, he who was going to lobby me and not I him. In fact, it might be as well to keep out of his way until after I had seen Nelson. Possibly until the meeting itself.

Not cockiness, not self-importance, I told myself. Just tactics.

The night in the plane had left me without any special feeling of sleepiness or exhaustion, but instead a slight and persistent headache and a feeling as if my engine was revving a shade too fast. A bath, a change of clothes and a strong whisky from Nelson, if anything, increased this a little.

The Nelsons lived in a flat in Hans Court, within walking distance of my hotel. The building was Victorian Dutch-imitation and the flat had been done up lavishly a few years before when dark red and dark green together were all the rage. Or so I guessed. Mrs. Nelson I had not met before, a tall woman with a deep voice. We made conventional conversation about the flight home and how expensive Bermuda was and how nobody had any time for you there if you weren't an American. Then, tactfully, she left us. I suppose she went and sat in her bedroom.

Nelson said, "I'm glad you were able to get home in time for this meeting. It may be important."

"I guessed as much when I got your cable. You aren't usually asked to fly across the Atlantic and back for a routine meeting."

He smiled faintly. "Directors' Traveling. It's a legitimate tax expense."

"Just as long as there's some income to be taxed."

The smile became less tentative and then vanished abruptly. "It's about this Finlay offer, of course. I was so glad to get your letter. We knew nothing about it at this end. At least I didn't."

I looked him straight in the eye. He had a rather quizzical expression, but we neither made any comment.

"I quite agreed with you. The board ought to have an opportunity of discussing such a major matter."

I wondered how he had engineered the meeting, but I thought it better not to ask at the moment. Anyway there were more important things on hand.

I asked: "Is there still something to discuss? I mean, is the offer still open?"

"Apparently. At least they're prepared to reopen it if we are at all interested. They understand the position perfectly," he added.

I nodded. So did I.

Nelson poured me out another drink and remarked, "You're in favor of this offer being accepted, then?"

"Yes." I almost added "in principle" or "provisionally" or "depending exactly on what the terms are" or some such proviso. But I let it stand as plain "Yes." It seemed better not to equivocate, if I wished to convince Nelson. Anyway the offer was fine.

Nelson sipped his drink and gazed at me thoughtfully. "I would have thought that you as a member of the family would have opposed something which will mean in effect the extinction of your family business." He paused. As I was about to answer, he said, "Or have you had enough of the family stuff in the last few years?"

I grinned and relaxed. We were getting through to each other. "Well, I've had quite a bit of it," I admitted. "And it doesn't seem to me the really vital factor. As I see it, it's a case of sink or swim. At least it will be in the end. And this offer provides a life-belt."

"You don't think we could carry on as we are now?"

"Oh, for a while, yes certainly. Especially if the bank doesn't turn the screws too tight." I waited but he didn't rise to that, so I went on: "We might stagger on for years. But in the end we shall just have to have the capital and the bigger base for operations, or we shall go under."

"We could wait till then."

"The offer may not be open then. And anyway, why wait? I want to get on and modernize that estate straight away. Do you know, we haven't changed a thing out there in the last fifty years?"

Nelson gave a faint smile. "I suppose this is the price we have to pay for getting young blood into the firm. It doesn't worry you about the family name disappearing?"

"Why should it? What's in a name? I shall still be called Pemberton. It's rather a silly name anyway." I thought of making a point about a girl not minding losing her surname when she married, but it wasn't really relevant. We weren't in love with Finlays. It was purely a *mariage de convenance*. I went on with a fine show of enthusiasm:

"The thing that matters is Malmaison, if you care about the family heritage. That's what old Samuel Pemberton really cared about, and my grandfather too. From the point of view of tradition, it's the estate and the factory we've got to keep going, quite apart from the financial angle and all the people who depend on it. It doesn't seem to me to matter much what the name of the company is."

There was a short pause. He said at last, "Yes, I gathered from your letter that that was how you felt. And of course you'd still be out there running it for Finlays."

"Well, they offered me the job of running the three estates for them." I made a gesture of vagueness. "But it was very much in the air."

"Yes, of course."

There was another silence. Nelson offered me a cigarette and lit it for me. I was wishing he would give his own opinion. Surely he must agree with me. If not, why drag me all this way to discuss it? But it seemed that he was carefully refraining from committing himself either way. Perhaps he felt that was not for him to do. In which case—

"You know your cousin doesn't share your views."

"Yes. I gathered that."

"He thinks it would be a tragedy if the family name were to disappear."

"Couldn't the name be kept in existence somewhere?"

"Oh yes. Finlays would probably keep the plate on their door. They'd have to, if the company wasn't wound up."

"Wouldn't that satisfy him?"

"Apparently not. The name wouldn't be in everyday use any more."

Again we sat in silence and smoked and drank. Suddenly I could bear it no longer.

"What are your own views about it?" I asked. "How do you stand?"

"Officially I don't stand anywhere. I'm merely on the board to watch the bank's interests and to advise on finance generally. A major matter of policy like this must be decided by the family."

"But surely—as our financial adviser, you must have a view. You must have a personal one."

"Oh yes. I find myself very much in sympathy with your views, especially as you've just put them." He smiled a little warm smile that softened his face. I wondered why I had ever thought him rat-faced. I gave a sigh of relief.

"Officially," he went on, "it's not quite so clear-cut. The bank doesn't want to lose a customer."

"But you wouldn't be losing us," I protested. "You bank for Finlays too, don't you?"

He let that go. "At the same time, we aren't very happy about having a lot of money tied up in a business which, according to its General Manager, is going to close down sooner or later."

I laughed at his little joke. "Well then!"

"Banks are very contrary people. We live off people having overdrafts and at the same time we're always wanting them paid back."

"Well, if you want ours paid back, you'd better see that we accept this offer. Otherwise it'll be centuries before you see your money again. There's a limit to what we can go on paying back out of our rather meagre profits. And it's all money that ought to be ploughed back into the business."

I looked at him. He was staring vacantly at the electric fire. I decided to jump in with both feet.

"The point is this," I said. "My cousin has an over-all control of this firm. If you don't support this deal going through, it hasn't an earthly hope."

Nelson glanced at me and then looked away again.

"Exactly," he said in an indifferent voice. "That's why we're here today."

I could have jumped to my feet and danced a jig, but I restrained myself suitably and merely said "Oh good!" and stubbed out my cigarette. Nelson got up, picked up the glasses and took them to the table for refills.

"By the way," he remarked over his shoulder, "you're wrong in thinking your cousin has complete control of the firm."

"Hasn't he? I thought his holding of ordinary shares was just greater than everyone else's put together."

"It used to be like that. I had the figures looked up the other day." He brought the drink and stood looking down at me. "Your cousin sold a big block of ordinaries to Mrs. Wright."

"Good God! When did he do that?"

"About ten years ago. Just after the war. I gather he was doing a certain amount of underwriting for one of these finance houses and he got badly caught in one or two issues. I suppose they gave him all the shaky ones to do. Anyway he had to fork up and so he sold some shares."

"Well!" I was amazed and then not so amazed. It was typical of Justin. I wondered if it was Brigadier Hope-Gordon who had landed him with the risky issue. The whole thing scratched just where it itched. I relaxed and grinned at Nelson. "And we none of us knew anything about it all these years."

He sat down again. "You wouldn't expect him to broadcast it, would you? No, it was news to us too. I just had the figures checked as a precaution. It was when I found out the real position that I insisted on the meeting tomorrow."

"Oh I see." Of course Hodges and the accounts department must have known all about it, and anyone else who had access to the books. Or who cared enough to look it up. But we were all so sure that Justin had complete control. It never occurred to any of us to doubt it, not even Diana. There was a moral in that somewhere.

"If only I'd known that earlier," I said. "No, perhaps it wouldn't have made any difference. Who controls the company now?"

He was sitting opposite me again, looking eager, his sharp little nose twitching.

"No one person any more. That's why the recommendations of the board at tomorrow's meeting will be so important."

"Ah!"

"If the board advises against the offer being accepted, the shareholders won't be likely to go against that. They're mainly the same people, besides."

"What do you think is likely to happen at the meeting?"

"I don't know. That's one of the things I wanted to ask you. We know the Chairman's views, and yours and mine. What about the others? Some of them I've never even met."

"Well, Muir isn't coming. He lives in Barbados and isn't well. Is Mrs. Wright coming, do you know?"

"I've no idea. I imagine she's been asked. What are her views likely to be?"

I shrugged. "I don't know. I've only met her once or twice in my life. She's very old and frail now, and virtually blind. I have a feeling she doesn't like my cousin very much, though of course that doesn't mean she'd necessarily vote against him." I smiled to myself as a thought occurred to me. "Her big thing is family pride, but it's Wright pride, not Pemberton. She doesn't like the Pembertons much. I think she feels they've always done the Wrights down, got them out of the big jobs, got them out of the firm altogether and she's the only one left. So I would think she'd be quite likely to support this deal, especially if it made her own income safer."

"Better a Finlay than a Pemberton. Is that it?"

"That's my guess. But she probably won't come at all. Not up to the journey. She lives near Eastbourne."

"We shall see. What about Sir Arthur Graham? I've only met him the once."

"Well, again he's got quite a journey and may not come."

"He came to that other meeting."

"Yes, he did. Well, perhaps he'll turn up. But God knows which way he will vote. I've always thought of him as Justin's stooge, I mean man. Justin put him on to the board when my father died. I've never thought of him as taking any interest in anything except grouse and salmon. But he's also my mother's trustee and he should be watching her interests."

"Your mother will lose some income if this deal comes off."

"Yes, but it'll be safe." I was feeling a bit despondent. "It looks as if he'll vote against the scheme, if it's presented that way. I mean, he'll probably vote as Justin wants him to."

We looked gloomily at each other. "Assuming Mrs. Wright doesn't come," said Nelson, "that'll be two on each side and the Chairman then has a casting vote." He smiled at me. "Oh, well, we shall have done what we could."

"If Sir Arthur doesn't come, we shall be two to one. But—I wonder if we could get hold of him tonight. I should have got his address from the office before it shut." I could have kicked myself. "Perhaps I could ring Miss Yorke at her home and get the number from her. If she knows it, and if she'll give it to me. She dotes on Justin."

"Oh, I shouldn't worry. He's probably coming on the night train from Scotland. If he's coming at all. You might try and have a word with him before the meeting tomorrow. I think it would be better if I kept out of all this lobbying myself."

"My cousin wants to see me half an hour before the meeting." I suddenly saw it. "Of course! That's to stop me lobbying the others."

"He may only want to lobby you himself."

"Oh yes." I looked at Nelson speculatively. "I suppose there's no way of persuading him to change his mind."

He looked at me with a smile under the surface. "There's nothing to stop you trying."

"I mean, couldn't you bring pressure to bear in some way?"

"We could hardly threaten him, if that's what you want. The overdraft is coming down satisfactorily, we have a representative on the board. We could hardly force him to sell the whole firm unless we applied for a compulsory winding-up order. I'm sure my own directors wouldn't agree to that."

"Anyway, I daresay my cousin would rather wind up the firm than sell it to Finlays. Dog in the manger."

"I don't know about that at all," said Nelson noncommittally.

I felt I was being a bit reckless in talking so frankly, but I couldn't bottle it up any longer.

"I imagine the real objection to the offer, from my cousin's point of view, is that he won't have a job in the new set-up."

"That is possibly an additional factor," said Nelson carefully.

"I wonder if Finlays would change their mind. Give him a seat on their board or something. It might make all the difference."

Nelson shook his head. "I made one or two tentative inquiries but I gather that just isn't possible. Not at present anyway."

I pursed up my mouth. I must have been looking pretty grim because Nelson suddenly leaned forward and patted me on the knee.

"We'll just have to do our best tomorrow," he said. "We can't do more than that, can we?"

What with the drink and the long plane flight I fell asleep the moment my head touched the pillow. But, unluckily, it didn't last. I woke in the dark hours with a thirst like a desert explorer's. I drank a couple of tumblers of cold water and turned off the light, but I couldn't get off to sleep again. I lay for an hour or so, speculating about the meeting, thinking about my talk with Nelson. Had I been indiscreet? How did Justin's sale of shares affect the matter? Was Sir Arthur such a fool as he sometimes seemed to be? How far was he Justin's stooge? Above all, was there something I ought to do which could just sway the issue the right way?

It wasn't a very good way of getting back to sleep and in the end I switched on the light again and looked for something to read. I hadn't brought a book with me and so I read *Vista*. The novels were reviewed by someone called E. P. Horrocks. My successor, I thought ruefully. He'd done it quite well, though I thought one or two of his remarks were a bit pretentious and didn't really mean anything when you thought about them. Still, it was an interesting notice.

I felt a terrible pang of longing. I wanted to have written that notice myself; perhaps they were the very novels Gatoff had sent to me and Diana had sent back. I had never seen my own reviews in print. If a complimentary copy of the magazine had been sent to me, which was unlikely, it had never arrived. I looked through it in case I might find *From Sanders to Scobie* but it wasn't there. Instead I read an article on modern French poetry, a new revaluation of the novels of E. M. Forster, a short story by Angus Wilson. It was like a hone for sharpening the wits and I felt exhilarated. The names of the contributors too, the aristocracy of the intellectual world, rang in my ears like the names of the galaxies. My world, I said to myself, that was my world before I forsook it. And it had never really stopped being my world. In my heart I was still there, in place of the usurping Horrocks, among Forster and Wilson and Modern French poetry.

I put aside *Vista* and picked up the copy of *Woman Today*. This was another world, Diana's world, the world of elegant professionalism and mass reader-appeal. There was nothing here on which to sharpen the intellect, but instead you were driven, reluctantly or readily according to your temperament, to admiration at the sheer competence and the startling sincerity of the final product.

It was, I always thought, a comforting journal. No hint of despair ever reached its columns. It never threatened you with radio-active dust or told you that you were experiencing the death-spasms of a civilization or called on you to make sacrifices without which there would be no survival. The personal problems it solved for you were always the same week after week. You could expect no help if you were in difficulties with a husband who was impotent or a Negro or a sadist or a homosexual or wanted by the police or senile or obsessed by the thought of suicide. Instead it would tell you, with little prompting, how to make a charming sweater for cooler summer days or how to turn that dark cupboard into a gay dining alcove or how to cure your spotty skin. At worst it would tell you how to cope with your illegitimate baby, but that was the limit. I found it very calming.

Miss Peabody's serial had evidently finished and the new one was about a young girl who came to the big forbidding chateau to teach English to the Vicomte's sickly little boy. The Vicomte had two older sons, by his first wife who had died tragically and mysteriously; one son was gay and charming, the other saturnine and haunted. I must remember to ask Diana which one she married in the end. The haunted one, almost certainly. No, on second thoughts, better not say anything about it to Diana. Poor Diana, with her restricted little community and her bridge and the circles under her eyes. No need to make her haunted too.

I got out of bed and sat by the window. Across the empty street the branches of the trees in Cadogan Place gleamed bare and wet in the lamplight. It was a world of its own, a dark winter city without people. With the room lights turned out, I brooded by the window for a long time. Away on the left somewhere was Nelson's flat. Over on the right, behind my shoulder, was the flat Fiona had had.

As I sat there, I went over the scene in that flat in detail, without pleasure, without anger and, now, without disgust. I went over again the great argument, all the different points of view—Justin's, Diana's, Nelson's, Walker's, my mother's, Arp's, Fiona's, my own—so vigorously, so excruciatingly pressed. I saw just how I had let myself be driven to the point where it was easier not to think, where reason was fogged and only sexual desire was sharp-edged. That had sucked me out of the miasma and I had been content, even eager, to surrender my free-will to my hormones. Glad, putting it bluntly, to sell my birthright for a pair of almond eyes and a nicely shaped bust, happy to be an animal.

There I had started the long journey which had led me away from everything I cared about, led me to take Diana even farther from her household gods and to live out our lives in the sort of place one can only bear to experience in other people's short stories. The only redeeming feature, though it was a huge one, was that Diana and I were now as close to each other as we always should have been. And that, I recognized humbly, was entirely Diana's doing. It was her submissiveness, her forbearance which had brought it about and I felt a twinge of shame.

Not, however, a very big one, not a kick in the stomach. I was too calm and dispassionate for much emotion. I was reviewing my life as if it were someone else's and I wasn't too impressed by it. I could think of Fiona's flat, not guiltily as the place where I had been unfaithful to Diana, nor remorsefully as the scene where I had betrayed my own integrity, but just as an ugly furnished flat where I had in my despair taken the wrong decision with the wrong person for the wrong reason.

2

DELIBERATELY I WAS late for the meeting with Justin. It seemed to me that the less we saw of each other, the less chance there was of open conflict before the meeting even began, and there might be some advantage in keeping Justin as long as possible in the dark about my own views and plans. Also there was a chance of running into Sir Arthur Graham in one of the office passages before we started. However, there was no sign of him, and in due course Miss Yorke ushered me into Justin's sanctum.

It was all exactly as it had been when I last saw it, the blue glass ash-tray, the one file on the glass-topped table, the shiny magazines on the side table. Justin was standing in front of the fire, looking both elegant and business-like in a very dark grey suit, a very dark grey polka dot tie and a stiff white collar. He was as brown as a berry.

"Good morning, Hugo. Glad you were able to make this."

The tips of our fingers touched momentarily.

"Good morning, Justin. Yes, I'm glad I could get here in time."

We were as amiable as long-parted clubmen. There were no feline undertones in our voices.

"Look, hang up your coat in the cupboard there."

I wondered if there was some significant honor in hanging up my coat in the Chairman's cupboard. My tweed overcoat looked scruffy and out of place beside Justin's black one.

"Did you have a good trip home?" he asked.

"Oh, not at all bad. You don't sleep much in those planes but at least we didn't get stuck in a blizzard anywhere."

"No, you must have been lucky in your weather, especially at this time of year. I was once caught at Gander in January for twenty-four hours. It wasn't at all amusing I can tell you. That's one of the reasons I always go by sea now, if I can spare the time."

He gave me a cigarette out of the silver box and I lit it with the big Ronson lighter. I wondered if he was deliberately wasting our few minutes together or whether he was, as usual, merely taking ages to come to the point. He certainly seemed not the least nervous or edgy. I thought that I too was in no hurry to come to the point and I let his conversational opening proceed on its leisurely amiable way.

"I only got back yesterday myself," he remarked. "Ran it a bit fine, but I was very anxious not to start chopping bits off my holiday. It's probably the only one I shall get this year."

I nodded sympathetically. He hadn't sat down and we were standing on opposite sides of the glass-topped table.

"You're looking very brown," I said.

He preened with pleasure. "Oh yes, the sun was wonderful out there. I suppose it's the way it reflects off the snow. Do you know I could lie on my balcony bare to the waist in the sun?"

"No! Could you really?"

"Yes. It was as hot as Cannes in August. Of course it was freezing out of the sun, but the hotel was nice and warm. It did me a world of good, just lying there and relaxing in the sun. I was pretty done up before."

"Yes, you must have been."

"And the air's so wonderful too. I suppose because it's so dry. It really does pep you up when you're down."

"It's just the time of year when you need pepping up."

"How right you are!" he said, delighted at the way I had taken his point so well. "I think it would be an excellent thing if more people took their holidays in the winter."

"Yes, I suppose it would. I must try it one year."

It was all perfectly silly. I only got leave every three years and whoever heard of a colonial planter taking his leave in the middle of winter.

"You're looking pretty fit yourself, Hugo."

I said nonchalantly, "Oh yes, we have a lot of sun too at Malmaison, though there isn't much time for lying about in it."

He hesitated between a frown and a smile. "Yes, you must have been a bit hard-pressed lately. Still, I shall be coming out next month to take the strain." He paused and looked at me, genial and serious. "As a matter of fact, Hugo, I wasn't at all sure that I ought to bring you away from the colony even for a few days. But then I thought, no one's as indispensable as that and you'd appreciate the excuse of a few days in the bright lights. Freshen you up. You've always been fond of London, haven't you?"

He gazed at me blandly. For a moment I thought I was going to choke, but I suppressed it. I don't think he noticed. He went on:

"And then it gave me the chance of getting the latest news from the colony out of you and giving you the picture as I see it. All the little things you can't really put down on paper. So I hope you won't think it a waste of time."

"Not a bit. There's always this meeting too."

He gave me a thick-as-thieves smile. "Oh, that! That's just a formality."

"Formality?"

"Yes, Hugo." He put on the air of one deliberating whether to take me into his confidence—or so I judged it. "I don't know if you've heard, but Finlays have made an offer to buy us up. Of course there's no question of accepting it, but Finlays are good friends of ours and I thought that out of common courtesy we ought to go through the motions of considering it formally. That's why I called this meeting today. But it's only a gesture."

"I see," I said innocently. "I should have thought there might have been some advantages in linking up with Finlays. The extra capital, the extra co-ordination, the—"

"You wouldn't get that in a larger firm, believe you me." There was an edge coming through Justin's honey voice. "Anyway it's not a linking-up, as you call it. They're offering to buy us up altogether and it's not a very good offer either."

"Perhaps we could push them up a bit."

"What, Finlays!" He whinnied with amusement. "Why, Hugo, they're not much bigger than we are."

"They're over twice as big."

He brushed that aside. "Finlays buying up Pembertons!" he chortled. "It's ludicrous. We could just as easily buy them up."

"Except that they've got the money, and we haven't."

There was a momentary scowl like the flash of summer lightning.

"We've got a better name than they have," he said defensively. "We're more respected. And we've been there longer too. Samuel Pemberton came to the colony nearly twenty years before old what's-his-name Finlay. Gosh, he'd turn in his grave to think of us even considering this offer."

"It wasn't Samuel Pemberton who founded Malmaison," I said. "He only started that grocery store. It was Ernest Wright who started the sugar business. He only took Samuel Pemberton into partnership much later on."

"Well, it's Pembertons now in any event. No one hears the name Wright any more. Pemberton is now one of the great names in the colony's history." He simpered, "You could almost call us the Royal

Family of Natividad. And that's how we're going to stay. We're not going to go out like the Wrights, not if I have anything to do with it."

"Not even to save the business?"

"Save the business? Hugo, how on earth do you save a business by selling it to someone else? Use your head, boy. Anyway, there's no question of saving it. We're doing fine at the moment. Crop's going well, we're over the strike, money's rolling in, everything in the garden's rosy." He moved round the table and took my arm. "Frankly, Hugo, I think a lot of it's due to the way you're putting your back into it out there. Of course, you were lucky the way the strike folded up so quickly. But there's nothing wrong with being lucky, is there?" He looked at me roguishly. "You're doing fine, boy. Don't go and lose your nerve now."

Miss Yorke put her head round the door and said, "Sir Arthur Graham's here, Major."

Justin gave an audible sigh of relief. "Ah, ask him to come in."

Sir Arthur bumbled in, greeted us both, hoped he wasn't late, explained that he'd come down on the Aberdonian and it was really very comfortable; thought I was in the West Indies, lucky man in this weather, and hung up his coat in the Chairman's cupboard. Two tweeds to one black, I thought, and hoped it was a good omen.

"I only got back from St. Moritz yesterday," Justin said. "Hence the suntan." He seemed a little peeved with Sir Arthur for not noticing it.

"Weather good?"

"Wonderful." We had to go again through it being as hot as Cannes in August and how you could lie bare to the waist on your balcony and the air which was so dry it really pepped—

"How was the skiing?" Sir Arthur interrupted. "Do the Corviglia?"

"Well, no. I messed about a bit on skis, but I'm rather rusty. I don't get the chance to keep it up nowadays."

"We none of us do," commented Sir Arthur. "I did the Corviglia a couple of years ago. It's a great run. You ought to make a point of doing it next time. Do the Cresta?"

"Heavens, no! I don't want to die yet."

"I used to do it quite a bit at one time," he went on smoothly. "Margaret made me give it up in the end, said my reactions were getting slow and it was a bit risky. Suppose she was right though I was sorry to give it up. It's a great run."

"Yes," said Justin. He looked a bit put out and turned eagerly to the door as Nelson arrived. Nelson greeted us formally and hoped he wasn't late. As he shook hands with me, he gave no sign that this wasn't our first meeting for six months.

He hadn't got an overcoat or hat—I suppose he had hung them up somewhere outside, but he politely commented on Justin's suntan. Justin warmed to him openly and told him all about it being as hot as Cannes in August and lying bare to the waist. Nelson nodded gravely and started to ask after the skiing, so Justin quickly told him about all the wonderful, marvelous, famous people who had been staying in St. Moritz too. Nelson listened attentively and seemed impressed. Justin beamed.

"Well," he said, making an elaborate gesture to look at the watch on the inside of his wrist, "it isn't quite eleven, but as we're all here we may as well get started."

"Isn't Mrs. Wright coming?" I asked.

"No, she didn't feel up to the journey. It's just the four of us."

Once we were in the boardroom we became grave and formal, as if we had put on senatorial robes. I suppose that is the point of boardrooms as in numbers we could just as well have had our meeting in Justin's office. Justin sat at the head of the table, Hodges with his minute books on his left, Sir Arthur with his pipe and tobacco pouch on his right. I sat beyond Sir Arthur, Nelson beyond Hodges. To my right the table stretched away, bare, brown and shining. I thought that the company hardly needed such a large boardroom table.

I settled myself in my seat and arranged my pencils and blotting paper. This was, I recognized, another of the crises of my life, possibly the biggest of them all, and I was fascinated to find that I had no trace of butterflies in the stomach, no hint of ache in my cheekbones. Perhaps I had conquered that at last, I told myself; perhaps I was at last fully master of myself. The thought bucked me up a good deal.

Justin was saying something to Hodges. I looked above his head where the portrait of my grandfather gazed solemnly down on our deliberations. Possibly it was a trick of the light but it didn't seem that he had as stern an expression as I had remembered. It was almost benign. I speculated whether he, like old Samuel, would turn in his grave at the thought of our even considering the Finlay offer. It seemed to me that he would turn far more violently if he knew we were turning down the offer and condemning Malmaison to a slow decline back into the jungle just because Justin didn't want to lose his job and his authority. Perhaps that was why he was looking so benignly at me. Then I told myself not to be fanciful. This meeting was a battlefield and you don't win battles by dreaming fancies about the expression of an ancestor.

Justin stopped muttering with Hodges and cleared his throat. "Gentlemen," he said in his high official voice, "as this is a special meeting, I think we might well omit the minutes of our last meeting. We can leave them till our next routine meeting."

There was a general grunt of assent. Sir Arthur was filling his pipe elaborately with a good deal of "business." The tobacco apparently had to be rubbed between his palms before it would go into the bowl. It was a memory-evoking sight, and they weren't very pleasant memories either.

"Well, gentlemen," said Justin, "it is my pleasant duty to welcome you here today. Mr. Muir and Mrs. Wright are unfortunately unable to be present but I am very grateful to the rest of you for coming. Some of us have made long journeys to be here today. Sir Arthur has come specially from Scotland, my cousin has flown back from the colony and I have returned from Switzerland. I only hope that you won't feel that you are wasting your time, though I feel possibly you may. As I said to my cousin earlier, this meeting is more in the nature of a formality than anything else."

No one said anything. I caught Nelson's eye but we were both expressionless.

Justin went on, "Before we proceed to business, there is one thing I should like to say. As you all know, during the summer Mr. Walker, our General Manager died. He had been our General Manager for—for over twenty years and he was also a member of this board. He was much respected and liked both inside the company and in the West Indian sugar world. I myself found him an admirable colleague and used to rely a good deal on his wisdom and experience. The board sent a wreath to his funeral and on your behalf I wrote to Mrs. Walker to sympathize with her. She has replied, sending her thanks for the kind message. Er, I don't think I need ask the secretary to read out the letter, but as this is the first opportunity we have had to pay tribute to his memory, I suggest that we rise in our places and stand for a minute in silence."

It was all rather trying. Sir Arthur had just got his pipe going, and didn't look at all pleased at having to lay it down. We shambled to our feet and stood in embarrassed reverence, missing each other's eyes, glaring at the table, wondering whether we ought to button up our coats again as tribute to the dead. I remember thinking that this was another trick of Justin's, a way of inducing in us a suitably reverent and sacrificial state of mind. It couldn't surely have been affection for Walker. Justin had been totally unmoved, at the time, by the news of his death. And then I thought, was this really the first board meeting since his death six months ago? Heavens, what a firm! I thought about Walker a bit too, how good he was to the firm and to me. I wondered how he would have felt about the deal with Finlays, and decided he would have voted for it. He wasn't so sold on the beauty of the name Pemberton that he was blind to all else. And then I wondered how much longer Justin was going to keep us all standing there, and whether anyone was timing the minute. It must have been a good three minutes. Finally Sir Arthur cleared his throat noisily. Justin glanced at him and at the rest of us, and then suddenly sat down. There was a faint and unsuitable smirk on his face.

When we had finished shuffling ourselves into comfortable positions, Justin said: "In his place we have appointed my young cousin Hugo Pemberton. As this is the first board meeting he has attended, I should like to welcome him here today. You will of course understand my own special pleasure at having another member of the family on this board. You may be interested to know that he is the youngest director this company has ever had, but I daresay none of us will hold that against him." The smirk was no longer faint but still, I thought, unseemly. "I can assure you gentlemen that whatever he lacks in experience, he will make up for in youthful enthusiasm."

Sir Arthur said "Hear, hear!" a little louder than was strictly necessary, and struck a match. I gave him a grateful look and said "Thank you." There didn't seem much else to say. Nelson nodded and smiled at me. I looked for the flash of irony in his glance, but I didn't see it. But then he wasn't a very ironical man.

"And now, gentlemen, to business. I don't think it need detain us for more than a few minutes. As I mentioned earlier, this meeting is really only a formality. Finlay Brothers, as you know they're the other family sugar business in the colony, they're a little larger than us though not so old or well-established, well they have made an offer to buy us up. It's not in my opinion a very attractive offer, but in any event there's no question of accepting it. We're not on the market, we're doing fine as we are. But Finlays have always been good friends of ours; Ned Finlay is a particularly close friend of mine and I thought we should do them the courtesy of discussing their offer at a board meeting, even though we don't mean to take it up. Nelson, as our finance man, would you like to explain the offer to us?"

Nelson folded his hands calmly on his blotting paper and said, "Thank you, Mr. Chairman."

He explained the offer clearly and coherently and I think even Sir Arthur must have understood it. It was all pretty well what McDougall had told me that night in Port Catalan. The purchase price figure of £400,000 was provisional and depended on our statement of assets and liabilities. £250,000 would be in cash, the remainder in specially created shares in Finlays which would be redeemed each year in proportion to the profits made by Malmaison. The company of Wright Pemberton would not be wound up but would become a wholly owned subsidiary of Finlays and its board would be reconstructed. The London and Port Catalan offices would be closed and as many as possible of the staff absorbed by Finlays. Those who could not be absorbed would be pensioned off or jobs found for them elsewhere. All the Pemberton pensioners would be taken over. The Malmaison estate would be integrated with the two Finlay estates and capital would be provided for its full development.

"Thank you, Nelson," said Justin. "Well, gentlemen, I think that's pretty clear. Not a very attractive offer is it? Either for our shareholders or for us."

Nelson looked calmly at him. "Oh, I don't think it's so bad, Mr. Chairman. It's possible that we may be able to persuade Finlays to better the offer, but even if they don't, I think it's quite a good offer for a firm with quite large liabilities and a rather precarious future."

The contradiction had sandpapered Justin's suavity and he glared at Nelson. "What do you mean?"

"Well, for a firm this size, it's a large overdraft. Over double the total paid-up share capital and—"

"Oh, that's what's worrying you, is it? Well, that's coming down nicely, we're keeping it below the limits you set. I think you'll find we shall pay off the overdraft much sooner than you think, given good weather and no more labor troubles."

Nelson said, "I don't think I could subscribe to such an optimistic assumption."

I was surprised at Nelson's outspokenness, but I assumed he knew what he was doing. If his object was to make Justin angry, he seemed to be succeeding. You could tell it by the look in Justin's eye, the way he fiddled with his pencils, the redness of his neck just above his collar. He seemed to be too surprised to speak and Nelson went on in the same calm voice:

"I was sorry to hear you say, Mr. Chairman, that this discussion was only a formality. I think we should give it very serious consideration. In fact, I would go further and recommend—"

Justin interrupted him roughly. "Just a minute, Nelson. I hardly think that this comes within your province. You're on this board to watch the bank's interest, not to give us your views on future policy."

"If I may differ with you there, sir, I am here both to watch the interests of the bank and to advise this board on financial matters. In both these capacities the important point is surely the future prosperity of the Malmaison estate. That is the thing we must safeguard at all costs. I think, sir, that I should be failing in my duty if I did not advise this board to give the Finlay offer the most serious and indeed sympathetic consideration."

The battle was joined, the first shots were exchanged. I think Justin was a bit startled by the violence of the onslaught. His eye roamed over the rest of us, over me silent and, I hoped, enigmatic, over Sir Arthur, sucking and bubbling in his private smoke-haze.

"That's the important thing," Sir Arthur mumbled. "Got to keep the wheels turning."

He seemed to regard his directorial function as an echo. It struck me that the whole battle would depend on whether, at the crucial point, he echoed Justin or Nelson or me.

There was a silence while Justin fidgeted with a pencil. I suppose he was considering his tactics for he evidently decided to revert to sweet reasonableness. He gave Nelson quite a good smile and said: "Well, I can assure you we all value your opinion. I just don't see what all the flap's about." I wondered if his informal language was an attempt at mateyness or whether it was a deliberate contrast to Nelson's. "What's all the fuss about, eh? I admit we had some trouble last summer, but we're over that. We're grinding steadily, making six hundred tons of sugar a week, the money's coming in, the overdraft's coming down, we've got new young blood out in the colony, labor's working well, the purity's averaging 79, we're going to be able to maintain our dividend. I can't for the life of me see what the sudden panic's about."

Nelson said, "I agree, sir, things are running quite smoothly at the moment. It's most satisfactory the way things have improved since the summer. Your cousin's appointment was certainly a most happy one. But I don't think we should let ourselves be lulled into a sense of false security. It's not this year I'm worrying about, or next. It's the future generally; it's thirty or forty years time I'm concerned with."

Justin gave a contemptuous leer round the table. "Oh that! I don't think that'll affect any of us here. Except Hugo there. It'll be his problem then." He waved airily at me.

I was astounded that he had the nerve to say it. Nelson's eyes met mine gravely. I murmured, "*Après moi la déluge.*" It was only a mumbled aside, but Hodges, scribbling frantically in his notebook, asked across the table how that was spelt. So I had to spell it out slowly and we all had plenty of time to mull it over. Nelson nodded in agreement, but I wasn't sure that Sir Arthur saw the point.

"Hardly that, Hugo," said Justin. "It's just that I don't pretend to be a soothsayer. I can't see as clearly into the very distant future as some of us think we can. It's the present I'm concerned with, the present and the immediate future. I think that if we cope with that all right, we're not doing so badly." He turned to Nelson. "What I don't see is why you think we shall do better under Finlays than under ourselves. They're only a small family concern like ourselves. Why should we be better off in thirty years time under their umbrella?"

Very patiently Nelson explained about Finlays' spare cash from their oil deal, how we badly needed the capital they proposed to invest, what an advantage it would be to us not to have to operate on a rather frayed shoe-string, how in these hard competitive days a larger firm had a greater chance of withstanding the draught than a smaller one. It was all quite ably presented but somehow it lacked the conviction of his earlier points. Most of it was clearly taken from my letter to him and expanded by him into formal boardroom eloquence. Perhaps something of its second-hand nature came through. He was speaking in vague generalizations without the mass of figures and details he had used earlier to buttress them. Justin pounced on the weakness.

"Thank you," he said genially. "Yes, that's quite clear—as far as it goes. The bit I still don't follow is why we should suddenly have to pour money into the firm now and why so much. What's it all in aid of?"

"Increased productivity," Nelson said mechanically. "The other colony estates—"

"Yes, yes, I know. But what exactly are we going to spend all this money on? What are all these items of equipment that we need so urgently?"

Nelson answered with fair confidence, "Perhaps, Mr. Chairman, that's something we ought to ask our General Manager."

He had side-stepped the question with some ingenuity but for all that it was a clear point to Justin and we all knew it. Justin hammered the point home.

"I see," he said. "Just theoretical modernization."

It was all very neat and aggravating. I said quickly, "Mr. Chairman, if I may—"

He interrupted me. "No, Hugo, not your turn. We'll have you in a moment." He threw down his pencil and leaned back in his chair and surveyed us with the complacency of one who is handling a tricky situation, extricating himself from an unexpected difficulty with his usual masterly skill. I expect he was enjoying himself quite a lot, though his expression was suitably grave.

"Well, gentlemen," he said, returning to his formal manner, "we have all heard Mr. Nelson's views with attention and I think respect. We haven't had the advantage of his counsels for very long in this company; he joined us, as you will remember, to advise us on financial matters on which he is, of course, an expert. But I think that for that very reason he is perhaps inclined to view things from an exclusively financial angle, not to take into account the other less tangible but no less important factors. No reason why he should, of course. He is not a member of the family and he has not been with us long enough to have a chance of acquiring that family tradition, that special sense of—" he hesitated effectively for the word—"of responsibility and trust which is the mainspring of our business. We listen to him with attention, but that does not mean we are not allowed to disagree with him and form our own view of this matter."

The plan was clearly to isolate Nelson, to show him to be an outcast, a stranger, a man outside our family, club, totem and tribe, who could not be expected to understand our wonderful ways and was only influenced by filthy lucre. I looked at Nelson and saw he was flushed with anger. Justin, on the other hand, had fully recovered his poise. The initial positions were reversed and I felt some alarm at the way Justin had recovered the initiative. No butterflies or aching cheek-bones, though; I was too caught up in the battle for that.

Justin went on majestically: "For myself, gentlemen, I need hardly tell you how completely I disagree with Mr. Nelson. Finlays are, of course, an excellent firm, though I like to think no better than ourselves. But that is no reason why we should sell ourselves to them in a moment of panic, particularly when there is nothing in the world to panic about. Even if there were, I should think we should have grave misgivings before selling ourselves to another firm. Additional capital is always a useful thing to have, I admit, but there are easier and better ways to raise it than by quietly committing suicide. We could raise it in the city; as you know I have good friends in the various finance houses and they have often expressed interest in this company. Or we could turn ourselves into a public company and get the great general public to invest in us."

Both Nelson and I stirred uneasily at this but Justin swept on.

"Over and above this financial angle, as I said earlier, is the more intangible but I think greater vision, the vision of the founder of the firm. It is something I would not willingly betray. I have spoken before of the part the family plays in the life and spirit of the colony, the way it enshrines in practical form the noble conceptions of fatherhood and brotherhood. The Pemberton family business seems to me an almost perfect example of this and we are consequently trusted and loved in Natividad. I will not break that sacred trust, gentlemen, no matter how hard some of you may press me. I have not become Chairman of this company to sell us and those who depend on us down the river." He broke off and swept us with a visionary glance. It made Grandfather's expression above him seem very practical and down to earth. "Before this meeting I used the phrase 'The Royal Family of Natividad'. I think the Pemberton family have some right to that title and I would resign from this board rather than see us abdicate that honorable and honored position."

He looked round at us again and then punctured our embarrassment with a deprecatory smile and a self-denying shrug. "I don't wish to labor the point, gentlemen. I only wish to say that it would be nothing short of a tragedy if we were to falter today and throw away both our great heritage and the bright future ahead of us. For I believe it is a bright future. I do not pretend to be a soothsayer, but at least I am no defeatist. The Pembertons were a great family in Natividad fifty years ago, and with your support, gentlemen, I know that they will still be a great family out there in fifty years time, or even longer. That is my credo and I am asking you to have faith in it too."

It was fine stirring stuff, the sort of speech that makes you either rise and cheer wildly or else be quietly sick into your handkerchief. It was sheer clap-trap, of course. None of it meant anything when you thought about it and I was sure Justin was no more taken in by it than Nelson or myself. I had been expecting some such outburst. The next move would be to ask Sir Arthur for his views. He would certainly echo the noble sentiments and then we should be nicely lined up two on each side with Justin able to give his casting vote against the deal. The battle would be over.

I looked at Sir Arthur with foreboding. He had produced a sinister implement from his trouser pocket and was jabbing it viciously into the bowl of his pipe. Smoking seemed to be more important to him than the affairs of the company. Or perhaps it was just an embarrassed reaction from Justin's rhetoric.

Justin said, "Well now, you've heard Mr. Nelson and you've heard my views. Let's go round the table and see what the rest of you think. Arthur, how do you feel about this offer?"

This was the crucial point. Sir Arthur was caught match in hand. Calmly he struck it and held it over his pipe, sucking noisily. Business could wait till his pipe was alight again. And then I suddenly saw it. I had perhaps five seconds grace. Never again shall I make an unkind comment on a pipe-smoker.

I leaned forward and said, "Mr. Chairman, perhaps as a member of the family I could come in next."

Justin threw me an irritated glance. "No, Hugo, let's go round in the proper order. We'll come to you in a moment. Well, Arthur?"

Negligently, unhurryingly, Sir Arthur waved the flaming match in the air and extinguished it. He leaned forward and dropped it in the ash-tray, puffing out billowing clouds of blue acrid smoke. He gave another two puffs and then at last said:

"Think Hugo ought to speak next. I'd like to hear his views. After all, he's the young'un, going to be his firm one day."

I could have hugged the man. Why on earth had I ever thought him a fool?

Justin forced a smile, but it wasn't a very good one. He said breezily, "Oh come, come, Arthur. I don't think experience ought to take a back seat. You know as much about this firm as any of us. I think we ought to have the views of an elder statesman next."

He gave an encouraging smile to show it was only half a joke but Sir Arthur just puffed away at his pipe. He never said a word. He didn't even shake his head. Justin waited hopefully for a quarter of a minute or more and then he turned to me. The redness was back on his neck.

"All right, Hugo. Let's hear what you have to say."

He couldn't hide the irritation in his voice. I thought, we're right back on the attack again.

I said with a careful avoidance of rhetoric but with a sincerity which wasn't the least forced: "As a member of the family and as General Manager I am deeply anxious about the future of the firm.

As you say, Mr. Chairman, it'll be my problem to solve, but I don't think it will be in anyone's power to solve if we skate over the real issues today. To my mind, our real duty to the ideals of the founder and to our shareholders and to our employees and to those who will depend on us in the future is to ensure that the Malmaison estate remains in maximum production and cultivation. I don't think we should jeopardize that just to keep the Pemberton name in the headlines of the colony's newspapers for a few years more."

Justin gave me a look of unguarded anger and started to say something, but I disregarded him. It was my turn now not to be interrupted.

I rammed the point home. "If the Pembertons have got to sacrifice their prestige and power in order to keep the estate going, then I don't think we should shirk making that sacrifice." I delighted in lecturing Justin on the need for sacrifice. We glared at each other. I looked away and picked up the threads of my argument again.

"You were asking, Mr. Chairman, just why we need so much money and what are the items we need to buy. I will tell you. No money has been ploughed back into the estate since 1939. First there was the war when machinery was unobtainable. Then afterwards, we were engaged in maintaining our dividend for prestige reasons and in trying to keep the overdraft within limits. But we can't go on indefinitely like that. Two of our vacuum pans are fifty years old and must be replaced. The No. 1 evaporator is nearly as old and very inefficient. It is always blocking up and then the whole factory has to stop until it unblocks. We need two new boilers to replace the old Stirlings. And of course a new continuous-still. In a couple of years we're going to need a new set of heavy-duty knives and a complete new battery of first curing. And there are lots of little things like the hopper and the juice-strainer and a new generator. It'll tot up into a largish bill. And then there's the mill itself, the crushers and rollers. Except for one roller it's the same mill Mr. Wright put in when he built the factory and it's getting pretty worn now. Not a very efficient mill, and the Chief Engineer reckons its maximum remaining life is ten years at most. That's a very expensive item to replace. We are, as you say, Mr. Chairman, making a steady six hundred tons a week, but we were doing better than that twenty years ago. I think it's almost a miracle that we've kept production up to that level and it is a tremendous achievement on the part of the engineering staff. But even they can't keep it going much longer—and that in a factory that should be capable of producing eight or nine hundred tons a week."

I had them all hanging on my words now, even Justin. Sir Arthur's pipe had gone out and he made no attempt to light it. I went on relentlessly.

"The position in the field is even less satisfactory. There we need, not replacement of existing equipment, but drastic new thinking about our methods of cultivation. We often speak here about the love and respect our laborers have for us. You don't hear so much about it in the colony. Indeed, when there are labor troubles, it's just as often on the family estates. I think it's time we stopped relying on these big uncertain gangs of men with forks and shovels. It's a slow and wasteful method even if the men work regularly, which, not being slaves any more, they don't. What we need are modern methods. We need tractors, ploughs, cultivators, bulldozers, irrigators, sprayers. And then we've got to reorganize the transport of cut cane from the field to the mill. We've got to get rid of those old ox-carts that take all day and hold almost nothing. We've got to run railway lines to all sections of the estate and for that we'll need embankments, bridges, lines, sleepers, engines, trucks. And for where we can't run a line we want half-tracks and six-ton wagons. It all sounds pretty ambitious, I know, but the N.S.C. and Finlays are going to do it. We shall begin to see the results in a couple of years. They'll start to go right away from us. If we can't raise our production to at least eight hundred tons a week, and keep our cost per ton sugar down to theirs, then we're going to sink. We shall drop further and further behind, become more and more uneconomic and finally cease production altogether. I see that happening in about fifteen years, perhaps less if there is a slump or a series of bad crops or labor troubles. The factory will be derelict, the fields will go back to being bush, the firm will be dead."

Ghoulishly I rubbed it in. I still held them taut with my glittering eye.

"You mentioned raising capital elsewhere, Mr. Chairman. That's been mentioned before but nothing ever seems to come of it. We've heard that these finance houses are interested in us but nothing concrete ever seems to emerge."

Justin moved to interrupt again and this time I let him in. "You're wrong there, Hugo. I spoke to Brigadier Hope-Gordon at Lehmann's a few months ago and he was most sympathetic. But it wasn't a good moment to press the point, with the strike on and Walker so recently dead."

"Exactly. It never is the right time and I doubt if it ever will be. With the state of the firm and the colony as they are now, can you see any firm wanting to put money into us? I can't, no matter how personally friendly the heads of the two firms may be. As for turning it into a public company, you'd never get anyone to subscribe the issue. Who would? I doubt if you'd find anyone to underwrite it—except the odd sucker."

It was an unexpected blow to Justin and I watched it go home. His face was changing color, his eyes were glazing.

"I think it's wonderful that Finlays want us at the moment. I'm sure if we turn it down, they won't reopen it. In ten years time they wouldn't take us as a present. I think it would be a tragedy if we were to lose this offer in chasing some pie-in-the-sky idea of raising capital elsewhere. If there were some concrete scheme before us, it would be another matter. But as it is, it's just a mirage. But we've got to have that capital if we're going to live and I'm convinced it's now or never. That is why I think we should tell Finlays that we accept their offer in principle and that we would like a meeting with them to discuss the details further."

There was a pause. Justin and I eyed each other balefully. Sir Arthur nodded heavily.

Justin said, "Not a very edifying performance, Hugo. I put you into your present job, rather against my better judgment, but I never thought you would turn against me quite so soon. I thought you would have more loyalty to your Chairman and your family." Anger was making him speak fast, stumbling over his words.

I was pretty angry too. "I have as much loyalty as anyone. But it's to Malmaison and all those who depend on the place."

We still glared at each other like cats. Justin said venomously, "I think you ought to know, gentlemen, that my cousin has been offered a fat job in Finlays if this deal goes through. So he's not really unbiased in his opinion, is he?"

The implications of his remark must have been obvious to everyone. Sir Arthur looked at him for a moment and then turned to me. "Have you, Hugo? That's good." He turned back to Justin. "Daresay we're all a bit biased in this matter."

He banged out his pipe loudly on the ash-tray. It reverberated impressively in the room. He seemed to be growing in stature every moment, almost to be dominating the meeting.

"Seems to me," he said after a weighty silence, "that Hugo's right. We've got to accept this offer, whether we like it or not. Got to have that capital. Got to think about the future. No use just saying it's Hugo's problem and waving it away. Got to do something about it now. I'm a trustee for Mrs. Pemberton, you know, got to think of her interests. If the firm goes bust, she won't have anything. And another thing. Seems to me we're in a pretty good mess out in the colony. Who's responsible for that?"

"That was an exaggerated picture," said Justin thickly. It wasn't very audible. Sir Arthur didn't hear, or didn't choose to hear.

"Got to look to the future," he repeated, "and that's Hugo's. He's the young'un. Leave it to him and Finlays to get us out of the mess we've got ourselves into. That's my view. Take this offer, sell the firm to Finlays. And the sooner the better."

It wasn't a very elegantly phrased speech but it was possibly the most devastating of the meeting. Justin was fidgeting in his chair as if it was red-hot, and he clutched a pencil in both his hands. His sunburnt face had a purplish tinge and his words were incoherent, almost slurred.

"I never thought you'd let yourself be talked round by a young whipper-snapper like Hugo," he said.

Sir Arthur just sat stolidly. His face was red, but then it always was. "Not a question of being talked round. I'm quite capable of making up my own mind."

"Nonsense, Arthur," said Justin. "All you ever do is repeat what the last person said. That's what you always do. God knows why we have you on this board."

Sir Arthur remained stolid, the sort of stolidity that had subdued centuries of rebellious clansmen. But he was angry enough.

"I'm not going to let myself be talked to like that by anyone. I didn't come here to be insulted. Know I'm not a financier but I've got a bit of common sense. I can still see straight, which is more than you can, Justin. Got to do my duty whatever you say. Never wanted to come on to this board, but I felt it my duty. Got to do my duty now and that doesn't just mean saying what you want me to say." He cleared his throat noisily and started to fill his pipe again. "Know what's wrong with you, Justin?" he said with sudden mildness. "You're going to lose your job with Finlays. You're not going to like that. No one to order about any more. That's why you don't like it. Eh?"

With a convulsive jerk Justin snapped the pencil in his hands. He threw the pieces down on the table. "Oh, go and stew in your own juice, the whole bloody lot of you!" He almost shouted it.

Nelson asked smoothly and correctly, "Just how are we meant to take that?"

"Oh, take it how you damn well please."

I looked round the table, Justin trembling and livid-faced, Sir Arthur, impassively filling his pipe, muttering to himself, Nelson impeccable and flushed, Hodges deeply shocked, cowering behind his books, not daring to meet anyone's eye. This was the moment of victory after the doubts and swings of the battle. This was the moment for the *coup de grâce*, for the cavalry charge that would put this issue beyond any possibility of reversal.

"Gentlemen," I said, "I think we will all have heard that news, the intimation of our Chairman's resignation, with regret if not with surprise, and I do not think we should let the moment pass without some expression of gratitude to him for his services to the company and to the family. As a member of that family, and as the junior director I should like to pay my tribute to him. I did not always find him an easy taskmaster but I always found him a man of vision and purpose, dedicated to his ideals." I hesitated. I was enjoying myself hugely but I did not want to lay it on too thick. I ended, "It must be a matter of great regret that his services should be withdrawn so abruptly and that his advice will not now be available to us in the great adventures which lie ahead."

I was rather pleased with myself. In a few well-chosen clichés of pompous pastiche, I had rid myself of the resentments of the past three years. I looked at Justin now without hate, without fear, without much pity. His mouth seemed weak and fleshy and worked in a lop-sided purposeless way. His eyes flashed murder.

Nelson followed me up, suavely, formally. "I should like to associate myself with that tribute. I too have not been a member of this board for very long, but in that time I have learnt to admire and respect the strength of Major Pemberton's convictions and the extent of his experience and knowledge. I can fully endorse my colleague's happily chosen phrase in calling him a man of vision. I am sure his counsels will be missed in the future on both sides of the Atlantic."

Sir Arthur contented himself with saying "Hear, hear!" in a rather unenthusiastic voice.

Justin sat, opening and closing his mouth as if he were about to say something but couldn't quite think what. The seconds ticked by. Gradually the bright light of triumph dimmed, the mists of embarrassment seeped in. Suddenly Justin coughed out something that sounded like, "God rot the lot of you." He scrambled to his feet and swayed out of the room like a drunk. The door slammed behind him.

There was a long empty silence when he had gone. Distantly we heard another door slam. I think we none of us quite knew the right thing to say next and were waiting for someone else to speak. Sir

Arthur lit up again and we watched the billowing curves of smoke with dreamy raptness.

It was Hodges who brought us back into the firing-line. "What record am I to make in the minutes?" he asked.

Nelson said, "Just a short entry, Mr. Hodges. Say the board discussed the offer from Finlay Brothers to purchase the whole of our share capital and decided to recommend to the shareholders that the offer be accepted, subject to the details being worked out satisfactorily. The Chairman tendered his resignation which was accepted with regret. Tributes were paid to him by members of the board." He glanced at me. "That all right?"

"Fine," I said. It was, after all, just what had happened.

As Nelson was taking his coat and hat from a peg in the passage, I remembered that mine was in the Chairman's cupboard.

"I'll have to go in and get it. Better make my peace with him at the same time."

Miss Yorke intercepted us outside his room. "The Major isn't in," she said. "He went out a few minutes ago."

"Out?"

"Well, I saw him going down the stairs. He didn't look quite his usual self." She looked from one to the other of us with open inquisitiveness.

We didn't enlighten her. I explained about the coats. She opened the door for us and then went back to her typewriter.

"He went without his coat and hat," I said when I opened the cupboard door. "In this weather."

Nelson said from the door, "He can't have gone far. He'll be coming back for them."

I pulled out the coats and helped Sir Arthur into his. I said, glancing round the room, "No, I don't think he'll ever come back here, coat or no coat. Not now."

"And good riddance too," Sir Arthur growled over his shoulder. "Telling me I didn't know my own mind. And all that pansy stuff about the family when all he meant was himself. Never could stand it. Thanks, Hugo."

He turned round and shook my hand. "Remember me to your mother." In the doorway he passed Nelson. "Good-bye, Mr. er—" and then he was gone, a great mountain of tweed, wreathed in smoke like Olympus.

"He turned up trumps, didn't he?" I said to Nelson. "Who'd have thought it?"

"Oh, I'm not altogether surprised. He'd better be Chairman, don't you think, during the interim. Or do you—"

"Oh no, he's obviously the man. Let us get on with the deal."

He nodded. "We'd better form a committee to handle the negotiations. Perhaps you and the company's solicitor and auditor."

"Not you?"

"No, better not. But you can keep me in touch."

"All right. I'll get going on it this afternoon. We might as well tell Finlays while we're about it."

We both laughed at that. He held open the door and let me go out of the office ahead of him.

In the street Nelson asked, "Which way are you going?"

"To the cable office. To send a cable to my wife. Tell her what's happened."

"I expect you'll be celebrating your new job with Finlays, won't you? By the way, I don't think I've ever congratulated you on it."

"Well, celebrating the merger coming off." I paused and then added, "But I'm not going to take that Finlay job."

He looked at me sharply. "Why not?"

"Just don't want it. I've had enough of that colony. I've done my job out there. I've got the firm salable, and that's enough. I'm not really interested in making sugar for its own sake."

"It sounded an interesting job."

"Oh yes. For the right man. But it wouldn't satisfy me. Nothing's so awful as spending your life doing something that doesn't really interest you. I've been finding that out."

Nelson was frowning a little. It might have been surprise or just the raw air in his eyes. "What'll Finlays say when you tell them?" he asked.

"Oh, I don't expect they'll mind much. They're not buying the firm just to get me. I'm not *that* good." We glanced at each other. "I'll stay on till the deal is signed and complete, of course, but then I'm going my own way."

"What way is that?"

The thing that had been in the back of my mind for the last few months, that had reached the front of my mind in my analytical vigil the night before, came out at last into words.

"I'm going to write," I said.

"Write?" He checked abruptly. "Oh yes, you were doing that sort of thing before weren't you? But—"

I broke in. "Yes, a few bits and pieces in magazines like this."

I pulled *Vista* out of my pocket and showed it to him. I went on: "Writing about other people's books. But that wouldn't satisfy me now. I'm going to write books of my own. Other people can write about *them* in here."

Nelson glanced politely at the magazine. "I'm sorry," he said. "Perhaps I should have congratulated you instead on your forthcoming best-seller?"

"Of course," I said with a laugh. But I wasn't laughing inside. The whole bursting, seething springtime of my great new world was breaking over me and I was almost dumb with excitement. So much to say, such a great world to conquer.

Nelson was looking at me with the humoring incredulous look you give to a child who tells you he is just going into the garden to saddle a white horse and fly away. As we shook hands and went through the formalities of parting, I thought: And that's just about what I'm going to do. Now I'm free, and at last I've got the nerve to do it.

As I walked away down Bishopsgate and turned into Threadneedle Street, I began to draft the cable to Diana in my mind. Supersuperpatrick. Something like that. She'd understand and be glad.